A SARAH BEAUHALL NOVEL
NIGHT TERRORS

A SARAH BEAUHALL NOVEL

NIGHT TERRORS

J.A. PITTS

WordFire Press
Colorado Springs, Colorado

NIGHT TERRORS: SARAH BEAUHALL BOOK 4
Copyright © 2016, John A. Pitts

ISBN: 978-1-61475-410-7

Cover design by Janet McDonald

Art Director Kevin J. Anderson

Cover artwork image by Ester Sanz

Edited by Bryan Thomas Schmidt

Book Design by RuneWright, LLC
www.RuneWright.com

Published by
WordFire Press, an imprint of
WordFire, Inc.
PO Box 1840
Monument CO 80132

Kevin J. Anderson & Rebecca Moesta, Publishers

WordFire Press Trade Paperback Edition April 2016
Printed in the USA
wordfirepress.com

ONE

Waking up at 3 AM, naked and cold is usually not something that bothered me. Katie was a blanket hog and I tossed and turned enough that I frequently shucked out of the concert shirt I wore to bed.

I rolled over and reached out for Katie, but she wasn't there. I was just trying to get my brain cells to fire in unison when I heard her vomiting in the other room.

That woke me right up. My head was still fuzzy from too little sleep and the couple bottles of wine we'd drunk, but adrenaline has a way of cutting through the haze. I rolled off the nest we had in the living room, hit the light switch, and leaned against the wall next to the bathroom.

Katie was on her hands and knees heaving her guts out into the toilet. I knew that feeling, could sympathize, my own gut churned at the sound of her combined moans and retching.

I grabbed a couple of washcloths off the stack by the sink and ran cold water over them. By the time I had them wrung out, she was sitting back on her heels and had flushed the toilet.

"Here," I said, kneeling beside her and handing her one of the wet rags. She wiped her face with it and leaned against me.

"I'm sorry," she said, her voice nearly a whimper. "I guess the wine didn't agree with me."

I took the wash cloth from her and handed her the second one, which she pressed against her eyes, sighing deeply.

"Not so sexy now, huh?" she asked as I helped her up.

"Oh, you're totally hawt," I drawled, steadying her on her feet. Of course she was white as a sheet. Even her lips had gone grey. She leaned against me as we crossed the few feet back to the living room, she collapsed onto the nest. We hadn't slept in the actual bedroom in months. Too dangerous with the shadow door on the far wall. It was closed for now, but I didn't trust it. I got her settled and pulled the blankets up to her chin. "I'll get you some water."

She smiled, but didn't open her eyes. By the time I got back she was breathing slowly, sound asleep. The color was coming back into her cheeks, though. The clock read three-thirty.

It had been a good day. I'd come home from working with Julie out at a bunch of farms in Redmond and Katie had arranged for Jai Li, our foster daughter, to spend the night at Black Briar. Katie wanted to have a romantic evening, so she insisted on cooking for me while I grabbed a shower.

The steaks were awesome and the wine had just the right amount of buzz to make her both horny and willing. She'd been recovering for months now. The battle with the necromancer just before Christmas had nearly killed her. She wanted to be better, insisted she was mending, but I had my doubts.

I set the glass of water on the coffee table by her side and went back into the bathroom. The cloth she'd used to wipe her mouth had traces of blood on it. I closed the toilet and sat on the lid, staring at the bright red of the blood on the cloth.

We'd been to see a few doctors who were all confused by what could be bothering her. Katie thought maybe she was getting an ulcer or something, but I knew better. I think it was the magic. Her songs were growing more powerful since I reforged my sword, Gram and I think they were wrecking her body—eating her up inside. Magic has a price. I was growing more sure the price Katie was paying was her life. Things had been spiraling out of control with her ever since we had fought all those spirits at Samhain.

She was getting weaker, frailer. It was the little things: like when she had to catch her breath after tying her shoes or wringing her hands like she was in pain. She faked it well enough.

Didn't think anyone noticed, but I did. I loved her more than breathing.

Our friend and confidant Stuart, one of the Black Briar leaders, had told me how Katie had nearly collapsed while battling the cultists during the winter solstice. Later, her brother Jimmy had found her face down in a pool of her own blood after the battle. She hadn't been physically wounded, but you can lose a lot of blood through a nose bleed. I hated thinking about how close I came to losing her that night. They'd given her two pints of blood and kept her in the hospital overnight. Thing was, she had no real symptoms. They just got her stabilized and suggested she see a specialist.

So, that's exactly what we did. With the help and guidance of Melanie, our doctor friend, we'd seen a series of specialists from infectious disease, to gastroenterology, and finally a neurosurgeon to make sure she wasn't having some sort of seizures or strokes.

We had another appointment later this week just to rule out anything mundane—like cancer or something. I hated it. This would be the fourth specialist visit in as many months. I wasn't dealing with the ambiguity too well. This wasn't something I could stab or punch or hit with a hammer. I couldn't bend it to my will like iron, or wrestle it to the ground like a dwarf. One thing I knew about myself, something I didn't need any shrink to help me figure out, was I did not take well to feeling helpless.

I'd killed a dragon a year ago, hunted the bastard down for taking Katie and my blacksmithing master, Julie. Oh, and killing too many of my friends. But this unknown malady was out of my wheelhouse and I was starting to get a twitch.

The last few days she'd been doing remarkably well. Maybe even turned a corner, or so she claimed. She hadn't had a nose bleed or anything for over a month. Heck, after Christmas we were so busy getting settled in with our foster kidlet—Jai Li—that we hardly had time to kiss each other in passing, much less do anything more strenuous. I kept an eye on her, and had others watching out as well.

Last night she'd been urgent, willing. But I wondered how much I'd overlooked in my own need. The sex had been good, and the evening as a whole was one of the best we'd had in months. Still, it seemed that maybe her health had backslid to where it was a couple of months ago.

I hated how wiped out she looked, even while sleeping; like she was withering away while I watched. It made my heart hurt. Maybe it was time for me to bring in my witch friend, Qindra. She could perform a series of magical tests or something. Hell, I'd gladly get further entrenched with her and the old dragon Nidhogg if it would make Katie healthy.

I sat on the rocker across from our bed and watched her until the sun started to rise. Another day of short sleep rations wouldn't kill me. I just couldn't stop watching her breathe.

Two

Katie had a follow-up doctor's appointment at nine. I grabbed a quick shower and made some tea before waking her up. She was a little groggy, but in a pretty good mood.

"Sorry for hurling last night." She sat on the edge of the bed, running her hands through hair. "I feel like a million bucks, though." she said, grinning. She stood, stepped over to me and kissed me on the cheek. "Morning breath, sorry."

I'd already brushed my teeth, so I know she meant her. Silly girl. I watched her walk to the bathroom, admiring her ass, remembering holding it in my hands last night as we rocked it for the first time in months.

Now I just felt guilty. Like maybe it had been too much too soon.

I stood in the doorway and waited until she was under the shower spray before I went into the kitchen and poured my coffee. Luckily we'd remembered to set it up before we'd gotten too far into the wine last night.

Katie already had a sub for the day and I'd rearranged my farrier work where I could, making arrangements for those who were willing to postpone a few days and getting Julie to pick up the rest.

Didn't matter, really. I was not missing this doctor visit with Katie. We were going to be discussing blood work with her general practitioner.

I stood in the kitchen drinking my coffee and making some dry toast to see if Katie's stomach would handle it, when the phone rang. Seven-thirty was damn early in anyone's book. I didn't recognize the number and almost let it go to voicemail, but decided to answer it just so Katie didn't try and rush to the phone and fall over.

It was Charlie Hague, the veterinarian I had met last fall, who just happened to be a member of the Order of Mordred. One of those watcher groups who kept secret histories of the dragons and their ilk. When that nut job necromancer murdered one of the horses out at Circle Q farm, Charlie had responded to help clean up the mess and check on the other horses. Of course, he was also scouting the scene for his order.

He was a cute guy, more Inspector Clouseau than James Bond in my mind. Nice enough, with some exposure to the occult and magic, but really he was an animal doctor who was fairly fresh from college. Still, I'd seen his secret order tattoo, and I bet he had some sort of hand book, as well. Very earnest guy. But in reality he was a message boy. I doubt he had any real clout in the organization. At least that's the impression he gave.

Of course, Nidhogg, the oldest and most bad-ass of the dragons looked like a frail old woman most of the time, so there's that.

"What's up, Beauhall?" he asked me, the cheer in his voice altogether too damn earnest.

"Pretty early," I growled, turning to face the cabinets so my voice didn't carry into the bathroom. "We'd about given you up as a lost cause."

"Yeah, sorry about that," he said. "Things are a bit crazy around here. Work has been a little steady with all the foaling and the fact we're shorthanded here at the practice."

"Yes, tragic." I had one ear out for the shower and I could tell Katie had just turned off the water. "Can we cut to the chase here? I'm not having the best morning."

"Well," he drawled. "I was hoping you and Katie would be free for lunch today."

Black Briar had been playing footsie with the Order of Mordred for a while now, and it was about time they made a move. Hell, I could get to first base faster than this group could commit to a meeting, and I was definitely not comfortable with groping anyone but Katie.

And here he was, finally making a move. I agreed to lunch in Bellevue at a quaint little Thai place over on Bell-Red. At least the food would be decent. I wasn't so sure about the business. I didn't have high hopes.

We were in and out of the doctors by eleven-thirty and cruised over to Bellevue for our lunch date. Charlie was in the restaurant when we walked in.

When I thought of secret societies, I tended to think of shadowy assassin guilds or ancient orders of knights who guarded a treasure like that old guy in Indiana Jones. What I didn't expect, honestly, was khakis, a pink Polo shirt, and penny loafers. Reminded me of pictures of my parent's generation. It just gave me the heebie-jeebies that today's clandestine operative would be comfortable in a John Hughes film.

Charlie was a total dork. Katie laughed when he stood up and practically dragged the teapot off the table along with the table cloth. As it was, his silverware bounced into the main aisle and the waitress skipped over it like she'd done it a dozen times.

She waved us to our seats while Charlie tried to clean things up. By the time we were settled with crab wontons, pineapple fried rice, and Hot Mama noodles on the way, he had begun to get his act together. Dude was seriously freaked.

"I'm really glad you both agreed to meet with me," he said, flushing. "I hope you're doing okay," he said to Katie, his eyes round. "The news about the necromancer and the blood cult," he swallowed hard and glanced at me. "We were afraid you'd think we were mixed up with them." He leaned forward, lowering his voice. "Things are a bit unsettled at the moment, if you've noticed."

Katie looked at me, raising her eyebrows. Was this guy for real?

He'd been so calm and collected when we'd interacted back in the fall. He'd taken the lead, been sure and cocky.

"I gotta be frank here," she said, picking up my glass of water. "You're not instilling a high level of confidence in your organization."

J.A. Pitts

"No shit," I said, glancing back toward the door. Charlie was glancing that way every few seconds. "You expecting someone?"

I looked at him as his eyes darted from Katie, to me, to the door.

"Not expecting," he said, his voice a little shaky. "Dreading, maybe."

He began tapping his fork on the table, a rattle that was quickly growing on my nerves. I slapped my hand down over his, stopping the noise. "Charles, get it together. What the hell is going on?"

There was a haunted look in his eyes. Not just fear, but resignation, defeat.

"Two of our people have died," he said, deflated. "Bobbi had gone into a meet with a prospective informant and the next time anyone saw her, she was washed up on the beach at Oak Harbor."

Katie shrugged and I pulled my hand away from him. He started to rattle the fork again, but stopped when I looked at him. "Sorry," he said, putting his hands in his lap.

"Where was the meeting? Who was she trying to get information on?"

"Deception Pass," he said with a snort. "She jumped off the bridge there. Three eye-witnesses."

"That sucks," I said. "Who was she trying to meet?"

He shrugged. "No idea. Madame Gottschalk won't tell me." He hesitated, taking a long drink of water. "One of the witnesses saw her talking to a middle-aged woman before she jumped. Real ugly woman," he recounted. "Guy was pretty drunk, just kept saying Bobbi's contact had a five o'clock shadow."

"How freaking odd," I said. The runes along my scalp had begun to prickle. There was something more here.

"Did he say anything else?" I asked. "This drunk witness of yours?"

Charlie grimaced. "No confirmation he was drunk, but his behavior …"

Katie looked at me sideways, smirking.

"After Bobbi jumped, they were all milling around. This guy saw the older woman, Bobbi's contact, moving away, but he said she looked younger, had lost the beard." He looked from one of

8

us to the other. "He had to be drunk."

My runes flared, burning for a split second. I doubted the guy was drunk. Why would this operative just jump off the bridge? How did this contact suddenly change appearance? Drunk maybe, but the way the runes were behaving I was betting there was something more there.

Which meant there had to be another player in the area. I was bone tired of all the interference. What the heck was Qindra doing letting all this crap go on under her nose? Of course, I was happy she'd overlooked Black Briar for so long. Maybe these Mordred folks were low key enough to ignore.

Katie spoke up. "You said there was someone else. A second order member to die?"

He nodded. "Don't laugh."

I shot Katie a puzzled look. This guy was really rattled.

"Go on," I said.

"Madame Gottschalk's talking cat."

Whiskey Tango Foxtrot ... Katie looked as bemused as I felt. "I'm sorry, what did you say?"

He put his head in his hands and sighed. "I know it sounds crazy and I'm not supposed to talk about the cat, but there it is." He looked up, his face pale. There were bags under his eyes that I hadn't noticed at first.

"The old lady you work for is a witch, right?" Katie was suddenly serious. "Like a real witch, not one of those wannabe pretenders."

Charlie just nodded. "Old school," he said, his voice barely a whisper. "And she's freaking out. The cat has been with her since the old country."

"What happened to the cat?" Katie asked.

"Which old country," I asked at the same time.

Charlie looked from one of us to the other again, his eyes practically vibrating in his skull. "Russia," he said, nodding at me, "and lightning" he said, looking at Katie. "Madam often sent the cat over to give me instructions. It carried notes tied to its collar. It had delivered a few messages before I heard it complain that I never tipped it. Imagine how surprised I was that the cat talked." He chuckled. "After that I always had a can of tuna handy."

He paused as the waitress set an order of crab wontons and a steaming dish of pineapple fried rice in front of us and refilled our water glasses.

"Some beggar had been hanging around my neighborhood," he continued, scooping rice onto his plate, "creepy guy with one eye. Anyway, one night last week, after the cat had delivered me the news of Bobbi's death and had finished his tuna, he decided to investigate our Dumpster. He did that, must be a cat thing." He smiled at us, but neither Katie nor I smiled back. This was the most bat shit conversation.

His smile faltered. "Anyway, this homeless dude was digging through the Dumpster and didn't take kindly to the cat's intrusion. One second the cat was hissing and shouting in one of the Slavic languages and the next this bolt of lightning flashed down from the sky and the cat exploded. It was crazy. When I could see again, the old man was bent down over the cat, poking it with his walking stick and laughing. *Tell the old woman I repay my debts,*' he said, and he struck the ground three times. Then the cat got up," Charlie paused here, his eyes wide. "I'm telling you, the damn thing was a blackened husk one minute, then it was up and stretching. The old man pushed the cat with his staff and laughed. *Four to go,*' he said. The cat arched his back, hissed at the old man and ran into the darkness."

Katie kicked me under the table. I knew what she was thinking. Odin was haunting Charlie's apartments. What's up with that?

"Have you seen this old man since?" I asked.

"Three times," he said, quickly looking toward the door. "I'm beginning to think he's following me."

Katie gave me a look and I grinned at her. Better him than us. He drew the wrong kind of attention, that crazy old man. I didn't relish being jumped by another pair of giants.

"So, about meeting up with Black Briar," I said. "What is in it for us to join forces with your lot?"

Charlie looked at me and had the good sense to look chagrinned. "We have contacts, lots of secret knowledge, and," he lowered his voice again, "we have new information about your parents' trip to Reykjavik." He was looking directly at Katie.

He wasn't grinning at her, just had his voice lowered and his face ducked down, like he didn't want to be seen. I thought he was acting pretty damned suspicious. That's probably why I didn't see Katie move.

She punched him, just above his right eye. His head snapped back and then forward, going nose first into his plate of fried rice.

"Ow, fuck," she said, shaking her hand out, her fingers loose.

The other patrons were looking at us. Our waitress stopped in the middle of refreshing water at another table, just staring at us.

"Why'd you hit me?" he asked, brushing rice from his face.

I reached over and put my hand on Katie's shoulder. She was going for round two.

"You know about my parents, you prick. You just tell me. You don't negotiate."

She was fired up. Charlie had a hand over his punched eye and his other eye was wide, scared. "I was gonna tell you. Geez." He scooted to the left, further away from Katie. "I wasn't supposed to tell you that yet. Madame will be pissed."

Katie slumped back with a sigh, the fight going out of her. "Why didn't you say so?"

He shook his head and reached for his water, watching her for any movement. "I wanted to get with you and your brother, tell you both at the same time." There was something scared in his voice, something that made the hairs on the back of my neck stand up. "We have something of theirs. Something they left in London before they went to Iceland."

"What?" I asked.

Katie was tense, her face taut and her mouth set.

He opened his messenger bag and pulled out a small envelope. He slid it across the table and Katie picked it up. For a moment I got a spark of green—made me think *sympathetic magic*. But it could've been a trick of the light.

Katie looked inside and went pale. She handed me the envelope and I looked inside. Laying in the bottom were a pair of wedding rings.

Her eyes were hard, her face tight. I placed a hand on her arm closest to me. She was tense. I squeezed her, lending her my support.

"They left these on the nightstand of their hotel," he said, his voice quiet. "They were protected by some sort of spell. The maid never saw them, but someone else did. A player named McTavish."

I glanced up at him, "Is that name supposed to mean something?"

He shrugged, obviously disappointed we didn't react. "Probably not. He was pretty active during the Troubles, real cat burglar type. Did some work for the IRA. Had a knack for getting into places no one thought possible."

"Why was he trying to steal my parent's wedding rings?" Katie asked, her voice deadly calm.

I watched her. Blood was slowly welling up from her left nostril. I handed her a napkin and she clutched it to her face, "Tell me."

Charlie's head snapped around and he had the strangest look on his face—part panic, part incomprehension.

"He worked for the Dublin dragon," he intoned, his voice wooden and strained. "The order thinks he was an elf, traveled through mirrors somehow. We've never heard of that before." His hands were shaking like he struggled to move them. "There's speculation it could explain some of the things we've observed out at Black Briar. I was thinking maybe you knew who he was in context, and why am I telling you all this." He was breathing really fast—his voice a staccato machine gun delivery.

It was creepy. I glanced at Katie and she was staring at him, mouthing the words that flew from his mouth.

"Touching the rings killed him," he went on. "Whatever wards were on them seemed to be gone by the time our operative arrived. The police wrote it off as electrocution and the body went into a pauper's grave. We acquired the rings and have been studying them for years." The tendons in his neck were standing out and his whole body trembled. "I just found out about them in the last few weeks."

Blood dripped down onto the table from Katie's fist. The napkin was a dripping crimson mess. "Katie?" I asked her, jostling her elbow. She was as rigid as Charlie, vibrating. She stared at him as if she was trying to bore a hole through his skull and see inside.

Maybe that was exactly what she was doing. "Katie!" I barked and snapped my fingers in front of her face.

She flinched and lowered her eyes. Charlie jerked back, gasping. "Sorry," she said, pushing her chair back and standing up. "Ladies room."

Charlie was wide-eyed with panic. "How did she do that?" he asked. "What did I say?"

"Stay," I ordered him, pointing at my index finger at his face. "Do not leave."

He nodded once and I turned to follow Katie.

That had gotten totally out of control.

I found her in the ladies room washing her face and hands. The blood had run down the length of her arm and her pale skin was streaked with lines of sticky red.

I stepped to her, put one hand on the small of her back and looked at her in the mirror. "Are you okay?"

She nodded and splashed water on her face. I took a stack of paper towels out of the dispenser and handed her a handful. She mopped up her arm and began washing her hands with soap and water again.

She wasn't crying, but there was something distant in her eyes. Something cold. What the hell was happening to her?

"Bleeding's stopped," I said, filling the silence. She nodded again and kept scrubbing her hands and arms. After a few minutes her actions became less frantic and her shoulders began to relax.

I stepped behind her and put my hands on her shoulders, kneading the muscles there. She was tight, like nothing I'd ever encountered.

"Come on, baby," I whispered into her hair. "It's okay. I'm here. It's over."

She shook a little, put her hands on the sink and sagged down onto her arms.

"I'm so sorry," she whispered. "I didn't mean to. He just ..." she trailed off.

"Shhh,..." I said, wrapping my arms around the front of her.

She grabbed my arms, hugging them to her.

"It was like I'd opened his head and pulling the words out," she said after a moment. "Like I was scooping them out with a spoon and couldn't stop."

"It's over now," I said, struggling to keep my voice calm.

She turned and pressed her face into my shoulder. We stood there for a few minutes while her breathing evened out. I stroked her hair and just breathed with her.

When we'd cleaned up the mess and left the bathroom, Charlie was long gone. The envelope with the rings was gone as well.

The server was clearing the food away and I dropped a couple of twenties on the table.

"You want food boxed up?" she asked, her Thai accent thick and sweet.

"No thanks," I said, trying to smile. Probably wouldn't go back to that restaurant for a while.

I helped Katie out to the truck, settling her in the passenger side and closed the door.

How the hell was I supposed to fix this?

THREE

I called Charlie and left him a voicemail. I didn't blame the guy for bolting. That was some freaky shit. Katie was quiet all the way out to Black Briar, but she hadn't shut me out. She kept glancing my way, keeping one hand on my thigh as I drove. It was a peaceful way to share each other's space. By the time I put the truck in park at Jimmy's, she had come to grips with the events of lunch.

"Thanks for loving me," she said, leaning over to kiss me.

I wrapped my arms around her and kissed her back.

"Have you done that before?" I asked her, thinking of other times she'd gotten pissy and demanding. All minor things, but when you see things like that, it brings everything else into question.

"Once or twice," she said, putting her head on my shoulder and holding my hands in hers. "Scares me. It's like I have this power to compel people to tell me things. Maybe even do things."

I squeezed her hands gently. "I'm comfortable at our current pace of sexual exploration," I said, wiggling my eyebrows. "You don't need to try that stuff on me, 'kay?"

She chuckled and hugged me again. "Makes my head hurt," she said into my shoulder. "Definitely not conducive to intimate moments."

We got out of the truck and slowly made our way to the house. It was a beautiful day and the sun was warm for a change. I held her hand and looked around at the farm. It was a good place.

I could see the Cascade Mountains climbing to the east of us—tall and snow covered even this late in the spring. Over top of it all was a sky so blue it made my eyes water.

I absorbed all that in the second it took me to turn my head and settle back on Katie. It all paled compared to the light in her eyes. I touched the side of her face, caressing her.

"We have dinner with Melanie and Dena later," she said, turning to kiss the palm of my hand. "I'll get a nap and we'll have a quiet dinner. Give them a chance to meet Jai Li. Maybe it will just be normal. What say?"

"If you're wiped out, we can reschedule," I said. "Your health is more important."

"It's been months," she said, smiling. "Melanie is going to show up on her own if we don't do it formally. She's beside herself about the kiddo."

I nodded. She'd seen Jai Li in the hospital after the battle with the necromancer, but a quiet evening of normal would be totally different.

That night we had one of the best nights in a long time. We let Jai Li pick out the music and we all played games. I knitted while the other four played Parcheesi. Then Jai Li convinced them to play Candyland for a while.

Dena was shy at first. I'd never gotten on with her very well, but Jai Li thought she was aces. Seemed to confuse the woman. Melanie and Katie had no trouble connecting again after a long dry spell. I felt almost like an outsider as the four of them interacted, and I was on heightened alert. Jai Li was too damned vulnerable and Katie too frail. After a bit I put aside the knitting and got settled into a wicked game of three way War with Jai Li and Dena while Katie and Melanie talked in the kitchen.

I knew Melanie was grilling her about her health. Being a doctor and an old lover gave her an insight that many people didn't have. Twice Melanie caught my eye and just shook her head. She was not happy.

We had popcorn and cider, told stories and generally enjoyed the peace of being surrounded by family and friends.

The night was so amazing that after everyone had gone home we got the nest built in the living room again. No way we were sleeping in the bedroom. Too risky in my book. I didn't want to wake up in the Sideways. Too many things wanted to eat me there.

I was beginning to hate this apartment, but tonight had been a slice of normal we hadn't experienced in a very long time. After Jai Li and Katie were asleep I sat up on the big chair, watching the street lights through the front windows with Gram on my lap. A night this peaceful had to be a precursor to something nasty.

At one, Katie came and dragged me back to bed. She even made me tuck Gram away. The apartment was still. Katie snuggled up against me, naked under her T-shirt, all curvy and warm. I pulled her against me, hugging her back to me, one hand over her breasts, and fell asleep. That night, for the first time in a very long time, I had no dreams at all.

FOUR

We went back out to Black Briar on Saturday. I needed to spend some time at the new forge and wanted to give my kobold buddy, Bub some one-on-one time. I felt like I'd been neglecting the little guy. Forget his unfortunate habit of eating anything that wasn't nailed down and his obsession for the old barn that had been burned down by dragon fire, he was great with the other kids and acted just like one most of the time. I tended to forget he was a fire being from another plane with a mouth that hinged open allowing him to eat things—or people—bigger than his head. It was rather creepy.

Of course, the second we got there, Jai Li took off like a shot, tackling the kobold and getting piled on by the troll twins. It had only been a few months since they'd joined our larger clan but they were already longer and leaner than the typical toddler. I bet those two topped seven feet by the time they finished growing. Glad they were being raised by our side. I'd fought their kin in the past. They were nasty fighters.

But Jai Li owned them. That girl had those three boys following her around like puppy dogs. It was comical, our little waif girl, a four foot tall scaly red kobold, and two troll twins nearly as tall as Bub though they were not quite a year old.

Trisha sat on the back porch mending something leather. An old hauberk, it looked like. One of the old sparring bits. I let the kids have at it while I chatted with her briefly, checking on things, exchanging kid stories. Soon enough I was waving at the kids and heading to the smithy. Katie went into the house to visit. I was itching to get back to some fire and steel. It had been more than a month since I'd been out here last and I was itching to make some blades.

We didn't have a good coal forge out at Black Briar yet, but it was on my Christmas wish list. I liked the way coal heated better than propane. Felt cleaner to me, a quality heat. Propane was fine, but it felt too modern, like cheating.

But that's what I had, so that's what I used. I had a dozen or so sword blanks prepped from old leaf springs we'd salvaged at a junk yard down near Lacey. I'd been doing some studying in guerilla smithing circles about using what is around in case of apocalypse—zombie, nuclear, alien invasion, or the generic technological break down. I expected that last one over any of the others. I'd fought the recently risen dead with the necromancer before Christmas and there's no way they could translate into a global epidemic. Not enough blood mages out there willing to keep them animated. They were not self-regulating. With the magic present in the battles I'd been in, firearms were problematic. Give me a solid hammer and Gram and I was ready to rock.

Leaf springs would be plentiful, no matter the apocalypse, if you knew how to salvage them off old cars. I figure I was just preparing for the end of civilization. It was silly, but I guess part of me wanted to be ready, just in case.

I was heating and punching out the first blade when Bub rolled into the smithy. I felt him before I saw him. The amulet around my neck was tuned to his presence—that thing that tied him to me. It had belonged to Anezka for a lot of years, but somehow it had given me its allegiance. I don't think she's that chuffed about it these days. At the time she was a little on the crazy side, in no small part because of the amulet's connection to the fiery little guy.

Of course, he kept the flaming rages to a minimum most days. If he got a little over excited or scared he would sprout blue flames, like burning off alcohol. I bet if pressed he could raise a righteous flame. Luckily I've never had the occasion to see him in full rage. The one time I'd fought him, he'd been toying with me, back when he was feeding off Anezka's crazy.

But, once the amulet transferred to me, he changed. His personality got a lot more mellow. Then we introduced him to Jai Li, and the troll twins, and he'd turned into a lovable muppet. And he kept the burning thing under control here at Black Briar. I think he'd become attuned to the place, felt it was home for him. It was bizarre. He called me master and wanted to be in my presence, but was at home here at Black Briar.

"More swords?" he asked after a few minutes. He'd just stood in the doorway and watched. He usually helped tend the forge, but with propane, there was no real need to keep the bellows rolling or stoke the coal.

I shrugged at him. "I like making them and it's Ren Faire season. Time to get some stock made up, ya know? Get some money rolling in."

Bub didn't have any use for money. Oh, I'm sure he'd love a lifetime supply of frozen bean burritos, but beyond that, what did he really need?

"You should make something for your motorcycle," he offered. "You have strength within you that you have not tapped."

It was strange carrying on a conversation with a smith. You could only get words in while the metal was firing. Then you had to wait while we pounded the metal in whatever fashion we were working at the time. Bub and I had a good rhythm. Didn't seem to miss a beat.

"The bike, huh?" I asked, setting the sword on the work bench and putting aside the tongs and hammer. "What did you have in mind?"

"You're a maker," he said, shrugging. "Make something useful."

"Swords are useful."

He shook his head and scratched his backside.

I grinned at him. He was very clear on his opinions. "Do you have any suggestions?"

The smithy we'd built here had the lifting walls like the one out at Anezka's place. They were hinged at the top, allowing me to push them out from the bottom and prop them open, leaving most of the four walls open to the outside. Only the load bearing parts didn't move. That and the doors.

Bub kicked his feet on the dirt floor of the smithy and shrugged again.

I caught a glimpse of Frick and Frack chasing Jai Li around the yard and up onto the deck of the main house—not looking at Bub, giving the little guy some space to formulate his thoughts.

"Well," he said. "You could put a rack mount for your sword instead of carrying it on your back. That way you could carry someone behind you without the sword smashing their face."

I sat on the work bench and thought it over.

"Bub, my friend. That is a smoking hot idea."

He beamed at me, raising his head and pulling his shoulders back.

"It'll take some design work but shouldn't take a whole lot of work to make it right." I walked over to the desk, pulled down one of the sketch pads we kept around, and picked up a charcoal pencil.

We spent the next hour drawing out ideas and calling up specs of the bike on my laptop. The bike was out at Circle Q in one of the barns. There was no place for it and the pickup at the Kent apartment. And I couldn't get both Katie and Jai Li on the bike.

In the end we opted for a latch mechanism that would allow me to lay the scabbard along the frame at a forty-five degree angle to the ground. It would rest flat against the bike to keep a low profile and not impact my leg position and allow for the tip to stop just to the side of the rear tire.

Looked good on paper. In the next few days, I'd drive out to Circle Q with Gram and see how it would lay out. It would definitely not fit with the sleek lines of the Ducati, but with the right push, the right bit of maker skill, and help from Bub's brand of magic, it should work. Hell, if the dwarves of legend could make a flying pig that glowed as it flew, I could adapt a rack for my sword on a motorcycle.

That was the theory. Bub was excited in any case. Maybe I'd get Gunther's opinion as well. He was good with tinkering with things. Couldn't hurt.

FIVE

unday afternoon we all had big plans at Black Briar. It was
coming up on the one-year anniversary of the battle with
the dragon, Duchamp, and his minions. We lost a lot of
good people that day and we felt it was appropriate to have
a little gathering to remember the fallen and the living. Rolph and
Skella were coming, but not Qindra. Jimmy couldn't take having
the witch there, even if he knew she meant us no harm. She was
still the dragon's, still Nidhogg's property.

We agreed to stay for dinner. No sense going all the way back
to Kent only to have to get up and drive back north for the
gathering.

Jai Li was excited to stay. She led a game of tag with Bub and
the troll twins, Frick and Frack, as soon as Katie had accepted the
invitation. I'd barely had time to wash up when Deidre was
shoving dishes into my hands to set the table

After dinner we sat out on the deck for a little while, watching
the kids play hide and seek. It wasn't too late, about eight, so the
kids were still wide awake. The trolls shrieked with joy as they
tumbled out of the barracks and tackled Jai Li. They didn't care
she was in a dress, and apparently neither did she.

We chatted with the permanent crew of the farm: Trisha and
her team, as well as a few new trainees who were on duty. Jimmy
said he had some work to do out in one of the sheds, so I
followed him out while Katie chatted with Deidre.

As we were heading past the barn, I saw that there was some construction going on out in the center of the fields where we had had our skirmish line set up the day the giants arrived by helicopters and we saw our first dragon.

I asked Jimmy about it, but he was noncommittal. Said I'd see what it was when everyone else did. I helped him work on the truck for a bit, then headed to the house. It had been a long day. I was looking forward to some sack time.

It was nice to stay with Jimmy and Deidre from time to time. Katie had grown up in this house, so she was comfortable here. Though she complained in private that it made her feel like a little kid again if she stayed too long. We got Jai Li bunked down in the living room after everyone else had gone. Katie and I would be staying in her old room now that Anezka had moved out.

Seems Anezka had moved in with Gunther. It was all hush-hush, but I'd be pressing him for details the next day. After her psychotic break, he'd been the one to help her find her way back. She wasn't one-hundred percent better, by any means, but she was stable and loved the big Viking. What could you do? I slept pretty well that night. Katie didn't have any more middle-of-the-night vomiting sessions so we all did pretty well.

The next morning was a blur of activity. We dragged the long tables out into the back yard, tapped a couple kegs, and generally cooked until we could barely stand. Deidre ran her kitchen like a drill sergeant. She had three different shifts, each for an hour or two, depending on the food being prepared. I was a gopher, running things out to coolers, or covering dishes for later. I was not allowed to actually assist in food prep if humans wanted to consume it later. Deidre was pretty blunt about my cooking skills, or lack thereof. Good thing I wasn't sensitive about it or anything.

Two o'clock rolled around and we had the food stacked all over the tables out in the yard—everything from roasts and whole chickens, to a dozen types of salads. There were desserts galore as well. I figured if I managed the day correctly I could easily gain a pound or two from carbs alone. Then there was the alcohol: mead and moonshine, beer and wine. This crew liked to party.

Rolph wouldn't show up until after dark, which was getting later these days, so we had to wait until then for the big unveiling out in the ruined hay field. We did some sparring, horseshoes and singing … lots and lots of singing. The more we drank, the louder we sang. It was like we were trying to make sure those we had lost over the last year could hear us singing their praises.

Just after dark, when the twilight hadn't faded and the stars were not quite yet out, Skella vanished to get Rolph. There was a mirror set up behind the barn, it turned out, a fairly wide one. I was surprised to find not just Rolph, but seven other dwarves trudging through the mirror and out into the field as the last rays of the sun fled the sky.

Deidre knew what was going on but wouldn't share. I was getting antsy with anticipation. The kids were dancing in the yard as Katie and a few of the others started another round of drinking songs.

At first there was a flash of light out in the field, like someone had touched a strobe light for one quick burst. The crowd fell silent and we began to hear the dwarves.

They were singing. Nothing too loud to start, more of a hint of sound, the deep rumblings of the sea. Then they raised their voices and the music became clearer. It was dirge, a song of mourning, and they sang it in their native language. I could pick out words here and there, something about rejoining loved ones after the end times, and passing across the black water. I wish I could've understood it all.

The crew got the point, though. People were crying and hugging each other. Jai Li made her way over to me and crawled into my lap. Bub ended up sitting at my feet, and Frick and Frack waddled back over to Trisha. We settled down and listened as the song went on.

I'm guessing there were eighteen or twenty stanzas in the song as they hit a chorus that many times. Each time I felt like a piece of pain was plucked from me and left to float up into the stars, preserving the memory, but easing the hurt.

When the eight voices finally fell silent, no one moved. Jai Li was holding her breath with her hand over her mouth. I could see Katie standing beside Deidre, her hands on the back of the wheel chair, with Jimmy beside them both. He had one hand on Deidre's shoulder and an arm over Katie's shoulders.

I know they were family and all, but I wanted her back with me, with Jai Li. We were her family, too.

Anezka and Gunther were sitting on a picnic table. He was nestled with his back between her legs and she had her arms over his shoulders.

Stuart stood by the kegs, draining his favorite goblet, the white foam of the beer glowing in the few hurricane lamps that were lit.

The dwarves were in shadow, silent and waiting for a signal. Jai Li finally took a gasping breath as the sky exploded in fireworks.

Great streamers roared into the sky followed by an assortment of flying Catherine wheels and shooting stars. The kids *oohed* and *ahhed*. People clapped and called out as each new light burst into the sky.

For the finale, a huge wall of white sparks shot up into the night. After the final spark died and our eyes began to adjust to the remaining light, we saw that the construction wall was gone.

A long statue was revealed. It showed several men and women struggling in battle with a giant while others pulled away the wounded. We began to walk forward as a series of spotlights came on, illuminating the statue.

It looked to have been carved from a single block of stone. Rolph glowed with pride as I followed the others in a hushed wave.

"This is but a token," he said, turning to face Jimmy, Deidre, and Katie. "My cousins who remain in Vancouver sought to make amends, pay the first drop in the long reconciliation with your clan. The last year has been unkind to all people of peace."

It was beautiful, and way beyond anything I'd ever dreamed of.

Jimmy strode forward and clasped Rolph in a wrist-to-wrist hand shake. They spoke to one another in hushed tones then they embraced. The hug was brief, then Deidre moved forward and Rolph knelt beside her chair. Jimmy moved down the line of solemn, bearded dwarves, clasping each in a warrior's hand shake, exchanging brief words. The crowd moved forward, each person either moving directly to the statue, or waiting their turn to shake hands with the dwarves.

Jai Li looked over her shoulder at me, eyebrows raised.

"Go on," I said, smiling. "Go see how well the carvers worked."

She hugged me, took Bub by the hand, and they scampered over to slip in and out of the crowd.

I sat on the edge of the deck, watching the survivors mingle around. There was a reverence here, a sense of honor and tribute.

Rolph finally pulled himself away from the crowd and came toward me, his arms flung wide and a huge grin on his face.

"Smith," he bellowed. I smiled and slid from the deck, letting him sweep me into a bear hug. He still smelled of the forge to me, hot metal and coal dust.

"Pretty amazing," I said, stepping back from him.

He shrugged. "They sought to honor you," he said, his voice dropping. "But I told them you would want no monuments in your name."

"Damn straight," I said, maybe a little too heated.

He looked at me, shaking his head. "You are a hero, young Sarah. Whether you want to hear it or not." He held up a hand to stop my protest. "No one asked your opinion on the matter. We were able to persuade them to honor more than just your deeds."

I knew I was blushing. Hell, I didn't want glory. I just wanted my family and friends to be safe.

"And the young elf," he said, gesturing over to where Skella stood laughing with Katie. "She has served as well, ferrying us back and forth each night for a month, letting us work when the sun was gone and the glory of the night embraced us."

"She's a good kid," I said. "She's done all right by us."

We turned to watch the crowd. I leaned back against the deck and he did the same, crossing his arms over his broad chest. "This is something my people can be proud of," he said, quietly. "There is much they have to atone for."

"So say we all."

Rolph made his way back into the crowd, accepting a huge mug of beer from Stuart. I made my way over through the crowd and took Katie's hand. She leaned against me and we studied the statue up close. I recognized the faces carved into that black stone. Each person who fought, whether or not they survived, was included in the long wall. The statue stood at least seven feet tall and ran twenty feet or more across the field. It wasn't a straight line, more of a wave. The lights shadowed several points and cast some into stark relief. In the distance you could make out the helicopters and the field of the dead. This was our final stand, just before the dragon took down Susan and Maggie. I remember it like it was yesterday.

Katie was crying quietly, holding my hand like she was afraid I would fly away. "It's beautiful," she said.

"Yeah," I breathed. "It's something."

We'd always have a place to honor our dead, but we also could never forget. I'm not sure which was better in the long run.

"Can we go home?" Katie asked me.

I looked down at her. "Sure hon, whatever you need."

"It's too much," she said. "I need a place to breathe."

I went and plucked Jai Li from the crowd while Katie went into the house to say goodbye to Deidre. We were leaving while the party was still going. I understood everyone's need to celebrate life, but there was a point where we just needed to pull away and find ourselves, even among the ruins of the past.

SIX

As I approached the house, I saw that Jimmy was standing in the kitchen, gesticulating pretty forcefully. By the time I heard the shouting, I handed Jai Li off to Trisha and asked her to cover for me while I went in.

Trisha grinned. "I won't deal with them when he's in a tirade," she said, hugging Jai Li to her chest. "I'll take her and the other kids over to the barracks to start settling down. They can play cards."

I nodded. "Thanks, Trisha. We'll come get her as soon as I figure out what's going on this time."

I hated when Jimmy and Katie fought. I'd thought they'd gotten past that little spat over the ring now that the necromancer was defeated. This was likely a new issue. I sighed and opened the door to the house, letting Jimmy's voice roll over me.

"Don't be such a damned child," he was bellowing.

Awesome. Just what we needed on this night.

Deidre made a face at me as I stepped into the kitchen—somewhere between run-for-your-life and get-me-out-of-here. A shame I was learning to gather that much from the set of her face and the nods.

"What's going on?" I asked loud enough to catch both Katie and Jimmy's attention.

Jimmy turned to me, his face livid. "You were with her," he said, pointing his meaty finger in my face.

"With her where?" I asked, calmly.

His nostrils flared and he blinked a couple of times before pulling his finger out of my face. "You met with the Mordred folks," he growled, swinging his attention back to Katie. For a moment, I thought he was going to hit her.

"Settle down, Jim," I said, taking a step between him and Katie. "Have you lost your mind?"

He shoved me in the shoulder, his fist up.

I stepped into him, grabbed his shirt in both of my hands, and slammed him back into the fridge. "You need to calm the fuck down," I said, pushing way from him and leaving him off balance. All that swinging a hammer and wrastlin' with horses gave me an edge.

He took one step toward me when Deidre barked out, "James, stop it."

That was the secret sauce. The fight seemed to fall away as his shoulders sagged and he lowered his arms. "You had no right," he said, the anger barely under control.

"No right?" Katie said. "They had mom and dad's wedding rings. Did you know that? Did you know that some elf died trying to steal those rings from their hotel room?"

Jimmy swallowed before answering. "No, I had no idea."

"It wasn't an official visit," I said, trying to be as reasonable as I could. "One of their people reached out to us. He claims he'd be in big trouble if his people found out he went around channels."

"Yeah, he works for a bunch of idiots like Jimmy here," Katie groused.

"Stop it," Deidre said, putting her hand on Katie's arm. "Not tonight. Let this go."

Katie whirled to face her, tears streaming down her face. "When then, huh, Dee? When do we talk about shit? When Jimmy's had his nap?"

"I'm your Seneschal," Jimmy growled.

"No," Katie said, turning back to him. "I'm not one of your little soldiers you can boss around. I'm your sister. And this is as much my house as it is yours. Mom and dad left it to both of us. So, you can get off your damn high horse and leave me the fuck alone."

That was news to me. Made sense; but Jimmy didn't like hearing it.

She turned and stalked down the hallway. Jimmy started to go after her, but I stepped in front of him again. "Let her go," I said. "You need to calm down and tell me how this got so far out of control."

Jimmy looked down at me, then turned to look at Deidre. She nodded and he stepped back, pulled a chair out from the kitchen table and sat down.

I took that as a good sign and did the same.

"She's up to something," he said, making two fists on top of the table. "I caught her sneaking around the house a couple of times and it's just creepy. I don't have anything to hide from her."

"Beyond the ring and whatever those other two statues are in your safe deposit box, right?"

"Don't you start, too," he said.

The family was coming apart at the seams. It had only been a year since the dragons went live in our communal psyche. We'd lost a lot of good people trying to fight back the crazy shit in the world. I just never thought I'd see Jimmy coming this unglued.

"So, what if she's poking around?" I asked.

"It's the journal," Deidre said. "Her mom's diary, the one that almost killed Jimmy."

"What about it?"

"It's missing," Jimmy said. "When I asked her about it she got pretty ugly."

"It's like she's another person," Deidre said.

I looked at her, then back at Jim. Was she another person? They've known her a lot longer than I have, but I was around her more and in more intimate situations. I didn't think she was a different person, like she was possessed or anything. But she was definitely changed by the events of the last year. Who wouldn't be?

"She's having a hard time," I said, confirming their fears by the look they exchanged. "The doctors still don't know what's causing her to be so wiped out all the time, and the nose bleeds haven't stopped."

"I think it's the diary," Jimmy said.

"No," Deidre said, shaking her head. "This started before I showed her the diary."

Jim glanced in her direction for a second, but looked down at his hands. There was bad blood over that decision. I was not going to step into this marriage, they'd have to come to terms with that on their own.

"It all started out at that house," Deidre continued. "Something happened when she was out there, the time the witch got trapped out there. I noticed things were different then."

That far back? I considered her behavior back to last fall, just after her birthday. Things have been crazy for a year. I was having a hard time picking out any particular event that was a change.

"You don't see it," Deidre said, patting me on the hand. "You're with her every day. These changes have been more subtle, building over time. We don't hardly see her anymore and the differences are noticeable."

"Like what?" I asked, suddenly very concerned.

"She used to be so damned optimistic," she said, smiling at Jimmy. "Both of them were."

Jimmy shrugged but I could tell he was calming down. There was a lot of anger boiling underneath the surface of that man. Anger made you reckless. I knew that first hand.

"But it's more than that," Jimmy said, finally. His voice cracking as he spoke. "She doesn't trust me. I can see it when she looks at me."

"What? No." I looked at him, but he wouldn't look me in the eye. "She loves you."

"Something's broken," he mumbled and pushed his chair back. Neither of us stopped him as he crossed the kitchen and went out the back door.

"He's right," Deidre said. "She's gotten pushy, demanding."

I thought about our lunch with Charlie Hague. "Has she tried to get you to tell you things? Like she was compelling you?"

Deidre quirked her eyebrows up, questioningly. "No, but Jimmy said something about that, how she had brow beat him into telling her about family stuff, trying to see if he was keeping anything back."

I sighed. She said she'd done it a time or two before.

"Did she have another nosebleed?"

"Yeah, vomiting and headache," she said. "Was a couple of weeks ago. She'd come out while you were out with Julie over in Cle Elum."

I remembered that day. Julie and I had driven over to visit with Frank Rodriguez. We were going to be gone late so Katie and Jai Li had stayed out at Black Briar. Katie had missed school the next day, sick.

"But Jimmy's losing it, too," I said. "Is there something else going on that I'm not aware of?"

She smiled at me. "Everything's changing," she said. "Gunther has moved Anezka in with him, so he doesn't come over as often. Stuart is making himself more scarce as well. I think Jim's just missing his friends, and he's worried sick about Katie."

"And the diary?"

She sighed. "I know Katie took it. The girl could never lie to me. She's got a right to it, but this is just childish behavior. Jimmy's afraid he's going to lose her. He won't admit it publicly, but," she leaned in, lowering her voice, "he's been having dreams where she's calling for help, lost someplace we can't find her. Night after night, he wakes up agitated. I think he was crying the other morning, but you'd never get him to admit it." She shook her head.

"Damn." I sat there looking her Deidre. We both loved the remaining members of the Cornett family, and they were both pulling away from us, lost in their own worlds of pain and fear.

"I'll talk to her," I said, pushing my chair back.

Deidre waved me toward the hallway. "I expect she's down in her old room crying her eyes out. Wouldn't be the first time."

SEVEN

I started down the hall and Deidre rolled out the back door after Jim. I checked in Katie's old room, the one we'd just stayed in, and she wasn't there. That was odd. I checked the bathroom, the other two guest rooms, and even poked my head into Jimmy and Deidre's room. She wasn't there. There wasn't a back door, so unless she crawled out one of the windows, she'd vanished into thin air.

The way things have been lately, that was a possibility. Hell, Skella could've grabbed her and taken her through a mirror, or Bub could've done a snatch and grab, porting her elsewhere.

But I didn't really think those were real possibilities. I was walking back down the hall to go outside and ask around when I noticed one of the wall panels was cocked up. I touched it and it swung open revealing a set of stairs going down.

This was the secret(ish) bunker of the Cornett's. I ducked and stepped into the shadows of the stairs and pulled the door closed behind me with a soft click.

"Katie?" I called softly.

I heard something down below. At the bend in the stairs I paused, remembering a story Katie had told me about the first time she and Jimmy had come down here. Her father and mother had gone off to help some refugees who were escaping from Canada and the dragon there. They were being chased by giants. Made my head hurt just to think of those events as someone's history and not fiction.

I turned and started down the remaining stairs, emerging into the bunker in all its eclectic glory. I'd been down her twice before, once with Katie, and once with Jimmy, Gunther, and Stuart. The place was a cross between Indiana Jones' secret lair and a rummage sale. There were artifacts stacked everywhere, over-flowing book shelves and display cases, and in the center of the north wall, the huge dragon map.

Opposite the map were two leather chair and a small table between them. Katie was curled up in one of the chairs staring at the map. I squatted down next to her and stroked her hair.

"Hey, babe. You doing okay?"

She didn't answer right away, but placed her hand on mine. We sat there quietly for a few minutes. I shifted and sat down on my knees and she sat up, rubbing her eyes. Her nose must have been bleeding a little because she smeared red across the side of her face.

"All those lights," she said, pointing to the map. "I dream about those lights." She turned in her seat, taking my hands in hers. "All those dragons, Sarah. How can we ever win?"

I squeezed her hands and smiled. "We win by staying alive, by loving each other, and by staying true to who we are."

More tears sprang into her eyes and she took a long shuddering breath. "I think I'm lost," she whispered. "I don't know if I know who I am any longer."

I leaned forward, pulling her into me, wrapping my arms around her. "I know who you are," I said, quietly. "You're Kathryn Elizabeth Cornett. You are a warrior and a skald, a teacher and a lover. And above all else, in my world, you are the sun and the moon." I paused as she squeezed me harder, like maybe she was drowning. "You're my one true love, Katie. Forever and for true."

We sat there for a few more minutes, just holding one another. Eventually she pulled back far enough to kiss me once on the mouth than sat back and rubbed her face. More blood.

I went to stand, but she held me back. "Wait," she said, pulling a pack of tissues from her pocket and wiping her face. She wiped a bit of wetness from my cheeks that could've been tears, I couldn't say for sure. Then she sat back with one hand holding a wad of tissues to her nose and the other clasping my hand to her chest.

I watched her face as she tilted forward to prevent the blood from draining back down her throat and choking her. She had her eyes closed, and by the little lines along the sides of her eyes, I could tell she was in pain.

Of course, by this time, my legs were starting to go numb, but I wasn't moving, not for anything. Not until she was ready.

First her breath started to calm and find a more soothing rhythm. Then she fluttered her eyes open, glancing first at the map, then over at me. Then she let my hand go and sat up straight.

"I'm sorry I'm such a jerk," she said, a wry smile playing on her lips.

"Do we somehow have our roles reversed?" I asked her. "Isn't it my job to apologize?"

She laughed a little, nothing too much, but a brief moment of quiet release.

I tried to stand then, but my legs were nothing but pins and needles. I leaned against her chair, and she stood, helping to pull me to my feet.

"Sorry," she said again as I waddled around in a circle, stamping my feet and gritting my teeth as the nerves starting firing all at once.

Once I was flexible again, I put my arms around her waist and turned toward the map, pointing to the upper left of the United States, toward the only light to be snuffed out by human hands in recorded history.

"We don't have to beat them all," I said. "We just have to defend ourselves against those that are monsters. I'm beginning to think that some of them may be redeemable."

She looked at me, quizzical and surprised. "Has Nidhogg converted you?"

I shrugged. "They're monsters, there's no denying that," I began, letting my thoughts fall into place, verbalizing something I'd been thinking a while, but never pieced together in a coherent sentence. "But I think they have the capability for compassion and that's enough for us to try. They're not all alike, and they definitely don't all get along."

"You think?" she asked, a bit of wonder in her voice as she stared at the map. "So we can turn them against one another?"

Interesting thought, but not what I'd been piecing together.

"Not exactly, but what if we can get the good ones to stop treating us like prey, open their minds, let them start seeing us as thinking, caring, viable entities that deserve their respect and their protection."

She raised her eyebrows at that, but let me continue.

"And not the protection in the way most of them do today, like we were cattle and they had to protect us from predators. More like partners in a peaceful and prosperous world."

She leaned into me, grasping my arm in her hands and putting her head against my shoulder. "I'd love to see that work," she said. "But I just don't know if they're capable."

"I can't speak for them," I admitted. "But I get the strong impression that recent events are forcing Nidhogg to rethink her position. And the deal with Frederick Sawyer before Christmas—something changed there. When Justin and his blood cult snatched Mr. Philips, I think Sawyer had a real moment there where he was lost without his most able of servants."

"I wish I could've seen Nidhogg protecting him there at the end," Katie said, her voice almost wistful. "It sounded majestic."

"Nidhogg was beautiful," I agreed. "And when she stood over Sawyer's broken body, I felt the same energy I felt from Trisha protecting Frick and Frack ..." I paused, turning her back to look at me. "The same thing I feel for you and Jai Li."

She smiled and nodded

"And the same thing I feel for Black Briar, for Gunther, Stuart, Deidre, and even Jimmy."

She pursed her lips at that and moved them to the side, thinking—her eyes narrowed like she meant to argue.

"He loves you the best way he knows how," I said, before she could launch a salvo.

"He's an ass," she said, but there was no heat in her voice. "And I know he loves me. It's smothering sometimes, you know?"

I nodded, letting her continue.

"I mean, look at all this," she said, stepping back, keeping one hand in mine and sweeping her other arm to encompass the room. "I had to badger him into letting me come down here. He thinks I'm a child and can't be trusted with any of this."

I glanced over to Jimmy and Gunther's swords and the great axe that Stuart wielded in the battle with the giants, trolls, and ogres. The blades were dwarven made, commissioned by Jimmy for him and his two best friends, back before they really thought of the consequences of war.

Many of the remaining objects had historical value, links to other groups, secret societies, and ancient lore, but they were scraps and cast-offs, useless in today's world.

"Do you think there are any true artifacts here?" I asked, stepping toward one of the glass display cases, pulling her along with me.

We glanced down at the torques, rings, bracelets, and charms. Nothing in this case caught my attention.

"Trinkets," she said, sighing deeply. "Detritus of a world that vanished long ago. Maybe you're right," she said, glancing back at the map. "Maybe we need to stop looking to the toys of the past and start making a new future."

We stood there in the semi-darkened room, watching the dragon lights; some bright, some dim, but all a point of power beyond any one of us, and maybe all of us if we remained afraid and divided.

We had to start working together. "We are stronger together than apart," I said. "You need to stop fighting with Jimmy and start putting together an alliance for us to move forward."

"You're right," she said. She dropped my hand, ran her fingers through her hair and straightened her shirt. "I'll go apologize to Jim and start a conversation about a partnership."

"Excellent," I said, hugging her again.

We turned to the long staircase upwards, hand in hand, moving to a new understanding of our little piece of the world.

I didn't have the heart to bring up the diary. One battle at a time. I just hope I didn't live to regret it.

EIGHT

Katie sat in her classroom well after school had ended the following Monday. Her room was covered in brightly colored pictures of elephants, unicorns, narwhals, and dinosaurs. She'd finished her planning for the week. Everything was graded and put away. She could've gone home an hour earlier, but she was studying her mother's diary.

She'd spent time after New Year's snooping through Jimmy's house any chance she got, looking for the book. Just recently she broken down and resorted to that song Sarah had picked up in Nidhogg's library—the secret finder that made the singer pay a high price. For days after she'd have headaches or nosebleeds. Usually both.

Sarah was getting antsy, sending her to see Melanie and then a couple of specialists. She thought maybe Katie had a brain tumor. Katie couldn't tell her she was using the song to find the diary. It was private. She had found it a couple of weeks ago and kept it stashed in her car at first. Someplace Sarah wasn't likely to go snooping around. Then she transferred it to school, hiding it in her desk. The children would never dream of opening her desk. It was safe there. Safe enough.

She hadn't dared open it, yet. This book had nearly killed Jimmy years earlier when he'd tried. Their mother had placed violent and dangerous spells on it to protect it. She wasn't just keeping out childish prying. This was serious magic—deadly.

Katie was bound and determined to figure it out—without Jimmy or Sarah. This was her secret.

Things had changed inside her since drinking that mead last fall, her power grew stronger and the consequences of her magic had gotten suddenly dangerous. Then, after they'd battled the cult before Christmas, things had started getting worse. There was a darkness in her, a voice that pushed her, a voice that dared her to throw caution to the wind. Life was too capricious, too violent and short to wait on niceties.

She'd learned that at the hands of the dragon Jean-Paul. Despite Sarah's recent change of heart, dragons were not fluffy bunnies. They were manipulative killers, torturers, rapists. Katie knew she had to find something to even the odds. Her new found powers with music was one thing, cute and helpful, but nothing compared to Sarah's Gram, or Qindra's magical abilities. Maybe, just maybe, this diary would give her the power to protect those around her. Something to prove she would never be a victim again.

Today she just wanted to look at the diary, maybe open it. It probably wouldn't kill her. She'd touched it with no repercussions. Deidre had handled it with no problems— something about sympathetic magic, she thought. Women's magic. Like the ring the necromancer had used to transform Trisha into a dragon. He couldn't have used the ring himself.

The diary cover was a dark leather that had somehow been molded to seal not only along the spine like a normal book, but also across the other three edges, hiding the pages within. It had taken her a few weeks to even hold the book for very long. She could feel the power in it, the way it wanted to leap from her hands if she gripped it too tightly. There were marks on it, a few cuts and a burn on the lower left corner, like a cigarette would leave. Careless marks, not mutilations.

Other than that, there were no other markings. If Deidre hadn't shown it to her originally, she would've had no way of knowing to whom it had once belonged. At least not visually. There was the one thing that happened when she held it gently and with care. Instead of a beast ready to spring, the book flooded her with that feeling that lingers moments after someone you love deeply releases you from an embrace. Twice, when she was just holding the book and letting her mind wander, she'd smelled lilacs and her mother's perfume. That convinced her of the books true ownership.

She let her mind drift as she stroked the book. Better to have an open mind, breathe a little. Her fears, and her worries were always at the surface.

Charlie Hague and the Mordred folks had been weighing on her mind. They knew things she didn't; had her parents wedding bands. Katie didn't trust them, though Sarah seemed to think that Charlie was a harmless enough guy. Katie just wasn't convinced.

On the home front, Sarah was totally supporting and Jai Li provided joy she had only imagined. But she knew she couldn't share these thoughts with them. And definitely not the diary. This was for her alone. And she had to keep it secret, keep it safe. Her thoughts drifted to Hobbits and birthday parties for a moment, and the irony of secrets blossomed brightly in her mind. She quashed the guilt and thought maybe it was time to go home. Jai Li would be missing her, and Sarah would be home eventually. Maybe she'd make some dinner.

She cleared the remaining papers off her desk and opened the drawer where she kept her purse. She was debating on putting the diary into her purse when voices from the hall startled her. Most everyone should've gone home by now. She dropped the diary into the drawer, stood, and walked to the open door, glancing down the hallway. Mrs. Danby was shaking hands with a young man in a white lab coat and carrying a medical kit. Katie was speechless for a moment: Was that Charlie Hague?

Once Mrs. Danby had walked back into her classroom and the young man had turned, Katie stepped into the hall. It was definitely Charlie Hague. Here, in her school. Alarms sounded in her head. She thought maybe she should go back into her classroom and shut the door, but he'd seen her and stopped, his face wary and his body tense.

"Hello, Ms. Cornett" he said. "I didn't expect to see you here." He stayed where he was, his medical bag clutched to his chest. He glanced down the hall to the exit. "I was down at Mrs. Danby's classroom'—he pointed back over his shoulder— "checking on her rabbits."

Katie leaned against her doorframe. "Are they in need of medical care?" she asked, watching him.

He laughed nervously, "Nothing too serious, I promise. Ms. Nibbles is going to have a litter anytime now. Mrs. Danby just wanted us do to a checkup. Can't have something horrible happen to the classroom's favorite pet, can we?"

She smiled. He was clean cut, dressed professionally. She could see a collared shirt and tie under the coat. He didn't look dangerous.

"I'm sorry about our last meeting," she said, taken suddenly with a need to justify her actions.

He held up one hand, forestalling her. "No harm, no foul," he said, but his eyes didn't speak of forgiveness. He was scared of her. "I really shouldn't be here, talking to you," he started walking, hugging the far wall, like he was afraid to get too close to her.

She stiffened, taking a quick look toward the door to the playground. "I promise never to do that again," she said, feeling like she meant it. There was another voice in her head, an angry voice that told her he didn't deserve her compassion, but she ignored it.

He seemed to relax a bit. "That makes me feel better," he said. "I'm sorry I don't have the rings with me." He stepped three more steps toward the exit, but kept facing her. "They're safe," he said, holding up his hands. "But we need an official meeting, I think. I got some heat from our last ..." he paused with the hint of a cringe, "... meeting. Madame Gottschalk was not pleased that I'd taken the initiative." He fished in his jacket and pulling out a card. "Call me when you want to set up a meeting and I'll make the arrangements." He held his arm outstretched, his card protruding between two fingers. "I really do think it would be in both our best interests to get together and combine forces," he shrugged. "At least share intelligence if we can't come to an outright alliance."

Katie crossed her arms and he let his arm drop with a sigh. "How do you know about us?" she asked.

"I'm really sorry," he said, taking a step nearer to her, holding up his arm once more. "I want to answer all your questions, but we have to do it properly."

"How do you know about me and my brother?"

He let his arm drop once again. "Fair question," he said, leaning back against the wall opposite her. "I have associates who are familiar with your"—he hesitated—"current activities, let's say."

Heat flashed through Katie. The thought of them spying on them, on Black Brair. Her thoughts flitted back to the bugs they'd found in Jimmy's house.

"Did you bug my brother's house?" she asked.

He sighed, his shoulders sagging and his confidence waning. "We did," he said, taking another step away. "I really just need to make contact with you folks. My order was on friendly terms with your parents. Before they disappeared."

Katie's head came up so fast, her teeth clacked together. "How do I know you didn't make them disappear?" she asked. Anger rose in her and the dark voice in her head started to howl.

"We're watchers," he said, holding up one hand, showing his wrist and the tattoo exposed under his coat sleeve. "Bestellen von Mordred," he said. "We shared information with your parents. We were allied, I swear."

Katie marched over to him, grabbing him by the shoulder. "Where are my parents?"

"Whoa, there," Charlie said, shrugging her hand off his shoulder and backing away. "I don't know much, honestly. I'm not even supposed to be talking to you, but I'll tell you what I know."

"Start talking," Katie said, squaring up to him and clenching her hands into fists. "Either tell me something I want to hear or get the hell out." Her temper was flaring to the danger zone.

Charlie held one hand up as if to forestall an attack. "Mrs. Gottschalk knows more than I do. We should really meet with her. I honestly don't know much."

"You," Katie said, poking him in the shoulder with one finger. "What do *you* know?"

Charlie paled, the fear coloring his features in shades of white and grey. That just made her even more angry. She wanted someone to throttle, not cow. "Iceland," he said, glancing back over his shoulder to the open doorway. "They were meeting some people about a new archeological dig. Rumor had it they'd uncovered evidence of Jómsborg."

Katie shook her head, confused. "Pardon?"

"Viking sect," he said. "Rumored to have a homeland in the south Baltic sea region. Crazy warriors according to legends. No real evidence they existed, though. Nothing concrete."

Katie's anger began to ebb. "They went to Iceland to look at an archeological dig?"

"That was their starting point, or so our sources say." Charlie looked innocent enough. Just a guy trying to have a conversation.

"Is that the official reason for the trip, or the secret reason?"

Charlie laughed a fearful guffaw. "Touché. That is the secret reason. Officially, they told both the Icelandic and United States governments that they were just sight-seeing."

Katie stepped back, leaned against the wall by her classroom door. "That makes sense based on what I know," she said. "But why are you talking to us now? Why haven't you contacted us sooner?"

She'd hit a nerve there. He looked down, shuffling his feet. "Politics," he mumbled.

"What?"

He looked up at her. "Honestly, political bullshit. Our order is afraid of every shadow, double-checks and rechecks everything just to make sure we're safe—in the shadows—in control."

Now it was Katie's turn to chuckle. "You sound disgruntled."

"Hell, yes," he said. Suddenly he looked more in control. "Gottschalk will totally kick my ass, but I have to tell you. They're scared out of their minds that you folks are going to fuck things up and bring the wrath of the dragons down on all of us."

Katie made a thoughtful pout. "That was brutally honest."

Charlie shrugged again. "Look, if Sarah has"—he leaned in to whisper—"really killed a dragon." He glanced over his shoulder and back. "They are gonna flip their shit."

"And do what?"

He pulled back, shocked. "You mean it's true?"

Now it was Katie's turn to shrug. "Why are you asking me? If you're watchers, wouldn't this be the exact kind of thing you should be watching for? If you don't even know if that much is true, how good can you guys be. Sheesh."

Charlie flushed. "They're a bunch of old women," he said. "All they do is drink their tea, bitch about the old days, and warn us against moving too fast. I'm the youngest recruit and I don't know much." This was something that had been eating him a while, it seemed. "Half the time I think they only recruited me because they needed a gopher—or more likely free vet care for their damned cats."

Katie smiled at that. That's how Jimmy made her feel. Like she wasn't good enough to play with the grownups. "I guess they saw something there," she said, feeling her anxiety drain away. "I'm sure you add something to the group." Suddenly she felt very sorry for young Charlie Hague. He was about her age, maybe a year older, and, it seemed, out of his league.

"Well, you'd think I had something to add," he started, getting a full head of steam. "Like speaking seven languages, having degrees in history, veterinary medicine, and theater?"

"Really?"

"Hey, I thought I was going into the CIA. I had no idea all this dragon bullshit existed."

They stood there a minute, quietly. He was looking at his feet again and she watched him.

"Okay, we'll call you," she said, holding out her hand.

He fumbled with his bag, shuffling it to his other hand and held up the now crumpled business card. "We can arrange a meeting anytime you want," he said, smiling. "Gottschalk will want things to be secure and obfuscated."

"Oh, we're all over that," she said, taking the card. "Let me make some calls and we'll get back with you."

He looked relieved, grabbed his pack to his chest and stepped back toward the door. "Crazy running into you. I really was looking in on Mrs. Danby's rabbits."

Katie waved at him as he hurried down the hallway and out the door at the end. She glanced down at the card. Crazy days.

She shut her classroom door and went back to her desk, dropping the card in a coffee mug she kept pencils in and sat down, rubbing her temples. There was headache building and she needed to either get some painkillers in her, or find a nap somewhere.

Instead she opened the drawer to her desk and pulled out her mother's diary once again. She stroked the cover, thinking. That was a lot of coincidence right there. He seemed harmless, but seriously ... She should go down the hall to Mrs. Danby's room, see if she was still around. The thought made her forehead ache. Better to sit here a minute, close her eyes and think.

For a few moments just having her eyes closed seemed to be helping. Then she felt a pulse from the diary. A tiny throb that barely registered against her finger tips. She cracked her eyes and looked around. She had a ground floor classroom, so anyone could be snooping out in the bushes. Better to take this someplace away from prying eyes.

She looked to the back of her classroom and saw the small bathroom. All the kindergarten classes had one. The little ones didn't always have time to make it down the hall.

The door shut quietly behind her as she flicked on the light. There was no sound in here. She lowered the lid on the toilet and sat down, caressing the book. Her mother's book. This held secrets of her mother that no one knew. Would it lead her to find her missing parents? God the pain of missing them was stronger these days.

Taking a deep breath, she began to sing the little ditty Sarah had found among Nidhogg's books. The discordant song that made her teeth ache and her nose bleed.

She sang quietly while tracing the edge of the diary. Her ears popped and the bathroom door began to vibrate. She finished the song through one time and picked it up again from the beginning. Along the spine edge of the book, runes began to glow with dull purple light.

By the time she'd finished the four stanza tune a second time, blood dripped from her nose. It caught her by surprise. The fat drop struck the diary cover and a bell sounded inside the small room—a noise so loud her ears rang for a moment. In her hands, the book shook once, as if giving a little sigh.

Instead of staunching her flowing nose, she leaned closer and sang the song again, letting the drops strike the book like the thrumming call of funeral bells. Her head swam and her vision blurred.

After the seventh drop, the book shuddered and a seam appeared along the edge opposite the spine. For an instant it flashed with a deep purple explosion and the sound of chains striking the floor echoed within the bathroom. The book rattled for another second and then lay still—the runes fading like the afterimage of a flash bulb. She opened the book, placed her hand on the first page and tried to focus. A spasm ran up her arm and the dark voice in her head rose in exultation.

Her head pounded and the floor rose up to meet her. The book tumbled from her hands as she struck the linoleum. She could feel the blood running down her face before she lost all feeling. The light faded and the ringing in the room grew louder. Somewhere in the distance she heard calling voices and slamming doors.

The last thought that flitted through her mind was the first words scrawled on the page in her mother's handwriting.

"You're dying, Katie love. The draught will be your doom."

NINE

I was in the back of the studio at Flight Test working on *Cheerleaders of the Apocalypse* with Jones and Carnes, my two volunteer lieutenants. *Grandma* Jones was a retired nurse who enjoyed being out with creative types rather than become one of those crazy cat ladies or hoarders. *Cry-Baby* Carnes was a twenty-year-old trust-fund baby who never had to lift a finger, so instead of being bored, he poured his ample free time into Flight Test. They were a good pair, she helped him see reality by taking him along on her forays into the homeless shelters and food banks that filled the rest of their days.

I'd been pretty rough on them during the shooting of *Elvis Versus the Goblins*, but they'd managed to see past my ass-hattery and stay on the movie. They were good people, better than I deserved some days.

We were working on costuming with the cheerleader brigade. Imagine a dozen well-endowed extras prancing around in low-cut sweaters and too short mini-skirts. Carnes was loving it, but Jones complained that these girls would catch their death of cold. I just couldn't imagine wanting to fight mutants in this type of outfit. It was so beyond silly it was offensive, but that's what the script called for, and Carl Tuttle, the director said it would increase sales. If Jennifer McDowell, our fearless co-leader and director of photography hadn't approved things, I'd have probably punched Carl for being such a pig.

Jones and Carnes had been with us on every movie Flight Test had done—all the way back to *Blood Brother One*, which had sold about twenty copies, if you didn't count the ones the actors picked up to preserve for when they got famous. I hadn't even been around for that, but JJ had. Joseph (JJ) Montgomery was the meal-ticket—our star actor, and he knew it.

JJ had been going through his lines, really kicking it for about the last hour. As much as it pained me to admit, the guy had major talent. And his personality was morphing. I don't know if he was smoking something other than cigarettes, but since the end of *Elvis Versus the Goblins* he'd started acting differently— nearly human. There *was* this girl, Wendy Lawson. The guy was smitten in the worst way. He usually chased strippers and the like, but since meeting Wendy he'd flipped. Honestly, I think it was love. I had no idea how they met, but while my life was going seventeen kinds of crazy, he'd met this hot young college chick and they'd co-written the movie we were now working on. It was nuts.

It rankled me exactly how good the script was. JJ may be a total whore, but he had a way with dialog that sang. When he delivered his lines in practice I was blown away. The young women we'd hired to play the cheerleaders for this film nearly all swooned when JJ was working.

It made me want to vomit a little. Just a little. Carl, the overall brainchild of Flight Test movie studio had mentioned he thought that this would be JJ's last movie. Jennifer was working the Wendy angle, digging for confirmation. It was more of a hunch, but we were small time. JJ was growing into an actor that would eventually catch Hollywood's attention. Whether he left on his own or someone came and took him away, he would not be stinking up this Podunk little outfit for much longer.

So Jones, Carnes, and I had our hands full of gotchas and hooters for the better part of the hour that JJ was dazzling the crew with his work. We could hear the rehearsal, but not really see what was going on.

Then all hell broke loose. There was this moment, right at five-thirty where a wave of energy broke over me—like something brushed my soul. It was magic, I knew it by the taste.

I looked up, turning to face the actors, when JJ made a gargling sound and fell to the floor.

"Shit!" Carl swore and dropped his clipboard onto the floor. "Beauhall," he called.

I was on my feet and half way across the sound stage before he took his second breath. He looked terrified.

"Call 911," he ordered. "Beauhall?"

"Here, boss." I skidded to a halt next to him and looked down. JJ was flopping around on the floor, convulsing. Blood was running from his mouth, nose, eyes, and ears.

I dropped to my knees and grabbed his head, cupping both sides with my hands and bracing it between my knees to prevent him from bashing his brains out. There was a lot of blood.

People were standing around us, watching like our species was born to do, mesmerized by pain and blood.

"Scatter," Cry-baby Carnes called, pushing through the crowd. Grandma Jones followed closely behind him.

"I'm a nurse," Jones called, squatting beside JJ. She didn't touch him, but watched as he convulsed, his feet drumming on the wooden floor.

"Don't touch any blood," Jones called to those around us. Everyone stepped back. Not me, of course, I was already holding his head steady. My hands were covered in blood.

"Ambulance is on the way," Nathan called from the back of the crowd. Nathan was our security guard. Good kid. Three tours in Afghanistan and a heart of gold.

Three and a half minutes. That's what it took for the EMTs to roll in with a stretcher. JJ convulsed the entire time. The crowd just stood there, watching. Several people were crying, and I think someone threw up. The whole world had narrowed down to this young, arrogant man whose life was leaking out of him for no apparent reason.

Then the crowd parted and two EMTs materialized beside me.

"Don't move," the first one said to me. He was gruff but gave me a quick smile. "We'll take care of things," he said again. "Just keep his head steady."

His partner, a young red-headed guy with a face full of freckles and green, green eyes was cutting JJ's sleeve open to expose his arm.

The ginger kid shot JJ with something that caused the convulsions to lessen and you could feel the tension in the room drop a few notches.

He'd lost a lot of blood, but he was breathing. The gruff guy was getting vitals while Ginger started an IV. Once the IV was in, they scooped JJ onto a body-board, got him onto the stretcher, and out the door. They were in and out in under three minutes.

I sat there while they disappeared. I couldn't move.

The whole time I'd been holding his head I could hear him screaming. Not out loud, but in my head. There was something deeply magical about all this. I couldn't tell if it was an actual attack or some external catalyst that had triggered this reaction in him. Whatever the hell had swept over the room, JJ was the only one affected.

A second ambulance showed up, as well as two senior fire and rescue folks who began asking all sorts of questions and cordoned off the studio. They checked each and every one of us to make sure no one else was affected, then they began testing the area for contaminants. I could've told them it was no use. The thing that had triggered JJ's seizure was long gone, a ripple in the fabric of reality that had washed over us all like a shockwave.

That's what it was, I realized. A shockwave. Somewhere, a magical explosion of sorts had happened. Now I just needed to know where the epicenter was. I couldn't imagine what it would have been like to be near ground zero. JJ's head may have exploded.

"As soon as the emergency folks clear everyone, send them home," Carl said to Nathan. "I need to find Jennifer."

"You got it, boss," Nathan said. He put his arm over Clyde's shoulder. "Come on, big guy. Let's see about the hospital."

"Harborview ," Grandma Jones said, standing and placing a hand on my shoulder. They'll chopper him in. He's lost too much blood. "

"Holy Jesus," Clyde said.

I looked up at him, caught by the sheer terror and despair in those two words. Clyde was one of those bearded and tattered men, mid-fifties, rough around the edges, but knew more about camera work than anyone I'd ever met. Of course, I was only twenty-eight. He and JJ were best friends, a relationship I never could figure out.

"We should call Wendy," Clyde said. "She'll want to go to the hospital."

"You can use the phone out at the security desk," Nathan said, steering the dazed man.

The room cleared and I just sat there and tried to find the thread of that wave, concentrated on the feeling that had passed over me. I wanted to burn it into my mind. I bet if I had Gram I could pinpoint the disturbance. As it was, I was afraid that if I moved I'd lose it altogether.

No one bothered me, no one asked me anything. I was an island of pain and concentration amid a maelstrom of chaos. Eventually the pins and needles grew strong enough to drown out the thread. It was definitely south of us, but I had no clear idea where. This was not my area of expertise. I was sensitive to magic, but to pinpoint it and follow it, that was beyond me.

When I was done, Grandma Jones helped me to my feet and back into the locker rooms. I ducked into the shower and hosed all the blood off me. I'd been in this situation more times than I like to remember. I bundled the soaked jeans into a garbage bag. My first inclination was to burn them. Maybe I'd take them out to Black Briar.

By the time I got back into the soundstage, Jones and Carnes were the only two left. They'd been mopping up, using a lot of bleach by the smell of the place.

Carl and Jennifer were closed up in his office. I could see them talking through the big window. Time to head out.

I thanked my lieutenants for all the help and sent them on their way with a promise to call once we figured out when we'd work again. With JJ in the hospital, we were out of commission. We'd been working this film for a few months. Shooting live for six weeks. Six weeks with JJ in the lead role. With him down, we either started from scratch, or gave him time to recover. I wasn't betting on a swift recovery—Hell, I just hoped he lived.

I walked back to the props cage and grabbed my personal kit. Jai Li might still be over at Circle Q with Julie, Mary, and Mrs. Sorenson. They did some part-time babysitting for us when

Katie's and my schedule wouldn't work out to keep her. I tapped on the office window and waved at Carl and Jennifer, pantomiming leaving. Jennifer gave me the universal hand signal for "I'll call you."

The parking lot was nearly deserted by the time I hit fresh air. Nathan stood there waiting. He wouldn't let any of us be here after dark without him. Good kid. I waved at him from my truck and watched as he settled back against the wall by the exit door. He'd stay until Carl and Jennifer left.

Katie didn't answer her phone. Since I didn't have any messages, I called Julie to let her know what was going on out at Flight Test. She said they could keep Jai Li until Katie came. Not sure what good I'd be, but I thought it best if I went over to see how JJ was doing. Carl and Wendy needed the support, if nothing else.

I expect Katie was on her way out to pick up Jai Li; it was still pretty early. She put in a lot of hours outside of the typical school day. I called her again, but it went straight to voicemail. I left a quick message about JJ and Jai Li. She must be in with one of her peers or something. Not like her to ignore my calls.

Good chance we wouldn't have any work for a few days with JJ out and things in flux. I hated that, damn it. Disruptions to the cash flow were less now that I was living with Katie, but old habits were hard to break, old worries too familiar a friend.

The whole way to Seattle the anxiety rode high in my chest. We'd had five months of almost normal. What crazy shit were we facing this time?

TEN

Clyde and Wendy were already in the waiting room outside the ICU by the time I'd found my way through the maze of corridors at Harborview. I collapsed onto the vinyl couch on the other side of Wendy and patted her arm.

"You doing okay?" I asked.

She turned and hugged me, burying her face in my shoulder. I stared at Clyde who looked down at his hands. I'd never seen him look so lost.

When Wendy had gotten herself collected a little, she let go of me and sat back, wiping her face. "Tha … Thanks for coming," she stammered, taking in halting breaths. "JJ always said you were good people."

Clyde's eyebrows shot to the top of his head, but didn't look up. He just studied his hands like he was hoping to find something new.

JJ thought I was good people? When had that changed? There was definitely something odd about his behavior. Was Wendy that strong an influence on him?

"What happened?" she asked.

"He was going over his lines, rehearsing, you know?"

She watched me, desperate for it to make sense.

"Then he just collapsed."

She touched her face, staring off into the vague distance.

"Blood started coming out of his mouth, nose, ears …" I trailed off. "His eyes."

Clyde grimaced and took her hand. She squeezed his in both of hers and rested her head on his shoulder with her eyes closed.

"It was horrible," Clyde whispered.

We sat there for a few minutes before the doctors came out to let us know that JJ was stable. They were doing everything they could for him.

So we waited.

It was going on nine when Clyde offered to go down and get us coffee. I could tell he was agitated with waiting. Didn't blame him. Wendy and I sat there in silence. Misery loves company, at least the pain can't overwhelm you with someone sitting with you.

She got up to go to the bathroom and I watched her. She was young, maybe twenty-one, but carried herself well. I was already impressed with her ability to write screenplays. Couldn't say I liked her taste in guys, though. JJ had always been arrogant and egotistical on a scale that rivaled his real world standing as a B-movie front-man. Maybe he'd changed. Didn't jive with my world view, but I've been wrong before.

When Clyde got back with the coffees he had Jennifer and Carl in tow. They came and sat with us. Carl said something quiet to Wendy, who hugged him, then he slid over to sit with Clyde and me across the room while Jennifer sat with her and chatted. She and Jennifer had been working pretty closely on the script together. Jennifer was closer to her than any of the rest of us, with possible exception of Clyde.

When it was clear that JJ was stable and his condition wasn't likely to change in the next twenty-four to forty-eight hours, I begged off to head home.

Wendy hugged me again before I left, thanking me again for coming. That girl was too good for JJ.

As I was climbing into the truck my cell phone buzzed. I looked down and saw that it was Jimmy. Not that ten-thirty was late for Jimmy, but why was he calling?

"Hey, Jim. What's shaking?"

"Sarah, where are you?" It was Deidre. "We're on our way to Valley Medical. Katie's in trouble."

A shudder ran through me. Not again. "What happened?" I asked, resting my head on the steering wheel.

"Blood loss we know," Deidre said, her voice stoic. "Janitor found her in the bathroom off her classroom. Lot of blood. Thought maybe she'd been attacked."

Attacked? That was nuts. I resisted the urge to start swearing. What the hell was going on? She should've been done hours ago. "Any idea how bad? Is she conscious?"

"No," Deidre said. I was beginning to hear the strain in her voice. "Jimmy's driving a little wild at the moment—"

That was directed at him.

"—but we should be there within the next twenty minutes. You in Everett?"

"Seattle, Harborview Hospital."

"What? Why? Are you okay? You weren't attacked as well? Were you?"

"Yes, no, I'm fine. No, I wasn't attacked. It's one of the actors. He collapsed, started hemorrhaging pretty bad. There was a lot of blood."

The phone went silent and I could hear Jimmy swearing in the background.

"Lots of blood?" Deidre asked. "That a coincidence?"

"Not one I like," I said, starting my truck. "I need to call a couple of folks, but I'll meet you in Renton in twenty minutes or so."

"Drive careful," she said, and disconnected the line.

I called Melanie and left her a message. She was most likely on shift, but she'd want to know about Katie.

Then I called Circle Q.

Julie answered. "Sarah?"

"It's Katie," I said, turning onto James Street. "She collapsed at school—might have been attacked, no one is sure yet. Jimmy and Deidre are on their way to Valley General."

"Damn," she said, "hang on." I heard her close a door. "They do good work there. Go on, we'll keep Jai Li overnight."

"Thanks," I said. "This is just fucked up." I gunned it and skated through two very deep yellow lights and turned onto Sixth Avenue. I got caught in a row of traffic to the onramp for I-5.

"Something funny's going on," Julie said. "Jai Li's been drawing some odd pictures tonight. I think she knew something was wrong. Started around five-thirty. See if that lines up."

I reached over the back of the seat and pulled Gram's case up into the front with me. If there was something funny going on, something that Jai Li picked up from the ether, I may be needing Gram. "Funny how?"

Traffic was just not moving, so I swung around and hit the HOV lane. I'd deal with a ticket another time.

"She was just drawing lots of pictures of Katie and that actor fellow you work with. Kept crying while she was doing it. Took Edith twenty minutes to get her to stop."

Holy mother ... I tightened my grip on the steering wheel and pushed the gas pedal to the floor. "JJ's in the hospital," I said, the willies creeping up my spine. "He collapsed around five-thirty."

"I don't like it," Julie said. "See to Katie."

Damn straight. "Watch Jai Li," I said, weaving around an eighteen-wheeler. Somewhere behind me there was the squeal of brakes and the honking of horns. Sue me. "Call me if she does anything else strange. And tell her I'm safe. That I'm going to get Katie, okay?"

Julie's voice softened. "I'll tell her. You just watch yourself. I need to go tell Mary and Edith. It's going to be a long night. Think I'll get out my shotgun."

"I'll call you when I know something for sure."

"No matter how late," she said.

I cut over onto the break-down lane and drove around the line of cars merging with I-90. This was too much bullshit. There was another call I had to make and I hated to do it. But if this was as fucking strange as it sounded, I needed some expert advice.

The phone only rang once when Qindra answered.

"What have you done now?" she asked. "Nidhogg is freaking out. I need to deal with this. I'll call you when I can."

"It wasn't me," I said, hating the defensiveness in my voice. Usually it was me, or actions related to me. Not like I went looking for trouble.

There were angry voices in the background and someone screamed.

Qindra's voice rose, shouting something I couldn't really understand. Not sure what language it was, but it had a lot of consonants.

Then the phone went dead.

ELEVEN

Katie was stable when I got to Valley Medical Center but they had her in ICU with stage four Hypovolemia. Fancy talk for shock and coma from sudden blood loss, which they estimated was just over three pints. They had her on an intravenous drip trying to get her blood pressure to stabilize, but adding too much fluid too fast could damage the brain, or so the doc said. Something about permissive hypotension.

I'd have Melanie explain it all to me in English later. Right now, I was freaked that Katie hadn't regained consciousness. That really worried the doctors. The blood loss and associated symptoms were manageable. Shock was the current worry, as well as figuring out just what the hell had happened.

Fortunately, there was no signs she'd been assaulted. There was a question as to why she had been found in the bathroom. The seat was down and she'd been completely dressed—no collapsing mid-pee or anything.

I wish either Melanie or Qindra would call me back. I needed answers.

Jimmy paced while Deidre rolled her chair back and forth, talking to fill the quiet. I sat on vinyl cushions combating a serious case of déjà vu.

Something didn't add up. Around midnight I called Julie to fill her in.

"Jai Li has been bouncing off the walls," Julie said when I called. "She's drawn a dragon now, and a blonde guy with a funky stringed instrument. We looked it up, it's a double necked lute called a chitarrone. Somehow that lute and the dragon are connected and they're tied in with JJ and Katie."

Wait, I knew a guy who played a chitarrone—Cassidy Aloysius Stone of the Harpers. We'd met the Harpers back in October when all that mess with the mead came up.

That was interesting. Was that a connection? What else had happened then? Maybe I needed to contact Frederick Sawyer and see what he knew about things. He'd gotten a sample of that mead. Nidhogg's had been destroyed or so Qindra figured, when the house in Chumstick burned down at Christmas. The final two had gone to Memphis and Dublin, so I doubted *they* were connected. On the other hand, we really didn't know anything about Mr. Stone, nor the rest of his band. Seemed like nice enough folks. Who knew what secrets they were harboring. I'd be calling him next. Katie had his number at home somewhere. I'd have to dig it out.

I rubbed my eyes. Not enough pieces to the puzzle. Besides, what did that have to do with either Katie or JJ?

"Tell Jai Li we love her and will come get her as soon as we can," I said, finally. I was too damned tired to think.

"She asked about Nidhogg," Julie whispered. "Said the dragon was angry about something." There was a long pause. "Sarah, how does she know Nidhogg's angry?"

My stomach was in knots. All I'd had to eat in the last twelve hours had been coffee. I needed something on my stomach or I was gonna hurl.

"I called Qindra," I said, turning away from the waiting room. Didn't want Jimmy getting his panties in a wad. "Nidhogg was going a little nuts. Qindra was dealing with it, but she hasn't called back yet."

"When is this going to end, Sarah?" Julie asked. "When is too much?"

What could I say? I didn't have any answers for her. "I don't know."

We let it hang there for a long time. I stared out onto the highway, letting the lights from the traffic hold my attention.

"Would you feel safer at Black Briar?" I asked finally.

Julie laughed an angry bark. "Hell no, we're not bolting. Mary has her hunting rifle out and I've got the shotgun. Edith is keeping Jai Li calm. No way we're letting a little fear drive us off the farm."

I smiled. House full of tough women. "I stand corrected," I said. "No one better to watch Jai Li for us."

"Be careful," she said. "I'll text if Jai Li has any new brain waves. Otherwise call in the morning."

I hung up and stared at the traffic a bit longer. What other enemies were out there? How was this related? Who else did we know who had ties to this shit?

Skella.

I called her and filled her in. Surprised to find her in Bellingham. She was hanging out with a group of college kids up there. The news about Katie and JJ didn't make Skella happy. She agreed to help if she could and I promised to call when I had more news.

Then I called Rolph and let him in on the situation. He didn't have any advice either, but the more eyes and ears we had on the ground, the better I thought we'd be. I told him to hug Juanita for me and left him to his family. It scared me how vulnerable we all were—especially the young ones, and Juanita was due any time now.

Deidre patted me on the knee when I sat back down again. Jimmy had gone off to get coffee. I told her about Jai Li and we lapsed into that silence that overcomes people in waiting rooms. The sheer volume of silence becomes too heavy a burden to carry.

So we waited. And oh, how I loved to wait.

TWELVE

The doctors came out again around two in the morning. Katie was stable. They were feeling much better about her condition, as the aspects of shock seemed to be lessening.

They were going to keep her in ICU for the immediate future, however. I shook the doctor's hand, thanked him, and let him move on.

Jimmy sat with his hands in his lap, wringing them to keep from punching something. He looked just like Clyde from earlier in the night. A lifetime ago.

Deidre was making noises about staying for the duration, but I could tell she was flagging. She'd been making excellent progress with her physical therapy over the last year. The wheelchair was second nature to her now. But she didn't have the stamina she used to. By three I pulled Jimmy aside and convinced him to take her home. I offered our apartment, but he wouldn't hear of it. Wanted her in her own bed.

I called Skella back to see if she could take Jimmy and Deidre home via the mirror travel and she was eager to help. By the time she could get away for a bit, another twenty minutes had eked by. It was good to see her. I'd grown fond of the elf. And I wasn't unhappy at all when she hugged me.

"Sorry," she said, giving me a final squeeze. "Call me if things change."

I envied her at that moment. I wish I had some action I could take, some way I could make a difference.

Jimmy would get his truck the next day. He and Deidre disappeared down an empty corridor. Several minutes later I got a text from him that they were home and that Skella was heading home herself. I was to call any of them if things changed.

I paced a little while, letting the blood work its way through my limbs. I was growing stiff just sitting there. Moving at least felt like I was doing something. Illusion was better than nothing. At three-thirty, I gave up and went back to the couch, letting my head fall back against the wall. The ceiling tiles were very white.

Sleep defeats even the greatest warriors. If that's not a famous saying, it should be. One of the nurses shook me awake around five to tell me that Katie's vitals were stable and that her color was coming back. She said I could go in and see her for a few minutes if I promised to go home and get some real sleep.

Katie had been in the hospital over Christmas for a couple of days the last time she'd collapsed from using her magic. She'd been in a private room with an IV. It was scary, but normal.

This was a totally different world.

There were wires and hoses running under the blankets that I didn't want to see where they connected. Her hair was plastered against the sides of her head and her face was puffy. I went to touch her, but wasn't sure if I was allowed.

"Best if you just let her rest," the nurse said.

I didn't argue, just looked down at Katie and tried not to cry. The pain was building in the back of my throat, a clawing sensation that was just as likely to turn into a howl as a sob.

"I have to go check something for a minute," the nurse said, patting me on the arm. "I'll be right back."

She walked into one of the empty rooms and stood looking at her watch; didn't look back at me at all.

I knelt down and kissed Katie on the forehead. She had a tube down her throat so I was afraid to get too close to her lips.

"I'm sorry, baby," I whispered to her. "I wish I could fix this. Wish I knew what the fuck was the matter with you."

The regular rhythm of the heart monitor never changed as I lay my hand on her shoulder. After three breaths, I kissed her again and turned away. I walked out of the ICU and didn't stop until I was outside. I waited until I got into the truck before I broke down and let the salty pain bleed out of my eyes.

I drove over to the apartment, grabbed a shower, and put together some things for Jai Li for a few days. By seven I was pulling into Circle Q. The clouds were low and heavy, threatening lots of liquid sunshine. We'd had a dry spell for a few days, quite unlike Seattle weather.

By the time my boots hit the porch at the Circle Q, the door slammed open and Jai Li launched herself into my arms. I dropped her sleeping bag and duffle bag onto either side and caught her. She sobbed into my shoulder for a very long time, just me and her standing in the chill morning.

I talked to her in quiet tones, explaining about Katie being okay, how she was going to come home soon, and Jai Li finally quieted. The women of Circle Q stood in the doorway, watching us. Mary was crying, one hand covering her mouth. Julie had her arms crossed but wiped at her eyes. Only Mrs. Sorenson—Edith—wasn't crying. She was watching me, appraising me. I looked at her for a moment and she nodded once, then turned back into the house.

I stood and carried Jai Li across the porch. Mary held the door and Julie stepped out and grabbed the things I'd dropped. I walked straight through to the back of the house to where Mrs. Sorenson was standing.

"Put her here," she said, pointing to a large bed covered with a double wedding band quilt. "She has not slept. Lay with her."

I nodded and set Jai Li on the side of the bed, kneeling at her feet.

"Come on, Big Girl," I said, taking off her shoes. "Time for a little rest, what do you say?"

At first she shook her head, but I slipped off her socks and tugged her dress over her head. Julie dropped the duffle at my feet and handed me a pair of pajamas.

Jai Li sighed and took the pajamas out of my hand, pulling the top over her head and stepping into the fuzzy bottoms. They were pale blue.

When I tucked her in, she grabbed my hand and pulled me toward her.

"Lay with her," Julie said.

I glanced over. "Not tired."

"That's what Jai Li says," she said with a smile, flicking out the light. "Lay with her a bit and get her to sleep."

I rolled my eyes and sat on the side of the bed to take off my Docs. Soon I was nestled in the bed beside Jai Li, who snuggled up to me and closed her eyes.

"Only for a few minutes," I said. I closed my eyes and tried to believe the lie.

THIRTEEN

Julie shook me awake late in the afternoon. "Phone," she said, handing me my cell. "Qindra."

I grabbed the phone and followed her out of the room. Jai Li was sleeping, one arm thrown over her head. Julie pointed to an office two doors down.

"Hey," I said into the phone, pulling the door closed and finding a large office chair to collapse in. "How are things?"

"Rough," Qindra said into the phone. "Nidhogg is sleeping, finally. I don't know what the hell happened yesterday, but it's a damn miracle we didn't have more casualties."

I rubbed my face, letting a huge yawn overwhelm me. "Sorry," I said. "I was dead asleep."

"Lucky you," she said. "I haven't slept. I hear we weren't the only ones affected by this, whatever it was."

"Wait, casualties? Did she freak out and eat people again?"

Okay, maybe not the smoothest way to ask that question.

Qindra sighed. "Tactful as always, Beauhall. She cleared her throat before continuing. "Minor injuries. One broken arm, two burns, nothing major. The staff scattered when she turned. Luckily, I was able to hold her attention long enough for the others to make it out."

"Not too horrible, then," I said. Of course, Katie wasn't conscious and JJ had seen better days. No one dead yet. Hell of a way to measure success.

I filled her in on JJ's and Katie's situation as well as Jai Li's antics.

She listened, asking probing questions. "Damn it, Sarah. I couldn't pinpoint exactly where the epicenter of this event was, but I know it was south, Kent area. And with Katie crashing and burning, I'm betting hers is the hot spot."

"Want to go over there?" I asked, climbing to my feet. "Scout out the place? I'd like to get a bead on what the hell happened."

"Interesting thought," she said. I could almost see the look on her face, that quizzical and determined look she got when she was narrowing in on something. That image was burned into my memory from when she was holding that dome together out in Chumstick. She'd held that against the wraiths and ghosties for months. Magic or no, I had no idea how she'd managed to stay alive, other than sheer cussedness, as my da would've said.

"Give me two hours," she said. "I want to make sure that Nidhogg is really and truly calmed down. Hell, I may even sedate her. A little wine should do the trick in her state. Just something to take the edge off."

I rocked my head around slowly, stretching the muscles and listening to the creaks of my spine. Sleep would be more prudent.

"Two hours," I said instead. "You know the place?"

Of course she knew the place. She had done her research the second she met Katie and me. I'm sure they had files about each of us somewhere in that huge old house.

"Yeah, I'll call ahead, get the principal's permission to search the classroom. You're known to them, right? They'll recognize you?"

I thought back to the faculty luncheon Katie had dragged me to before the last school year ended. Back when she was afraid she may not teach again. "Yes, they'll know me."

We said our pleasantries and I left the office to gather up my boots.

Julie had them in her hands when I opened the door. I hugged her and she made shushing sounds, pulling me down the hall to the kitchen.

Edith handed me a chicken salad sandwich and a large glass of milk. I ate the sandwich quickly and downed the milk.

I hugged her, which seemed to surprise her, and headed out to the truck. Julie handed me a sack with another sandwich and a thermos of coffee. I hugged her, too. I needed the human contact.

"Watch out for Jai Li," I said. "I'm going over to Katie's school with Qindra. See if we can figure anything out."

"Assumed as much," Julie said. "You had that look on your face that tells me you are going to do something rash and probably painful."

I laughed. "Hopefully neither of those, but I reserve the right to do what it takes."

She hugged me again. "Of course. Find out what this is before anyone gets killed. Then we need to seriously discuss moving someplace with fewer dragons and necromancers and shit."

Did such a place exist? Or were we just screwed in general. "Don't pack up yet," I said. "The grass isn't always greener and all that jazz."

She waved as I drove away. There was something comforting about seeing her there. Safe and sound—that's what it meant for me. A person who loved me unconditionally. Folks who were in my corner. Good to know I had a place to come home to.

Now off to find the witch and track down just what the hell happened to Katie. It felt good to have a plan. There was definitely something wrong here and if Qindra and I couldn't get to the bottom of it, no one could.

At least that was the hope.

FOURTEEN

I got to the school ahead of Qindra. Must have been tougher to get away from Nidhogg than she thought. Even though it was after five, there were several older model sedans in the parking lot. Katie's Miata was still in her spot. I'd tell Jimmy to have some of the Black Briar crew come move it. No reason to leave it here longer. Kids would just vandalize it. I headed into the office to see who I could see.

Principal Nutter was still in his office and rushed out when he saw me.

"Any word?" he asked. He was pale, his pencil mustache the only real color on his whole bald head. "Is she okay?"

I put my hand on his shoulder. "She's stable," I said, trying to smile. "Doctors are baffled."

He looked like he wanted to ask something else, but it was stuck in his throat. There was definitely something there.

"She wasn't attacked," I said. "If that's what you're worried about."

"Oh, good," he looked around quickly then leaned in toward me. "No subtle way to ask this." He licked his lips. "Is there any drug use or anything we need to be aware of?"

"What?" I took a step back. "Are you kidding me?" I felt my shoulders tensing up. Seriously?

His face fell, embarrassed and horrified. "No, of course not. I just ..." he faltered. "The district is very concerned here. Ms.

Cornett has had a series of unfortunate events over the last year or so. The superintendent was just thinking of the children's safety." He didn't look at me, kept his eyes downcast.

I let out a long breath. Guy was scared and worried. That was his job.

"No, no drugs. Nothing we can pinpoint at this time, either. If she comes out of the coma, we'll ask her. What say?"

He jerked his head up, shock painting his face. "Oh ... of course ... Coma?" I'd always had the impression this guy was decent enough. Tough position for him, I'm sure.

"Is there something else I need to know about?" I asked. "Something you've observed?"

"Nothing in particular," he said, fretting. "She's fabulous with the kids, as always. But a few of the other teachers have noticed that she looks fatigued, run-down." He looked up at me, careful to hold my gaze. "We think the world of Kathryn. It's just worry, is all."

I thanked him for his time and got his approval to pick a few things up from Katie's room. He offered to escort me, but when I said I knew the way, he went back into his office relieved. Guy carried a heavy load.

Qindra arrived five minutes later. Mr. Nutter didn't even notice. I met her out in the parking lot and we walked around to the far side of the building where the kindergarten classes were located.

"Let me try something," Qindra said in the little garden courtyard outside Katie's classroom. Actually three classrooms opened onto this courtyard. It made a lovely place for the kids to work with plants. Katie loved it here; said it was peaceful.

I watched as Qindra pulled out her wand and began to do her little squiggle magic. There had to be a pattern to it, but I couldn't figure it out. It just looked like she was wiggling the wand around randomly and muttering under her breath. But I could feel the magic. At first it was a tickle on the back of my neck, then a breeze that ruffled the hairs on my arm. Finally, several small sparks flew into the air and coalesced into a diamond pattern, settling onto the surface of Katie's classroom door.

"Interesting," she said. I watched her, expecting more, but she didn't divulge. Instead she walked over, tapped the door with her wand, saying a quick "Alohomora," and it clicked open.

"I have a key, show off. Did you just say 'Alohomora'? Is all that real? You know, wizards and Harry Potter?"

She grinned at me and shrugged. "No, I'm just screwing with you."

I looked at her appraisingly. I didn't know her to joke, this was a change. Odd time for it, but what the hell.

"So, what's interesting?" I asked, going back to her previous comment. We walked into the cool classroom.

"Magic," she said. "Chaotic. Not something I'd expect to find in a school."

Well, that sucked. "Right, then. Chaos magic. So she was attacked?"

"Not necessarily," Qindra said, glancing around the room. "Let's not be hasty."

The classroom had been mopped down and all the papers cleared off Katie's desk. While Qindra walked around doing her hoodoo, I ransacked the desk.

Didn't take me long. Mostly papers, crayons, safety scissors, unopened pack of little kids' underwear in case one of them had an accident. Old pictures and stacks of graded papers. Nothing exciting. In the bottom-right drawer, however, was her personal stuff. Inside was her purse, some cards I'd sent her over the last couple of years, and the first scarf I'd ever knitted. It was folded neatly under her purse. I took out the purse, set it on the desk, and grabbed the scarf. Inside was a stack of five pictures. They were all of me: sleeping, working at the studio, hammering a sword on the anvil at Julie's old smithy, she and me dancing out at Black Briar. The fifth one was of me in the hospital after I'd killed the dragon.

I sat there with those pictures on the desk, trying to see myself the way she saw me. The pictures were intimate, quiet.

What the hell would I ever do without her? I closed my eyes and breathed deeply, fending off tears. I had to figure out what had happened here. That was my mission. Then I could figure out how to bring her home.

I wrapped the pictures back in the scarf and left them in the bottom of the drawer. I'd take her purse with me when we left.

I leaned back in her chair and stared out across the room. The desks were tiny. All along the walls were brightly colored posters with Muppets, actors, and athletes saying things like "Gym time is fun time" and "Milk makes you strong". Katie hated them. Said they were paid advertisements, but it drew money into the schools, helped buy pencils and paper.

Qindra meandered around the classroom for a few minutes, then made a beeline back to the bathroom.

"They cleaned up in here," she called, stepping back to look at me through the open door, "but they did a piss-poor job. Come look at this."

I leveraged myself out of Katie's chair and wove between the desks. This was her domain. Every inch of it radiated Katie.

I leaned around the doorframe and followed where Qindra was pointing. In the very corner of the room was a supply cabinet. Underneath it something glowed purple, like neon running lights on one of those souped-up street racer cars.

"What the hell is that?" I asked, squatting down and craning my head sideways.

"Not sure," she said, looking at me. "Started glowing when I cast a revealing charm on the room. But I'm not touching it."

"Seriously?" I went down onto my knees, lowered my torso and reached for the cabinet when Qindra grabbed me by the shoulder and pulled me back.

"You neither," she said. "That'll kill you."

I looked between her and the purple glow. "And you know this, how?"

She squatted down beside me and waved her wand in front of the cabinet. She drew three runes I was beginning to recognize from her: Perthro, Nauthiz, and Ansuz. Each one formed the point of a triangle which created a lens to look through. It revealed hidden truths. She'd used it to show me just how utterly fucked up the house out in Chumstick had been with all the necromancer bullshit present.

I had a flash of *CSI: Seattle—Special Dragon Unit*. Qindra could have her own television show. Or maybe I just needed more sleep.

The runic filter showed us the impression of blood on the walls and all across the floor. The janitor had used either bleach or ammonia to mop up, but the psychic residue was not so easily removed.

As she moved her wand, the lens floated around letting us examine the whole room before she settled it once again near the floor in front of the cabinet.

It didn't look like it was going to explode, or bite us, or anything. There was just this hint of secrecy and danger.

"Blood is powerful," she said, quietly. "Taints an area. Hard to purge."

"Burning sage and lilac helps," I said, absent-mindedly.

She looked at me funny and nodded. "Yes, that's true. You surprise me."

I shrugged at her. I'm a quick study. And we'd used it to clear away the negative stuff out at Circle Q after the necromancer had slaughtered Blue Thunder.

"Maybe we can move the cabinet, see what's under there without reaching with our hands. What do you think?" I thought it was a grand idea.

"I don't know," she said. "Let me try something else, first."

She went back out into the classroom and over to Katie's desk. She poked through the pencil mug she kept there and drew one out that had teeth marks in the wood. She tapped it with her wand once, then brought it to me. "Hold this."

I took the pencil and immediately got the strongest sense of Katie. "Yeah," I said. "This is definitely hers."

"Good," she said, plucking the pencil out of my hand again. She tapped the wand against the pencil again and spoke some words I recognized as probably being Latin. Might have been some German thrown in, I couldn't rightly tell.

The pencil glowed a solid throbbing green, calm and peaceful. She squatted down again and rolled the pencil under the cabinet. Whatever was under there didn't mind the pencil visiting, because the purple glow strobed a couple of times and became green for a few heartbeats. Then the purple began to once again overtake the green.

"Okay, sympathetic magic," she said. "Whatever is under there belongs to Katie."

"Good enough for me." I stood up and grabbed the cabinet with both arms. I leaned back, heaving it off the ground and stepped back with my left foot, pivoting. Basically I swung around like a barn door and set the cabinet down with a grunt.

Qindra whistled. "I forget how freaking strong you are," she said.

I shrugged, embarrassed. "Side-effect of the smithing," I said.

We peered around the cabinet and saw that the glowing thing was a book.

"Looks like a diary," Qindra said.

Diary? Holy cats, was this her mom's diary?

Qindra studied the book through her magic lens for a moment, then looked at me shaking her head. "There's more wards and spells on that book than I could muster in a year," she said. "If that belongs to Katie, then Black Briar is way beyond anything we'd considered."

Frak.

I squatted down, picked up the pencil and poked the book with it. Qindra started to protest, but didn't stop me in time.

Nothing happened.

"Your turn," I said, handing her the pencil. She looked at me dubiously but took it. She leaned in and moved the pencil toward the book, slowly. At about four inches away, the pencil burst into flames.

Qindra dropped back, swearing and holding her hand. The pencil hit the floor, blazing.

"Graphite is a conductor," she said, putting the palm of her against her lips and sucking the burned point.

"Okay, I can move it, you not so much." I took a paper cup from the dispenser by the sink and filled it with water, then I poured it over the pencil. The flames went out immediately. The pencil wasn't damaged. "Freaky."

"Indeed," Qindra said, examining the angry red welt on her palm.

I picked up the pencil with no trouble. "Here goes nothing." I reached over and poked the book with the pencil. No flames.

"I still wouldn't touch the book itself, if I were you," she said. I think maybe she was pouting a little.

"Think I can pick it up if I only touch it with something of Katie's?" I looked back at her for support.

"Can't leave it here, that's for sure," she said. "First person to touch it is getting fried."

"Good point."

"I'd like to bury it somewhere and forget we ever saw it. I have a bad feeling." She looked worried, that was true. But also frustrated.

I poked the book again. "Well, we're not burying it, and since you can't touch it, I'm taking it out of here. It may clue me in about what happened to Katie."

She sighed. "I think if we can wrap it in something of hers, we may be able to pick it up."

Okay, she was still in the game. I grinned up at her. "I've got just the thing." I got up and went back to the desk and took the scarf I'd made for Katie out of the bottom drawer. I was careful to leave the pictures. Those were hers alone.

"How's this?" I asked.

She did her little sympathy magic charm and nodded at me when the scarf glowed green.

I bent down, lay the scarf over the book a couple of folds. The stitches were not the tightest weave.

Hey, it was my first knitting project.

I held my breath and scooped the book up. Nothing happened. I walked across the room, set the book on Katie's desk and pulled the scarf away.

It didn't look dangerous, but I understood the nature of magic. Size was not important.

Qindra performed several more spells on the book, yelping once as whatever spell she'd used rebounded and punched her in the face.

"It doesn't like to be examined," she said, rubbing her eye. "But I can safely say whatever exploded out and swept over this region started with this book."

I sat on the edge of the desk and poked the book with Katie's pencil. "Great. Now we have to find out what the hell Katie was doing with it."

Qindra looked at me questioningly. "Secrets between you?"

I shrugged. "Don't start," I said. But I didn't like that thought.

"Sorry," she said, nodding. "Your business. Still. I'd like to take the book, but I'm afraid it would explode."

I looked up at her, thinking. If this was Katie's mother's, then she and Jimmy would kill me for letting it fall into Nidhogg's domain. On the other hand, I didn't know any other witches.

I plunked the pencil back into the coffee mug with all the others and saw a business card tucked inside. I pulled it out and glanced at the name.

Charlie Hague. Things just got a whole lot more complicated. "Christ," I breathed.

"What is it?" Qindra asked, reaching for the card.

"Oh, nothing," I said, pocketing it. "Katie has a doctor's appointment. Guess that's a moot point now, huh?"

She looked at me. No idea if she saw the lie or not. She didn't have her wand waving around at the time, but you never knew for sure.

"And the book?" she asked.

"I'll take it," I said, dropping the scarf over it again. "If this is that dangerous, I think I should hang onto it a bit, see what Katie says when she wakes up."

She didn't like that answer. Qindra was not used to asking, and definitely not used to being denied a request.

"Fine," she said, tucking her wand back into her purse. "We know the source of the event. Shall we tend to the victims?"

"Do you think you can do something?"

She smiled a sad smile and patted me on the arm. "As you've pointed out, I have a knack for healing. I'll do what I can for them. Then I must get home to Nidhogg."

I didn't blame her. Nidhogg had proven to be more than a little unstable of late, what with her flying out to Chumstick and mixing it up for the first time in a few hundred years. Qindra thought Nidhogg was even more erratic.

Erratic dragons were not fun to have around.

"I'll put this someplace safe," I said, wrapping the scarf around it and tucking it inside Katie's huge purse.

"Fair enough."

We walked out into the courtyard and made our way across the parking lot. I hated lying to her on Katie's behalf. If I have to choose sides, I'll always err on the side of Katie. I just wish she'd told me about the book.

And what the hell was she doing meeting with Charlie Hague? Had she met up with him before or after the crazy meeting in Bellevue? Were he and Katie keeping this from me?

I didn't like it, not one little bit. Secrets got people killed.

I'd get a hold of Charlie at the next free moment, but in the meantime I wanted to see what Qindra could do. If she could push Katie on the right path to recovery, I'd love her forever.

FIFTEEN

We drove out to Valley Medical since we were already in Kent. While Qindra stripped off several pieces of jewelry and arranged some things in her trunk, I grabbed Katie's purse. I had no intention of leaving that out here for someone to snatch. I waited by the elevator while Qindra finished up.

"Going in as incognito as I can," she said, smiling. "Too much of the woo-woo stuff, and the electronics get a little wacky."

I nodded. All hail the woo-woo stuff.

It was surreal riding the elevator with her. The music was an odd string arrangement of an old Clash tune and the juxtaposition there made my head hurt.

We made it all the way to the nurse's station before anyone even looked at us. Busy people, lots of folks going up and down the halls. And not many people making eye contact. This was a place of hope and pain.

Qindra did something that allowed her to slip into the ICU unnoticed while I chatted up the charge nurse. There was a lot of equipment in the room, electronics and such which didn't like magic. Qindra didn't spend much time in there. She did something, no idea what, because all the alarms started going off and the nurse whipped around and dashed into the room, grabbing a crash cart on the inside. I looked around and Qindra was gone. Could she teleport? Or somehow turn invisible? How awesome and scary would that be?

While the alarms were still going off, my cell phone rang. It was Qindra.

"I touched her head," she said, panic leaking into her voice. "I was using something quiet and low-key to encourage her body's own abilities to heal when a presence pushed me away. It was strong, Sarah. Something nasty. Then the alarms started going off. Katie opened her eyes, snarled at me, and everything went black."

"Where are you?" I asked, glancing around. The hallways were deserted. Several people stuck their heads out of doors along the corridor, but no one was running down the hall or anything.

"I have no idea what the hell is going on," Qindra said, getting control over her panic. "She dismissed me. One minute I was examining her and the next I was standing outside my car."

I stood by the nurses' desk, looking in through the huge glass windows, watching them work. Katie was moving around. I saw one arm rise in the air. When the nurses moved around I saw one of her feet wiggling.

"She's moving," I said into the phone. A rattling noise caught my attention and I turned to see Katie's purse vibrating. I looked inside and to see the book was convulsing. Holy crap.

"We may have a problem …"

"I have another call," Qindra said, clicking over.

I waited, holding the purse closed and watching the nurses work. A doctor ran into the room after a minute and then a second. Katie was starting to fight them. One of the nurses inserted something into her IV and she settled down.

So did the book.

"I have to go," Qindra's voice echoed out of the phone. "When I touched Katie, Nidhogg had another fit."

The line went dead and I slipped the phone into my pocket. "What the hell is going on with you, Katie?" I asked no one. "What have you gotten into?"

Or, maybe the question was, what has gotten into you.

The doctors came out after another five minutes. Katie had never really woken up, they said. She was fighting in her sleep and ripped off several sensors. They were pleased she was showing signs of life. One of them was sporting a fat lip. "She's a fighter," he said, grinning.

I sat in the waiting room and called Jimmy to tell them about Katie's condition. He tracked down Skella on his own, and within twenty minutes he was chatting with the nurse while Deidre and Skella sat with me, waiting.

I held the purse in my lap in a total death grip. I wasn't letting that damn thing out of my sight. I was strongly debating having it around Katie at all.

I needed to know when she'd taken the diary. Before Christmas Deidre had refused to give it to her, said it was too dangerous. Hell, it had almost killed Jimmy when he touched it a decade earlier.

But it was her mother's, right? Why would it be so damn dangerous?

Did it have something to do with Katie's parents disappearing? Was there a connection here we hadn't figured out? It all gave me a headache. Maybe I should just give the damn thing to Qindra and let her figure it out.

On the other hand, the diary reacted pretty damned negatively to Qindra. I sure as hell didn't want her getting killed. Who else would control Nidhogg?

I looked down at my phone. It had been a couple of hours since Qindra had to rush home to a dragon in fits. Had she been in time.

Which got me to thinking on the nature of magic. How come Qindra could use a cell phone? Maybe she wasn't leaking magic all the time. I bet when she was doing her squiggle magic, none of the phones worked.

Timing, I guess. It was just so damn confusing. I'd test the theory at some point.

I held Katie's purse against my chest and felt the book through the thin leather. As I sat there, I noticed that it throbbed ever so slightly, like a heartbeat. I stood and went to the window, looking in on the room where they had Katie restrained and sedated. I could see the heart monitor, watched as each beat spiked and fell. Spiked and fell in time with the pulsing of the book.

Maybe this wasn't Katie's mother's book any longer. Maybe it was Katie's, like the amulet I wore became mine when Anezka had me hold it that first time back last fall. Made me consider if magic was sentient somehow.

Like my sword, Gram. She spoke to me, sang in my head. She was willful and had her own agenda. Why wouldn't other artifacts behave the same. Gram chose me, the amulet chose me. This book chose Katie.

I just wish I knew why it was so damn dangerous. Was that what Qindra had sensed? A connection to the book? I needed more information. Needed to ask questions, but hell if I knew who to ask.

SIXTEEN

JJ died on the operating table around the same time Qindra had touched Katie. I'd bet money it was within seconds. Jennifer called me to let me know. Wendy had to be sedated. Her parents were coming up from Lacey to take her home with them for a few days, to let her find some balance. It was all so damned useless.

Melanie knew one of the nurses at Harborview who told her that it was like JJ's head exploded. They were prepping him for surgery when a piece of his skull the size of a quarter erupted, spraying the operating theater in blood and brains. No one had ever seen anything like it. Except maybe from a bullet. There was no bullet, though. Not a physical one, that is. More like a psychic magical trigger of some sort. She said several pieces of the equipment were also fried at that exact same time, like a power surge. Really bizarre.

I know the book had something to do with it. It may not be the cause, but it was involved. The way it pulsed in time with Katie's heart beat freaked me out a little. Part of me wanted to burn the book. I just didn't know what would happen.

This was so far out of my league.

What the hell was I going to do? I knew deep down I was going to have to open that book, explore the pages within. The very thought scared the crap out of me. If me mucking around hurt Katie, I couldn't live with myself.

In the meantime, I'd try and keep life as normal as possible for Jai Li. What else could I do? I'd figure something out, eventually.

SEVENTEEN

I split my time between Circle Q and the hospital in Kent. Katie hadn't made any further progress. The doctors had her on an IV but said she didn't need any extraordinary life support. She was fairly strong. She just wasn't waking up.

Reminded me of Gletts, the elf boy who'd fallen fighting the wraiths last October. He was in a similar state, body on pause, but his spirit was gone, fled into the mirror land—the sideways. Was that what had happened to Katie? Could I see the thread that tethered her spirit to her body if I slipped sideways?

I'd seen the silver thread that connected the various spirits to the bodies of the wounded when I visited the house of healing at the elf compound in Vancouver. Those lines were so fragile it amazed me we managed to survive all this time.

Maybe that's what I had to do. Maybe I needed to go walkabout, get my astral projection on and see what I could see with Katie. Was worth a shot. I hadn't done it in a while. I'm sure it wouldn't be any harder than it had the last time I did it, up in Chumstick. Only this time, I hope I don't run into the spirits of any more serial killers. There was that one guy in the top hat that totally freaked me the fuck out. He was bad news of a special sort. Like dragon level pain.

Flight Test was on hiatus and Julie was managing the smithing work without me. The rent was due on the apartment and I think I had enough in my account to cover that and the utilities. Would make things like gas and groceries a little thin, but we'd make do. Hell, being out at Circle Q saved us a ton on food. Those women sure loved taking care of Jai Li and me.

They had JJ's funeral a week after he died. It was strange thinking about my life without him in it. The guy was a pig and I'd wanted to stab him on more than one occasion, but he'd been changing. Wendy had done something to him, or maybe he had already begun to change which is what made the whole Wendy thing possible. Either way I was going to miss the guy and that is not something I'd have thought in a million years.

I discussed it with Julie and the girls and we decided to leave Jai Li on the farm with them instead of taking her to the funeral. She was so young and had been through enough hard times in her life. Besides, she was pretty freaked out about Katie still and I didn't want to add any more stress than we had to.

The funeral was at the Universalist church over in West Seattle. I'd never been there, but it had a good sized hall. I got there thirty minutes early, only to find the place almost completely full, with more folks coming in.

I grabbed a seat with the rest of the Flight Test crew. Jones and Carnes made it a point of corralling me and sitting me between them with a box of tissue shoved into my hands. My people. I didn't deserve either of them, but luckily no one asked my opinion.

After the preacher spoke, people began to go up to the podium and give their remembrances of JJ. I was feeling a bit nauseous at that point. You'd think the guy was up for a Nobel Peace Prize or something. I must have voiced my incredulity a little too loudly, because Grandma Jones dug her elbow in my ribs and gave me a scathing look.

I shrugged innocently and sat back, listening to the testimonials.

I held it together with my sarcasm and cynicism intact right up to the point that Clyde got up and spoke.

Clyde had pulled his thick, shoulder length gray hair back into a ponytail and trimmed his usually unruly beard into something neat and stylish. He had on a pretty good suit, like from a suit place, not a throwback to the eighties or something. He looked nice.

His voice had that gravel edge of a pack-a-day smoker and it reminded me that he and JJ would stand out back of the studio on their breaks and talk about the women on the set. Since Wendy had showed up, however, that behavior had gone to the wayside. It's like they both wanted to be a better person by knowing her.

He spoke of friendship and second chances. Carnes was crying quietly and I was having a hard time in that arena myself. I was fighting the tears and had begun to work up a head of pissed-off-by-it-all when Clyde finished. I didn't really hear his closing remarks, my brain was firing too quickly. Too many memories, too much pain. I wish Katie was here beside me instead of Carnes and Jones. They were nice enough people, but I missed Katie.

Wendy spoke for a couple of minutes, and then JJ's parents got up there and hugged her, thanking her for loving JJ. The father spoke of an honored son, how proud they were with his success and finally finding someone as wonderful as Wendy. Then the mother pulled the father away from the podium and the preacher came up again. There was to be a graveside service

The crowd began to break up and I moved to the side of the hall, watching as small clumps of people consoled one another, or as individuals shuffled out, heads down. Skella stood in the far back, closest to the door, with several kids I didn't know. Probably part of the Bellingham crew she was hanging with these days. She waved at me at one point and they all left, heading for their car. I didn't follow. I could see her later, and I was in no mood to meet new people.

Once the crowd had thinned down to a mere trickle, I paid my condolences to JJ's parents, spent a few minutes letting Wendy hug me, then headed out a side door, hands in my pockets and my mind pinging all over the map, worry and anguish about Katie blurring the world around me.

I couldn't do this with her as the guest of honor. I think I'd die of heartbreak. I had to do something, figure out what the hell had happened to her. I couldn't lose her.

I pushed out through one of the side doors and stopped, shocked. Sitting in a wheelchair beside a dark blue Hummer was Frederick Sawyer. His able assistant, Mr. Philips, stood behind him, one hand on the wheel chair, one hand holding an umbrella over Mr. Sawyer, blocking the weak sun.

They were talking to Qindra and Nidhogg.

My heart began to race. Nidhogg was out of her house again? And at a funeral? What the hell was going on in the world?

I strode across the parking lot, my eyes boring a hole in the back of Qindra's head, willing her to turn around.

Nidhogg saw me first. She stood to the right of Sawyer, leaning on her cane with one hand on Frederick's shoulder. This made Mr. Philips uncomfortable, by the way he kept glancing down at that hand. Nidhogg said something too quiet for me to hear, but all four of them turned, facing me, expectant looks on their faces.

"Good," Nidhogg said. "Now that we are all here, we need to find a quiet place for lunch. I'm starving."

I stopped in my tracks. "I'm sorry, what are we discussing?"

Qindra smiled at me and Mr. Philips nodded.

"Lovely to see you," Frederick Sawyer said.

The man looked haggard. Doubly so since he was also a dragon, and even in his human guise, he had always been a shining example of virility and good health. Now he looked broken and drained.

"I know a quiet place," Qindra said. She took a card from her jacket pocket wrote something on the back and handed it to Mr. Philips, who glanced at it and nodded.

"Very good," he said, his voice calm and smooth.

He wheeled Frederick away to a Hummer. Qindra motioned for me to follow her and Nidogg to a Town Car that was waiting in the back of the lot.

"Ride with us, Sarah," Qindra said. It wasn't a request. I shrugged and caught up with them, walking on Nidhogg's right.

She placed her hand on my arm as we walked, letting her set the pace with her cane. The *tok-tok-tok* of the cane on the blacktop parking lot mirrored the pounding of my heart.

What the hell was going on? My mind, over-flowing with thoughts of Katie, was suddenly in full panic mode. Nidhogg had only left her house once in a few centuries, and that was this past winter solstice, when we fought the necromancer and his blood cult.

Nidhogg in her full glory was a sight to behold. She was both beautiful and terrible, but I hadn't killed her, hadn't killed Sawyer either. Oh, the sword wanted me to, in a big way, but I held my ground, let Nidhogg shelter a broken Sawyer under her wings.

And now we were all going to lunch like an old family. There was something critical I was missing, and I didn't like surprises. Especially not when the dragons were involved.

Qindra glanced at me over the top of the car, just before she got in. Her face was stoic, but she gave me a quick wink.

Okay, maybe I wasn't going to be killed right away. Not that any of them had considered it lately, but I was going to worry.

The thought of it all kept my mind split, the anguish of Katie tempered by the spiraling unknown.

EIGHTEEN

We ended up at a small Mediterranean place off Anchor. Qindra spoke to the little man who was doing the seating and he swept us into a back room, segregated from the rest of the restaurant. Without us ordering he placed hummus and pita bread, along with a collection of other spreads: olives, pickled garlic, and feta cheese.

There was a pecking order to our seating. It was not spoken of directly, but Nidhogg sat next to Sawyer. The servants sat beside their respective masters, and I sat opposite them, a Ronin amidst the vassals and lords.

Nidhogg ate quietly, scooping hummus, fat green olives, and chunks of feta onto a triangle of pita and nibbling them into oblivion. After a minute, Frederick began to eat, which was the signal for Qindra and Mr. Philips. Once they had both taken their first bite, the old man scampered into the room and poured glasses of water, tea that smelled strongly of mint, and some pale golden wine with a rich fruity bouquet. I stuck with the water.

By the time the hummus and the rest were mostly devoured, large dishes of moussaka, lamb, rice, and little morsels wrapped in grape leaves arrived. Every dish was passed and we waited for the proper order before taking the first bite of the next course.

This went on for three more courses, including a hearty lentil soup, and ending in a small dishes of dates and figs.

The food was amazing and I ate pacing Nidhogg. When she ate, I ate. When she stopped, I stopped. This felt like a ritual and I didn't want to be the one to blow the rhythm.

Once the food was cleared and we were served thick, dark coffee in tiny cups, Nidhogg nodded at Qindra. She sat her coffee down, cleared her throat and the show began.

"Things have shifted," she began, glancing at me briefly before settling her focus on Frederick. "There are forces moving on the periphery, forces that seek to overthrow the natural order of things."

Frederick waved his hand, dismissing her words. "There are always wolves in the wild lands. Every now and again one pulls down a sheep, but that is no reason to panic."

"Be quiet and listen," Nidhogg chided him, prodding his elbow with her cane. "Let the girl finish her speech." She winked at me, which was the weirdest thing. "She's been practicing," Nidhogg said, nodding her head toward Qindra.

Qindra blushed, cleared her throat, and went on. "We believe the time is drawing near for a closer alliance between our two kingdoms."

Frederick looked surprised by this, and Mr. Philips took out a notebook from his breast pocket and began to scratch down notes.

"Nidhogg—She Who Must Be Obeyed …"

Nidhogg grinned and nodded once.

"… believes that we must pool our resources, reach out to those who currently govern Vancouver and prepare for dark days ahead."

I yawned. I couldn't help it. I had not been sleeping well with Katie in the hospital, and all that food was dragging me down.

"Drink your coffee," Nidhogg said, motioning to my untouched cup. "The caffeine will keep you awake."

The coffee was very strong and very sweet. If it had had chocolate I may have orgasmed.

Qindra droned on about borders and tariffs, obligations and treaties. My head just wasn't in the game, right up until my name came into the picture.

"Therefore," Qindra continued. "We propose that Sarah Jane Beauhall be given diplomatic immunity within our two kingdoms, and be given free rein to pursue our enemies with limited interference from either ruler."

"Wait a moment," Frederick said, sitting up in his wheel chair and scowling. "You propose to let this dragon slayer have free reign within my protectorate, and I'm expected to turn a blind eye?"

Nidhogg sighed. "Be reasonable, Frederick. Of course the girl will check in with you or Mr. Philips when in your territory, I just want it established that she has my blessing and yours, if you'll agree. It should help smooth things over if my worries begin to become reality."

Mr. Philips leaned in to whisper something in Frederick's ear. Whatever he had to say, Frederick didn't like the words. A grim look flitted across his face for a moment, then his mask of reasonableness and cooperation fell back into place.

"I see now why you've brought her here," Frederick said, looking at Nidhogg. "I do not forget her part in rescuing Mr. Philips, nor your own, mother, in protecting me there at the end of the that unfortunate business over the winter solstice."

Nidhogg nodded at him.

"But why do you feel she would have need of anything within my borders?" he asked, genially.

There was definitely a hint of something there—something he was afraid to have exposed. Something that Mr. Philips had felt the need to warn him about.

Interesting.

"I appreciate all this," I said, speaking up for the first time. "I realize our relationships have evolved"—they all four looked at me like I'd grown a second head—"but I'm not a tool to be passed around at your whim. While I am more than willing to entertain a partnership between us ..."

Nidhogg coughed and Frederick laughed out loud.

"Partnership?" he managed. "You an equal?"

I sat back, crossed my arms over my chest and grinned. "If you'd rather consider me an adversary, I can plan for that as well," I said.

"There's no need for threats," Nidhogg said, waving Frederick's next emotional outburst down.

I shrugged and flourished one hand, signaling that she should continue.

Qindra looked slightly affronted, and a little amused.

Mr. Philips' face was a mask of stone, though his eyes did flick toward me briefly.

Frederick was stunned, his eyes wide and his mouth slightly open. He was definitely out of his element.

And Nidhogg, that sly old beast. She looked at me, a twinkle in her steely eyes and a smile on her lips. Either she was going to back me up here, or kill me. At the moment, I wasn't sure which way she was going to go, but I knew I was in no mood for their feudalistic bullshit.

"I think 'partner' is a bit presumptuous," she said, her voice oily and smooth. "But she has a point." She turned to Frederick and gave him her most regal glare. "There is precedent amongst the council for one such as she." She gave me half a nod and looked up at Qindra. "Qindra, darling. What do they call those landless gentlemen in the Orient that wander around doing good deeds, selling their swords to the righteous?"

"Or the highest bidder?" Frederick asked.

"Ronin," Qindra said, echoing my earlier thought. "I believe that is the word you are searching for, Mistress."

"Ah, yes. Ronin. I do think our Sarah here is similar in calling, don't you agree?"

"Yes, Mistress." Qindra looked relieved. I hadn't noticed how tense she'd been until I saw her relax. She seemed to shrink a full inch.

"But she fights for love and honor," Nidhogg said, returning her gaze to Frederick. "She does not seek wealth or personal gain. I have seen this for myself over the last year."

I knew she'd been watching me, following me around, magically if not physically.

"And what of that band of hooligans she has aligned herself with?" Frederick asked.

"The ones that put their lives on the line for the likes of Mr. Philips?" I asked. "That bunch that died in fighting the bastard Jean-Paul?" I could feel the heat rising in me. I hated the look of condescension on his face.

"You dare?" he gasped. "To openly boast of such deeds? To even conceive of them is a crime punishable by death."

It was Nidhogg's turn to laugh. Her voice was brittle and sharp. "Flesh of my flesh," she spat at Frederick, who recoiled. "It is my judgment in that matter which holds sway and I have forgiven the girl."

I looked at Qindra, who ever so slightly shrugged the shoulder away from Frederick. This was a surprise to her as well.

"Jean-Paul debased himself, fell from his position of glory and earned his fate. You of all should know that to the victor go the spoils."

Frederick growled low in his throat and for a moment I saw the fire reflected in his eyes.

Mr. Philips leaned in once more and whispered something to Frederick. I had the feeling that despite her advanced age, Nidhogg had no trouble hearing what the man said. Mr. Philips seemed to know it as well and was unconcerned. I couldn't make anything out, and that seemed good enough for them.

Are you suggesting, "Frederick began, "that this ..." he searched for the right words, and I watched him closely, waiting for the misogyny to spew forth.

"... this *woman*," he finally spat out. "Who at best should be servicing me in my bed, should be granted lands and titles as befitting one of our kind?"

Nidhogg reached across the table and placed a hand on mine, giving it a bony squeeze before laughing aloud. "This one would likely prefer my bed to yours," she said, winking at me. "Though as I understand it her heart beats for another."

"Damn her heart," Frederick grumbled. "She can love whom she pleases as long as she pleases me."

My chair scraped along the floor as I came to my feet, leaning across the table, prepared to punch the pompous pig in the face. The fire in him be damned. By the time he shifted, I could be out of the restaurant and have Gram in my hands. He'd find me more than he could handle.

BAM! I jerked back as Nidhogg brought her cane down on the table lengthwise, startling us all and scattering the dishes.

"I rule here," she spat, poking a bony finger into Frederick's chest. "And you survive due to my grace, and the strength and courage of this young woman and her clan."

I sat back down, taking deep breaths, listening to She Who Must Be Obeyed defending me.

"This is not a debate. I am granting this woman my protection and my seal," she took off a ring from her left hand and pushed it across the table at me.

I stared at it, shocked. I recalled that symbol from a dream I'd had a year ago, a dream where we had been branded by Nidhogg to prove that we were her chattel.

"Take it," Qindra urged.

I looked up from the ring and the memories. Nidhogg looked at me with an air of maternal patience. Frederick had gone pale.

I reached out and closed my hand on the ring. It was warm to the touch, warm from where it has rested on her hand for as long as I'd known her.

"It is done," Nidhogg said with a satisfying nod. "Sarah Jane Beauhall, I grant you rank and privilege in my domain equal to Qindra. While she is the mouth of She Who Must Be Obeyed—"

A shock wave careened around the room. There was power here, magic of an ancient form. The runes on my forehead flared to life and everything and everyone in the room shifted to clearer focus.

"You—from this moment forward—shall be my Fist."

Silence filled the room. I don't believe anyone breathed for a full thirty seconds. Mr. Philips swallowed loudly and pushed his chair back from the table. Frederick's face was difficult to read—mainly shock, and maybe a little horror.

Qindra's was a mixture of shock and pleasure.

I nodded, and Nidhogg turned back to Frederick.

"So shall it be," she intoned, leaning forward toward Frederick.

There was an air of expectancy in the room. A calm before the clap of thunder.

"So shall it be," he replied, his voice dry as a grave.

A bell sounded, deep and sonorous, three deep strikes before fading into oblivion. No one outside the room heard those ringing notes, however. I'd bet my life on it. This was magic deeper and older than anything I'd ever encountered.

Nidhogg clapped her hands twice, and a smattering of waiters came into the room and began clearing away the remains of our meal.

I pushed my chair back, my head spinning. I gripped the signet ring in my right hand and watched Frederick. He leaned in and began talking with Nidhogg in hushed whispers. Mr. Philips stepped away giving his master space, and the waiters left, leaving the two of them huddled across a cleared table.

Qindra walked over to me, pulled me up into a hug, and stood back, looking into my face.

"We'll have to talk," she said, smiling. "This is a game changer."

Qindra and Mr. Philips walked me to my car. Qindra hugged me, promising we'd meet soon to go over what the hell had just happened and let me ask questions. Mr. Philips waited until Qindra walked back to stand by the door to the restaurant, waiting for him before speaking.

"Ms. Beauhall," he began, his face as flat and expressionless as I'd ever seen on a human being. "Mr. Sawyer will be in touch about the particulars for your situation as it pertains to his territories. Please contact me if you have questions or if we may be of service to you in any manner."

He held out a business card which I took and slipped into my jeans pocket.

"Your boss is a very strange individual," I said.

He looked at me, considering his words. "I am aware that his actions are not what one would expect of a person of his position, but let us be perfectly clear, Ms. Beauhall. He is not a person. Not a human such as you or I. He is greater than that, greater than most in this world we find ourselves in."

"Grander and more beautiful?" I asked, catching his vibe.

"Immeasurably so," he agreed. "There is such compassion and glory within him that they overwhelm any sin he may commit."

He believed it, would follow the dragon into the very fires of hell, I had no doubt. Too bad, truly. For while Frederick had shown great moments of loyalty and bravery, he was vain and self-serving. He did not deserve the love and loyalty of Mr. Philips. Sawyer's wrath was awe inspiring, and in the end he took what he wanted and believed he was above the rest of us.

As much as the thought pained me, I had a fifty-fifty chance, as things stood, that I'd be hunting him down one day. Made me sad a little. Made me think of JJ, honestly. There had been good in him after all. Maybe Sawyer was evolving in his own way.

"Call if you require any assistance," Mr. Philips said. He turned and walked back into the restaurant.

Qindra looked back at me, her hand on the door and paused as I strode toward her.

"Tell her," I called to Qindra. "My people are safe, not to be touched."

She looked at me curiously, as I closed the distance between us, so we wouldn't have to shout. "Which ones are your people? Black Briar, the women at Circle Q, the fine folk at Flight Test?"

"Yes," I said. "All of them. They are my clan. They have my protection." When she didn't say anything else, I pressed on. "And I don't do anything I find morally reprehensible, and I don't kill the innocent. I'll be her *Fist*, but I will not become Jean-Paul. I will not commit atrocities."

She studied me for a moment and nodded. "I told her you'd say as much." She smiled. "She said those are the reasons she has chosen you. She does not need a hired killer, Sarah. She can make people disappear with a whim. No, she needs someone who is strong, who sees the world in a certain way." She paused, collecting her thoughts.

"She says the wheel has been broken too long, Sarah. She believes it is within your power to set that to right."

Lightning flashed in my mind. The old man, Joe or Odin, had told me the same. The wheel, always the wheel.

"Fair enough."

She hugged me and kissed me on the cheek. "We are sisters now, you and I. There is much we need to discuss."

And she turned, walking toward the restaurant.

"And my family," I called after her.

She paused, looking back.

"My mother, father, and sister," I said.

She nodded and went in the restaurant.

"Maybe some more people," I mumbled. "I'll get back to you."

I stood in the fading light, thinking about the totally psychotic world I found myself a part of. I just wish I could talk about all this to Katie. She'd help me sort through it all.

And why not? She may be in a coma but I could still talk to her. Maybe she'd hear me. It was a possibility, and it sure beat crying myself to sleep later.

I drove out to the hospital and sat with her, listening to the machines and the monitors and spoke to her in hushed whispers.

"You are not going to believe this," I began, toying with the ring. "No chance at all."

NINETEEN

I was thinking that Qindra's trip to the hospital had helped
Katie, but I had no real proof. As it was, she was stable
enough to be moved to a private room. It was nice to have a
place without all the chaos of the ICU. This way, we could
settle into a normal routine, for what it was worth.

I stayed out at Circle Q most nights, giving Jai Li as much
attention as I could. I even brought her to the hospital a couple of
days a week to see all the stuff going on. She was pretty
insistent—made sure there were plenty of pretty pictures in
Katie's room so she'd know she was loved. Then, she would sit
and wait, doing embroidery or more drawing. She had the most
patience of any kid I'd ever known. Had to do with all that time at
Nidhogg's knee, I'm sure.

The hospital staff loved Jai Li. She drew pictures of each of
them as they appeared. Her drawings started showing up at the
nurse's station. The staff was amazed at the girl's talent, as I'd
come to expect. Jai Li didn't want for attention or treats.

Some days she stayed out at Black Briar playing with my
kobold buddy Bub and the troll twins—Frick and Frack. On
those days, the staff was visibly and verbally disappointed. That
girl had a way of getting under your skin.

Basically we all put our lives on hold. Even Flight Test was on
hiatus while Carl and Jennifer tried to figure out what to do about
the movie. JJ's death was hard on everyone, but they had an

obligation to keep the business running. They agreed to hold a wake out at the studio for the crew and any family that wanted to come. Apparently, JJ's parents were coming back up from Portland, and Wendy would have her parents there as well.

Clyde texted me daily with updates on Wendy. He had begun to think of her and JJ like his own kids. The poor guy was devastated.

Skella visited us every day, either at Circle Q or the hospital. Frequently she talked about the Bellingham kids. She was hanging out with them more and more, pretending to be normal. She couldn't just step into a mirror with them around or anything, so it put a crimp into her mirror taxi services. I was just thrilled she'd found friends outside her own community. They had always been an insular bunch, and with Gletts in a coma himself, she'd been lost.

Between the hospital where Katie was improving, if not actually conscious, emergency meetings with Carl and Jennifer on movie matters, smithing and Jai Li—May slid into June in a haze of unexpected laughter, crazed boredom, and never ending pain.

Julie picked up more and more of my share of the farrier work without me even asking. It made me happy to see her growing stronger—finding her way back to her old life. Mary and Edith were also great, mothering Jai Li and me like we were their own. I guess that's the lesson I was learning. Our capacity to love and envelope others into our circles of protection had no real limits. I don't know how I would have made it through without them.

The whole time I carried that damned book in Katie's purse. Jimmy asked me why I suddenly decided to carry a purse, smirking. Deidre told him it was Katie's purse and that he should just let it go. For a moment he looked at me with an odd expression, then he hugged me. He didn't mention the purse again.

I didn't mention the book.

During the days I tried all I knew. I held Gram, searching for answers, cut myself and smeared the blood over the runes on my body, looking for a flash of understanding. I talked with Bub and Anezka, Gunther, Stuart, Trisha, Jimmy, and Deidre. Consulted our doctor friend, Melanie, and even called Rolph, thinking the dwarves may know something. Skella spoke with her grandmother, who only sighed and offered her sympathy. Gletts was in the same state.

I spent long hours in Nidhogg's company with and without Qindra, then hours with Qindra alone.

I even asked Jai Li to draw pictures of Katie awake, just so I didn't leave any options uncovered.

Nothing worked. No one had answers I didn't already have. And all the time the book remained a cipher. Twice I reached into the purse to remove it, and both times I withdrew. The magic there caused my runes to light up, and not in a good way. I was missing something here, and I couldn't figure it out. To be totally honest, the book scared the crap out of me. I was half-afraid that if I handled it, whatever happened to JJ would happen to Katie.

In the dark of night, as Jai Li slept at my side, I would lay and stare into the blackness and begin to imagine what would happen if Katie didn't come back to me. I'd never felt so desperate in my entire life.

Sometimes, when Jai Li was too wound up to sleep, we'd sit up alone in the kitchen at Circle Q and have cocoa and cookies, just like ma used to do with me when I couldn't sleep.

There was more than one deep night cookie session where I'd pull my cell phone out and call up their number. I know they'd be asleep, but I thought if I could hear ma's voice for just a minute, that I could find a bit of peace.

Then I'd look over at Jai Li and wonder how I'd ever merge my new family in with my old. Felt like an either/or choice that I couldn't find a way to resolve.

In the light of day, I let the old habits take over, and calling home lost its luster. Still, I needed to do something. I wasn't going to be any good to anyone, including Jai Li before too long.

Then, one night, as I was hovering in that between space where you begin to dream, but know you're dreaming, I felt her. Katie was there, somewhere in the ether. It was the first breakthrough in weeks and weeks. She said my name, like a prayer, and I sat bolt upright, expecting to see her standing before me.

But I was at Circle Q. Jai Li was asleep at my side, and the house was quiet. Katie was not here.

Eventually I tried to go back to sleep, straining to hear her voice again. The morning came too early and too bright. I don't think I'd slept more than ten minutes at a time. I kept waking myself up, trying to keep that fugue state. Jai Li knew something was going on, though and tried to let me sleep in. I must've dozed a little, but by the time I got up and staggered into the kitchen, the whole house was alert, drinking coffee or juice and watching me like I was going to sprout a second head.

I told them about hearing Katie calling me. They watched me, each of them keeping her thoughts to herself. It was damned frustrating.

Finally, Julie piped up. "Wishful thinking," she said, patting me on the shoulder.

Jai Li smiled and made the sign for hope in that optimistic way kids have. Soon she and Edith were spinning a tale of daring rescue and Katie waking to my kiss. That morning I had a modicum of sanity, a few moments of light.

Mary hugged me and told me to go kiss Katie again, just to be sure. It was all very sweet. Of course, they damn near drove me nuts. Platitudes were awesome and all, but I needed expertise.

So, I called Qindra. We met for lunch over in Bellevue. For her to make the long trek over the water spoke volumes about her concern for me. I was a little oblivious to most of it, however. While she agreed there was a possibility I truly heard Katie calling me, she doubted it was anything but wishful thinking. Made me consider that Julie and Qindra were talking behind my back. Not that far-fetched.

"There is more to the world than I know about, sister, mine," Qindra said over her Caesar salad. "Things the wisest only hint at and fools embrace with conviction." She took my hands when she was telling me this, as if to lessen the pain. "Only you know the truth of it."

Great, that wasn't ambiguous or anything. I thanked her and went back to Circle Q more depressed than I'd been. Was I losing my mind here?

TWENTY

I took to half-sleeping more and more, so I could search for Katie in that between-space where the conscious mind slips into the deep waters of the great unconsciousness. I knew this term from a poetry teacher I had back in college. She believed that we as a species were all connected in this great underground sea of thought and dreams. It was this place where ideas were germinated and shared; how the same ideas could emerge in the world on different continents at the same time, even back before the creation of high-speed travel.

So I went diving into that metaphorical warm underground lake hoping to find a hint of Katie; another moment where her voice called out to me. It was frustrating at first, just hoping beyond hope that I'd find her in a fictional ocean where billions of other minds mingled and coalesced.

This went on for days. I stopped working, stopped doing much of anything really. I only ate when Julie and them forced me to. There were points where I know I was hallucinating, and Jai Li would wake me up. Eventually she started sleeping in Edith's room. One morning she refused to hug me, told me she was scared. That almost did me in. Seeing the look on that little girl's face was almost enough. But I loved Katie more, and I would sacrifice anything to get her back.

I even had a moment of guilt. I'd taken this child in, promised to be a mother to her, to raise her, keep her safe. But without

Katie, with this unknown hanging over my head, I wasn't good for anyone.

Melanie started talking about depression, and Julie told me if I didn't get my shit together she was going to drag me to therapy if she had to hogtie me. Funny, I believed her. But I had to keep trying.

It was Edith who had the right of it in the end. She was cleaning the house, going through things, dusting and making order of the general chaos five of us had wreaked on the house since Jai Li and I had taken up residence. No one complained, but I could tell we were straining things to their limits. It was inevitable at some point. And I knew it wasn't even Jai Li. It was me.

They were watching me, pacing me, conspiring against me. I wasn't exactly paranoid or anything, but when you see people whispering, heads together, then they separate and dodge into different rooms when you show up, it makes you wonder.

Of course, it could also be I was losing my shit. Yeah, that was happening.

It was the middle of the afternoon and I was once again hiding in our room out at Circle Q. We'd had three days in a row of overcast, and I had blankets jury-rigged up over the windows to block out what weak light we were getting. I had the light out and was thinking, wandering in my mind with only the glow of Gram to cut the absolute blackness of the room. Apparently I had been singing something nonsensical loud enough to be heard in the hallway. I honestly have no idea what I was singing, something about apples and pain, I think. I'm pretty fuzzy on the details. As I said, I was searching for ideas, thinking about Katie and letting my mind wander where it wanted, listening to the roaring in my ears.

Edith slammed my door open and stood in the glare of the hallway light with her fists on her hips and a scowl on her face that would make a Navy Seal cringe and call his mama.

"You have to sleep," she said, her voice stern.

I sat up and shielded my eyes, but couldn't see her, not with the hallway light creating a penumbra, casting her features in shadow.

"Drink this," she said, walking into the room and handing me a travel mug full of something warm.

I sniffed it. It smelled like milk with nutmeg and honey.

"No thanks," I said, holding the cup out to her. "I'm not thirsty."

She stepped back, her hands up to her shoulders. I couldn't make out her features, but she came off as smug.

"Drink it anyway," she said, leaning against the doorframe. "You need to sleep, or I will beat you into unconsciousness."

My eyebrows darted upward, and I squinted at her.

"You're kidding, right?"

Mary appeared at Edith's elbow, both hands on the handle of a broom. "Drink it, Sarah. Just sleep for a little while. You're driving us all crazy."

"Where's Jai Li?" I asked, sitting up straighter and laying Gram on the bed beside me.

"Julie's taking her to Black Briar for a couple of days," Mary said. "You drink that and you sleep, or so help me I will hold you down while Edith forces it down your throat."

This was exactly the opposite of anything I could imagine coming from these two women. Mothering and caring were the first two words that came to mind. Protective and matronly. Thugs threatening a beating was not on my radar.

"Jesus," I said, sitting up straighter. "I thought you people said I was sleeping too much."

They looked at each other. Mary spoke first. "You haven't slept for more than twenty minutes in the last four days. You're scaring Jai Li. She says you're losing your mind."

"Bullshit," I said, swinging my feet around to the side of the bed.

Edith stepped in and held a hand up. "What day is it?"

I smirked, looking between the two of them. "Thursday."

Mary shook her head. "Try again."

I looked at her, really took her in. There was a desperation there that finally got through to my brain. "Friday?"

"Sunday," Edith said. "Drink this, or so help me god, you can leave here and never return."

Mary shot a worried look to Edith, but didn't object.

"Fine," I said, sagging back. Maybe I was losing my shit after all.

I drank the milk in one long pull. It was sweet, and a little bitter. "How long will I sleep for?" I asked, handing over the mug and wiping my mouth.

"No more than a day," Edith said, smiling. "Now be a good girl, lay back and close your eyes."

I sighed again, they were so acting like lunatics. I did what they asked, however. Right before I slipped out of consciousness I noticed that Edith leaned over me and grabbed Gram by the hilt. She was wearing oven mitts.

What in the seven hells was that about?

TWENTY-ONE

I found myself in a foreign place, strange and dangerous. I was dressed in civilian clothes, jeans, T-shirt and my Docs. No Gram, though. That was a shock. There was something else, however; a presence that throbbed in the back of my mind. A powerful object that whispered to me, called to me. It was the book—Katie's diary. I had it locked in the closet down in the Kent apartment, but I could feel it.

I walked down deserted streets, trying not to be totally freaked out. There were things in the shadows, things that watched me with hunger in their eyes. Some of them were large, bigger than a dog, but most were smaller, rat-like things that scurried away as I approached. Twice I turned to find a shadow creeping up on me, but the light from my gaze sent it back into the deeper shadows.

After a few minutes I realized it wasn't my gaze. It was the runes on my forehead. The runes that Odin had marked me with the day I saved him from those giants. The runes that allowed me to have flashes of insight, moments of clarity.

I shuffled toward the center of the street, away from the deeper shadows as the sun continued to fade. I had no real desire to enter any of the buildings, but instinct told me I didn't want to be caught out in the open when the last light faded. If I had Gram I'd feel different, but Edith had taken Gram from me. Was it to prevent me from hurting myself while I slept, or was there some more nefarious meaning? I shook my head, trying to clear the rising despair.

Edith wasn't out to get me. No more than Mary, or any of my other friends. It had to be exhaustion ... or perhaps the general depression I was drowning in.

I sped up, looking from side to side, trying to find a building I could hole up in while I waited for the dawn. My feet began to feel leaden as the shadows pushed closer, narrowing the band of street for me to run down, pell-mell.

A flutter to my rear and the gut-wrenching dread caused me to spin, the light of the runes arcing a bright red line across a shadowy figure that had risen behind me to strike. It was something like a great bear, but with three heads and claws like knives. The red light severed one head and burned a slash across its body like a laser. It stumbled back, black blood spattering the ground between us.

Eaters ran from the blackness around us, dashing in to gobble up the blood. I'd seen this before. These were spirits, haunts that fed off the spirits or energy of the living, or the remains of each other. I felt bile rise in my throat as more, larger scavengers emerged from the alleys around us and brought the great bear-thing down.

It didn't go quietly. I stumbled back several steps as it tore at its attackers, two heads snapping into wisps of smoke that held malevolent intent. But something greater was coming. A cold wash of fear fell over me and I suppressed an urge to vomit. Carrion and pain. That's what was coming; something so far beyond the bear-thing that my mind was having a hard time staying in the game. A whiteness began to cloud my eyes and I let my arms fall to my side, weak and lifeless.

Run, a voice whispered in my head. There was a moment of bright golden light, a spear of power that pierced the fog and caught the corner of my eye. I spun and sprinted down the cobbled street ignoring the stream of eaters that flowed toward the feast and headed in the direction of the flickering golden light.

For the first dozen or more steps I had no other thought than to run and hide. The terror drove me on blindly. Once I was far enough away, the sudden wash of fear left me and I slowed, exhausted. I'd had fluffier nightmares in my time, and I'd battled a dragon. Whatever was there, whatever was coming to feed was beyond my wildest fears. At least I didn't pee myself this time.

The golden light winked out, but I had a good idea of the direction now. The city streets were giving way to parks and open ground. In the distance, there was a small outcropping and what had to be a cave. That's where the light had come from. There was safety there. An ally perhaps.

The cave led to a series of roughhewn tunnels—chopped out of the raw earth—with dangling roots and crawling things. For a moment, the peace and confidence the golden light had brought me had fallen away. This was a place of death and decay. A flash of stumbling across Katie's broken body clawing its way from a moldering grave rose up in me, and I nearly froze once again.

Move, the whisper came again. I'd come to a complete halt at the intersection of three tunnels—one ran downward out of sight; one upward, which made no sense as I'd not gone down and the surrounding area had not risen, as far as I had seen on my way here. The third tunnel was likely my best bet. It was wider and ran forward with a smooth tunnel and torchlight ahead. It seemed the right thing to do.

Left, the voice said again, as I took a step straight ahead to the well-lit tunnel.

I looked around. The left tunnel went down into darkness. There was no real sense of well-being there, only damp and cold. I took three more steps into the clear tunnel and stopped beside the first torch, looking ahead.

Back, dear god, back, the voice begged me. I stopped, looked around again and shook my head. All my senses told me to go forward to safety. Even the runes had no opinion here. But the voice had saved me from whatever was coming on the surface. Should I trust it? Or was it luring me back to be eaten?

I reached out and took the torch from the sconce to my right. A little part of my mind wanted me to listen to that voice. There was something familiar about it. It wasn't Katie, but it had a certain timbre, a specific pitch I almost recognized.

The next step down the tunnel in front of me came without conscious thought. My body was going on autopilot and all sense said to go forward.

I guess it was the stubborn streak, and what da said was my innate need to be contrary that saved me in the end. I turned back once again. The tunnel led up a just a little ways ahead and it seemed sunlight streamed out. Only a few more steps forward and I'd be able to see the sun again. I tried to shift the torch to my left hand but found that I couldn't let go of it. I grabbed it with my left hand, attempting to pry it out of my right, and the world shifted. What had appeared to be a torch was a winding tendril with a glowing tip, and it had wrapped itself around my right arm and was ever so gently tugging me forward.

The image of the sunlight exit wavered, and for a split second I could see another image. There at the end of the tunnel was an enormous gelatinous mass—writhing and pulsing with fairy lights. I could see into the translucent form where corpses, human and otherwise, hung suspended inside, each in a different state of decay. As I watched horrified, a small human skull was pushed from the undulating body to hit the cave floor with a *crack*, and roll toward me. The bone was polished and shone white in the glow of the lights.

The floor around me was littered with broken skulls and bones of a thousand other victims, each digested by this great eating blob. And the tendril pulled me forward another step—so close I could lunge forward into the muck.

I pulled back, but the tendril stretched lightly and another shot forward, wrapping around my right leg. I jerked to the right, using my left hand to support my right, and smashed the glowing tip of the tendril into the cave wall. The glowing bulb at the end exploded in a spray of light and pain.

The creature gurgled as the tendril ripped backward, leaving ripped flesh in its wake.

Pain flared from both the burning spray and the tearing flesh of my right arm. I twisted, stamping down on the tendril that had captured my right leg and it burst like a water balloon, more acidic fluids splashed my boots and jeans.

I stumbled back three steps, the pain finally destroying the illusion before me. Three more steps and I'd left whatever part of myself that was in this world behind forever.

I had no trouble making my way back to the intersection after that. The monster had plenty who would wander down its passage to keep it growing, I'm sure. But not me, not this day. I juked toward the lower hall and staggered down, letting the moist air take the edge off my burning flesh.

At the very bottom the tunnel opened into an immense cavern with a clear lake. Stalactites hung from the ceiling and the walls were adorned by many similar features. I rushed forward into the shallow water, realizing the alkaline water would offset the acidity of the gelatinous goo all over me. Bathing my wounds helped immensely. The pain didn't magically disappear, but the burning stopped.

I lay on the edge of the lake panting and trying to clear my head. Part of me wanted to sleep, but I realized I was asleep. In my room at Circle Q. Edith had given me something to sleep and here I was.

Get up, the voice said again, and I struggled to my feet. So far, it was batting a thousand. I tried to ignore the way my right arm didn't want to work, and the way my feet and legs felt raw and weeping. I looked around, saw a golden flicker to the left side of the lake and began making my way around.

The next tunnel was crystalline, fetid and abandoned but with a hint of something lurking, something hungry. My thoughts raced with an urgency that had no specific focus, but which drove me forward nonetheless. The voice did not return, but the very air grew more visceral.

Eventually I became aware of other entities sharing my tunnels, hunters and hunted. There was a force, a malevolent hunger that dogged my trail. It followed me through my sleep, never drawing nearer, but always there, in the back of my mind, a presence that spoke of pain and death.

Once more, before I woke, just as the crystalline tunnels began to fade, the voice came to me one final time.

She is not here, it said, full of sorrow and pain. *Do not return.*

Then the sudden light of a new day flooded the room where I slept. I moaned, covering my face with my arms. First thing I really noticed was that my limbs weren't burned, physically in any case. I felt drained and weaker than normal, like maybe I had been battling the flu or something. But I distinctly remembered the burns. I blinked my eyes open and moaned.

Julie stood over me, the blankets I'd tacked up over the windows in her hands.

"Time to face the world again," she said, sitting on the edge of the bed and brushing the hair from my eyes. "Time to see your daughter, and time to talk about next steps."

I sat up and she reached for me, pulling me into a hug.

"I know you miss her," she said. "But you can't give up your life. You have things you need to do."

I cried then, letting the grief and anguish I'd been holding inside flood out in hot, wet tears. What scared me the most was the undeniable feeling that I had narrowly eluded horror beyond my imagination. Not the gelatinous mass. That wasn't a thinking creature. No, the thing that had scared me so bad was when the three-headed bear had fallen. The thing that pursued me through the crystalline tunnels at the end. I was being hunted, or rather, something hunted for the thing I hunted.

My deepest fear was that this entity was death, pursuing Katie. No matter what the voice had said, I knew I was right. Katie had been there, had passed through those lands at some point. The runes throbbed with a comforting assurance. I just needed a way to find her.

I'd slipped sideways in my dreams. I knew it in my soul. My dreams were merging with that place of eaters and wandering spirits. I wondered if every dreamer went to this world from time to time. Was this the source of nightmares, the land of the fear? Or was it reserved to those marked by ancient gods, claimed by magic swords, or on the verge of losing their one true love?

TWENTY-TWO

Apparently I'd slept for thirty-two hours. I was stiff and sore, but a hot shower and a steaming mug of chocolate and coffee had me almost feeling human again. I sat at the kitchen table, struggling to focus, reliving moments of my dreams in my head while the three Circle Q women sat with me.

Edith refreshed my coffee, Mary slid a second helping of scrambled eggs in front of me, and Julie upended a bottle of chocolate syrup over my coffee until there was barely room to dip a spoon in to stir it.

"Thanks," I said, glancing at the three of them each in turn. "Thanks for everything."

Edith patted my hand, Mary smiled, and Julie sat back, crossing her arms across her chest.

"I'm giving you thirty more minutes to get your shit together, then we're heading out."

I looked at her, watched the way her eyes danced, and nodded. "Yes, ma'am."

She nodded back and took up her own cup of coffee. The three of them chatted about things that needed doing. Mary was going to run out to the Grange for a bit to talk to one of the other farmers out here about leasing him twenty or so acres.

"I'm just too beat to do much more farming," she said with a smile. "I'll keep the horses, but there's nothing wrong with letting

Lester and his boys put in some wheat. We'll both do all right, I reckon."

We spent the next thirty minutes on minutiae, and I loved it. It let me settle my head before the drive out to Black Briar. By the time I'd polished off the food and coffee I was ready to face the world. I went in the back, changed into my normal attire, and came out to meet Julie at the truck. Of course, I'd brought Gram. I'd decided it was stupid of me to ever go anywhere without her, honestly.

Nidhogg had named me her Fist, whatever that meant, and there was something hunting Katie, or me … or both. Julie just watched me for a minute then motioned me to her truck. As I slid in, I set a sheathed Gram on the seat to my left. I looked back as we started the truck and saw that Julie had her shotgun behind the seat. All right then. We were in agreement.

On the ride out to Gold Bar, Julie filled me in on the last several days while I had gone mentally AWOL. Katie's condition had improved to the point that the doctors considered her stable and had suggested that she be moved to a long-term care facility. There was nothing physically wrong with her that they could detect. She just wouldn't wake up.

Jimmy flipped his shit over that suggestion. She was to be brought back to Black Briar, he insisted. They'd look after her. He'd arrange for a hospital bed and a nurse to check in on her daily. Everything else would be taken care of by family. We had a couple days to decide.

I already knew what Jim was going to do. It's what I'd do in his place. Hell, if I could afford it, I'd do it out at Circle Q, but we didn't have the room, the money, or the staff. No, Jimmy would do what he thought best, and as long as it kept Katie safe and sound, at least physically, I was all for it.

I wasn't going to lose my head again. Didn't mean I wasn't planning to explore the dreamlands as best I could, but I'd only do it during normal sleep. I had things to take care of.

When Julie and I arrived out at Black Briar, Jai Li was sitting at one of the communal picnic tables, coloring with Bub. Frick and Frack were having a late breakfast. It was just after nine.

J.A. Pitts

At the sound of the truck, Bub looked around, but Jai Li resolutely kept coloring. She hunched over and began bearing down on her page with the crayons, to the point that, by the time I was out of the truck and moving toward her, she snapped one in half and threw it back onto the table.

"Hey, big girl?" I said.

She may not have a tongue, but I knew she could hear. Her language skills were decent. I squatted down between her and Bub and signed hello. She turned away, not acknowledging the greeting.

"Hi," Bub said, grinning at me. Of course, he grinned most of the time, it came with having a head full of teeth. Like a carnivorous Muppet.

"Hello, Bub. How are you?"

He shrugged. "I've been better. We've missed you."

Jai Li pushed him and scooted down. I almost grinned. Obviously that was a secret that he'd betrayed.

"Me, too," I said. "All this stuff about Katie had me out of it for a while."

"We're scared, too," Bub said, putting one clawed hand onto Jai Li's shoulder.

Jai Li shot him a glance that would've made milk go bad.

"Except Jai Li. She's not scared. She's angry."

"I figured as much," I said, reaching over to brush the hair out of her face. "And I've been a bad person to ignore her for so long."

"Grownups do that sometimes," Bub said with a sigh. "Even when they love you, they abandon you when they go crazy."

I reached up and hugged the little guy. "I'm sorry," I said, cupping his cheek. "You're right. I've been a real jerk."

He shrugged, but the tension went out of him. I glanced over to see Jai Li watching me, her eyes full of tears.

"You want a hug?" I asked, turning to her.

She didn't move, but Bub nudged her. "Come on," he said. "You know you want to."

She gave him one final look of betrayal and scrambled from the table and ran back toward the new barn.

I sighed and stood, thinking to follow her.

"Wait," Bub said, placing a hand on my arm. "Let me talk to her. She's not as mature as me."

I nodded and he tore off after her, his little spindly legs a blur as he tried to catch up with her. As he rounded the side of the barn, I heard a wail of anguish.

Not a sound that made me comfortable, so I ran after them. At the last minute, I paused. I could hear Bub talking to her, hear her sobbing.

"You'll be okay," he was saying. "Sometimes the moms do stupid things, but they always love us."

I walked away, head down, letting the pain of his words settle into my heart. I had two kids. How had I abandoned him here to ghost amongst the others. He needed a home as much as Jai Li did.

The picnic table was strewn with colorful pictures. I sorted through them, amazed as always at the girl's talent, but heart broken by the scenes I saw. Had I really yelled at her? Was that why Edith and Mary had finally pushed me? There were scenes of me lost in the dreamscape: one of the three-headed bear that made me shiver, a dark cave with something pulsing green at the end, an entity who did nothing but consume and spit out the bones.

No princesses and unicorns for my girl. Nope. Nothing but the finest nightmares for my girl.

I turned at the sound of them coming back. They walked hand in hand, but I could tell that Jai Li was not ready to forgive me yet. Hell, I didn't blame her. What were we putting her through?

She wouldn't approach the table, just stood near the edge looking at her feet.

"Come on," Bub said. "Get it over with."

"No," I said, standing. "I've been pretty bad to Jai Li, and she has every right to be angry with me."

Both she and Bub looked at each other, their eyes wide.

"I should be grounded or something. Time-out maybe?"

Jai Li got very serious then, took a step back and signed something to Bub.

"She's not teasing," he said, nodding. "I can tell when she's lying. She means it."

Huh. He could tell when I was lying. Had I lied to him before? How many times and for what reasons? "Man, we grownups get lost in our own little worlds, don't we?"

I sat back down, hanging my hands between my knees. Was I doing to them what ma and da had done to me? Was all the controlling behavior because they were afraid of other things. Jesus. I hadn't been exactly selfish or anything, kids needed their parents *and* needed to have their freedoms as well. It was a wonky balancing act that apparently I totally sucked at.

"I'm sorry, Jai Li. You don't deserve how I've treated you. I'm just so scared for Katie that I lost sight of what I should be doing." I stood, shoving my hands in my pockets. "I'm gonna go into the house and talk to Deidre and Jimmy."

She just watched me, her face a mask of wonder and tears.

"You deserve better. If you want to live somewhere else, I'll do what I can to help you have a better life. But if you want to live with me and Katie, I promise to try harder."

She nodded once and didn't move otherwise.

I brushed the top of Bub's head with my hand and shrugged. "I'll be in the house. Julie's in there as well. When you make up your mind, let me know."

Of course, it was a shitty move. Putting all that pressure on the girl, but I couldn't dictate to her. She'd had a hard enough life so far. Maybe I was bad news, and she needed someone who could care for her better. Someone like Edith, Mary, and Julie. They'd take care of her. I'd leave Circle Q, head back down to the apartment in Kent, and let them raise her.

No matter the outcome, I thought maybe I had a slightly better insight to my life growing up, and a deep abiding hatred of being a fucking grownup.

This all just sucked.

TWENTY-THREE

Julie headed back to Circle Q and I stayed out at Black Briar for a couple of days, nursing my relationship with Jai Li and Bub, while just regaining my strength.

Jimmy had Katie's old room converted to a hospital room. He had a full hospital bed brought in, as well as all the equipment needed to monitor someone in a coma. The hospital was not pleased but couldn't really refuse him. He had staff who could watch her around the clock and hired several nurses to come in throughout the week. He also had Melanie to help coordinate all the care. She was just as safe and cared for there as she would've been in a long-term care facility.

After a couple of days, Jai Li began coming around me again. I was working in the smithy there, spending time with Bub, just making swords and trying different techniques. I sparred with Trisha and her crew and really pushed my body every day. I needed to feel fitter. The time in the dreamscape had taken something out of me, but the days at Black Briar were helping me rebuild it.

In the end, it was Jai Li who really accelerated the healing. Once she decided she could forgive me, I started feeling much better. I didn't shirk my duties, either. I let her pick my punishment and spent another three days helping the Black Briar crew dismantle the old barn. Bub wasn't going to be living there anymore. I was going to build him a place at the smithy, and then, when we got our own place, he was going to come live with us.

He was very excited by the whole prospect but insisted he had to stay near the forge. Jai Li assured him we'd have a forge at our new place. She even drew him a picture of the house she wanted with the fence and the roses. Only now, it had a smithy in the back with a house for Bub. It was all cute and healing.

By the time they had Katie settled into the house, we were a family again. But Jai Li insisted that Circle Q was our current home and we had to go back there. They missed us, she assured me.

We settled into a solid rhythm out at Circle Q. I started back to working with Julie, letting the hard labor of shoeing and mucking stalls beat my body down, so I could sleep long and deep at night. I was open with everyone, explaining how I was dreaming about searching for Katie. Jai Li knew how serious it was and approved, even if the others thought it was silly and dangerous.

One afternoon, after a long day of shoeing horses, Julie and I stopped out at the County Line for a beer before going home.

"I know you and Jai Li have made up," she said, toying with her glass. "But I've been asking around, and I think you're playing a dangerous game."

I patted her arm and smiled. "I won't lie to you, Julie. It scares the hell out of me, and I don't go into that place every night, but when I do, I know she's out there. You don't know what it's like. I can sense her, you know. It's dangerous, and frankly scares the bejesus out of me, but what else can I do?"

Julie got her boss face on immediately. "This is that sideways place, right? The place between the mirrors where the eaters live?"

I could tell she was worried. I wondered who she'd been talking with.

"And Jai Li keeps drawing you in danger," she said. "Have you seen the pictures? Giant glass spiders and hate-filled spirits hunting you through dark tunnels."

I shivered. That pretty much described the way the latest trip had ended up. I'd barely escaped again. Just the thought of that last encounter gave me a shiver. I had been so close to losing it. I took a deep breath, pulled on my best suit of bravado and smiled.

"Home again, home again," I sang as I walked into the house, just ahead of Julie. Jai Li came tearing down the hall and was about to throw herself into my arms, but stopped herself. She held her nose and shook her head, signing for shower.

I bowed. "You are so right," I said, grinning. "Mucked out a few stalls today to help out Mr. Peters."

"He's a nice man," Mary said, coming out of the kitchen with a dishrag in her hands. "But you go take a shower, then come into the kitchen to help your girl with her work, while Julie showers."

She didn't wait for an answer, but turned and walked back into the kitchen.

"I guess we know who's boss," I said, quietly.

Jai Li snickered.

After a quick shower, I sat beside Jai Li at the kitchen tables and worked through a math workbook with her. As we were home schooling her for the summer, there was no real break. Also no real class times. We studied as we could.

When Edith came in carrying a bag full of groceries, Julie and I hustled out to the truck to bring in the rest. When I got in, Jai Li and Edith had their heads together plotting.

Jai Li nodded, signing something I didn't catch, and Edith nodded.

"She wants me to show you the pictures she's been saving," Edith said, standing. "The girl's like a machine when she's on, just creating one picture after another, colors and shadows ..." she waved the thought away. "Let me show you."

I sat at the table and pulled Jai Li into my lap. She snuggled against me, the top of her head under my chin. I loved the way she felt in my arms, the way she smelled.

I drew a deep breath and let it out slowly. I was worrying that I was becoming obsessed with this dream fugue thing again. The nights were getting rougher, which told me that either I was getting closer to finding Katie, or whoever was hunting us was getting closer to me.

I had to remember that Jai Li needed me, even more now that Katie was lost to us for the moment. Only for the moment, damn it. My throat clenched, and I squeezed Jai Li tighter, making her yelp in surprise.

"Sorry," I said, lessening my death grip. "I just missed you so much."

She cooed and ran her small hand over the side of my face. Her smile was a miracle, a moment of sunshine in a gray day. I turned my head and kissed her hand. She laughed. Guess it tickled.

When Edith came back in the room, she had Julie with her. They sat across from us and Mary came around to sit at the head of the table—her spot.

Jai Li held only my arm, one hand to her mouth as Edith laid each picture on the table in front of me.

There were so many. The world of sideways was immediate, the crystalline landscape, the shadows, and especially the eaters. Most were rendered in black and white, which fit the worlds I visited in my sleep.

She drew page after page of the eaters, from the smallest, about the size of her thumbnail, all the way to one that was nearly as big as Nidhogg in her full dragon form. And Jai Li had seen Nidhogg, so I knew there was no exaggeration in the scale.

This last one was not made of smoke or crystal, but meat and pain. I didn't know how I knew that, but it was pretty clear in the pictures. Jai Li could capture emotion as well as form. It was a little terrifying.

Several pictures showed me jumping over lakes of fire, sliding down dunes made of broken promises, and delving through caves of forgotten dreams.

I touched each picture, getting the flash of their true meaning, understanding the world this child saw when I delved into the sideways.

I squeezed her hand and looked down at her. "Are you sure you're only six?" I asked. She shrugged and hid her face against my chest as Edith brought forth the final batch of pictures.

They were odd portraits. Some were us as a family: Katie, Jai Li, Bub, and me, usually with horses in the picture somewhere. She did have her first and true love there.

But in every one there were our shadows. Mine was nearly always a boring smudge of gray, while Jai Li's had no shadow. For some reason that made me sad.

Katie's picture was the clearest. Her shadow was dark, darker than mine. As every picture was laid out on the table Katie began to fade and her shadow grew more distinct.

"We're losing her," I said, touching the papers carefully. "She's fading."

Jai Li nodded, but pulled my hands back, holding them in hers.

Safe, she signed, pointing between me and her.

"Yes, you and me, we are safe."

She tapped Katie's last picture and shivered, signing *danger.*

I nodded, not saying anything else.

Finally, the last three pictures were different. These weren't about any of us, nor of the typical denizens of the Sideways. These showed a shadow—a wraith, like one of the hungry spirits that had been trapped in the house out in Chumstick. It was the ghost with the bowler hat. The one that promised to watch me suffer. He was drawn in such a way that if you turned the picture ninety degrees, it looked like the focus was on him, and Katie, Jai Li, and I were the shadows.

He stood there, as I'd seen him that dark night. He had a bowler hat in one hand and a dripping axe in the other. A skeletal frame peeked out from beneath his shoulder-to-ankle trench coat.

He'd been just inside the dome Qindra had erected over the house, a shield to keep him and his ilk contained. As I traced his outline with my finger I could hear his voice in my head.

When you die, I'll be waiting for you. Waiting to play.

The last picture was of him and Katie, superimposed over one another in one frame, then another where Katie lay on the floor of her school and her shadow and the Bowler Hat Man's were both flying away as the book obviously exploded.

Her spirit was blasted out of her body, as I'd suspected. But was this proof she hadn't been inside there alone?

I covered my face with my hands, leaning back. "Burn those, please." I said, my voice muffled behind my hands.

"Dark portents," Edith said, gathering the stack of papers.

Where did Stuart find Katie after the Solstice battle? Was it within the boundaries of the dome? The dome had blown by that point. And the spirits had been siphoned into the rituals of the blood cult. But had this one eluded them? Had he somehow marked Katie?

I excused myself quickly and ran down the hallway. I made it into the bathroom just before the bile rose in me and I spewed the beer Julie and I had drunk an hour earlier.

Was that who hunted us? Had he latched onto Katie somehow to withstand the necromancer's summons? Had that mass killer been inside Katie when we'd made love? Was he looking out of her eyes, hidden in the darkness, feeding on her nightmares and fears?

I had to call Qindra. Hell, maybe I needed to call an exorcist.

TWENTY-FOUR

Qindra didn't answer her cell phone, and when I called the house, Zi Xui, the head of Nidhogg's servants, assured me she would take a message and see that Qindra got it. She said that Qindra had gone that morning and was not expected back for a few days.

I thanked her and hung up, looking down at my cell phone. What the hell was I supposed to do? Maybe the wraith had been destroyed when the diary had gone off like a magical nuke. Or, maybe he was just in the sideways, following me around when I was looking for Katie. That seemed more likely, now that the initial shock had subsided. Jai Li drew vivid pictures, but I was the one drawing the conclusions.

With the shock, and my extended absences, we decided to stay at Circle Q, do a little bonding and see if we could get some answers out of Jai Li without totally freaking out the child. I found it bizarre to be relying on her abilities, but she saw things we didn't, or saw them in ways we hadn't thought to consider.

It was almost as if she was an antenna into the psychotic and crazy that had sideswiped our lives in the last year. Of course, she was part of all that, having been a servant of Nidhogg her whole short life.

We had a quiet evening of knitting, games, and stories ... lots and lots of stories. She especially wanted to hear silly things like The Three Pigs, The Three Bears, and Humpty-Dumpty. She thought they were high art. She'd begun to read on her own, as well. I think she just liked hearing me read. And it was something she hadn't experienced frequently in her time with Nidhogg.

Of course it reminded me of the homey night I'd had with Katie, Melanie, and Dena the week before Katie's collapse. It made things a little more manic, a little on edge. Not sure Jai Li noticed, but I think the others did. We called it an early evening and I trundled Jai Li to bed. Maybe I needed some sleep to help clear my head. Something without being hunted.

Jai Li must have been a good shield. I didn't have any memorable dreams and felt better rested than I had since before the collapse. After a hearty breakfast of steel cut oats and fresh fruit (I thought we could've used some actual meat) we went for a horseback ride out to the wooded trails that backed up to Circle Q.

We all went, five women on horseback, riding out with a picnic lunch, more books, and a Frisbee. We were in no hurry and I really enjoyed the ride. It was peaceful. We rode for a couple of hours, had a nice lunch in the bright sunshine on of a wooded clearing, and threw the Frisbee around for a while.

When we were packing up, Jai Li and Edith were talking, their hands flying back and forth. I really needed to take the time to improve my signing. I had no idea what they were talking about. I was barely at the alphabet stage, and maybe the baby-words portion of the education.

When I asked what they were talking about, Jai Li pointed at my hair and drew her hands far apart, frowning.

"She says you have lost your way," Edith said, stuffing a few loose folding napkins in her saddlebag. "You've let your hair grow out, and she thinks it makes you look funny."

I ran my hands up through my hair, contemplating. I normally kept the sides shaved, but with all the crap going on since fall, I'd let it go. I pulled the sides of my hair and could tell it was down below my ears.

"You don't think it's pretty?" I asked.

"Oh, I think it looks a sight better than you normally keep," Edith said.

"I agree," Mary chimed in, grinning as she checked the saddle of her horse. "You're a beautiful woman," she said. "But you definitely don't look like yourself."

I helped Jai Li up onto her horse and mounted my own. "Okay," I said, looking over at Julie who was just shaking her head and holding up both hands.

"I'm not sure how I feel about it at the moment," I said with a laugh. It was true. I hadn't given any thought to how I looked, honestly. Oh, I still had my jeans and my concert Tees, even my Docs. But before I'd been cultivating an image of the rebel. Now, it didn't really seem to matter.

Jai Li pulled her horse around close to mine and leaned out, patting my leg. I looked at her, and she signed quickly. I let her finish and looked to Edith who had been watching.

"She said you need to find yourself before you can find Katie."

I drew a deep breath, taking in the clean country air and clearing my head of cobwebs. "Find myself, huh?" I asked.

Jai Li signed a response that I understood. *Yes,* she signed. *We need you.*

We rode back to the farm, one of us adults keeping pace with Jai Li, but the others rotating back to carry on conversations without the girl. She was happy to take point on the trail.

"Wouldn't hurt you to start working out again," Julie said, grinning. "You're getting a little soft, or so the girl says."

I looked down. I didn't have a paunch or anything. But I hadn't gone on a run for a while, and I can't remember the last time I did sit-ups. Maybe I was depressed. Maybe exploring the Sideways was an excuse to not really do anything.

It was hard to tell. Was I wasting my time? Or, maybe I was just going about it wrong.

On the ride home, I decided I'd call Gunther, let him know about the wraith and see if he knew anything that would keep it away from Katie. I had a hunch that the magicked fence out at Black Briar could probably keep the wraith away. Would also explain why he had been following me. If he was still haunting Katie, he'd be there, not chasing me.

That thought buoyed me a little. Not that being hunted by eaters and wraiths were simple things. But them being after me meant they weren't after Katie, and that was a relief.

Unless they were really looking for Katie and I happened to be in the same vicinity. Circles within circles. It made my head hurt. I rotated up the line to ride beside Jai Li and try and settle my whirling thoughts.

Time to get back onto my routine, do some smithing, restart life. Katie wouldn't want me floundering around. And if Jai Li had to point that out to me, it must be pretty bad. No more dreamwalking for me. Time to face the real world.

TWENTY-FIVE

Then in the third week of June I got a surprise I hadn't expected. Jai Li and I had pretty much moved full-time into Circle Q, so I drove down to our apartment in Kent to grab some odds and ends Jai Li and I needed.

I was in the kitchen debating if I had time to make a pot of coffee and go through the mail when I heard a voice calling to me from the old bedroom.

I spun around, reaching for Gram who was in her case in the living room. I vaulted over the bar, rolled over the top of the couch and ended up on my knees on the floor, pulling the case toward me, flipping open the latches, and grasping Gram by the hilt.

The world shifted like it did every time I held her—sounds were sharper, the world was a little crisper. We hadn't slept in the bedroom since the night I went walkabout of my own volition months earlier. Astral projection, some called it. Like dream walking, but when you're awake. It was crazy and damned dangerous.

At that time, I'd been exploring the apartment when I found we had a shadow door between our apartment and the next. It gave off that haunted house vibe, but I've never been one to be afraid. Being afraid was a good self-defense—a lesson I had a hard time retaining. I'd tried to push through the shadow door, like a ghost walking through the solid wall that it really was in the normal world. Just an experiment, to see what would happen. I expected to feel funny, maybe get cold or hot, something like when you walk through a ghost in movies. What I hadn't expected was being sucked into the Sideways. Not the dreamscape, the real and for true land of eaters and malevolent spirits.

I could barely bring myself to walk into the room after that. Katie had humored me, and we moved the bed into the living room. Made having company a little awkward, but we didn't entertain all that much. The place was too small as it was.

Katie had this ancient old mirror she'd inherited from her mother long before I'd met her. It had hung in that bedroom as long as I'd known her. She loved that mirror. I hadn't thought much about it until I walked into the bedroom, looking for the source of the voice.

I got quite the surprise. In the mirror, glowing like an angel, was the elf boy Gletts—Skella's brother—who'd been lost for so long. He'd rescued me from being pulled into the Sideways the day I'd discovered the shadow door. And lo and behold, here he was in Katie's mirror.

His body lay in a house of healing in Stanley Park, Vancouver where his grandmother held vigil waiting for his spirit to return. I'm the one that told them his spirit was wandering the Sideways. They hadn't been pleased.

His gran, Unun, was out of her head, worrying. I wasn't sure she'd ever recover. It scared Skella. I think that more than anything was what was driving the girl to Bellingham and new friends—the grief and the madness brought on by the helpless waiting.

Pretty much how I felt with Katie.

My mouth went dry.

"Why are you here?" I asked, striding across the room. "Why don't you go home, back to your body? Your grandmother is mad with grief."

He held up his hand, grinning like an imp. "Keep your panties on," he said.

I glared at him and he blushed.

"Or don't."

Such a boy. He'd gotten bolder since I'd seen him last.

"Why are you here, besides concern for the state of my underwear?"

The look on his face spoke of fear and nervousness. "Have you given up the search?" he asked.

It had been a few days since I'd gone dreamwalking. Is that what he meant?

"If not," he rushed on, "you need to come up with a better plan. You've been searching in the wrong places."

He looked like a normal gaunt Goth kid I'd first met, too thin, hair in his face, black eyeliner and fingernails.

"What do you know about it?" I asked.

He rolled his eyes. "Who do you think has been keeping you out of trouble, geez." He pulled a face—petulant and exasperated. "You go running through places even the most experienced travelers fear, screaming your fool head off. It's been damn close a few times, you know."

"So it was *you*," I said, finally putting the pieces together. "You're the one who's been guiding me, that voice in the dark."

"Yep," he said, grinning. "It was fun at first, following you, keeping the crawlies from catching you, but that was before *he* showed up."

My blood froze. "Who? Who showed up?"

He leaned in toward the mirror, his face suddenly getting a little distorted. "The man in the bowler hat," he said, shivering. "I'll take the meanest eater over him any day. At least the eaters only want to eat. The hat man, he wants to hurt."

I closed my eyes for a moment, trying to settle my breath. My heart was pounding like I'd been running.

"Is he chasing me, or looking for Katie?"

A grimace flitted across Gletts's face. "Katie," he said. "I've heard him talking to some of the others. Some he negotiates with, some he tortures and kills. Eats the dead," he stammered to a halt, his voice quivering. "Not afraid of eaters or anything in there," he said, looking up. "I think they've started being afraid of him."

"Thank you," I said, shivering. "Thanks for helping me."

"Katie's holed up somewhere," he said. "Scared. I'm betting she's waiting for a time she can come home, if she's not so lost she can't find her way."

"Maybe I need to start hunting the hat man."

He stepped back, hands up in the air, shaking his head. "He's bad news, Sarah. I'm not sure you can handle him."

"I'll think on it," I said. "Thanks for the warning." I looked at him. There was more, I had a feeling. "What have you been doing?" I asked. "Why aren't you going home to your family? To your body?"

He shrugged. "I was busy before you started running around like a crazy woman." He pulled his shoulders back and raised his chin a little. "I'm on a quest. Doing important things and you're keeping me from them."

"What things?" I asked. "And I can most likely defend myself, even against a wraith."

He laughed at that. "In the meat world, sure. But when you're spirit walking, you should at least carry that sword of yours. I know you can take it Sideways, you told me."

I looked at him. So I was definitely slipping from dreamland to the Sideways. I thought of my promise to Jai Li—my promise to stop dream walking and live in the real world—but this changed things. Maybe I should start sleeping with Gram in bed with me again. Probably not totally crazy. I'd had her the first time I met the bowler hat scumbag.

"Have you seen any clues of Katie?" I didn't want him to hear the desperation in my voice, but he already knew. He'd heard me calling for her night after night.

His grin faded. "No, I'm sorry."

"What are you doing that is so important, then?" I asked.

"You aren't listening," he said, glancing over his shoulder. "I can see it in you, the way you stand, the way your eyes are. You think you can beat anything, you think you can't die." He paused, gulping, and turned to the side. "I don't want you to get hurt," he said, quietly, not looking at me. "And Katie isn't here, she's not in any part of the Sideways I've explored. And she's not in any of the between places I've been to. She's someplace else, hiding."

"Hiding?" I asked, really not expecting an answer.

"Yeah, I'm sorry. I just don't have any idea where." He shook his head. "I know something happened to her. There was a ripple affect across the worlds. Surely you felt it."

Now it was my turn to nod. "Oh, you have no idea. Things have been crazy."

The mirror behind him shimmered with golden flames, made me think of Bub. "Where are you?"

"Not sure," he said. "Funny that no matter where I search, I can always find a window to you and Skella."

That was sweet and creepy.

"So, dish. What're you doing, exactly?" I asked again. "What keeps you from coming home?"

"That's just it," he said, smiling. "I'm searching for home."

"Can't you follow that thread back to your body?" When I'd gone walkabout in Vancouver at his grandmother's insistence, I saw that each of the wounded and the lost had their spirits connected back to their bodies by a gossamer cord. Once that cord was severed, the spirit moved onward and the body died. Gletts's cord had been strong. Not like some who yearned to move to the next place. "Your grandmother misses you."

He shook his head. "Not that home. Álfheim. Our true home. I think I've found something you could help with."

I watched him, considering all the crazy shit in my life. "My priorities are with Katie," I said. "Sorry, she's more important."

He sighed, pursing his mouth into a pout. "When you find a way to bring her home, will you help then?"

Heck yeah. That was exactly the type of thing Odin wanted me doing. "Absolutely."

"Excellent!" he shouted, doing a happy dance. "It's in Bellingham, I think. South of Vancouver, anyway. But I'm pretty sure it's in Bellingham." He was excited, joyous. "Skella's been searching, but she hasn't found it yet."

"You talk to Skella?" She never told me.

"Not directly," he said, shrugging. "I talk to her in her sleep, but she listens. She thinks she's dreaming. I've gotten that good. I tried it out on Rolph, your dwarf friend at first, but he doesn't sleep very well, and besides he's pretty grumpy."

I chuckled. "Yeah, funny, that."

"But, I finally got the knack of it. It took me a while, but I've convinced her to search Bellingham for signs of a way home, a way off this mudball."

"Wait," my head was buzzing. "Do you think you've found Yggdrasil, the world tree?"

"Maybe," he said, thoughtfully. "That could be it. I just see it as a portal from this side. Another junction between one place and the next." He looked thoughtful for a moment, edgy. "The problem is, it doesn't stay put. I've seen it a few times, but it flickers, waxes and wanes."

"So, go home, get your own body, and come back here."

He shrugged at me, that old familiar reticence I'd come to recognize with him before he'd fallen. "Can't see it from meat space," he said. "If I can find this, figure out how to get my people off this world and onto our own, I'd die happy."

I understood the sentiment. Needs of the many outweigh the needs of the few. It was also bullshit in most cases. "Let's see if we can find it, and get you home," I offered, smiling. "Win-win all around. What say?"

He looked up at me, his hair covering half his face. For a moment I thought he was going to laugh at me, throw his head back, and cackle in the face of my absurd suggestion. Instead he smiled shyly and nodded. "I'd like that."

"I'll call Skella," I promised. "You go take care of yourself. Don't get eaten by … well … eaters."

He grinned, and that rakish look I'd seen before returned. "They can't catch me," he said. "You'd be surprised what I've learned here."

"Like secret passages to other worlds?"

"So much more than that," he replied, suddenly serious. "Did you know another drake has come into the world? First in a century."

"A new …?" I stared intently at him. "When? Where?"

"Not sure, exactly," he said. "Direction and distance are not very relevant here. But I'd think you should check in on Frederick Sawyer. See what he knows. It's definitely south of you, but it's all a little vague."

"Okay, I'll check into that. Anything else?"

Gletts pursed his lips, thinking.

"Anything," I said. "Even if it seems strange. You never know what's important."

He laughed. "You don't know the half of it." There was another moment, where he seemed to be wracking his brains. "You know, there's this beacon I can see from time to time. Like a searchlight, only sometimes it's green and sometimes it's purple."

Sympathy magic? Like with the diary. "Where?" I asked, suddenly excited again.

"Near here," he said, shrugging. "They don't like it here, whenever one of them gets too close to that light, they get zapped. Fries them in a heartbeat. Would be a powerful weapon to have, if you can find it."

Maybe it was the diary. Who knew how far its magic reached. Something I'd look into, for sure. If it didn't scare the hell out of me and everyone who knew of its existence.

"There's a book," Gletts said, off-handedly. "Not sure what kind, but I overheard some of the Bowler Hat Man's minions talking about it. Something he wants pretty badly. Almost as badly as he wants you."

"Like a diary," I asked, a little weirded out that he was almost reading my mind.

"Could be," he said, "Now that you mention it. Seems that either the book leads to you or Katie, and any of the three of you leads to the other." He tapped his chin, thinking. "You know, makes me wonder which he's really looking for. You, Katie, or the book."

I nodded slowly. "Freaky," I said, my mind running in circles.

"He's a freaky dude," Gletts said, nodding sagely. "But I should run, can't stick around too long in one place, except for the few safe-houses I've discovered."

"We'll have to talk about all that after you've returned home," I said, with a smile. "Now go home and stop making your grandmother go insane."

He looked at me, his eyes reflecting the golden flames all around him. "Soon, I hope." He gave a quick wave and stepped exit stage left. One moment he was gone, then Katie's mirror was full of flames. Then I only saw myself reflected back.

Holy crap. Was he after the book? That made no sense. And a way home? Just the fact I had spoken with Gletts was gonna totally freak out Skella. Odin, on the other hand, was going to freak, but in a totally different manner. I looked forward to his next poetic ramblings. And what the hell was that about Frederick? My head was spinning. Diary, new Dragons, Yggdrasil. A path away from this world. A chance to explore other worlds.

But not without Katie.

That stopped the spinning. Other worlds or no, I wasn't going anywhere without her. I'd promised her. Never again.

When Qindra called I'd see if she had any news of Frederick. It could explain some of his behavior after JJ's funeral. If Katie was awake, I would've driven down to Portland and visited the great lizard myself. The battle with the necromancer had not been kind to him, but he'd lived. Too bad many others couldn't say the same.

Katie first. If she was hiding someplace, as Gletts suggested, then I had to redouble my efforts. I'd take Gram with me and maybe scare up some more help. Wherever Gletts had been reminded me of Bub. Maybe he'd have a clue. The diary may hold some answers as well. Had he seen the light from the diary, or was it something else? Was that the key to bringing her home? Something in my gut told me it was all related.

Yep, I'd have to really explore that scary ass book. I just hoped like hell it didn't kill me when I touched it in meat space, as Gletts called it.

And how embarrassing would it be to be killed by a diary, I mean, seriously.

TWENTY-SIX

I called Skella and she agreed to come to the apartment. She said she would get here as quick as lightning once she walked over to the cave she kept the mirrors in—her little subway stop through the Sideways. It had taken me about thirty minutes to drive down to Kent, a drive I would be happy to never make again, frankly.

Traffic was not getting any better on the Eastside. We needed to find a place north, way north. I was thinking Marysville or the like. Maybe I'd start looking for a realtor. It was past time. Besides, living above a gun store had its charms, but the place was feeling less like home every time I walked through the door.

I had my gear, including Gram, stacked on the dining table, and I was stretching. I was a little stiff from not working out and a lot grumbly. Nothing food wouldn't cure.

Of course, Skella only had to step through a mirror. She'd stopped to pick up Chinese takeout, which very likely made me love her more than before. I took that as a good opportunity to get down a couple of glasses of water, paper towels, and plates. I was afraid to open the fridge after all the time away.

"Thanks for calling me," she said, pulling a pair of chopsticks from their paper wrapper and snapping them apart. I mimicked her and we both sat there rubbing our chopsticks together, worrying off the splinters.

"Unun is becoming despondent," she said, sliding a box of steamed dumplings my way and nabbing the box of mu shu pork.

"I keep telling her that Gletts will come home when he's ready, but she's losing hope."

"How much longer can his body stay alive without his spirit being there?" I asked.

She shrugged. "There are signs that he's beginning to fail now. He's the last of the fallen in the great healing hall. The others have either passed on, or recovered enough to return to their families." She shoveled a mass of pork into her mouth and paused to chew.

"I thought he was in some sort of stasis," I said. "While he's out wandering the spirit world."

She drank half her water, wiped her mouth on her sleeve and grabbed a dumpling out of the box in front of me.

I dumped most of the remaining pork on my plate and sat back, watching her. I wanted to tell her about talking to Gletts, but I wanted to see if she'd tell me about her dreams first.

"Tell me about your sudden interest in Bellingham," I said scooping rice into my face.

Skella shrugged, began digging the last vestiges of rice out of the take-out container.

"I was thinking about going to college. Learning new stuff, you know?"

"That's cool. It's a good school." I watched her, waiting for some other reason.

"You've met some new folks, what did you call them? Hamsters?"

She laughed. "Yeah, Bellinghamsters, ya know? It's punny."

I rolled my eyes at her. "Great. Folks your age?"

She shrugged again. "Either in college or just out. They've got some strange ideas about the world, but they're pretty cool."

"College kids are all mostly strange," I agreed. "But what made you go down there instead of one of the Vancouver schools?"

"I don't know. Why?"

I wasn't sure why I wanted her to broach the subject first, but that was failing, so I jumped in. "I spoke with Gletts."

Her chopsticks clattered to the floor followed by the mostly empty takeout carton. Tiny grains of rice and bits of pork scattered across the floor.

"You what?" She leaned forward in her chair, reaching across the coffee table toward me. "Where? How?"

"Here, actually." I stood, waved her to follow. She scrambled out of her chair, kicking the rice container across the room to bounce off the bar that divided the dining area from the kitchen. "Careful there," I said, smiling.

"Right, sorry." She composed herself and followed me into the bedroom. I pointed to the mirror hanging there.

"I came by this morning to pick up a few things for Jai Li and me when I heard him calling to me."

She went over and touched the mirror causing the surface to shimmer like water, rolling back and forth in the frame.

"Gletts?" she asked, looking in the mirror like a window. "Gletts, where are you?"

He didn't appear, not that I really thought he would. "Sorry," I said when she stepped back dejectedly.

"That's twice you've seen him," she said, leaning against the wall, staring into the mirror.

Scenes flashed by at her touch. Black Briar, Monkey Shines, the bathrooms at the driving range near her home in Stanley park, on and on, faster and faster, like she was riffling the pages of a book.

"He said he's been coming to you as well," I said, quietly, placing my hand on her shoulder. "Told me he's been talking to you in your dreams."

She stiffened for a moment, then let her shoulders slump. "So those are real?" she asked, turning to me. Tears streaked her face. "I even went to Bellingham in the hopes they were real, but I haven't found what he's looking for. He scares me sometimes," she said, taking a deep breath. "He sounds so desperate; like he's running out of time."

"Isn't he?"

She turned back to the mirror and continued flipping the mirror from place to place.

"He was really happy," I said. "Said that he'd found a way home, back to Álfheim."

"Could be," she said, shrugging. "Or he could be delusional. He's been away from his body a long time. There is no way of telling if he's lost his mind or not."

Good point, that. But I didn't think so. "He seemed lucid to me, even managed to get a comment in about my panties."

She barked a laugh then, wiped her face with one hand, and turned away from the mirror, smiling. "He's such a boy."

I smiled back. "Always. So, what do we do? How do we proceed here?"

"I'm not sure," she said. "There's something about the place my friends live—Sprocket and Dante. It's a boarding house. The place is amazing. I've been there dozens of time. It's safe, homey. But there is a power there. Something I can't define."

"Could it be the portal Gletts is looking for?"

She shook her head. "Not that I've been able to figure out. I've checked all the mirrors, snuck into all the rooms. Really the only thing odd is the woman who runs the place—an odd duck named Mimi who's obsessed with karaoke."

"She sounds charming." I hated karaoke. Made my head hurt. Horrified me, really. Being up there with all those people staring at you. I shivered.

"All the Hamsters hang out over there," she continued, ignoring my comment. "It's a cool place. But I haven't found anything out of the ordinary. I'm not sure it's the place, but it's close. I can feel it."

"Maybe when Katie's better we'll head north and check it out."

She smiled big at that, changing her face from sullen and pinched to open and pretty. I bet without all the heavy, dark makeup she'd be cute. Not that I was into changing people's appearances. God knows I'd had enough of that as a kid.

She passed her hand over the mirror again, returning the reflection of us and the room. "Tell him to come home," she said, quietly, staring into her own face. "I miss him so much."

"I told him," I said, sliding my hand across her shoulder and giving her a squeeze. "He said finding the way to Álfheim was more important than he was."

"He's a fool," she said and walked out of the room.

We cleaned up the spilt food before Skella headed home through the hallway mirror since it was tall enough to walk through. She paused and stared at the bedroom mirror for a bit first, calling to Gletts, willing him to make an appearance, to no avail.

As she stepped through the mirror and back to Vancouver, she glanced back at me and waved. "Tell him I love him," she said, and was gone.

TWENTY-SEVEN

I packed up Jai Li's undies and a few nightshirts, grabbed a couple of books, some packs of needlepoint floss that had fallen under the coffee table and a couple skeins of yarn; I wanted to start knitting some gloves. That was my next project before I thought about tackling something complicated like socks or, heaven help me, a sweater.

I called out to the farm to make sure Jai Li was ready to go out to Black Briar. We were going to visit Katie, see if talking to her would help in any way. Jai Li wanted to make her a new cross-stitch and I was going to knit while I talked. Okay, talk between rows. If I tried to talk while I knitted most days, it ended with swearing and tinking. That's the polite way of saying unknitting. I had other words for it that were not for polite company.

Sitting with Katie would be peaceful and unnerving at the same time. Not relaxing, exactly. More of a helpless time where I gave up the urgency and the need to solve everything in favor of just being with my family, being in their presence.

I rolled into Circle Q and packed an overnight kit for me and the girl, just in case. Jai Li asked about the Ducati which was stored out at Black Briar. She asked if we could ride it home later.

"Well, honey," I started, but I looked over at the women of Circle Q who all gave me that mom look that told me I was about to do something really stupid. I think Edith would've punched me if I tried, Mary just looked disappointed that I even considered it, and Julie shook her head, giving me the boss look that told me I was contemplating a child protective services-level event. Tough crowd.

"When you're older," I said, poking her pouty lip with one finger and smiling. "You won't like it, it's very loud."

She made a face, and shrugged.

Whatever, she signed. That was one I'd picked up. Girl had a bit of sass in her.

I know how to pick my battles. Most of the time, anyway. So we drove out in the truck. Jai Li twirled through the radio stations, bypassing anything I found to be palatable, to land on something that made me think of bubble gum and sock hops. I grinned as she bopped along, wiggling and dancing in her seat belt. Would've been enjoyable if the music didn't make me want to scream.

Jimmy was out working with the horses and Deidre was in town with Trisha getting groceries when we arrived. The farm was pretty quiet. Stuart was at the house with the nurse, watching Katie, but he'd gotten a call from work, so he was glad I was there to relieve him.

Jai Li and I set up shop in the room, taking our normal places and began working on our individual fiber projects. It scared me sometimes how absolutely quiet the girl could be. I had to look up and make sure she was still in the room. Of course, when I dropped a stitch (which I did twice in two rows) or started reducing when I wasn't supposed to, I swore, which made her giggle.

I may have said a few minor swear words just to check she was still breathing throughout the afternoon, but the girl's giggles were better than alcohol for buoying my spirits.

Nancy and Gary from Trisha's squad had the troll twins under wraps, but when they woke from their nap, Bub came in to alert Jai Li. There was no holding that girl in the room with that news. There was tag and hide-and-go-seek to be had in the world. She tucked away her needlework as fast as her little hands would move and hastily kissed Katie on the cheek.

"What about me?" I asked, as she dashed past. She rolled her eyes, ran back over, and patted me on the leg, not even pretending to give me a kiss. Then she dashed from the room, grabbing Bub's hand on the way and dragged the four-foot kobold down the hall. I quite enjoyed his laughter as well.

"They're good kids," I said to Katie, knowing she wouldn't respond.

I told her about the meeting with Gletts and Skella. Reminded her of the first time we'd met the elves, lamenting the missed weekend when they'd poisoned us so they could try and steal Gram. Good times.

"I've been thinking," I told her, setting my knitting aside and taking her hand in mine. It was warm, but stiff. The nurses moved her limbs every day and kept a set of pressure stockings on her legs which inflated and deflated at regular intervals. It was supposed to help keep blood clots away. There were too many machines in that room. The noise was driving me bonkers.

"We should move," I told her. "The apartment is really too small, and Jai Li needs her own space. It would be nice to have our own room again, you know?"

This wasn't the first time we'd discussed it. But we'd been ignoring the conversation while Katie was still teaching. She loved her kids, loved being a teacher, and didn't want to leave them while school was still in session. Of course, all that was moot now. The school had brought in a sub for the rest of the year, and Katie was in a coma.

Jimmy came in a little while later and poked his head into the room. "Saw Jai Li terrorizing the boys," he said, grinning. "Thought I'd find you in here. Where'd Stuart go?"

"Got called back into work," I told him.

Katie's breathing was slow and steady, the sound of her breather a counter point to the heart monitor and the leg cuffs. It was a cacophony.

"Been meaning to talk to you, anyway," he said, straightening up. "Mind if I come in?"

I shrugged and waved him to an open chair. He turned around, sat facing me, and took off his ball cap, running one hand through his hair. He pulled out a long piece of hay and tucked it in his shirt pocket.

"Gunther has done some poking into the Mordred crew," he said. "His order knows a bit about them. Pretty hard to be active in this region and not be noticed by the monks, ya know?"

"Have you ever met them? The monks, I mean. I know he was raised by them as a tyke, but aren't they like cloistered or something?"

He nodded. "Yeah, it's strange. They live in a monastery over in Seattle, near Montlake. Over by the gardens there." He waved his hand. "Not that it matters. They rarely leave the place. I have no idea how they know so much and keep an eye on so many things when they never leave the property, but that's a mystery for another time."

I smiled at him, letting him ramble.

He smiled back and paused, looking at me. "You letting your hair grow out?" he asked.

I sighed. "Not you, too. Jai Li was pointing that out the other day. I just haven't had time to take care of it. Is it that bad?"

He laughed. "Hey, I don't care how you look. That's between you and my sister." He glanced at Katie and the smile died on his lips. "Damn it, Sarah. What are we going to do?"

"Maybe we could contact the dwarves," I offered, thinking. "Maybe they could make a box out of crystal like they did for Snow White."

"Keep her preserved?" he asked, smiling again. "I don't think we know the same dwarves," he said. "But you can ask Rolph what he thinks about the idea. I just want my little sister back."

"She's not so little anymore, Jim."

He reached over and placed a hand on her blanket-covered ankle for a moment, then jerked his hand back as the cuffs began to expand again.

"I hate this," he groused.

We sat there for a few more minutes, watching her.

"What about the Mordred crew?" I asked, breaking the silence.

"Good and bad," he said, turning his head toward me slowly. "Your boy, Hague, is who he says he is. Newly recruited, veterinarian, and all the rest. But the rest of them, the old guard. They're something else entirely."

"Gottschalk is an old school witch, right?"

He raised his eyebrows and nodded. "Russian, been here since before the gold rush."

"That's old."

"And she has ties back to Minsk. Gunther's crew thinks maybe she's tied to the dragon there. There's no clear connection, but she's got some powerful allies in that region. The kind of allies that can make people disappear, explode, spontaneously combust, or generally kill themselves in nasty and creative ways."

"Lovely. So, bad guys?"

He shook his head. "Not clear. No friends of Nidhogg, that seems to be clear. They were routed out by Qindra's mother before she died. Several of their cells have been destroyed since then, but our guys don't think Nidhogg and her crew knew they were all part of the same faction."

I got up and went around Jimmy to look out the window. You could see the fence from there, the one that we'd secured with magic, the one that the necromancer had breached. We'd resealed it once we learned what had happened, but it felt vulnerable.

"Do you feel safe, Jim?"

"No," he said, immediately. No hesitation. "But I asked my dad that same thing before he and mom left for Europe. He said that when you felt safe, that's when you were in the most danger. Made you careless."

I stared out over the fields toward the road, thinking. Nidhogg had named me her Fist without talking to me about it, and I hadn't spoken up to argue against her. "Something's happened, Jim. Something I need you to know about."

He didn't say anything, but the tension in the room went up several notches.

"It's Nidhogg," I went on. "She's offered me a deal. A deal to protect us, protect Black Briar."

"Bullshit," he growled, standing.

I didn't look over, but I heard his chair scraping across the floor.

"She named me her Fist," I went on. "We met with that dragon from Portland, Frederick Sawyer." I caught a glimpse of Jimmy in the window, vague and distorted. He stood by Katie's bed, his shoulders hunched and his hands in fists.

"There's more going on than we're aware of," I continued. "It was me, Nidhogg, her witch, Qindra, whom you've met."

He nodded without thinking.

"Also Frederick Sawyer, the dragon guy, and his assistant, Mr. Philips."

"That was the guy the blood cult snatched as bait, right? Guy they dangled from the side of the mountain to draw Sawyer out."

"Yeah."

I could hear him breathing, trying to calm down. He thought I should've killed Sawyer that night, killed Nidhogg. Or given it my best shot. We'd argued about it later.

"They aren't the only dragons," I said. "There are more like Jean-Paul out there. Dragons that seek carnage and battle. Those that want to make open warfare on the dragon council and break the Veil. Rebels and anarchists who want to shatter the world order and send us all down into chaos."

I turned, looking at him. His eyes were wide.

"There's a war coming," I said. "They haven't said it outright, but I can feel it, Jim. All this activity, all these players coming out of the woodwork."

I stepped over to Katie and brushed my hand across her cheek. "In the meantime, she's lost. Her spirit is somewhere in the Sideways and I can't find her."

He sat in the seat I'd been in earlier and put his face in his hands. "I can't lose her, Sarah. I've already lost our parents. And Deidre's paralyzed. And Maggie and Susan, all the others ..."

I could hear the anguish in his voice. The strain of trying so damn hard to keep things together.

"And we don't have much magic," he continued, looking up, his face red and his eyes shining. "Trinkets and a few weapons. Trifles." He paused. "If Nidhogg named you her Fist and she tells you to come after us, what then?"

I shook my head. "No deal. I told them you were clan, you were family. You, the Flight Test crew, Julie, Mary, Edith ... my family. All safe, all have my protection."

He looked at me, his fear and anger warring with one another.

"We'll never be safe, Jim. But we'll have powerful allies."

"I don't know," he said. He stood, squeezed Katie's shoulder and walked to the door. "Do you trust them, Sarah? Honestly?"

I nodded. "Yeah, I do. I trust Qindra, and I think Nidhogg is scared. She keeps talking about the wheel being broken. Remember,

I told you when I first met her. She thinks it's her fault, for leading the rebellion against Odin and his lot. She thinks she broke the wheel and that's why the world is going to shit."

"And you want me to ally with her?"

"No, I want you to trust me. I'm taking that responsibility. I just want your support. I want your guidance and your advice. You're my Seneschal, Jimmy. I need you. Katie needs you. Our daughter needs you."

He drew a deep shuddering breath, cricked his head to the side, popping his neck. "You love my sister," he said finally. "You came back for her, you protect her. That makes you family."

He stepped forward and held out his hand. I grabbed his forearm, a warrior's grip.

"Keep your friends close and your enemies closer, eh, Beauhall?"

I squeezed his arm and shook.

"You never know," I said. "The players are shifting. I think we need to be damn careful with the Mordred crew. Shall I ask Qindra about them?"

He stepped back, his face lost in thought. "Don't give anything away, but dig around. We'll set up a meeting with them."

I remembered the business card from Katie's pencil jar at school. "I think Katie met with Charlie Hague sometime before she collapsed," I said, thinking back.

"Definitely want to talk to them personally," he said. He was pulling himself back together. I knew he wasn't happy, but he was going to cope.

"Very soon," he continued, turning back into the hallway. "I'll keep you up to speed."

I sat back down beside Katie and picked up my knitting. Jimmy was golden as far as I was concerned, but we were all dancing in the shadows. I hated not knowing, and so did he. Two peas in a pod. Made me grin. I sat there for a couple more minutes, but my mind was racing and I was restless. I dropped my knitting in the basket, kissed Katie on the cheek, and went out to the front of the house. I called Jimmy back in from the deck where he was watching the kids run around like wild things.

"Need to get the girl back in time for dinner," I said when he looked back at me. "You know how important schedules are to a little one."

He made a face, but nodded. At least he didn't try to talk us into staying again. I called to Jai Li, let her dash in and grab her cross-stitch and kiss Katie goodbye. She returned with my knitting as well. Guess I could work on it back at Circle Q or something. Then we piled into the truck. She waved at the twins and Bub. They all three chased the truck to the end of the and jumped up and down, waving as we pulled out onto the main road.

I noticed that none of them went past the fence. Maybe they were aware of the protections on the farm. Maybe they felt them in some way. Or maybe they'd been forbidden by the adults to go past a certain marker and they were just good kids.

Nancy wasn't too far behind the twins, so I knew they wouldn't run out into the road. Not that it got much traffic this far into Black Briar territory. There were bonuses to being at the end of a road and shoved up against federal lands. Allowed for some decent isolation.

As I drove through Gold Bar I thought about our allies. Who did we really have besides Black Briar? Who could we really trust? Maybe Mordred were bad guys. Didn't make Charlie one. He just may be a patsy. I'd keep an eye out for him.

In the meantime, I needed to talk with Qindra. Time to get some more information on exactly what the hell was going on.

TWENTY-EIGHT

After we got back to Circle Q I let Mary take Jai Li out to brush down a couple of the horses and went into the room we'd been staying in and unpacked my knitting. I'd been thinking on the way back to the farm, and I decided I needed to do something better with the diary than to leave it in the back of the closet.

I had the diary wrapped in one of my old scarves, so it was pretty camouflaged, but I was feeling like I needed something more. Jai Li didn't usually nose around in other people's things, but I suddenly felt like I'd been lax in that department. Someone could've been killed.

I went into the kitchen, dug around until I found a good-sized Tupperware container and took it back to the room. I put the scarf wrapped diary in it and put the whole thing in the top of the closet, all the way in the back. I left it there about three and a half minutes before I pulled it out again, raided the kitchen a second time, and ended up wrapping the book in aluminum foil—careful to only touch it with the scarf, then rewrapped the scarf, and shoved it back into the Tupperware. I figured all those crazies who wore tinfoil hats to protect their brainwaves may have had something going for them. I had no idea how magic actually worked.

I was watching the box, waiting for something to happen, some stray magical beam or something to erupt after all the handling. I hadn't felt anything, but you couldn't be too sure. I'd have preferred a lead-lined box; I just didn't know where to get one. But I could do something else. Back when Mary's favorite horse, Blue Thunder, had been ritually murdered out in the main barn, Katie had the idea to burn lavender and sage to clear the last vestiges of magical taint. Purify the area. The next time I went out, I'd pick up some of both and add those inside the box. May help to pick up stray bits of magic that could leak out. It was a good idea. Not that we had any way of telling what exactly was going on with the book. I, for one, was in no mood to explore things further.

I felt kinda bad for not telling Jimmy I had the diary. That was on Katie to confess when she pulled through this mess. Right now I wasn't pushing the subject. Not like we could sneak it back in and pretend nothing happened. This was big shit. And the worse part, I was pretty sure it contributed to JJ dying.

What did I do with that? *Sorry, mister and missus Montgomery, your son was killed by the side effects of my girlfriend's magic diary?* It was just fucked up.

I spent a few days puttering around with Julie, hitting a few small farms, and working a ton at Circle Q. We repaired about a million miles of fencing in the back of the farm and did some work on the acreage that Mary was going to lease to Lester Boudreaux and his boys. Mainly marking off where a new fence was going in, then spending two days digging holes. With Mary and Julie helping, we had a whole new section of fence up in just a few days. It was hard work, left me sore and bone tired, but it was a good sore.

Finally, I decided I'd had enough of being a homebody. The conversation I'd had with Bub was weighing on my mind, so I decided to go back out to Black Briar, without Jai Li, and give the poor guy some TLC.

After dinner I dug through a stack of papers I'd been meaning to do something with and found the designs Bub and I had drawn up—schematics for adding a set of clips onto the Ducati so I could attach Gram's sheath to the bike. Then maybe I'd take him out for a ride. Depending on his fear factor. Never knew what was going to upset him.

I made a few calls, making sure Gunther and Anezka were going to be out at Black Briar on Saturday, then arranged for a pickup from Skella. That way I could ride the bike back to Circle Q later.

I showed Julie our designs once we got Jai Li into bed. I let her laugh at first, then listened as she had some good ideas on placement of the connection points for the sheath clips and a better angle to avoid interfering with a passenger. The Ducati was not the best bike for carrying a passenger, so I really didn't want to have something that would interfere with the foot pegs in the back.

There was a certain joy in designing. It tickled the runes on my scalp and made me feel smarter. I had lots of ideas I needed to get around to working. When I built the gate to put into Nidhogg's place I learned a ton about engineering, physics, weight distribution, and overall aesthetics. I needed to do more of that.

I needed to prove that I was more than a grunt hammer swinger. I had a degree, for goodness sake. Okay, it was in English Literature, but I knew about learning. And I was a Maker. I had to explore more of that side of me. Maybe all this magic had some positive things about it—contrary to the evidence so far.

I was really looking forward to trying my hand at something new and creative. I wanted to show Katie something when she finally woke up. Something she'd be proud of.

TWENTY-NINE

Gunther and Anezka were already at Black Briar when I arrived bright and early Saturday morning. Gunther hugged me, and Anezka nodded at me from beside one of the workbenches. She'd been banging on a long, curved piece of steel when I popped in, and she wasn't in the mood to stop what she was doing just to hug me. She was like that.

She was mostly not crazy anymore, or so Gunther told us. I guess I should trust him on that, but I had some pretty scary memories of her losing her shit out in Chumstick. Deep breathing and patience were definitely needed when dealing with her.

I called Bub over, showed him the mods Julie and I had made to our original sketches.

"See where she shifted the second weld down several inches so it could run along the bottom of the support beam instead of the top. Gives us a few more centimeters of length and moves it out of the way of the passenger."

He picked his teeth with one claw, studying the drawings.

"These look good," he said. "Maybe we can work on your making skills as well, distort reality a small bit. What do you think?"

I felt the amulet flare against my chest. Three hot pulses as he watched me. I pulled the amulet out, watched as it strobed a couple more time and watched him. I thought he was causing it. "Was that you?" I asked.

He nodded. "I can nudge you in certain directions," he said. "Nothing too blatant, but enough to keep you on the right path."

"Bloody nuisance if you ask me," Anezka said, putting down her hammer and stepping over. "Never really found it helped me much." She stopped next to Gunther and snaked her arm around his waist. "But you may have different results."

Gunther put his arm over her shoulder and squeezed. "It's Sarah's now, right?"

Anezka shrugged and pulled away. "Barely feel it anymore," she said. "Bub is hers now. No regrets." She stepped toward me and held out her hand. I shook it, and she went back to Gunther and sat on the workbench beside where he stood. He was tall, very Viking, and she was not so much.

"We have something for you," Gunther added. "You want it now, or after?"

Anezka was smirking, and Bub shrugged.

"Now is good. I like surprises."

Honestly I dreaded surprises. Lately they've involved crazy psycho killers or giant raging dragons.

Gunther handed me a nice set of saddlebags to replace the ones that had gotten wrecked in the battle with the necromancer, the dragon, and all those walking dead.

"It was a miracle the Ducati didn't suffer much more than scratches, though the paint job on the tank was pretty trashed."

"Bike survived," I said. "With all the death and destruction, I'm thankful for whatever I have."

The saddlebags were nicely tooled leather with a pair of crossed hammers in the center, an image of Gram level across the top of them and a set of runes along the bottom. The runes matched the ones on my calf.

"Nice work," I said, impressed. "Real quality there."

Gunther shrugged. "Anezka did the design, and I know a guy."

I hugged him, then hugged Anezka. She was stiff at first, but loosened up into the embrace. It was nice. She smelled like the forge to me. Not quite like Rolph, but similar. More earthy, somehow. With an undertone of hops. Of course, maybe she'd just been drinking.

Inside the saddlebags was a first aid kit, flashlight, water, protein bars, and my two battle hammers. "Very nice," I said, pulling out one of the hammers. They felt so light in my hand, fit right in my palm like they were made for me.

"They're not normal," Anezka said.

"No," Bub agreed from beside the drafting table. "They have taken on some of the properties of their defeated foes."

I had noticed that the last time I used them. They felt different, more attuned to me.

Gunther and Anezka both looked at my designs for how we'd mount the clips before we got started. They agreed with the changes Julie had suggested, so while I got my supplies ready, wheeled out the oxygen tank to prep the kit, Gunther went back to the shed where we'd stored the Ducati and pulled it around.

All three of them were staring at me as I worked, almost annoyed. I didn't let them get to me. I know I took my time setting up my workspace, but I didn't want to leave anything to chance. I grabbed gloves, a throat-to-knee apron, and my welding mask. I had everything I needed, the clamps I'd be attaching, the cleaning solution to prep the surface, and a fire extinguisher handy just in case.

I clapped my hands and rubbed them together. "Let's melt some steel."

I turned around and froze.

They'd had the bike repainted. The chrome had been repaired and the normal red and white of the original design had been replaced.

The tank had been painted with a battle scene, the top was a giant white dragon, with her wings flowing down the sides of the tank, her head toward the front forks. It was beautiful.

"What the hell?" I started, and Gunther laughed.

"About time you noticed," Anezka groused. "You are the pokiest damn apprentice I've ever had."

Bub chortled and walked around the bike. "Notice they replaced the damaged foot pegs from where the bike had skidded on the road the night of the battle."

I walked around, looking where he pointed. The pegs looked like thick-headed hammers, like the ones I used in battle. The exhaust had been replaced by a slightly larger bore pipe that flared out at the bottom, ending in the roaring mouths of dragons. The front skirting was painted differently on each side. The left showed a blacksmith, probably supposed to be me, standing in front of an anvil with her back to the viewer, hitting a glowing sword with a hammer.

The right side of the skirting showed a winged horse flying towards the mountains just starting to lighten with the dawn.

"Holy shit," I said, making the full circuit and leaning back against the central anvil. "That is some serious custom work. How much does something like that cost?"

Bub coughed and Anezka frowned.

"Poor form," she said, grumpily.

But Gunther laughed. "Bartered for it," he said. "Parted with a vintage seven-inch vinyl of the Sex Pistols, 'God Save the Queen'."

Anezka harrumphed. Gunther ran a jazz record store and collected some real esoteric shit. "God Save the Queen" by the Sex Pistols. That was worth more than my bike, I was pretty sure.

"It wasn't in the best shape," he said, smiling. "Someone had written on the label. Shame really."

"So, this is a big deal," Anezka said. "We'll leave you and Bub to adding your little addition, but do not fuck up the paint job."

She turned and walked out of the shop.

Gunther shrugged and followed her.

I turned to Bub and looked at him. "You knew about this?"

"Yeah," he said, grinning his toothy grin. "We'll be extra careful, and maybe do something really fancy while we're working. Maybe bleed the paint job up over the clamps to hide the welds. Wanna try it?"

"Hell, I'm half afraid now."

He chuckled and went over to stand near the welding gear, within easy influence range but not between the equipment and the bike.

I took an abrasive and scored the area where I'd be adding the clamps. The support I'd be adding them to was not part of the major paint job, but they were colored to blend in with the general theme.

Once that was done, I put away the abrasive and got my welding gear on. "Here goes nothing."

Bub held the first clamp while I used a long welding rod to secure it into place. I took my time, not wanting to use too much of the steel rod at one time, and not wanting to totally screw up the paint job. As I used the torch to melt the steel, I felt a flow from Bub, via the amulet and down my arms. There may have been oxygen burning and steel melting, but the weld was as much magic as chemistry. It was a strange damn feeling.

It really only took me thirty minutes to attach the three large clamps.

The design reminded me of how the old cowboys used to carry their rifles on their saddles, slung down to the side. Bub and I rigged the three clips to hold Gram in her sheath, along the side of the bike from the front of the frame closest to the forks, backwards below the gas tank and half under the edge of the seat. I could ride the bike and carry Gram with me. After the year I'd had, I wasn't inclined to go around unarmed ever again. From giants running me off into the quarry yard a year ago, to the necromancer kidnapping Jai Li in the fall. Things didn't go down when it was convenient for me.

Gram normally rode in the truck behind the seat along with my old saddlebags. But today, with the new rig in place, I'd be able to carry Gram on my newly painted beast. I could deliver an ass-whupping and still satisfy my need for speed.

I locked Gram in place and stepped on the bike. There was plenty of clearance for my legs, and the sword was nearly concealed unless you were looking for it. I notched that up to my budding *maker* skills.

I stepped back off the bike and stood back, looking at the handy work. It flowed, following the lines of the bike, and the calipers blended in with the paint job—camouflaged, as it were.

Bub went to fetch Gunther and Anezka who apparently hadn't gone very far, just to the picnic benches beside the shed.

They came in, made appropriate noises about the sword mount, and helped me clean up. Once all the gear was put away, Bub disappeared for a few minutes and Trisha and her squad came into the shed carrying two large boxes. Frick and Frack trundled along behind them, hand in hand with Bub.

"Presents for you," Trisha said. "These are from the squad for your help." She paused, her eyes full of tears. "And for keeping Frick and Frack safe." She hugged me and stepped back, wiping her eyes.

Nancy, Gary, and Benny stood with her, each of them smiling.

There were two large boxes. I had a good idea what they were.

Inside were two helmets. Each with a custom paint job. One had the crossed hammers and sword design that was similar to the original helmet that Gunther had gotten me. That one had been lost in the battle. It also matched the design on the new saddlebags. The second helmet was midnight blue with a guitar on one side, and a crossbow and short sword crossed on the other. That was Katie's.

There was much crying and hugging all around. Jimmy and Deidre came out of the house to join in, and several other folks from the farm buzzed in to comment on everything.

I was overwhelmed and ready to collapse in a puddle of too much emotion.

I took the helmets into the house and sat with Katie for a long while. She needed a guitar in the room. That's what was missing. I'd get her one as soon as I could. She never moved, but I had to show her what our crew had done. Had to let her know how much I missed her and that I was looking forward to riding with her again soon.

Eventually I had to get back to Circle Q and Jai Li.

I walked back out into the yard. Bub was off with the twins, and the rest of the crew were scattered doing their daily routines. Deidre and Jimmy saw me out of the house, passing hugs around, and leaving me to my leaving.

I attached the saddlebags, put on my helmet, locked Katie's in place, and hit the road.

The bike roared between my thighs as I pulled out of the farm—the sound of the engine drowning out the voices in my head.

THIRTY

Qindra called me after dinner that night. She wanted to get together and check up on all that had been going on—talk about the whole Fist thing. She'd also gotten some information from Mr. Philips on what they had noticed down in Portland when Katie had collapsed. The ripple effect had been noticed as far south as Salem officially, but they suspected it may have dispersed further than that. The waves may have diminished, but there was no reason to think anyone who was sensitive to such things wouldn't have noticed all the way to Mexico and beyond. There was no official position from Mr. Philips, but Frederick had suspicions that it was somehow linked to JJ's death. Go figure. I'd gotten there already.

I found it interesting that Mr. Philips wasn't a witch or anything. He was just very well organized. After I'd left the restaurant the day of JJ's funeral things had gotten a little strange, she informed me. She was sure they were hiding something but she had no proof. She had no reason to question the truthfulness of Mr. Philips' replies, it just felt wrong to her. Frederick Sawyer hadn't been outright deceitful either, but she had the distinct impression he was protecting something.

Qindra didn't like things being out of sorts. Untidy meant more work for her and probably more danger for the thralls of Nidhogg. So she asked for us to meet for coffee. We made an appointment for the next day and left it at that. Hell, I coulda used some coffee right that minute, but she was a busy witch.

After I got the kidlet down for the night, I sat with Julie and discussed the bike mods and how it felt to be working with Bub. It was good to trade ideas with her. I loved the way her brain worked.

I excused myself earlier than normal and went back into the laundry room where I did a bunch of sit-ups and push-ups. I needed to get my edge back.

By the time I'd worked up a decent sweat and done some stretching, I thought it would be a good idea for a shower. As I padded through the house, Julie gave me a thumbs-up.

I slept well that night. Twice I dreamed about Katie. Once was just a dream, nothing more complicated. Once I could hear her somewhere. Her voice was muffled, but it was definitely her, talking with someone.

When the sun finally broke over the mountains to the east, I was already up and into my second cup of coffee before anyone else in the house stirred.

As for coffee with Qindra—Monkey Shines was my first choice, of course. Home turf. It still pained me to walk in and not see the regular barista Camilla there making the espresso and flashing her amazing smile. She'd been murdered by the necromancer in his attempt to get to me. Such a fucking waste.

I left Circle Q around nine-thirty, taking the bike, and headed into Redmond proper. Qindra arrived only a couple of minutes after me, so we grabbed our coffees and made our way back to the crowded seating area. I had my saddlebags on one shoulder, one hand looped through the full face mask of my helmet and holding Gram. In the other hand I had my coffee with a plate of scones on top of it. It was quite the juggling act. I had mad skills.

Most of the tables were full with business types on their laptops but there was one fairly good-sized table with only one young guy playing a racing game on one of those tablet thingies. I looked around. The only other available seats were at the counter along the windows. I turned to ask Qindra what she wanted to do, but she'd leaned in and was saying something to the young guy. Color me surprised when he nodded and began gathering up his gear.

"One of your people?" I asked as the guy picked up his tablet and coffee and moved to the far window seating.

"Just asked nicely," she said, smiling. "Honestly, Sarah. Common courtesy often works. Maybe you should try it sometime."

I sat my coffee down and flipped her off.

She laughed as she sat down across from me. "Your mother must be so proud."

That was below the belt, and she knew it. She just grinned at me and took up her large mug of java.

I settled all my crap on the wide seat, the saddlebags over the back and Gram in her sheath on the floor under my feet. Qindra watched me with raised eyebrows but didn't say anything. Not yet, anyway.

"I heard an interesting rumor that a new dragon had been born," I said, watching her as I settled back with my own chocolate infused coffee. "Not necessarily the best source, mind. But credible enough to follow up on."

She was shocked. That surprised me.

"That's news to me. Did you hear where? Surely not in Nidhogg's territory."

I shrugged. "South of here is all I know. Who's south of us besides Frederick?"

Qindra tipped her hand to the side, ticking off her fingers. "Frederick controls Portland. Then there are dragons in northern California, Utah, Nevada, two in southern California, Mexico, and all the way down through Central America and South America. If you just say south, it could be anywhere, practically."

"No skin off my nose," I said, smiling. "Just thought seeing how territorial Nidhogg is, that maybe you'd want to check into it." I loved that I knew something she didn't.

"Oh, I'll look into it," she promised. "Right away." She blew on her coffee and studied me. "Tell me about Jai Li."

Now it was my turn to be surprised. I figured we go straight for Katie and the diary. Or maybe Gram, since I was carrying her around. Jai Li was not first on my agenda. But I had to remember that Qindra loved the child, and Jai Li loved her. She had a fair right to ask. I had planned to show her some of the pictures Jai Li had come up with, ask for her interpretation. I just didn't expect that to be the opening round.

We discussed Jai Li's reaction the night of Katie's collapse, examined the drawings and discussed her initial insistence that Nidhogg was angry. That seemed to concern Qindra more than anything.

"She and her twin sister, Mei Hau, were gifts to my mistress from the Beijing dragon, Fucanglong," she said.

I snickered, and she rolled her eyes.

"Don't be childish," she said, kicking my foot.

"Does he have a Fucang crown and everything?"

She kicked me again.

"We were discussing Jai Li?" She raised her eyebrows and sipped her coffee.

"Yes, fine." I waved my hand in between us, clearing the air. "I'll try and be a grown up." I struggled not to grin.

She plowed on, the trooper. "We knew Jai Li and Mei Hau were special, definitely the favorites of the mistress." She paused, lost in thought. "When the great mother raged in response to your actions—"

She meant me reforging Gram. Not something we discussed. Hard to know one of the thralls had a weapon built to kill dragons. Don't ask, don't tell.

"—Mei Hau was in the room with her." She examined the pictures Jai Li had drawn. "Maybe their gift was to keep her calm."

Interesting thought. "Together, you mean. When Nidhogg transformed into her true form, she didn't seem to see Mei Hau as anything other than an hors d'oeuvre."

Qindra grimaced, the pain naked on her face. "Perhaps it was Jai Li's place to watch for danger signs." She waved her hand in the air. "We are merely speculating. What's done is done."

"Sure, I suppose. But would the Beijing dragon know they had abilities beyond the norm when he sent the twins to Nidhogg?" It seemed a reasonable thought. "If Nidhogg was the mother of all dragons, wouldn't they all have a desire to placate her?"

"It is possible," she said, quietly. "But again, we are in the realm of speculation. It's not as if I can call Beijing and ask." She rifled through the pile of drawings and pulled out the picture I thought was Cassidy Stone and tapped it. "Do you know who this is supposed to be?"

I glanced down at the paper, stalling. "Not so much. Does the dragon in the picture look familiar?"

She looked up from the drawing. "I haven't met all the dragons," she said with a laugh. "I have attended one meeting away from this region that involved dragons. This one does not look familiar to me. Of course," she shrugged. "They usually don't go about in this form, now do they? I may have met this dragon in her human form and never known it."

I highly doubted she wouldn't have known a dragon when she met one, but I let it drop. I caught her meaning.

"Funny you said she," I said, setting my coffee cup on the table. "What makes you say she?"

"Huh," she grunted, holding the picture up to look at it. "Coloration, maybe? I'm not really sure." She did look genuinely puzzled. "What do you think?"

I took the picture from her. Jai Li had a very distinctive style. This was fairly detailed for crayons. "Definitely female," I said. "Though I can't tell you why for any good reason than it feels right. It's what Jai Li intended when she drew it."

We both looked at the picture a bit longer, and then I added it to the stack on the table.

"She's an interesting kid," I said, finally.

Qindra nodded and we sat a few more moments in contemplation.

"There is one more picture," I said, needing to get this out in the open. "Frankly, it scares the hell out of me."

It was the picture of the man in the bowler hat.

Qindra stiffened as I slid the drawing around toward her. There was a moment of panic in her face, then it was replaced by her placid calm.

"How does she know this man?" she asked, her eyes darting to me for a brief moment, before returning to the picture.

It nearly pulsed with negative energy. The thing made my stomach hurt.

"I've met him once," I said, explaining about the night in Chumstick when I'd visited Qindra when she'd been locked in the dome.

"I saw him," she said. She had her hands crossed in her lap, and her knuckles were white. "I even looked into him right after Katie and Stuart freed me …"

She trailed off, a mix of emotions racing around her face. It was the way she said Stuart's name. Almost wistful. Odd.

"Did you learn anything?"

She shook her head. "No. It wasn't a very in-depth search. Just a cursory look." She sighed and sat back, taking her coffee with her, distancing herself from the picture. "The necromancer spoke with him several times. I took it he was a serial killer of some infamy, but I didn't find anything."

We both stared at the drawing for another few seconds before I covered it up, sliding the whole stack back into my saddlebags.

"I think he's hunting Katie," I said, explaining about the trips to the Sideways.

By the time I finished describing what had been going on, my coffee was cold and Qindra was dry.

She went up and got us both fresh coffee, and we resumed the conversation.

"One could assume he haunts this area because he died here," she said. "And with the bowler hat, he can't be older than the Victorian era. Gold Rush, maybe?"

"Lot of people coming in and out of Seattle at that time," I mused. "May just be a good time to be a serial killer."

"Let me do some research," Qindra said. "No promises. You are delving into realms I've never plumbed, my sister. Areas where my experiences are only hearsay and rumor."

That was not the most happy-making thought.

"That's me, going where angels fear to tread."

She just shook her head, not amused. Things grew quiet as we both fell into our own thoughts. I know I was missing something. Some connection.

"What of the diary?" Qindra asked after a few minutes. "I've watched for further indications, further disruptions."

I looked up, very glad for the distraction. The train of thought I was following with the Bowler Hat Man was not pleasant.

"I've actually got it hidden someplace I'd rather not discuss."

She nodded. "Prudent. I would still like to interview Katie when she recovers."

I could've kissed her for the way she worded that. "When she wakes up, I'll ask her," I said, really not wanting to have that discussion. "Not likely to happen anytime soon, though."

"I'm worried about the number of magical objects in your orbit," she said cutting to what I figured was the real purpose of our meeting.

Can't say I was surprised, frankly. I knew it would happen sooner or later. "Which objects are you interested in?"

"There are three that concern me at the moment," she said, folding her hands on her lap and leaning back in her chair. "The sword, the shield, and the book."

For a moment I thought that was the beginning of a really old joke. She didn't mention the amulet, so I didn't correct her.

"Well, I've already told you, the book is hidden away. I can't risk anyone else getting their hands on that. Especially with Jai Li around. That girl is curious like a cat."

She smiled at the image and nodded. "I assume the sword is equally off the table?" She casually waved her hand toward the floor near my feet.

I just looked at her. Was she kidding?

"Of course," she said. "That leaves the shield."

The shield. That was intriguing. I'm not sure how I felt about the shield. Justin, the necromancer had done some crazy shit with that, soaked it in his and the dragon's blood only after my own had been soaked into the leather and the wood.

"I can loan you the shield," I said. I'd really like to know what it was capable of. "But it is a loan, you understand?"

Qindra sipped her coffee and shrugged. "But of course."

We continued to discuss Jai Li—her education and well-being. I was starting to feel like a real parent. Not just a babysitter.

Now I just needed to start thinking about getting our life back to what resembled normal these days. This was nice, just chatting with her. Oh, there were a few raw spots, but I was going to like this aspect of the whole *Fist of Nidhogg* gig. I liked feeling like I belonged at the grown-up table for once. And Qindra was great to bounce ideas off of.

"I've asked Stuart to accompany me down to Portland," she said, setting her coffee cup on the table and folding her hands in her lap. "He's hesitant, as you may imagine."

I looked at her for a couple of seconds before I realized I had my mouth open. I closed it and blinked a couple of times. "Um … My Stuart?"

Qindra chuckled. "Well, I'm sure he's his own man, but yes. Stuart Black, I'm sure you know him."

I swallowed. Stuart had pulled her out of the house in Chumstick. He'd been very protective of her that night. I guess it didn't stop then. "He's his own man, for true. I just didn't realize the two of you had kept in touch."

Qindra shrugged. "We've shared a meal or two in the intervening months. I quite enjoy his company."

I was stunned, frankly. And was Qindra blushing?

"Surely you're not asking my permission?" I asked.

She shook her head, "Of course not. We're both adults. I just thought it may be easier if you were aware of it rather than finding out from other sources."

She was sweet on him. I'd have to pump him for information the first chance I got. The old dog. I thought he'd given up on women.

"So, are you asking me to nudge him along the direction of going down to Portland with you?"

She shrugged again, the color in her face deepening. "I've never had a …" she bit her lip, thinking of the right word, I'm sure. "Companion."

I couldn't help it, I laughed. "You're smitten."

She sat up straight, her back stiff. "I'll thank you not to belittle my situation, Sarah."

I held up both hands, shaking my head, the laugh dying on my lips. "No, I'm sorry. I think it's odd, but somehow intriguing. I love him," I said, realizing I really meant it. "He's one of the good guys. Don't hurt him."

She smiled demurely, "I have no intention of hurting him."

This was strange. I was terrible at dating, and here she was seeking my help. My how the world turns. "You know," I said, sitting back and cradling my coffee mug against my chest, "it may be a good idea for Stuart to get a lay of the land down in Portland. Check up on Frederick, make sure nothing negative is going to impact Black Briar."

Her eyes brightened. "Excellent suggestion," she said. "I'll mention it."

We finished our coffee discussing Stuart and the different views we had of him. I'd never had a girlfriend like that, talking about dating, comparing notes on the folks we crushed on. It was nice.

The fact she was a witch who worked for a dragon didn't really seem to matter in that moment. Of course, I worked for the same dragon now. Katie would find this whole thing charming.

Jimmy, on the other hand, was going to flip his shit. His inner circle was being compromised into the world of the dragons. The lines were blurring and the enemy was not so easy to discern. So much for the Tolkien view of orcs and goblins. Maybe the enemy was not always quite so obvious.

Unless they were about to kill you. That usually cleared things up. Of course, there was that one time, when the dwarf Rolph came after me with an axe.

Of course, I was about to give Gram to the awful fucking dragon, Jean-Paul in exchange for Katie and Julie.

He had a different view on things. Some days I'm surprised we're still friends.

And that's when I suddenly realized that I had some of the strangest friends. Ma and da wouldn't recognize me. Maybe this was what it was like to grow up. I could get used to the change. Too much angst just makes me tired.

THIRTY-ONE

Meeting with Qindra had given me a few ideas. I rode back to Circle Q, grabbed the diary and put it in my saddlebags, giving it the right side to its lonesome and putting the rest of the gear in the left side. I left the hammers in the bottom of the closet and closed the door. I had Gram, hopefully I wouldn't be meeting anyone that required hammering.

I wanted to get all the pieces of magic in one place, see if they influenced each other. I debated taking Bub with me, but thought twice about it. This wasn't a smithing problem. It was a discovery issue.

Back to Kent I went, this time on the bike. I got a few honks and waves, which was not something that normally happened. I chalked it up to the kicking paint job and the mufflers.

The gun store which sat under our apartment was open, but I didn't have time to run in and see Elmer. Besides there were a bunch of people milling around inside, so he was busy.

Instead I unlocked the door between Elmer's gun and knife store and the ... I stopped to look ... bakery. That place changed over pretty frequently. This latest tenant, a cupcake maven, had some strange damn hours. Thursdays were eleven-thirty to three-forty-five. What the hell was that about? I didn't understand how she stayed in business.

I jogged up the stairs with my gear and opened the door. The place had grown cold, devoid of love or joy. Most of our stuff was there, scattered about in the way that happens when you live a full and busy life. But now, things looked abandoned, wasted.

There was nothing of the passion Katie and I had shared here. We'd made love in this place, sometimes quiet, sometimes crazy. These walls were witness to some creative debauchery and more love than I ever thought I'd be blessed with.

Now it was empty. Even when she came back to me, came back to Jai Li, we couldn't live here. We needed a new space to grow into. A space that glowed with joy.

I called Qindra, explained I was going to try something she wouldn't like, and for her to make sure Nidhogg was in a safe place, that the staff were busy elsewhere. I told her to expect something within the next hour.

She was not happy, nor supportive. But assured she would keep her clan safe.

I washed dishes, cleared the counters, folded bedding and generally cleaned up while I gave Qindra time to prepare. I needed to do something here, something to unravel this damned mystery.

The apartment looked fairly good for the amount of work I'd just done. It's amazing how much you can get done in just an hour. Maybe I should do this more. Take care of the little things before they got out of control.

The real trouble was, beyond laundry and dishes, knowing which of the little things you could deal with was a real bitch to get a grip on.

After the hour mark, I gathered my things and prepared.

I sat down on the couch setting the saddlebags at my feet and holding Gram on my lap. Gram was another lover. That is how she saw it, in any case—that black blade who sang to me of battle, who cried for the blood of the dragons. She needed my touch as much as I needed to feel her in my hands again.

I grasped the pommel, letting the power of her course through me, and pulled her free of her sheath. This was power the likes the world had not seen in generations. This magic blade, tuned to me, embodied the power to slay a dragon, to bring down giants and trolls. The runes along her fuller glowed a soft, deep red when I turned her from side to side, letting the light play across her lines.

The amulet on my chest pulsed as I gripped Gram tighter and opened to her, allowing my true self to meet the sentience of the blade. For the briefest instance the room flared with light, crisp and clean. This was one of the gifts of Gram. The world became clearer, the good and the bad, the broken and the beloved—each shone with a clarity that I didn't experience without her.

This place, this apartment was dead to me. I could see it even more clearly now that I held the black blade. One of my top priorities had to be finding us someplace we could call home. Someplace to raise Jai Li.

I set Gram across my knees and pulled the diary from my saddlebags. The book leapt from my hand, landing against a pillow, the tinfoil showing between the loops of scarf.

"Calm down," I said. Everything was more—amplified. I took a deep breath, watching the book. It throbbed, almost as if there was a heart beating under the tinfoil. I carefully pulled aside the scarf, and using one edge of it, unwrapped the tinfoil. The book pulsed with energy I could see with Gram in my hand: sometimes green, sometimes purple. It was at war with itself, I suddenly understood. Two owners, two factions, two masters. This wasn't Katie's book after all. Was it her mother's?

I thought about the possibility that touching the book would kill me, but I had to try something.

The cover was dull leather underneath the strobing glow. There were cuts and burns on the surface, and the three sides away from the spine edge were ragged, like it was trying to grow together, like a healing wound.

I reached out and placed my hand onto the cover.

Screaming filled my head. Between one breath and the next the world exploded into a cacophony of anger and fear.

I didn't die. That was a bonus. But I'm fairly sure if I hadn't had Gram held in one hand, I would have.

As it was, power surged from the book, through me and into the blade. The runes that ran down the blade faded, the usual red, like burning coals, were overcome by throbbing purple and green light. Eventually, as I sat there, stunned by the amount of energy flooding through me, the flames began to rise along the fuller, pushing back the invading colors until once again the warm glow of the forge emanated from Gram.

Alone the book would've killed me. That much was clear. As a team, however, Gram and I together could take the full measure of what the book had to offer. At least for now.

The edges of the book were clean once again, the ragged wounds had been burned away in the energy pulse. I flipped the cover over and glanced down at the first page.

The page was blank. I flipped through several more pages, each blank.

I rifled through the whole book, looking for any mark, any drawing all to no avail. Every page was pale cream parchment without as much as a smudge or a doodle.

That was rather anti-climactic.

"Well, aren't you a disappointment?" I said to the book, setting it down on my lap and flipping back to the front cover. Nothing there either.

I closed my eyes, rubbing them with my free hand while I kept a death-grip on Gram. The book was open and taunting me.

What a total waste. For this, Katie was struck down? It was so damned unfair.

Maybe I was looking at this all wrong. Maybe this book was darker than I'd thought. I thought to the shield, the one I'd used to slay the dragon Duchamp, the one the necromancer had butchered the dragon on and infused the metal with my blood, his blood, and the blood of a dragon.

It was dark, that shield; powerful. I set the book down on the couch and went back into the bedroom. I checked the mirror, just to make sure Gletts wasn't watching for me, but the mirror remained empty. I opened the closet door and looked down at the shield. I'd debated taking it out to Black Briar to store in their underground bunker, but it felt right to keep it here, where I could reach it.

Qindra had wanted to study it, and I'd agreed. I just hadn't said when, and she wasn't currently pushing me.

I picked up the shield, the leather strap across the back was stiff with old blood. As I walked by the mirror, Gram in one hand, the shield in the other, I looked pretty damn scary. A force to be reckoned with. Even in my Death Pixies T-shirt and my hair longer than it had been since before I went away to college.

I was a badass.

The book hadn't moved, which was good. I lay the shield on the floor, backside up and knelt beside it, Gram firmly gripped in my left hand. I'd seen the necromancer do something in my vision the first time I touched this shield that may have some bearing on this.

I sat on my heels, leaned forward and ran my thumb over Gram's edge. A scarlet line appeared quick and clean. Blood was powerful, that much I'd learned. We'd seen the effects of blood magic when we fought the necromancer before Christmas. Crazy powerful and dangerous as hell. Just what the doctor ordered, I figured.

I smeared my thumb across the back of the shield, painting an arc of red across the blackened wood. There was a flash of smoke and the stench of burning meat then the shield vibrated against the floor, dancing about for the briefest of moments before settling down to a quiet hum.

Then I lay the book inside the curved shield, just above the leather strap and flipped it open to the first page. Here I smeared my bloody thumb across the page and sat back.

For a moment nothing happened. The bloody smear looked as you'd expect. Then it began to move, to be absorbed into the book.

Aha! Victory. The book required blood. Either it was hungry, which suddenly scared the heck out of me, or it needed a sacrifice of some sort to work.

The book throbbed, an insistent pulse like it had done near Katie. I pulled the book into my lap, keeping a death grip on Gram and grabbed the edge of the shield. "Open sesame," I whispered.

My mind exploded in a flash of magic. For the briefest of moments, the only things in the world were me, the book, Gram and the shield.

Then I was falling sideways.

THIRTY-TWO

Qindra waited in her rooms, watching for the danger to her and her wards. Why was everything with Beauhall reckless and dangerous? If Nidhogg reacted, she knew it would be Beauhall's doing. But it would be Qindra who was at fault for not stopping the Mistress's new Fist.

Zi Xiu gathered the little ones in the kitchen having them help roll out dough for dumplings. The head of the household had never questioned Qindra, just set about rearranging the kitchen schedule to make things flow smoothly. She was a wonderfully efficient servant.

The new Eyes was in with Nidhogg reading to her from one of the ancient tomes they had in the great library. Only the foot servants were in the room with them. It was all that Qindra dared alter without raising too much suspicion. Nidhogg would allow no fewer servants to be nearby.

Qindra was sure Nidhogg suspected something, but the trust there was irrefutable. If Qindra thought things needed to be altered, within reason, the great mother was amenable to the change.

Now, if things would just progress. Waiting was worse than dealing with the aftermath. Any minute now something was going to happen.

And so it came. Near on to five in the evening, Qindra's baubles and trinkets began to glow with a warning as something passed over the house. This wave was small compared to the previous ones. Nothing broke, no vessel was overfilled with energy and exploded.

Was this the end? The final blow or was this the first drawing down before the tsunami?

She cast down into the shallow basin where the lights of the thralls could be seen if one knew where and how to look. While it did not encompass all of Nidhogg's territory with any kind of detail, it allowed her to keep an eye on specific powerful agents. She touched the surface of the water with her wand and whispered Sarah's name. A cluster of lights swam in the water, one shining brighter than all the others. Many other lights moved among the greater blur of their demesne, but none rivaled that of Sarah's. Not unless she looked inward toward Nidhogg, or south toward Frederick Sawyer.

Suddenly, next to Sarah's will-o'-wisp a second glow pulsed, black as a bruise, sucking in the light. It flitted for a moment, nearly blotting out Sarah's own light, then it faded into nothing. The contrast was so stark, it took her a moment to realize that Sarah's light had gone out as well. It hadn't faded, like when one dies. It had just ceased to exist.

THIRTY-THREE

I stood on a hill overlooking a great battle scene. The dead lay across the horizon in any direction I looked. The night sky bore down on me from above, the thick mantle of stars like so many accusing eyes. In the distance buildings burned, the great fires sending mounds of smoke into the air. I brought my gaze back to my immediate surroundings. The ground at me feet was covered with the broken bodies of creatures that at once reminded me of Bub, but not. He was a creature of fire and flame. Those at my feet were ice and frost. They were similar in form, but they bore no semblance of higher thinking—animals—wild things. Most had attacked with claws and teeth, but there were a few among them fallen who had borne rough shields and clubs.

There was no one living as far as I could see. Below the hill, toward the rising moon, there was a building of some sort. I began to pick my way through the dead, trying not to lose my balance in the patches of ice and snow. I stumbled once, catching myself on my outstretched arm, realizing that I held the shield in my right hand. Gram was in my left.

Halfway to the building, I made out a glow coming from within a smoking building—a glow that pulsed between green and purple, subtle colors like old bruises and decay. I thought for a moment that maybe I was dreaming, but I knew I wasn't. Not for any concrete reason, other than I was still wearing my Death Pixies T-shirt, jeans, and my Docs. I had no armor, no helmet and amazingly enough, no wounds.

The building was low, a single story built from rough-hewn logs and a thatched roof. It was a long house, like those the Vikings built. The door was torn asunder and bodies of young men and women littered the ground before it. They'd died defending what rested inside, the glowing light.

I stepped over the young bodies, no more than teenagers, with rent limbs and horror stricken faces. Death had not been kind to any of the fallen—the ugly, the beautiful, the weak, or the strong. Once the fatal blow fell, the body collapsed into a misshapen pile of meat.

The stench of the dead was not so overwhelming due to the cold. But inside, a dying fire burned in a hearth large enough to drive a team of oxen within. This was the house of a great chieftain, a leader of many men. The great long tables within had been pushed against doors and windows, and yet the bodies within, old men and women, and babes too small to take up arms, all lay broken before the great hearth.

"Who did this?" I asked the dead.

None answered, thank the gods.

Near the hearth, propped in the corner closest to the dying fire, an old woman sat crumpled on her side, the green and purple glow pulsing from beneath her slashed and battered form.

I set Gram into her sheath over my shoulder, slung the shield around my back and knelt at her side. There was no blood in the building, I realized. None of the fallen here had slashing or bashing wounds.

I placed my hand on the old woman's shoulder and righted her, pushing her back against the wall of the lodge. She weighed next to nothing, her frame stick thin. Her face was contorted as if in great pain, and in her hands she clutched a glowing book. It looked so familiar, like something I'd seen in the past. A noise rose in my head—a great rushing of wind and the distant howling of wolves.

Something yet lived, whether friend or foe, I had no idea. But wolves rarely meant safety. I was tired, exhausted from days of what? Fighting? My clothes were whole and I had no wounds. But my arms felt like I'd been working the forge, or swinging Gram for far too long a time. The book called to me, the pulsing of the light echoing my own heartbeat. Was it the key? Would it lead me to my goal? I glanced around the room one final time, making sure nothing moved, then wrenched the book from the old woman's dead hands. The world exploded.

THIRTY-FOUR

Mrs. Gottschalk woke with a shout as a spike of pain pierced her head. A pride of cats scattered screeching and yowling into the furthest reaches of the house. A platter of sandwiches and tea set crashed to the floor at her feet.

"Attend to me," she bellowed, grasping her head in both hands.

Two young women scampered in from an adjoining room, and one of the cats returned, slinking around the edge of the doorway.

"Clean this mess," the old woman croaked, her head throbbing like an overripe melon.

"You," she pointed to the closest woman who knelt, gathering sandwiches and broken crockery. "My medicine, bring it to me."

The girl ducked a quick bow and scampered across the room, dumping the collected detritus onto a side table.

"Get a broom, stupid girl," Gottschalt spat, as the second girl knelt to finish picking up large broken pieces of pottery. "Is there no one here with an ounce of sense?"

"What is it, Madame?" came a male reply.

Gottschalk looked up, saw the boy, Hague, with a cup in one hand and a napkin in the other. "What is it that ails you, Madame?"

"Bring me my tarot deck," she barked, regretting the volume. "And kick that slug who is fetching my medicine. My head is like to split open."

Hague turned, set his cup and napkin to the side and stepped past the girl who was digging through a cupboard and handed down a large bottle that sloshed nicely. The girl carried it over to Madame Gottschalk and handed her the bottle, pulling her hand back quickly, looking as if she may catch whatever was afflicting Madame.

The old woman pulled the cork from the mouth of the bottle and bent it to her lips, drinking down three quick sips. The vile cat and the boy stayed in the room as she sat back and closed her eye, letting the poppy solution dull the pain.

"Something has happened," she said, trying to keep her voice as calm as possible. "Similar to the last time. Bring my cards, boy, and lay them before me. Let us see what has shattered the peace of the day."

He pulled a folding tray from the corner by the large television and set it up before her. The cards whisked pleasantly as he shuffled them.

"Careful not to bend the edges," she whispered, feeling the poppy trickle through her mind like icy fingers soothing a burn.

"Lay them out for me," she continued, her breathing beginning to settle.

"Show me what the cards have to say."

Let it not be our doom, she thought as the boy placed the first card down on the tray.

The smith. She grimaced and closed her eyes, not daring to see the next turn.

THIRTY-FIVE

I ran through an alley, my Docs echoing off the damp cobblestones. Gunfire blossomed behind me, far enough to not be a worry, yet. Somewhere in the distance an air raid siren wailed. Smoke choked the air as buildings on both sides of the street burned. Back the way I'd come the screams of the dying overwhelmed the sounds of gunfire and filled my head with the flavors of their pain.

Here the battle had passed already, a previous wave of carnage and loss. Uniformed men with guns lay sprawled in the streets, their bodies broken and slashed. Other men, civilians, lay shattered, their bodies riddled with bullet holes. These men bore axes, broken masonry, and lengths of broken pipes. These were those who were defending their homes. These dead outnumbered the men with guns ten to one.

I stood at the mouth of an alley, listening. I glanced to the left, past the group of dead men, toward an empty town square. To the right, the road angled back in roughly the direction I'd come from. Nothing that way but horror. I glanced back to the town square. There was no sign of movement within sight. I sheathed Gram, slung the shield over my right shoulder, and stepped out into the street. I paused at the closest gunman, his face smashed in by an axe handle, and knelt to check his gun.

The metal was old and the clip was empty. Other clips littered the ground. Others had looted here before me. I couldn't stand around. I barely had my shit together as it was. There were things coming after me. I didn't waste my time checking the other guns.

I dropped the machine gun onto the dead body of the soldier and drew sword and shield once again. If I ran into trouble, I'd be handling it the old fashion way. The row of shops that lined the street had been gutted by fire. I darted across to a smoldering bakery that was only identifiable by the sign hanging over the sidewalk.

I glanced inside but turned my head quickly away. There were more bodies inside, burned and barely recognizable as being human. I ran along the shop fronts in a crouch, keeping my profile low and pausing at the next alley. I took three deep breaths to calm my nerves and glanced around into the pitch-blackness between the two buildings.

I could see about three feet into the gloom, and the rest was lost. I had no desire to walk into a place I couldn't be sure was free from the enemy, so I darted past the mouth and continued on toward the central square.

A fountain lay shattered in the middle of a large cobblestone commons. There were fewer bodies here, but these were mainly women. Buckets and jars lay scattered among the dead. They'd been trying to get water from the fountain when some sort of explosion had wrecked the square.

There were three main roads out of the square not counting the one I'd just come down. Of the three new paths, two were blocked by overturned wagons and dozens of fallen defenders. That left a final road clear of rubble or overturned wagons, and it ran straight toward the rising moon, like a pathway into the heavens. Of course, it only ran up hill toward the outskirts of town. If I could make it up that road and beyond the burning buildings, I would be home free. The woods outside of town would give me better shelter than this village of the dead.

But there was something I needed to find. My head hurt. There was a buzzing that seemed to overwhelm thought. I had to remember, it was critical. There was something important … No. Not something—*someone* I needed to find. She had been here, I was sure of it. I could feel it.

I looked back the way I'd come, making sure I didn't see pursuers. They were back there, the unknown enemy, and they were getting closer. If only I could remember who they were, who I was looking for, and how I'd gotten here.

I scampered across the open ground and squatted beside the rubble of the fountain. Water still burbled from the shattered statue of a rider on a winged horse. The wings lay across an old woman, pinning her broken body to the cobblestones, while the head of the horse lay out in the courtyard, gouged and forlorn.

The water was cold and clean. I drank until my teeth chattered and my head hurt from cold, but the buzzing seemed to taper off if only briefly. I was definitely looking for someone. A woman and something about a book.

None of the dead around me were Katie.

That's who I was looking for. Katie whom I loved above all else. Why was that so hard to remember? I drank once more before I crossed toward the only open avenue out of town.

If I left without finding the book, would I lose Katie again? Did she have the book? I remembered finding it in another lost village, a place of great death and destruction from another era. I remember taking the diary from the old woman's dead hands, then nothing.

Gunfire brought me around. Closer this time. Soldiers were coming, and I had no chance against so many. The buildings directly in front of me were more intact. There had been no fire here. The windows were shattered, probably from the explosion that destroyed the fountain, but the buildings themselves looked solid.

I couldn't leave without a sign of Katie, and I sure as hell didn't want to get caught out in the open. I ran from doorway to doorway crouching in the shadows, glancing into the ruined interiors looking for a sign.

The third shop was a dress shop. There was a woman standing in the back, frozen in fear. I wanted to call to her, but couldn't risk it, just in case someone heard. Instead I threw caution to the wind and stepped over the broken windowsill, the glass crunching beneath my boots. I was careful not to grab a hold of the window frame. I had no desire to slash open my palms.

I glanced down. My hands were already bandaged, the blood crusted and old. Okay, I had no desire to slash my hands open again. Funny how they didn't hurt.

The woman in the back didn't move as I approached, and I saw that it was a mannequin in a wedding gown. By the light of the full moon, and the glow from the shield I carried, I could tell the hand beading and delicate stitches made this dress stand out in this shattered town.

Cries brought me back to myself, and I spun around. Three large creatures slunk near the edge of the square, great many-legged beasts with soldiers riding on their backs.

My heart stopped for a moment as one of them stepped from the road and into the light of the courtyard. It wasn't him, the Bowler Hat Man who hunted me. These were just henchmen, deadly in their own right, with guns and the great eaters they rode.

I crept around the long counter that stood behind the mannequin and squatted down in the shadows. A cash box lay shattered on the ground here, and coins I didn't recognize lay scattered across the floor.

The way the scarce light flickered across the coins held me rapt for far too long. I couldn't stay here. I had to find Katie, had to find the book. And then there were the soldiers.

If these three had come this far, there had to be others nearby. Maybe the bulk of the great man's army wouldn't come into this village, but they might. He was a fickle man, quick to murder and filled with a raging fire.

I drew a shuddering breath, blurred memories of my most recent escape filled me with anger and fear. I gripped Gram tighter, willing my runes to flare to life, for some insight to come to me. I looked down at my hands, wondering at the old wounds there.

I pulled the saddlebags over my head and looked around. I had been drawn into this shop for a reason, and I knew things rarely happened in this land of the dead without a reason. The trick was living long enough to understand the puzzle.

This village was not unique by any means. The method of the killings, the age of the town, and the state of decay the only markers of change. It was the same in all the villages and towns.

All dead, all massacred but in each held a sign or marker. Some puzzle piece that drove me to Katie. A clue to where she'd run.

I scooped a handful of the bright coins into the saddlebag and inched my way toward the doorway into the back of the store. That way was filled with darkness, and where it was very dark, crawling, biting things lived. I pushed myself back into the room, scooting on my bottom and glanced around the end of the counter. One of the soldiers stood in the courtyard between me and the fountain.

He would be like the others, misshapen and vile—a monstrosity. He had a pistol on his belt and his rifle stood propped against the fallen wings of the horse. He drank from the fountain, removed his helmet, and splashed water over his burned scalp. I crept toward the front of the store, looking for his companions. One I saw moving back down the first road, searching each building. Another was inspecting the furthest blockade. The great, horrid mount, an eater like a giant, mutated tarantula stood at the fountain, a line tethering the great beast to the broken statue.

It stood a good six feet off the ground, but it was mainly legs. It had two large mandibles that could cut a man in half. I'd seen them in action in other towns, but it was lying down, its head toward the fountain, either resting or asleep.

My attention went back to the rifle that leaned against the stature. I wanted that rifle. There was no way I was getting it without alerting both its owner and the great beast. I didn't care to take them both on, if I could arrange better odds. There was no way I was going to get out of this building without making a noise, so maybe I needed to bring that warrior inside.

I picked up a piece of glass, careful not to cut myself, and backed to where the moon's dazzling light pooled near the wedding gown. I took cover behind the mannequin and as far behind the counter as I could. Then I used the glass to reflect the moonlight, flashing it across the water.

The warrior didn't notice at first. I kept at it, angling the light to strike the water near his head when he bent to drink. For an instant he paused, and I knew I had him. He whirled, snatching up his rifle and sited into the shop. I dropped the glass shard as he fired three shots into the mannequin. I held my breath, gripping Gram in my fist and straining to hear him come in. The shots had echoed loudly in the room, and my hearing was suddenly filled once again with the roaring white noise of the void.

I took a shallow breath and listened harder. In the distance I heard the warrior's companions shouting to him, laughing as he called out about the mannequin. I smiled as he stepped over the windowsill, his boots crunching on the broken glass.

His voice was harsh, the language guttural, but for some reason I could understand him. I thought of it as Orcish in my head, but it was probably something less exotic. Once again, Gram translated the language into something my brain would recognize.

The man stopped, pushed the bullet-riddled mannequin with his rifle and sniggered. "Pretty thing," he said, his voice almost wistful.

I saw his hand as he reached down and grabbed the mannequin, righting her and straightening the dress. "There you go, beautiful one. Good as new."

He didn't see me until I'd rolled out and swung Gram up in an arc, bringing the blade down across the arm that held the rifle. He looked at me, his mouth agape as I spun, bringing the blade around and through his neck. Blood sprayed the beaded dress and he fell forward against the counter, his body twitching as his limbs registered there was no longer a brain at the other end.

I snatched the rifle off the floor on the first bounce and fell back against the side of the counter, the dress blocking me from the window. I checked the clip, seven shots, plus the one in the chamber. Maybe enough.

The shot from here, across the courtyard was not impossible. I'd managed against worse odds. But I could only take out one of the soldiers. If he fell, his friend would have me pinned down.

I sat there watching as the man's blood pooled against the hem of the fallen dress and debated my next moves. In the shadow between the headless torso and the pooling moonlight, I saw that the once-man had worn a necklace. It had fallen off when his head departed from the neck. I reached over, grasping the ruby pendant and suddenly my head flared with clarity. This was my amulet. This was my connection to the forge, to the flame. To Bub.

And this was how they had been tracking me. This was blood of my blood, tuned to me in a way I didn't fully comprehend. I couldn't recall where I'd lost it, but now that I had it, memories strobed through my mind like watching every third frame of a movie. I worked in movies. I was a blacksmith. I was searching for my true love who had been lost into the wild lands.

I squeezed my eyes closed as the images flashed faster and faster, a quantum filmstrip of my life. When I opened my eyes, the world was clearer, the darkness not so dense. But my danger had not diminished.

The first soldier—Alpha—had dismounted and was looting several of the fallen soldiers at the closer of the two barriers. The second soldier—Bravo—rode his mount toward the fountain, calling to the soldier who lay at my feet.

I braced myself against the counter and took aim. The first shot went wide, but the eater Bravo rode reared up, nearly throwing him. I worked the bolt, driving another bullet into the chamber and fired again. This time I hit the eater in its head, one pincer exploding. Bravo dropped his rifle, grasping the reins with both hands. The great beast bucked twice then rolled over, smashing the man beneath its great bulk.

A shot ricocheted into the building as I spun to look for Alpha soldier. The first rider's mount at the fountain was on its many legs, spooked by the screaming of its fellow monster, the sound of the gunfire, or some other reason I didn't care to know about. I put two bullets into it, sending it rolling to the extent of its tether, its many legs scrambling across the cobblestones before it collapsed.

A second shot rang into the shop, blasting through the mannequin, sending it toppling over me again. I kicked it aside, rolled behind the counter, and crawled to the other end, poking the rifle out first to see if a shot would follow. When nothing came, I poked my head around and saw Alpha soldier creeping over the windowsill, his rifle ready, heading toward the mannequin. Like his brother, he appeared to believe he'd shot the villain. I fired twice, killing him in a spray of blood and bone.

He went down, and I lay there, waiting for the eaters to arrive, or the last soldier to come in and finish me off. I waited as long as I could stand, then crept toward the Alpha soldier, checking that he was indeed dead. There were two large holes in his torso and he'd bled a very lot.

He'd not be following me again. I checked his rifle and found that he was out of ammunition. That's why I got the best of him then. They were running low on supplies. Explained why he was looting those who'd fallen at the roadblocks.

I stepped out of the building, looking toward the square, looking for the last soldier. Two of the eaters were down, and a third stood tethered to the roadblock, straining against the ropes that kept him bound. Him I'd deal with later.

I ran across the open square, keeping the fountain between me and the fallen Bravo soldier. His mount lay to the side, its legs curled up to its bulbous body. I used to think they were spiders, but I realized that some of them had more than eight legs, some fewer. They were monsters of the Sideways—eaters who lived to consume. We just tried to attach a label to them to keep from losing our minds.

The soldier lay beneath the eater, broken by the great beasts writhing. He was not dead, however. He reached for his rifle, straining to move his body from beneath the mass of his dead mount. I stepped up to him, pointed the rifle at his head and pulled the trigger.

His head exploded like an over ripe pumpkin.

I checked his rifle. No ammunition there either. They had nothing worth taking that I'd be willing to soil my hands with, so I left them. I tossed the rifle into the fountain and rinsed my hands. The water was so cold it made my fingers ache, but it was worth it to get the feel of them off my hands. I drew Gram and pulled the shield around on my right arm. I wasn't leaving the remaining mount alive.

I'd killed dozens of them by this time, and I knew their dance. Gram made short work of the thing. After two strokes of the black blade, I drove it between the three masses of eyes, ending its pained shrieking.

I stood there, afterward, breathing and scanning for more things to kill. Feeling my blood writhe and boil. Unfortunately, there was nothing left but the dead. I turned, listening in the distance, straining to hear more gunfire. Nothing.

The village, though. It held me. There was something here, something I needed, but I had no idea what. At least I had my amulet back. That was something. I knew who I was again, which was more than I had had before. As the moon rose higher into the sky, I returned to the dress shop, checked the soldiers for their pistols and found them without ammunition as well. I left those in the wreckage. I didn't need the weight.

Before I left, I went behind the counter and grabbed my saddlebags. As I sheathed Gram and settled the saddlebags over my neck and the shield over my right shoulder, I stepped over to the mannequin.

"Twice you saved me," I whispered, kneeling as far as I could from the congealing blood. The dress was ruined, all those beads, all the hours of hand-sewn stitches ruined by blood and gunfire. I reached out, stroking the bullet riddled bodice and noticed that the intricately beaded veil had fallen toward the back of the shop, away from the blood. It had been missed entirely by the battle. I picked it up and tucked it into my pack. Time for me to move on.

Katie was not here, but I had to believe I was catching up to her. Somewhere along the road there would be another town. And, if I lucky, I was far enough ahead of the hunters now that they would never catch up.

A girl could dream.

THIRTY-SIX

Jimmy was shaken awake by Katie going into convulsions. He fell out of the chair he'd been dozing in. The hospital bed rocked so violently that it hopped across the floor, knocking over one of the monitors.

"Angela," he called, picking himself up out of the floor.

"Coming," the nurse called, running down the hall.

She didn't say anything, just opened the mini-fridge near the bed, took out a small bottle of Lorazepam, and loaded a syringe with clear liquid.

"Hold her down," she said, glancing at Jimmy.

He dove across Katie's legs, keeping her from kicking as Angela injected the sedative directly into Katie's arm.

"I'll have to start an IV," she said, once Katie started to calm down. She checked Katie's eyes with a penlight, checked her pulse, and pulled out her cell phone and made a call.

"Melanie, yeah. Seizure, pretty dramatic. Yeah, moved the furniture and she wasn't strapped down."

She glanced at Jim and made a face he didn't like. "Yeah, I agree. Okay, do I call 911 or can you come out?"

"Call 911," Jimmy said, pulling out his own phone.

Angela reached over and grabbed his arm. "Okay," she said, shaking her head at him. "We'll see you soon."

She hung up the phone. "She was already on her way out here," she said. "Was at the coffee hut in town. She'll be here in less than ten minutes."

Jimmy sat down, and ran his hands across his scalp. "Jesus, that was terrifying. What the hell happened?"

"Seizure," she said shrugging. "No idea why, yet. Let Melanie examine her and we'll go from there." She moved around Katie the whole time, checking her pulse, feeling her limbs, checking her temperature.

"Nothing I can see," she said to Jimmy's look.

Melanie arrived shortly after, and they ran Jimmy out of the room. She and Angela worked on Katie for nearly an hour before she came back out, leaving Angela to keep an eye on things.

Deidre handed her a cup of coffee as she sat at the kitchen table.

"Well?" Jimmy asked, his own cup growing cold on the table.

"Nothing," she said. "Pulse is fine, heart rate is fine. She's responding to touch and light. Her limbs are responding to stimuli. I can't explain it."

She took a sip of her coffee and grimaced. "Better than the hospital coffee," she said. "But too sweet."

Deidre rolled over with the pot and a fresh cup. "Sorry, I was thinking of Sarah."

Melanie smiled. "I hope she has a good dentist."

"So, what do we do?" Jimmy asked, annoyed.

"I got nothing," Melanie said. "If you want, we can take her into town, get an MRI. But I think we're wasting our time. The brain is a funny thing, Jim. Who knows why she went into convulsions? Frankly, it doesn't shock me."

Deidre put her hand on Jimmy's arm and nodded to him.

"Let's do the MRI," he said. "Just to be sure."

"You got it, boss," Melanie said, taking out her cell phone. They watched her as she called in a private ambulance company.

"Maybe she needs to be in a hospital," Deidre said, leaning against him. "You know, after we get the MRI."

Jimmy ground his teeth, but took Deidre's hand. "I want her here."

"And if she dies because we can't provide the care she needs?"

Jimmy didn't say anything else, just walked out of the room and down the hall to stand in the doorway to Katie's room.

Angela was straightening up, righting equipment, picking up fallen books.

"We're taking her to the hospital," he said. "I guess you can take off, then."

"I'll wait until they get her away," she said, turning to him. "If that's okay with you."

Jimmy shrugged. "Suit yourself." He stepped into the room, dragged the chair to Katie's side and sat down, placing his hand on her arm. "She's been dormant for weeks, not moving, barely alive."

"But alive," Angela said. "Coma patients are tricky. We just never know if they are going to come out again."

"She's got a good, solid brain wave pattern," he said, defensively. "She'll wake up. I know it."

Angela patted him on the shoulder and leaned against the wall. "You betcha," she said.

Jimmy watched her, wishing he had any idea what had happened. "We need to call Sarah," he said, standing up.

"I'll go tell Deidre," Angela said. "You stay here."

Jimmy sat back down once again. "She'll want to know," he said.

Katie didn't reply.

THIRTY-SEVEN

They'd dogged me for three long nights. I'd normally have said days, but here, when the moon finally set, it just rose again. There was no day. My leg hurt from where I'd been clipped by a crazed hammer-wielding dwarf. He'd been covered in tattoos from head to toe, with only a loincloth to go with his great two-handed hammer. He'd been hard to kill. I wasn't even sure he was with the pursuers. I was pretty sure he was another one who was lost in this world, another traveler fallen into the madness of this place. I hated to kill him, but he left me no choice. I couldn't leave him here wounded, with the Bowler Hat Man closing in on me.

I needed water and food, but wasn't likely to find either. Several towns back there had been a fountain. The town where I'd recovered my amulet, the town where I'd killed the three soldiers and their mounts. Since then I'd only seen the enemy in the distance, riding along the tops of ridges as the moon set behind them, an army of monsters and the beasts they rode.

The shadows in the wild were not nearly as scary as the dark places in the towns and villages. Here the world was clean, at least cleaner than the places the dead were piled in great mounds. I'd gotten lost in the last village, nearly gotten killed by that damned dwarf, but Katie had never been there. There was no sense of her in those ruins.

Once I'd gotten away from the village with the wedding gown, I'd picked up the trail again. Holding Gram in my hands and directing her around, I could pick up the thread of magic, that line that drew me to Katie. She was here someplace, running from place to place, scared and alone.

I took a deep breath and stood, kneading my left thigh where the hammer had caught me a glancing blow. I was lucky the dwarven brute hadn't gotten a solid hit, or he'd have shattered the bones. As it was, it hurt like hell just standing.

I sheathed Gram, slipped the saddlebags over my shoulders, hefted the round shield and headed up the hill toward the rising moon. I know I'd been going in the same general direction since I started out. I just couldn't remember how long I'd been here searching, running, surviving.

As I crested the hill, I saw the spire of a church. The thought of another dead place wasn't exactly uplifting. But after the battle with the dwarf, the trail had grown thin. I needed to find another link.

The village was not too large, several dozen buildings clustered along a riverbank with farmland stretching out beyond. Unlike most of the others, this one had already burned, the fire so old, there was no pungent reek of smoke. The buildings on the outskirts were ruined shells, first ravaged by fire, then by wind and rain. I paused at a few of the huts, but found no signs of life.

This was the land of the dead. No one lived here any longer. Any living being here had come from outside, from some place beyond the dead. Perhaps where I was from.

I thought hard, my mind a blur. Where was I? Was I truly here, in this necropolis, or was I really someplace else? As I thought it, the vision came to me of an apartment. I had been in our apartment, examining the book.

The book I'd taken from the fallen crone in the burnt out Viking village. That was Katie's diary. I remember opening it, glancing at the first page ... and I was suddenly here, running across the land of the dead.

Katie was here somewhere. I'd been following her. I just needed the book, I think. The book, the sword, the amulet, and the shield. What was I missing? What clue did I need to find Katie? And when I found her, how did I get us home?

Noise brought me back around. The enemy was drawing nearer. I had to press on, or be trapped in these woods, with a broken village blocking my path. I was so tired. There was no telling how long I'd run, how many nights I'd searched. Hunger had long since lost its hold on me. Now there was only the weariness and the ever-increasing thirst.

Maybe I'd skirt this town. Surely they would search for me there, slowing them down further. But if Katie were inside, hiding, I would be abandoning her to torment. I hefted my shield, adjusted my gear, and trudged down the hill toward the cluster of buildings just this side of a wooden bridge that spanned a river.

I paused. This river ran swiftly toward the village. It was probably free from the taint of the dead. Not like it mattered, hell I was so thirsty, I'd drink from a mud puddle. I began a staggered run down the dirt road, sending shallow plumes of dust rising behind me. River meant water. Water meant life. I had to recover my strength and push onward.

I skidded down the embankment and threw myself down at the river's edge, cupping the icy water to my face in frigid gulps. After half a dozen swallows, I ducked my head in the running water, letting the cold seep into my head.

For half a breath I thought how easy it would be to give up and just let go. Take a deep breath of this icy flow and end the madness. No more pursers, no more villages filled with bodies.

Or, I just wouldn't care anymore. I'd just be another member of the citizenry here, all broken and decaying. I pulled my head out of the river when my lungs began to burn and sucked in several lungfuls of crisp air. Not ready to check out yet, no matter how seductive the thought had been.

It made me wonder about this land. Maybe this was the place of the dead. I had seen the Valkyrie choosing from our fallen, deciding who would be taken to Valhalla. Perhaps this was where the rest went. It was a bleak land, covered in the beginnings of winter and the never-ending night.

The wheel was broken, so said Odin and Nidhogg. Was this the domain of Hel, the ancient child of Loki who ruled over the dead not worthy to battle at Odin's side? Would Hel, that dark lady of eternity, let my pursuers rape and pillage her holdings, or were they the last of her followers, ravaging in her good name?

THIRTY-EIGHT

Julie pulled in front of Elmer's Knife and Gun Emporium, parking the truck behind a bike that had to be Sarah's. She glanced over at Mary. The last time she'd seen the bike it had been red and white, but the hammers, swords, and dragon paint job was a pretty good giveaway. She'd have to ask about it once she made sure Sarah was okay. Maybe after she'd kicked the girl's ass for being gone for so many days.

Mary slammed the truck door as she stepped out and turned, anger flashing across her face. "You mean she's here?"

Julie shrugged. "Let's just hope she's being a dumb ass and isn't hurt or worse."

Mary made a tight mouth, but nodded. "If she's okay, I'll be giving her a piece of my mind for abandoning Jai Li like this."

Julie reached over and put her hand on Mary's shoulder.

"I'm serious," Mary said. "If this is how she's going to treat that girl, I don't think we can let them stay with us. I can't condone this level of callous behavior."

"I know, Sarah. This isn't like her. She promised she wouldn't be gone over night without keeping us in the loop." She sighed. "She doesn't tend to make the same mistake twice."

Julie paused, thinking back. "Okay, that's not totally true, but when it's about something like Jai Li, she wouldn't screw around. There's something wrong."

"God I hope not," Mary sighed, the fight draining out of her.

They went to the door and hit the buzzer, but Sarah didn't answer.

"Okay, time to bend a trust," Julie said, digging a set of keys from her pocket. "Sarah's emergency keys."

"We'll apologize later," Mary said. "Let's just get in there and make sure she's not dead."

Julie winced as she unlocked the door. "God, not dead. I'm hoping for drunk and passed out at worse."

Mary growled. "If she's drunk, I may do something violent."

Julie stepped into the vestibule, holding the door open for Mary.

They climbed the stairs and turned toward Sarah's and Katie's apartment. While Julie unlocked the two deadbolts, Mary looked around. "Who lives next door?" she asked pointing to the door down at the end of the short hall.

"No one," Julie said, opening the lock on the door handle. "Been empty as long as Sarah's known Katie."

She opened the door and looked into the living room.

"Oh, my god," Mary whispered.

Sarah sat in the middle of the room, a glowing book on her left thigh, Gram in her left hand, and her right resting palm down on a shield on the ground. The place was disheveled. Everything that wasn't nailed down flowed, floated, or wiggled around the room—chairs, pillows, books, socks, toys, playing cards, and dishes—each falling into a pattern of intricate swirls, spiraling through the room in a decaying orbit around Sarah and the artifacts that glowed around her.

"What in heaven's name?" Mary asked, reaching over Julie's shoulder and plucking a toothpick out of the air. As she held it, her bracelet began to pull away from her wrist, wiggling along her arm, tugging toward the gravitational pull of whatever held Sarah frozen.

"I think we're in trouble," Julie said, pushing Mary back out into the hallway.

Mary gulped, dropping the toothpick which floated in the air for a moment and began to gracefully reenter the orbit of floating things. Julie looked back, feeling her hair lifting back toward the vortex.

"Magic?" Mary asked, her voice quiet and strained.

"Oh, yeah," Julie agreed. She backed up, pushing Mary with her, and pulled the door most of the way closed. Her hair fell back to her shoulders.

"I recognize the sword and the shield," Julie continued. She leaned against the doorframe and rubbed her eyes.

"What about Edith?" Mary asked, her voice a whisper, as if the magic could hear her. "Do you think she'll know something?"

Julie shook her head. "I'm gonna try something here. You stay back. If anything happens to me, call Edith. Hell, call Jimmy out at Black Briar." She paused, taking a deep breath, all the old fears suddenly rising in her. The dragon Duchamp breaking her thigh for the pleasure of hearing her scream; the giants and trolls leering at her, waiting to play with her as soon as the dragon tired of causing her pain. She squeezed her eyes shut tighter, willing the memory away. Her leg began to throb, even though the bone had mended. Psychosomatic, she knew, but her brain registered pain nonetheless.

"You know, forget that. If something happens to me, call Qindra."

Mary blanched. "The dragon's witch?"

"Oh, yeah. We're definitely out of our league."

Julie poked her head back into the room briefly, watching as the smaller items in the room flowed ever so slowly in their languid progression into Sarah's orbit. Like a black hole, sucking in matter, Julie thought. But small, a pinprick, nothing too severe. Maybe it wasn't too late yet.

"You know what?" she asked, turning and digging her truck keys out of her pocket, careful to keep Sarah's spare keys in her pocket. "Could you run down to the truck and grab my first aid kit out of the tool box in the back?" She handed over the truck keys, and Mary nodded.

"Back in two shakes," she said, hurrying down the stairs.

"Good enough," Julie said, stepping back into the apartment, knocking several small items out of their spiral, but they just found their new position and began the slow fall in toward the center of the anomaly. She let out the breath she'd been holding, turned and threw both deadbolts. "Sorry, Mary," she said, her face set.

She set Sarah's spare keys on the table by the door and they began to twitch, scooting toward the edge of the table. She glanced over as a playing card completed its final orbit and flared in a brief flash of green fire as it got too close to the glowing book next to Sarah

"Shit," she said, looking down at the keys as they slid off the table and found their buoyancy in the twisted gravity of the room. "None of that," Julie said, snatching the keys back up and shoving them into her pockets.

Ignoring the way her hair floated about her as if she were immersed in water, Julie focused on Sarah, who was thinner and looked to be in some sort of distress. Julie imagined this was what Qindra looked like when she held the dome in place out in Chumstick last year. That level of concentration, that out-of-body feeling that said lights are on but no one's home.

She knelt down, bringing herself eye level with Sarah and studied her for a second. The buzzer on the wall began to make a racket. Mary was trying to get back into the apartment.

Julie ignored it, reached her hand across the room, testing the air for anything. When she didn't meet an invisible shield or something, she inched forward, keeping herself low. She made it almost within kissing distance of Sarah before anything happened.

The book shook, its pages ruffled, and a burst of green light blinded Julie. She drew back, covering her face with her hands and squeaked in surprise. It was like a breeze of frigid air had swept from the book, forcing her back, taking her breath.

She lowered her hands, blinked a few times and started forward again, slower than last time. This time she touched the shield under Sarah's hand. A shock flowed up her arm, almost a mild electrical current. It didn't hurt, so she didn't let go. Next she reached for the book again, but the light flared, a tendril of green snaked upward, reaching for her. She pulled her hand back. *That looked like it would be a bad idea*, she thought.

Gram lay angled across Sarah's knee, the fuller pulsing with the red light of a solid coal fire.

This I know, she thought and reached out. She touched Sarah's hand where it grasped the hilt of the sword and more energy poured into Julie, through her and into the shield. Voices rose in her head, screaming and dying voices. Anger and battle cries.

Then Sarah drew a breath, a deep gasping thing that made Julie look over at her. "Sarah?" she asked. She started to release her hand from the shield but the power surged and she couldn't let go. Magical energy flowed through her like she was a switch, connecting a circuit.

Her vision blurred and suddenly she could see the lines of energy flowing around the room. The book was definitely the center—a pulsing orb of conflicting sources, battling for control of the artifact. This was way out of her league. The book's energy flowed into Sarah, but the sword pulled it, as did the shield. The extra pull of the sword and shield were the only things keeping Sarah from being totally burned out by the overwhelming energy. And as she watched, the power seemed to be growing.

"What have you done?" Julie asked in a whisper.

With a great effort, Julie was able to slide her hand forward, over the rim of the shield without breaking contact. It was like pushing her hand through tar, the resistance almost too much for her. Once she had her hand over the rim, she grasped it and tried to pull it toward her without allowing it to break contact with Sarah. Then she lifted it up, fighting the death grip Sarah had. She managed to get it up onto Sarah's lap and pushed it against the book.

Immediately green energy flared from the book and raced across the shield. Sarah shuddered. Julie slid the shield forward a bit more, scooping the edge under the book, feeling the room begin to vibrate under her. The vibration was growing at a rapid pace, and her eyes were beginning to lose focus. She pulled Sarah's hand with Gram in it, pushing the book from the left and continued to push the shield from the right. With a flip of her right wrist, the book hopped into the air and landed in the shield. There was a burst of green light like a flash bulb, and she yanked the shield up and to the right. The book sailed across the room with a dull clatter. Julie fell back, releasing the sword and shield as the detritus of the apartment fell around her. Then, after a heartbeat, Sarah screamed.

THIRTY-NINE

I crept into the village, alert for enemies. By the number of bodies scattered along the streets, there'd been fighting here recently. The center of the village held a raised platform with a statue of a tall woman with a book held above her head, and a sword in the other hand, held parallel to the ground. Thirty or so bodies lay scattered around the base of the statue, like they'd taken a final stand there. A great wooden cross sat propped against the statue and hanging from the crossed beams, a small figure hung loose, bound by ropes.

I saw no one alive, no monster men, no eaters.

The village had been prosperous once, tinkers and smiths, coopers, bakers, cobblers, and taverns. Each with a sign outside their establishment, each dulled by the elements, scarred by battle, and darkened by fire. But I could make out each one as I crept through the village streets. I had to see who was crucified. Had to know if it was Katie.

It began to rain then, the first rain since I'd come to this land, and it stung as it struck my exposed skin. There was as much ice as water in this slushy mix. I held the shield over my head and cut across an alley, past a small house and into the main courtyard. The crucified body was small, a child perhaps. The rain made details difficult to make out, so I took the plunge and dashed across the courtyard, leaping over the slashed and broken bodies of a small militia, their weapons rusted and their leather jerkins rimed with ice.

The base of the statue was a circle about ten feet across. It rose about hip height above the cobblestone square. I leapt up onto the platform and squatted down before the small body. The ropes were tied across his small chest, keeping the tension off the shoulders. It was a boy. Thank god it wasn't Katie. I took a deep breath, trying to slow my racing heart and reached forward. He hung leaning forward with his head bowed and long hair down the front of his face. I gently pushed the hair out of his face and he gave a weak cry.

It was Gletts.

"Holy Jesus," I said, my voice croaking like an old hinge.

"Trap," he whispered, his face a broken mess.

"Oh, god, Gletts," I set the shield on the ground the touching his face.

He winced. "Go," he gasped, his voice a ragged sigh.

"I'm getting you out of here," I said, leaning my shoulder into his chest and slashing at the ropes that strung him up to the tall cross. He dangled there, pulled forward by gravity, his arms out behind him.

But his arms had not been pulled from their sockets. As the ropes gave way, I lowered him to the ground, holding the shield over his face and glancing around quickly to see if anyone was coming.

"What happened?" I asked him.

"He came," Gletts croaked. He pointed to the right.

I raised my head. On a high road, just outside of town, the man in the bowler hat sat atop a writhing creature with a billion legs. I hadn't seen him coming into the village. The town hall had blocked him.

"Poison," Gletts choked. "Run."

"No!" I said, standing over him. "I won't leave you."

He watched me for a moment, "Fool," he whispered.

I reached down, offering him my hand as lightning flashed in the skies overhead. The Bowler Hat Man had not moved, just watched us as the rain grew stronger and the wind began to howl.

The second Gletts's hand touched mine, I could feel a bit of my life force flow into him. For a moment he shone brighter.

"Can you kill him?" he asked, his voice weak with pain.

"You bet your ass I can," I said, drawing Gram and stepping to the edge of the platform.

"Come on, you bastard," I cried, shaking Gram and the shield into the air. "Come face me like a man."

His only response was laughter. He raised an axe above his head, swung it once in my direction and eaters poured out of the shadows.

"We are so fucked," Gletts said, crawling back to the feet of the statue, her flowing cloak a stone alcove to protect our backs. I stood before him, ready to protect him.

I spun once, there was no way out. Every alley and lane was filled with biting, writhing things, each bent on eating us.

"Yeah," I said. "Fucked is right."

I had moments before the fastest eater would reach us. I bent, pulling my pant leg up with one swift motion. Gram thrummed in my fist as I pushed aside the bandages on my right hand, revealing several healing cuts. I dragged the edge of the blade across my palm, bringing forth a swell of blood. I ran my pulsing hand down my calf, feeding the runes. Obviously this wasn't the first time I'd performed this ritual since coming to these dead lands.

Strength blossomed in me, a rush of silver and pain. I squeezed my right fist against the stained bandages, pulled the shield up, and turned to face the oncoming hoard. It was as good a day as any to die.

I danced that night, danced and fought with the drumbeat of my heart releasing the berserker within. Time slowed. The enemy crept toward us, their sudden charge a piteous crawling mass of targets.

The smaller eaters were easy to dispatch. One flick of Gram and they fell into wisps of smoke. The larger ones, those that had flesh to rend, they took effort. The dead were piled at the base of the statue—but Gletts and I were cut and torn from the pincers, claws, and ragged horns of the eaters.

Twice Gletts intercepted a scuttling biter, kicking it away, earning a new wound for each effort. He saved me. I saved him. The endless night grew colder.

I kept waiting for the rifles to start, but no shots rang out.

They couldn't stand up to Gram and the shield. Any touch from either sent the crawling things shrieking back or reduced them to bubbling ooze. Gletts kept the riffraff away, allowing me to keep the larger ones at bay. We held the high ground against a relentless tide. But we were growing tired. Each bite, each scrape or nip drained us, bled our spirit.

Then, like a miracle, there was a moment when nothing came at us. I was winded, desperate for breath. Had we defeated them all? Really?

I sheathed Gram, jumped onto the plinth, and pulled myself up onto the statue's arm, using the formed stone cloak as a step. I wanted higher ground, a way to see beyond our little island. Scrambling a little, I was able to wedge my feet into a fold of the cloak, and the crook of the arm holding the sword. I stood, steadying myself against the arm that held the book aloft and looked across the valley.

Pouring over the edge of the hills surrounding the village things squirmed and shuddered, scuttled and writhed, flowing toward us—a sea of hunger.

"Dear Odin," I grunted. I couldn't breathe. We'd already lost. There was no chance. I looked down at Gletts. While I'd been climbing, he'd jumped down, grabbed a rusty sword from the dead and now sat huddled against the foot of the statue, his knees up to his chin and a blade held tight in one fist. He stared out across the commons, staring toward the Bowler Hat Man.

I didn't want to die, damn it. Tears, hot and bitter, burned my eyes, and my throat clenched. I needed to find Katie. I needed to get home to Jai Li.

The adrenaline was ebbing out of my system and my limbs were starting to shake. A despair began to creep into the sides of my psyche. Hope fading to a distant memory.

"What happens to us if we die here?" I asked, my voice steady but my heart thudded against my chest.

"Dead is dead," Gletts said, standing.

We didn't say anything for a moment, listening to the whispering tide of eaters as they flowed over the lip of the valley and made their way toward us.

As I stood there, angry and impotent, the great statue turned its rocky head toward me and opened its mouth.

"Sarah?" it boomed.

I nearly fell from my perch as my name echoed off the buildings and hills surrounding the town.

The book above me, the one held by the statue began to glow green and purple.

"What have you done?" the voice said. It was Julie.

Gletts looked up for a moment, gaped at the book which was growing brighter. "Is that your book?" he asked. "The one you carried the last time we talked? The one you used in your dreams?"

I paused. "In my dreams? You mean this isn't my dream?"

Gletts laughed, a sad and mournful sound. "No, Sarah. This is something beyond dreaming. This place is beyond the Sideways, beyond the land of dreams. This is one of the old worlds. Hel, I'd have to guess. The land of the dead."

Something moved in the shadows, something malevolent and hungry.

I dropped from the statue and landed on my feet, knees bent. I swung around, bashing the shield at a four-legged bug the size of a Volkswagen. It staggered sideways like a crab as I smashed in its long snout. The vanguard of our final death had arrived. At the last minute, a long proboscis roped out of the great beast and scored the side of my ribs. I screamed as it burned like fire.

Gletts leapt forward slashing down with his short sword, severing the wounded beasts head. I staggered back, gasping for breath. That really hurt.

"Julie," I shouted. "Can you hear me?"

"Sarah?" Julie called again, the great statue bending down.

"I need the book," I shouted, pulling Gram free and swinging her around in a wide arc, sending several other bugs scattering back.

"Take it," she said, smashing the great sword into a scorpion the size of a terrier.

I held the shield out to Gletts. "Take this, and grab a hold of me."

He tucked the rusty blade under his arm, hefted the shield, and grabbed my elbow. I reached up with my free hand and grasped the proffered book.

Light exploded outward—a great wave of green that scoured the shadows from the village around us, vaporizing the eaters that poured into the square. A heartbeat later a purple pulse followed the green, a deep thrumming chord that rang through the valley. Finally, a red wave followed, emerging from both the book and Gram, a dual blast of cleansing fire that caused the very essence of the world around us to ablate away in fine particles of reality.

And suddenly we were in a place of nothing, a void of shape and form.

There was nothing but Gletts and me. The village, the statue, the Bowler Hat Man, all gone.

"Are you okay?" I asked Gletts.

He grunted, dropping the shield and falling to his knees.

"Where is this place?" I asked.

"Nowhere," he gasped. "A place beyond the places. I've been here once before, but I can't stay here. We can't stay here long and survive."

"Can we find another place, a place to rest?"

He shook his head. "Yes, give me a moment."

I bent down and touched the side of his face. When he glanced up, I kissed him on the forehead. "Thanks for saving me back there."

He blushed and took my hand. I held the book and the sword. Saddlebags puddled at my feet. Gletts had the shield.

There was a moment of tension, then my ears popped and we were in a meadow with a crescent moon setting in the far horizon and trees to our right. I glanced around, looking for enemies, but nothing moved.

Gletts collapsed.

I knelt down, rolled him over onto his back and brushed the long hair from his face. He was breathing, but in short choppy gasps.

"We need to get you home," I said.

He opened one eye and let a ghost of a smile grace his lips. "Kiss me again," he whispered. "And I'll go home."

I thought of Gunnr, the absolutely breathtaking Valkyrie who demanded a kiss in payment. That had turned out okay. What did I have to lose? I bent down, pressed my lips to his, and he exhaled.

For a moment I thought we were back in the void, but when my eyes cleared, I was sitting in my apartment, staring at a wide-eyed Julie.

"Hey, boss." I croaked and fell sideways, dropping Gram and the book at the same time. The saddlebags slid from my shoulders, hit the floor and gold coins spilled across the floor. A beaded veil lay half in and half out of the leather bag.

Huh, I thought as Julie's voice echoed somewhere in the background. *Didn't expect to bring that home with me.*

Then the world faded, and I had no memories for a very long time.

FORTY

I woke up twice in the next thirty hours. Both times I had to pee. Mary made me drink a godawful amount of Pedialyte to keep my electrolytes up. I'd been gone several days and I was famished when I finally got up. I ate triple helpings and then slept for another seven hours. After that, I seemed to be over the worst of it.

I spent the next two days caving at Circle Q just trying to get my shit together. Mary had wanted to take me to the hospital, but when I protested, Julie just told her to let it go. I didn't talk much during those two days, just sat with them, being a family. Jai Li drew a dozen pictures of me in that time, each one lighter and happier. It was like each drew some of the dark from me, lightening my spirit.

I didn't know how I felt about things. The Bowler Hat Man was out there still. I don't think I killed him. Hell, for that matter, I don't think I killed the eaters. I wasn't sure they existed like that. I think they manifested themselves from the pain and misery of our lives and dispelling them, perhaps, lightened the load on the rest of us. It was the theory I was running with, in any case.

The gold coins and the veil I stashed in the dresser drawer where I was keeping Nidhogg's ring. I knew they would matter one day, I just didn't have a clue when. Jai Li loved playing with the coins, though. Thought they were pretty.

We talked about what happened to me, just us adults. I even called Qindra to check in, make sure nothing I did had caused too much damage. She was surprised how little affect she'd seen.

At Julie's request I went to work on Monday, falling back into my apprentice role, letting the sheer joy of work fill my mind. I loved the strain of my muscles, the feel of the hammer in my hands, the way the horses smelled. It filled me up, pushed aside the melancholy and the pain. Especially the horses. It was as if they sensed my need and filled it with a nudge of their head, or a gentle bump with their hindquarters. Whoever thought horses were dumb beasts had no idea what the hell they were talking about. They're intelligent animals, beyond a doubt. As we drove away from the second farm, I was feeling near enough to my old self to start asking Julie questions again.

By the time I climbed into the truck after the fourth farm, I was exhausted and smelled like horse and sweat. It was wonderful. On the way home, Julie pulled into the County Line, turned the truck off and looked over at me, her arms across the steering wheel, and her cowboy hat cocked back.

"I think you need a drink," she said.

I shrugged. "Whatever you say, boss."

"Good enough," she said, reaching over and swatting my thigh. "Let's get you liquored up."

I followed her into the bar, passing the farm trucks and the bikes. This was one of those places where bikers, truckers, and farmers mingled with a sort of détente that I'd grown to like. There were occasionally fights, but really, everyone was tired from a hard day's work and just wanted to unwind a little.

After the first beer, I felt my shoulders start to relax. I leaned back, letting the ambiance of the place wash over me and pushed my hair out of my face.

"You gonna do something about that hair?" Julie asked me.

I shrugged. I'd really lost the ability to care about that.

"I'm worried about you," she said, draining off the last of her beer. She waved the waitress over, ordered a couple more beers and some hot wings, then settled back, setting her hat on the table next to her and running her hands through her amber hair. It was thick and long, growing longer than I was used to her wearing it.

"What about your knitting?" she asked, pushing her glass back and forth between her hands, letting it slide on the condensation on the table. "You were going to learn to knit socks, right?"

I shrugged again.

She reached over and took my hand. "Listen, Sarah."

I looked up at her, the act of focusing on her took more energy than I wanted to expend.

"You're depressed and you're not dealing with it."

I pulled my hand back, scrubbed my face, and folded them on the table in front of me. "Depressed?"

"Yes, depressed. I haven't seen you this bad, ever. Hell, when you and Katie were having all those problems a year or so ago, you were more you then, than you are now. It's like you've given up. It's like you've let them win."

I laughed dryly. "Them, who, Julie? The dragons? The ghosts? The crazy homeless guys or the giants?" I leaned over, cupping my hands over the top of my tall beer glass and resting my chin on my hands. "Point to something I can take care of and get Katie back, and I'll be all over it."

I slumped back and let all the breath I had out in one long sigh.

The waitress showed up with our beers and the hot wings. I took a half-hearted sip of the beer and pushed it away.

"You can't fix everything," Julie said, taking a wing from the platter and ripping off a hunk of meat with her teeth.

I watched her chew for a moment, but couldn't get those eaters out of my head. Those crawling, biting things that consumed everything in their path.

I slid out of the booth, standing. "Can we go?"

Julie looked at me and took another bite of her wing. "Nope," she said and went back to chewing.

I turned and went to the bathroom. There were two women in there touching up their makeup, so I shuffled around until they cleared the sink. Then I stepped forward and splashed water over my face. I had straw in my hair and it needed to be brushed out. I hardly recognized myself. My hair was longer than I remembered it being since high school. My eyes were sunken and bruised. It looked like I spent all day crying.

I felt flabby and weak. I needed to do something. When was the last time I'd gone for a run? When was the last time I felt badass? I remember thinking I looked badass, before the book had taken me into hell. That had been fun.

I picked the hay from my hair, scrubbed the dirt from my hands and dried off. I thought of Gletts and how we'd battled side by side. He'd been looking for me, looking for Katie. And he'd nearly died for it. Had he gone home? Hell, I had no real idea what was going on in anyone's life. Time to fish or cut bait.

I smiled at my reflection in the mirror, feeling the rush of endorphins that it caused and pulled my shoulders back, standing tall. I walked back into the bar, slid into our booth and took a long drink of my beer. Julie just watched me as she wiped her mouth with a napkin. I grabbed a thick chicken wing and ripped into it, letting the sour tang of the sauce and the heat of the spices flare up in my mouth, burning into my sinuses and filling my head with a wonderful pain that I'd forgotten could exist.

"I need a plan," I said, talking around a mouthful of chicken. "I'm out of ideas and I need some help."

Julie nodded, nursing her beer and listening.

I polished off the last of the wings, knowing I'd likely regret them again later, but cherishing the way I was feeling something real.

"I'm calling Skella," I said. "Maybe her grandmother will be able to help me figure all this shit out."

Julie continued to stare at me, smiling and nodding.

"Maybe I'll see Rolph, too. See what he knows about all this."

"Qindra, too?" Julie asked. "She does know a lot of things outside of our regular channels."

I wiped my hands on a napkin and took a deep drink of beer, polishing off the tall glass. A burp the size of Texas ripped out of me, and the guys at the table in front of us applauded.

"Yeah, Qindra, too," I agreed. "Hell, I'll ask Nidhogg. And if they don't know anything, I'll drive down to Portland and get in Sawyer's space. Maybe they know something I'm missing."

Julie finished off her beer, dropped a couple of twenties on the table, and stood up. "Let's get that wing sauce off our hands," she said, grabbing me by the elbow. "Don't want to get that in your eyes."

I let her lead me back to the bathroom where we washed up.

"Make sure you eat dinner tonight," Julie told me as we got into the truck. Jai Li is helping Edith cook.

"Oh, my," I said, thinking about Jai Li in the kitchen. I laughed, the first happy thought I'd had in days. "Is that why we got wings, just in case?"

She shrugged and started the truck. "We'll see, won't we?"

It was pleasant riding home then, listening to Julie's country twang as she sang along to some old Patsy Cline. Music wasn't half-bad.

We rolled into Circle Q, unloaded our gear, and headed into the house.

Mary shooed us down the hallway, keeping us out of the kitchen. On my way by, I saw Jai Li standing on a stool, stirring something in Edith's large stockpot. It smelled tomatoey. Girl loved tomato soup.

Julie grabbed a shower in the master bedroom while I grabbed one in the hall bath. I looked at myself in the mirror, waiting for her to shut the water off. Two running at once made for a weak shower, and I wanted it full blast and as hot as I could make it.

While I watched my face, turning this way and that, studying the way my cheekbones looked in the light, I made up my mind.

I went back to our room, grabbed a box from the floor of the closet and traipsed back into the bathroom. I rummaged around in the box and pulled out my hair clippers. I knew one thing I could fix.

As I ran the clippers along the sides of my head, up and around the ears and across the back, I dropped long strands into the sink. I felt a bit of pain and uncertainty being stripped away with each pass.

I collected all the hair, dumped it in the trashcan and stripped, climbing into the shower. I loved the way my scalp felt as I rubbed shampoo into the hair that remained. Not a Mohawk, but high and tight on the sides and longer on the top. Just like I liked it.

With one towel around my girly parts, and another wrapped around my head, I lugged my stinky work clothes to our room and changed into clean jeans, my favorite Johnny Cash T-shirt— the one with him flipping off the camera—and looked at myself in the floor length mirror on the back of the door.

Not too bad. At least I recognized myself. Been too damn long.

FORTY-ONE

Dinner was great. When I walked into the dining room, I got a standing ovation. Jai Li led the way, hooting and clapping. Edith was a little more old school, so she gave me a sideways glance, her eyebrows lost in her hairline. But Mary and Julie cheered.

"About time," Julie said, hugging me.

Jai Li jumped into my arms and ran her small hands over the shaved parts of my scalp.

Very nice, she signed.

Mary got us all settled down, and Jai Li seated us all by her own choice. I sat on her left, and she left an empty chair to her right. "For Katie?" I asked.

She nodded, her face so serious. I bent down and kissed her on the top of the head.

Mary sat at the end closest to the window, and Edith on the end closest to the kitchen. Julie had the far side of the table all to herself. There were name tags, homemade place mats, and cloth napkins folded like swans. It was all very elegant. Edith, Julie, and Mary had wine, while Jai Li and I had sparkling cider.

We had like five gallons of tomato soup, two huge platters of grilled cheese sandwiches, and some kind of fruit salad that looked to be three parts whipped cream and one part fruit cocktail. I ate extra helpings of everything and made a lot of noise about just how delicious everything was.

Jai Li was tickled beyond belief. She beamed with pride as she stood on her chair to serve us all a third helping of soup. I was near to busting by the time everyone else gave in. Great comfort food.

As we cleared away things, we shooed Jai Li and Edith into the living room. They cooked, we cleaned. They loved it and went in to play cribbage while we danced round the kitchen to some new boot-scooting tunes that Mary favored. I love all kinds of music, but I was afraid that they were swaying Jai Li a little too far into the whole Country & Western scene. Time for a little Black Sabbath cleansing. I considered playing her some thrash metal, but I wasn't worried about the lyrics just yet.

Mary, Julie, and Edith were settling down for a quiet evening when I decided we needed ice cream. Jai Li made no objections, just grabbed a sweater and ran to the door. I smiled, seeing her so excited.

No one wanted more food, but I wanted the ride. We piled in the truck, got the girl buckled in, and headed down to the corner store. Of course it was several miles down the road to the nearest town, so we got a good long dose of Black Sabbath. On the way home I switched it up to Iron Maiden. Turns out she really liked *The Prisoner*. Who knew?

When we got back, there was a small white BMW in the yard in front of the house. I kept Jai Li in the truck, making her lock the doors. I had the keys just in case. I walked up to the porch and saw a squat woman in a charcoal gray suit jacket with matching skirt and shoes that I bet cost more than I made in a month standing in the kitchen. Mary leaned against the counter. Julie stood in the hallway, her arms crossed and her boss face on. Edith was nowhere to be seen.

I opened the door and stepped through the short hall and into the kitchen. By the time I'd entered, everyone was facing me. No one was smiling.

The newcomer looked me up and down, smirked, and handed me an envelope.

"You've been summoned," she said, gathering up her briefcase and walking passed me to the hall. I turned, following her.

J.A. Pitts

"What? Who are you?"

She waved at me over her head. "Read the card."

She opened the door and let herself out. I followed her onto the porch, making sure she got into her car and didn't go near the truck. Once she'd pulled around and was heading down the long drive toward the gate, I pulled Jai Li out of the truck, retrieved the ice cream, and hustled us back into the house.

"How long has she been here?" I asked, while Jai Li dug in the cabinets for bowls.

"She got here about three minutes after you left," Julie said, obviously perturbed. "Wouldn't say anything, said she had to hand you that thing directly."

She pointed to the envelope I'd laid on the dining room table. Edith walked out of the back and started digging spoons out of the drawer.

"Guess I'd better open it, huh?" I asked, pulling a butter knife out of the dish drainer and slitting the envelope.

It was white card with gold embossed lettering.

"I'll be damned," I said, passing it over to Julie who looked a little stunned. "Jai Li and I are being summoned to Nidhogg's place, tomorrow for brunch."

Mary snorted. "All that for brunch?"

Jai Li set the bowls on the table and clapped, jumping up and down.

"I guess you want to go?" I asked, the answer obvious.

She just nodded and took the ice cream scoop from Edith.

"I guess when you're the mightiest dragon of them all, and that old, you like to do things a certain way." I took a bowl of chocolate and slid down on a chair, grabbing a spoon from the pile in the middle of the table. "Glad I just fixed my hair."

Everyone laughed. How utterly bizarre.

By the time Jai Li finally succumbed to the food coma and was brushing her teeth half-heartedly, everyone else was ready for bed.

"I'll iron her dress," Edith said, patting me on the shoulder. "You may want to consider something a little more dressy than your usually fare."

"I know just the T-shirt to wear," I said, smiling at her.

She shook her head and went off to her room. I got Jai Li tucked into bed and read to her from our current book, *The Black Stallion*. Once she'd drifted off, I slipped into my jammies and crawled into bed.

The invitation to Nidhogg's place didn't offer a chance to refuse. Oh, I guess I could've risked pissing her off, but the invitation was only for brunch, and I'd been over there enough not to worry. But Jai Li hadn't been back since her exile. What did this mean? Was Nidhogg rescinding our fostering of Jai Li. I think Qindra would've warned me if that were the case. Besides the girl was very excited at the prospect of returning to the only other home she'd ever known. How could I tell her no? Those other kids, the rest of the staff at Casa del Dragon, were her family, had known her way longer than Katie and I had.

When I came out into the kitchen the next morning, Jai Li was working on her math packet while Edith was slicing apples.

"Something light," she said, placing the plate in the middle of the table and nudging Jai Li with her elbow. Jai Li grinned, snagged a slice, and went back to her math. She really understood what she was doing so far. At the pace she was learning math, we'd have to get her a tutor soon. I was an English major for a reason. When the girl started getting into calculus I was screwed.

All morning Edith was cautious, talking to Jai Li in fast sign language, expressing her frustration. I have no idea how she'd picked that up so damn quickly, but they were like two peas in a pod.

By ten-thirty, we were ready to roll. There really wasn't anything else for us to do. Edith was not the happiest, but she eventually caved.

Stay safe, Edith signed.

Jai Li smiled, lunged forward, and hugged the old woman. That was the final straw. Tears filled Edith's eyes, and she hugged the girl back.

After a moment, Jai Li pulled back, placed her small hand on Edith's face, and kissed her on the nose.

Edith laughed and hugged Jai Li again, standing with the girl in her arms, spinning around once, then setting her down. Jai Li giggled and turned, racing down toward our room to get some things.

Edith straightened and turned to face me.

"If you let that bitch hurt our girl here," she said, her voice as quiet and deadly as any I'd ever heard in my life. "I will hold you personally responsible."

Anger flared for a moment, but then faded. "We all love her," I said. "I'll protect her."

She nodded once, then went into the kitchen. "You must take a gift," she called. "I will put something together. It is only polite."

Mary and Julie had been actively ignoring us up until that moment. "I'll help Edith," Mary said, setting her knitting aside and scuttling out of the room.

Julie put down the book she was reading and smiled at me. "I trust you," she said. "This just makes us nervous as hell."

I nodded. "I know. I'm a bit nervous as well." I sat on the couch with my hands on my knees. "But I talked with Qindra. It is truly just lunch. Things are changing with Nidhogg. This may be a good chance for us to figure out exactly what. You've seen the affect Jai Li has on people." I glanced to the kitchen.

"Oh, yeah," Julie said, standing. "No matter who she meets, they want to protect her. Let's hope Nidhogg is not immune to her charms."

She patted me on the arm and then went into the kitchen. I didn't bring up the necromancer and how he tried to sacrifice her. Felt like a buzz kill type of thing to say. I sat back and listened to the three women as they argued about taking soup, cookies, or wine. I'd just trust their judgment.

FORTY-TWO

We breezed through security at Nidhogg's place with a wave and a smile. We were definitely known and welcome here. We were allowed to park on the long circular drive in front of the manse. Jai Li was very excited. A little scared, too. She sang a little, making breathy, throaty sounds as well as mouth pops and grunts for syncopation. She'd never win any singing contests, but she sounded like an angel to me.

If I had one wish, I'd spend it on getting that child's tongue restored. The fact that it was cut off as a baby seemed like one of the worst things anyone could do to a child, but she coped. She didn't really know any different. I know she was frustrated some times in communicating, but the sign language was working out pretty well, and I was getting the hang of it a little. Katie was better.

I had to pause there, let the fear and anger subside before we got out of the truck. Too much in this life was not fair. But I didn't need to bring that energy into this meeting. Nidhogg was not always stable. I wasn't really sure what this was all about, but I wanted it to be painless, pleasant for the girl, and over as quickly as possible.

Qindra met us at the enormous front doors and ushered us into the great hall. The halls were deserted, and Jai Li slumped a little. She handed a small box of cookies to Qindra who commented on the beauty of the bow on top. Jai Li smiled a little, but looked around, hoping to find her little friends, I bet.

"This way," Qindra said, smiling.

"Come on," I said, placing my hand on Jai Li's back and guiding her across the great hall and onward to Nidhogg's sanctuary. Jai Li had spent her first years in that great space, serving the dragon with her sister Mei Hau. Only Mei Hau had died at the tooth and claw of an enraged Nidhogg. Dementia, I guessed. Nidhogg was ages old.

Qindra pushed one of the huge doors into Nidhogg's inner sanctum open, stepping to the side and ushering us within. We were met with a cheering mob of women and children—the servants of Nidhogg. Each was dressed in fancy outfits and wore decorative hats. Even Nidhogg, who sat in her usual position by the fire, wore a wide brimmed hat with a huge peacock feather on it.

"What is this?" I asked, laughing at the splendor, caught up in the joy of the moment?

Jai Li tugged on my sleeve, motioning toward the other children.

"Go ahead," I said, and she flew across the room, skidding to a halt in front of Zi Xiu, the woman who ran the household, threw her arms around the woman's legs for a quick hug, then tackled one of the livery boys who stood a full head taller than her. Everyone was shocked at the roughhousing, but when Nidhogg waved her hand at them, giving her permission, the children fell on the other two, and the room turned into a huge scrum.

Everyone was laughing and cheering as, one after another, the servants hugged Jai Li.

"Welcome home, sister," they whispered.

"We've missed you."

"You've grown so tall."

And on and on. Qindra put her hand on my shoulder as I watched them, my heart full of joy.

"This is quite unexpected," I said, turning toward her.

Nidhogg laughed and clapped along with the children while the adults looked on with broad smiles and quite a bit of wonder and surprise.

"Nidhogg has declared a feast day," Qindra said, her face alight with joy. "She has not done this since my mother's time."

So we partied like it was fourteen-ninety-nine. There was music and food, games and small presents for everyone. Zi Xiu got a brand new set of spoons, while the two chambermaids each received a box of ribbons. Each of the livery boys was given a new uniform and a small toy—carved wooden animals, boats, and trains. They were amazed by the largess.

The young girls each got a small box with a new uniform as well as a puzzle and books. Two girls received wooden animals like the boys—one lion, one giraffe.

Finally, Jai Li was presented with a box containing a rainbow of embroidery floss, several new hoops, and a roll of white embroidery canvas.

Qindra was given a tiara with many colored gems and a pair of small bells which she openly wept over.

And before she was done, Nidhogg handed me a box of my very own.

I sat on the ground in front of her, legs crossed, and opened the delicate wrapping paper and ribbons, exposing a box the size of a large book. There were intricate carvings in the wood, and the hinges and clasp were of forged steel.

"Do not open it here," Nidhogg said to me with a wink. "We will adjourn to the library directly, so we can talk."

I rose, kissed the old woman on the cheek, which seemed to surprise her, and went back to stand with Qindra, looking over the amazing scene before us.

Several of the girls were trading ribbons, this color for that, while the rest were having a great parade with the wooden animals. It was wonderful and innocent.

"Too bad they go back to being slaves tomorrow," I whispered to Qindra, who frowned at me and shook her head.

"Do not spoil this," she said, patting me on the arm. "Times are changing."

Before the food was served, the other servants dragged the cooks out of the kitchen and set them at the great table. Everyone pitched in, carrying platters and dishes, glasses and great bottles of juices and water.

It reminded me of a Christmas feast, but it was June. Solstice, perhaps?

Once the meal was well underway, Nidhogg excused herself, taking Qindra and myself with her, out of the great hall and into the library. Several of the servants tried to follow her, to bring her things, but she shooed them away, directing Qindra and me to bring wine, glasses, and a tray of pastries that had avoided the grasping hands of young children.

Once we were ensconced within the great library and the doors were shut against the sound of revelry, the three of us settled down before a burning fireplace, taking up three glasses of wine and toasting the good health of everyone present. Nidhogg drained her wine and set the empty glass on the table between us, waving away Qindra's offer to refill it.

"The world is falling into chaos," Nidhogg said, her voice firm and confident. "It is beyond time to set things aright."

I looked at Qindra, who looked as confused as I did.

"But mother," Qindra began, but Nidhogg waved her down.

"I have chosen this wild woman as my Fist," she said, gesturing toward me. "And I do not regret that decision. She is brash and unafraid."

She leaned forward, poured herself another half glass of wine, and sat back, stamping her cane on the floor between her knees.

"I have come to a decision," she said, staring first at Qindra then at me.

"There are those in the council who will be outraged if they learn of our conspiracy," she said, her voice sure and her eyes as clear as I've ever seen them.

"What conspiracy?" Qindra asked.

"This one," she pointed her cane at me, a feral grin on her face. "I blame her for breaking me out of my torpor, forcing me to face the world again, and showing me the enormity of my sins."

My mouth fell open as the old dragon looked at me with fire in her eyes. There was a depth of history there, a power beyond anything I'd ever seen. Jean-Paul in all his black and silver glory; mighty wingspan and fiery breath was nothing compared to the fire in this woman's eyes.

"Oh, shit," I breathed. We were screwed.

"But, mother," Qindra began, moving to the edge of her seat, reaching one hand toward Nidhogg. "I don't understand."

"The wheel, child," she said, giving Qindra a patronizing smile. "Have you not understood the portents and the signs? The wheel has been broken for time out of mind. But it grinds along its broken toothed gear, struggling to move once more, small jerks and starts that rock this world and remind us that our doom is inevitable."

I watched her, shuddered, and saw the great wheel in my mind. The same wheel that Odin spoke of, the great cycle of life, the beginning and the end of things. The wheel that Nidhogg shattered when she slew the gods, preventing Ragnarök and the end of the world.

"How?" I began, setting my wine on the table and sliding to the floor at her feet. "The gods are dead. The end cannot come."

"They are being reborn," she said, her voice sly and her face alight. "And we shall find them. Only this time we will provide them a place of safety. We will nurture them, here in my kingdom."

Qindra fell back, her hands to her face. "Truly?" she asked, her voice tremulous.

"I will right the long wrong I have wrought," Nidhogg said, a look of pure joy on her face. "That is the only way to counter the chaos." She suddenly grew stoic once again. "If we do not act, the Reavers will shatter us and bring us to doom. We must find a way to repair the wheel. You," she pointed at me, her finger crooked. "Stand child. You are a maker, a warrior, and my Fist. You have shown me the way of it. You who stood against the necromancer and protected Frederick Sawyer, who put the love of Jai Li and many others above your own safety.

You who slew the child of my womb in order to preserve love and righteousness. You have given me hope in a life that has been bereft of it for far too long."

She turned to face Qindra. "And you, daughter. My heart. You who have guarded me and guided me beyond all reason. Even when I slew your mother, and so many others in my blinding rages, you loved me beyond reckoning. I release you from your obligation. You are free to choose your path, your life."

Qindra gasped. "No, mother. Do not send me away."

Nidhogg chuckled. "Nay, child. I do not banish you. I just give you your freedom. You may stay here if you choose, but it becomes your choice, no longer an obligation."

We fell silent. I sat on my knees at Nidhogg's feet, shocked and confused. What the hell had just happened?

I got up, slipped back into my chair, and drank my wine, watching Qindra's face as she processed everything that had happened. Nidhogg sipped her own wine, waiting for us to decide.

"I'll help," I said. "But I want Black Briar brought into the fold. I want them to be the ones to harbor anyone we find."

Nidhogg nodded. "As you see fit."

"What of the servants?" Qindra asked, her voice quiet. "Will they be given their freedom?"

Nidhogg smiled. "Yes, daughter. Each shall be given their freedom. But we will not abandon anyone in this harsh world. Those who are too young will be educated and when they are of age, may choose to leave us as they will. But they may never speak of this household. You must see to this precaution. If they leave us, they may never return, and they will be given a new identity."

"Holy shit," I said, my mind reeling.

"Indeed," Nidhogg said, breaking into a broad grin once again. "I do so love shaking things up. It makes me feel alive after a very long time of darkness and fear."

"How will this work?" Qindra asked. She was struggling to keep up.

"Conspiracy and revolution," Nidhogg said. "This cannot be my way. This must be something you sow beyond my household. No one can think I know anything of this. You must play your parts well. Operate without my knowledge, never bring another word of this to me. This is my one and only time to openly discuss this."

"Why?" Qindra asked.

Nidhogg pointed at me. "This one," she said, chuckling. "She has shown me my path forward, and I go forward unto glory, toward my very death, but with a glad heart."

Did she mean I was going to kill her? This was crazy.

"But," I began, standing. "Your death?"

"No more," Nidhogg said, struggling to her own feet, leaning on the cane. "Take Jai Li home, berserker. Give her a place built on love and joy."

"I'll try," I said, my world spinning, nearly out of control.

"And bring your young Katie home," she said. "You disturb my dreams with all your wanderings and thrashing about." She reached out and took Qindra's arm, the two of them ambling out toward the front of the library.

"Like a herd of elephants, you are, tromping around in the land of dreams. She is not where you seek. Didn't that silly elf boy tell you as much?"

At the doorway, they paused, and Nidhogg turned back once more. "Look to your heart, warrior. You have the answer within you."

I sat back down, trying to catch my breath as they left the library.

Look to my heart? What the fuck did that mean? And how come everyone but me knew Katie was not in the Sideways or the dream lands? Where the hell was she?

As to this revolution—secretly sanctioned by the overlord—how the hell did that work, exactly?

I drank my wine and stood up. I'd wander back to the party and grab Jai Li, get her home. But maybe I'd let her play with her friends a little longer. Life was too short.

FORTY-THREE

I thought about Nidhogg's words all that week while I worked the farms with Julie like old times. As much as I'd loved that first time I was the lead, took the checks, planned the work, there was something immensely satisfying in playing second fiddle to Julie. She was a damn fine teacher, and I still had things to learn. Patience being among the top items. But more than that, it was glorious to see her rebuilding her life one day and one person at a time.

The dreams I had at that time were mundane things, peaceful or anxiety riddled, they didn't involve eaters or murderous spirits in bowler hats. What I did dream of was Katie. Every single night I dreamed that she was calling me, that she was someplace I knew, and that I was just looking in the wrong places. It wasn't like I was walking the dreamscape, or anything. I had that connection down cold. This was just my brain working through Nidhogg's words. What was I missing?

I started keeping a dream journal. Each morning, before I got out of bed, I wrote down what I could remember. Then I set it aside and went about my day.

Days turned into a week, then two. I was gathering my strength, connecting with my daughter (man, that sounded so strange) and fortifying myself for the next big push. I had to go out again, but this time I was doing some significant scouting and research. I wanted to talk to Unun, Skella's and Gletts's grandmother. She knew about going walkabout. She understood the rules of the road.

One thing, though, that came up in every single dream journal entry was the apartment. That was the key to things, I was convinced. I hadn't been back to the apartment since Julie had helped rescue me. But I was going back. I needed to get the mail and pay the bills. I needed to walk around the place and differentiate what it was and what it wasn't. This was the real world, not the dream world. There the madness and chaos ruled.

Knowing what happened the last time, I took Gram with me, of course, but the book and the shield were stored in the closet in the bedroom of the old apartment. I didn't want either of them around Jai Li, and I sure didn't need them in my smithing work. I'd just do a quick rundown to Kent, grab the mail, and be home before dinner. I made sure Julie and Mary knew I was going down, so if I didn't return, they knew where to come beat my ass.

The mailbox was over stuffed with a note that the mailman wouldn't deliver any new mail until we came down to the post office and cleared things up. Seemed reasonable, seeing as we'd really abandoned the apartment. Maybe I'd get a P.O. box in Bellevue or Redmond. I didn't want to have the mail forwarded. Felt too much like giving up.

After a quick discussion with the postal czar, I loaded up the saddlebags with weeks' worth of mail and headed back to the apartment to sort it all. But mainly I wanted to go back to the scene of the crime—put some things in order, hide the book again, get it wrapped up. Julie had just left it and the shield where they lay when she and Mary pulled me out of the apartment.

When I opened the door to the apartment, I was shocked to see the oddly symmetrical chaos my time in the Sideways had caused. It was the book, of course, I noted it laying open near the bar, page down, like someone had been reading it and couldn't find a book mark.

"You suck," I said, grabbing a pair of tongs off the living room floor. I tried not to think about the way all of our possessions had been in a three dimensional orbit, flowing in toward the book. Julie said a card burst into flames when it touched the book. What would have happened when one of the bar stools had connected? I shuddered to think about it. Of course, nothing was happening now with it laying open, face down on the floor, but I guess without me or another person touching it, the book wasn't exactly triggered.

I'd have to check downstairs with Elmer to see if his guns had been moving on their own, just in case.

I got the book wrapped in tinfoil again, wrapped it in Katie's scarf, and shoved it into a large freezer bag along with a handful of sage and lavender. Then I took it and the shield, stashing them both into the closet in the bedroom. The place felt even colder, more dead space than ever before. I touched the mirror on the way out and pulled the door closed. My stomach was beginning to hurt, so I stepped into the main room and sat on the floor, doing some good cleansing breathing like Sa Bum Dim Choi had taught me back in Tae Kwon Do. Release the tension, release the fear. Bring in cool, cleansing breath, bring in strength and calm.

After a couple of minutes, I opened my eyes and rolled my shoulders. I felt a lot better. Then I realized I was in the same position I had been in when I tapped the book, and got up hastily, brushing loose bits of paper from the back of my jeans. Really needed to sort out the place again. Maybe I'd just get a shovel and put it all into the Dumpster out back.

I clapped my hands and picked up the saddlebags. "First things first."

I went to the kitchen, pushed the table away from the cabinet where it had been stuck as it tried to go into its orbit. I righted the chairs and grabbed a glass off the cabinet. Several of the glass ones had broken when Julie sprung me. Would need to be extra careful where I walked. Grabbing a plastic cup, I got a glass of water and sat at the table, separating the mountain of mail into three stacks—one for recycling, one with bills and finally one for personal items. The personal things were all for Katie. The first two stacks were fairly even by the time I had dug through the majority of the mail. Apparently there were a lot of grocery store sales in our area.

In the end I had to run to the recycling Dumpster in the back alley of the apartment. Seeing the jumble of garbage and the huge containers, I thought of the homeless guy, Joe, and his ongoing flirtation with actually being Odin. If I could see him right now, I'd even ask him about Katie, even though I knew his answers would be in riddles, or just gibberish.

I was slogging back up the apartment stairs when I heard my cell phone playing "Unknown" by D.O.A. I'd left it on the table by the bills. Who had this number that I didn't know?

I ran up the last few steps, slammed the keys into the locks, and flung myself across the main room, jumping over a barstool and slid into the seat at the kitchen table. I flipped the phone open and hit talk without even looking at who it was. Was probably sales call or something.

I was wrong.

"Hello," a woman's voice said from the other end. There was a trepidation in those two syllables. "Sarah?"

I stopped breathing. I knew that voice.

It was my kid sister.

"Megan?" I asked when I found my voice again. "What happened? Are you okay?"

She didn't answer right away, and my heart pounded in my throat.

"Can you come meet me?" she asked. "Please?"

"Jesus, Megan ..." My mind was spinning out of control. "It'll take me forty minutes to get over to Crescent Ridge. Where are you?"

"I'm at a payphone outside the Barnes and Noble in Federal Way."

Federal Way? That was pretty close. "Why Federal Way?"

"Sarah, please?" she begged. "Just come get me."

I think she was crying. "Yeah, sure. Give me twenty minutes. Go inside the store. People won't bother you in there."

"Okay," she said, and the phone went dead.

Christ on a crutch ... I sat there with my head in my hands, trying to hold in my thoughts. All I had was the Ducati. Luckily I carried Katie's helmet with me, just in case.

I grabbed all the bills and personal mail, shoved them into my saddlebags, grabbed Gram and glanced around the apartment once. Felt like I was missing something.

I locked the place up, making sure I'd turned off the lights first, and pounded down the stairs. My mind was racing with all kinds of possibilities. Was someone hurt? Were ma and da okay? Had Megan run away?

By the time the bike roared to life a thousand possibilities had flitted through my brain, none of them good. I kicked the bike into first and gunned the engine. I darted out from behind Elmer's Gun and Knife Emporium fearing the worst.

I should've called Julie, let her know what was happening.

Too late, of course. I was already on the road. And besides, Megan was waiting.

FORTY-FOUR

I pulled the bike into a space in front of the bookstore and climbed off, leaving Gram and the saddlebags in place. I wasn't going to be there long. My heart was in my throat as I unstrapped my helmet and peeled off my leather jacket. Seven years was a long damn time. I ran my hands through my hair, worrying the tangles loose and pushing it all back off my face.

Fear rode in my chest, fear and seven years of lousy excuses.

I pulled the doors open and stepped into the vestibule. It reminded me of an airlock lined with bargain books. Once through the second set of doors I noticed they had a coffee shop inside. Maybe I'd buy her a drink, talk to her a bit. The store was fairly busy. People milled through the book aisles chatting or grabbing books off the shelves. There were a lot of people here, and none of them looked like Megan.

I walked through the store three times, up and down every aisle, into the bathroom twice and once through the coffee shop. She wasn't there.

I started to panic. I knew Megan's voice. But had someone tricked me to get me here? Maybe I was getting too paranoid. I took a deep breath and decided to do the logical thing and ask.

The girl at the information desk was tall and slim with long black hair and a quick smile.

"May I help you?" she asked.

I looked down at her nameplate. Cassie. "Yeah, Cassie, I'm looking for my sister," I said, pulling out my wallet. Inside I had that picture Ma had sent me last year, of Megan leaning against the truck with her purple streaked hair and an old beat up pair of Doc Martens.

Cassie looked at the picture and brightened. "She was in her a few minutes ago, but she left."

"Left? When? Did you see which way she went?"

"She walked out with a young guy, early twenties maybe."

Guy? Twenties? "Did she know him?" I asked. "Did he force her?"

Her face fell. "Force? No, I don't think so. She was surprised to see him, actually. But I thought she went with him willingly. Let me check with Sally."

She walked around the end of the counter and walked over to a young redhead who was working the cash register. I glanced around at the books, fretting. Why would she call me then leave with some guy? And how did she know twenty-year-old guys? Church maybe?

"Sally says they left together," the information girl said. "She heard him ask her why she was in Federal Way and she told him she was supposed to meet someone, but they'd pulled a no show. He didn't press it. Said he'd take her home."

"Did she mention any names?"

"No, I'm sorry."

I thanked the girl and went out of the store to stand by my bike. It took me twenty-seven minutes to get here from Kent. Was she that impatient?

I called Julie. The phone rang a few times and rolled over to voice mail. Speaking of patience. Not that I'm really paranoid or anything, but I immediately called Circle Q.

Mary told me that Julie was out working with some of the horses and that her phone was on the counter with her keys.

I left a message, saying I had to run out to Crescent Ridge and that I'd be back to Circle Q late.

Mary jotted down the message and said she needed to go fix dinner, but admonished me to be careful.

It was early, about four-thirty. I could totally make it out there, see what happened.

I pulled on my jacket and helmet and climbed on the bike.

Seven years between conversations and she leaves without waiting for me?

We'd exchanged two letters over the last five months. We used the Tae Kwon Do school as our safe place. Sa Bum Num Choi was amenable to our subterfuge since we asked politely. I sent my letters there, Megan picked them up when she taught. We were still at the pleasantries phase, not really getting into too much. I knew she was much happier at the high school than being home-schooled. I knew she liked boys, and I told her I didn't.

That had been in my last letter to her. That was almost five months ago. I sent the first one just after Christmas and the second one in February. She had a lot of hurt. She felt abandoned and rightly so. I hadn't even tried to justify myself. Not yet. Telling her about Katie was as far as I'd managed. Then things had gone dark.

Frustration and anger warred inside me as I started the bike and pulled through the parking lot. What was I going to do, ride up to the house and confront her there in front of ma and da? I hadn't spoken to da in seven years either. I sure as hell didn't want to start now.

I idled at the parking lot exit, waiting for an opening in the traffic, debating on turning back north for Black Briar or heading south to Crescent Ridge.

Fuck it. I turned south toward Crescent Ridge and merged in with traffic. She called me for a reason. I'd avoided her long enough. Time to pay the piper.

Traffic was pretty heavy, but I made good time.

I pulled off onto 410 in Sumner and hit a gas station. I needed petrol in the worst way. And it gave me a chance to avoid getting there by a few more minutes. I was going, no doubt about it. Didn't mean I was looking forward to the confrontation.

To stall as long as possible, I hit the restroom before getting back on the road. I was walking back to my bike when a black and white Pontiac Fiero from like a million years ago pulled up to the pumps across the aisle from me.

I straddled the bike, helmet in hand and saw that the young

227

woman in the passenger seat was Megan. She looked so much like ma my heart clinched. I was pissed.

The guy started pumping gas when I carefully stepped off the bike and placed the helmet on the seat, but I kept on my leather gloves. Megan looked like she'd been crying, and this guy looked like the kind of guy who made girls cry. I may need to punch him a bit.

"Hey," I called, striding across the lot. "Megan?"

The guy looked over, surprised, and Megan did a double-take as I pulled the car door open.

"What the hell?" the boy called, but I ignored him.

I reached to pull her out, but she beat me to it. I had one hand on the open door and the other reaching in when she bolted from the car and into my arms.

The boy had the look of someone contemplating violence until he saw Megan's reaction. I staggered back a step as she wrapped her arms around my chest, buried her face in my shoulder, and started to cry.

I looked at the boy while I stroked her hair and told her things were going to be okay.

He stared at me like I had a third head. I gave him my best stern look, then closed my eyes as Megan shook in my arms.

This was right. This, more than almost anything in my life.

How had I abandoned this girl?

This I could fix. I had to. She needed me, and that was something I needed.

FORTY-FIVE

The guy's name was Dennis, and he was one of the instructors at the Tae Kwon Do school. It had been a total coincidence that he ran into Megan at that Barnes & Noble.

We moved our vehicles to the side of the gas station and he grabbed sodas while Megan and I sat on the curb and talked.

"Why'd you ditch me?" I asked when the crying was as dry as it was gonna get.

She looked at me sideways and shrugged. "I was scared. You took a long time."

"Twenty-seven minutes," I said, exasperated. "You couldn't wait a few more minutes?"

She looked down at her hands and shrugged again. "Wasn't sure you were really coming. When I saw Dennis, I thought that was a sign from God that I should take the gift presented and catch a ride with him instead of being ditched by my ... by you."

Harsh. I reached over and took one hand, squeezing it.

"I'm sorry I never came home."

She started crying again. Quietly, but enough that she wiped her face with her free hand and continued to look down. Her hair was well below her shoulders now, longer than in the last picture I'd seen.

I reached over with my other hand and pushed her hair up over her ear. "Da let you cut your hair last year?"

"Ha!" she barked. "Him? No way. He freaked." She glanced up at me "We saw your picture in the paper last year, when you saved those people from that fire. The parental units were apoplectic. They were very proud of you," she looked up fully, earnestly. "You have to know that. Da beamed, showed the article to everyone at church."

I found that hard to believe. "I must've looked like a disgrace." The picture the paper used was one of me working at some Ren Faire event from a couple of years before. I'd been maybe twenty-three, twenty-four with the sides of my head shaved. "I bet the deacons had a thing or two to say about my picture."

She grinned at me. "Oh, no. He didn't show them your picture. He cut that out, just took the article. I have that picture in my memory book." She looked down again, the smile fading. "Thanks for sending me those pictures of you and Katie. She's really pretty."

I must've stiffened because she squeezed my hand really hard until I relaxed. "Yeah, she's awesome."

Megan smiled at that, the grin creeping up over her face, but she didn't look around. "Ma thinks she's pretty, too."

I thought back to ma visiting my apartment last fall, mistaking Julie for Katie. "She's not freaked I'm a lesbian?"

"Not freaked exactly ..." She looked up and over to her other side as Dennis reappeared carrying sodas. He handed around three tall bottles of orange Crush. They were in glass bottles, from Mexico with real cane sugar. I twisted off the cap and took a long pull. It was definitely sweet.

Megan introduced Dennis, explaining he was a third degree black belt and taught a lot of mixed martial arts in the adult class. "Good guy to have in a fight," she said.

"I'll keep that in mind," I replied, giving him the once over. His hair was cropped very short, and he had wide shoulders and a broad chest. Not the tallest of the bunch, I was sure. He was maybe five-ten, five-eleven. He was cute enough, and his eyes were full of light. Excited about the world, and protective of Megan. No crush there or anything, not that kind of protective. But clan tight, like Black Briar. Different from how I assumed he was at first. It's all about perspective.

Dennis was going to Pacific Lutheran University, getting a degree in business and finance, so he made the drive north several days a week. He'd stopped at the bookstore to get his mother a birthday present.

After a couple more minutes of introductions and examinations, he excused himself and went to sit in his car and study while we continued our chat.

"Nice guy," I said once he'd closed his door.

"Yeah. Da actually likes him, even though he doesn't go to our church. Says Lutherans are okay by him as long as they're God-fearing."

"How is he?" I asked, taking a drink of my soda so I didn't have to look at her when she answered.

"This last year hasn't been too good," she said, quietly. "He's scared, Sarah. He tries to cover it up, but I can see it."

I glanced over at her and she was wiping the condensation off her soda bottle with both thumbs. She was staring into the distance, deep inside her own head.

"It was early last year, before the whole 'you becoming a hero thing,'" she glanced over quick, then back down.

She was nervous.

I placed a hand on her arm and she seemed to calm down.

"I've heard him and ma arguing a few times. He wants us to move. Says it isn't safe here any longer."

"Ma mentioned that in a letter," I said, quietly. I watched her face. She was such a beautiful girl. Strong and determined. But scared, too.

"Ma won't go, though. I heard her tell him that if we ran, we'd never see you again."

That was a nice surprise.

"It put him off for a few months, but last year, between Thanksgiving and Christmas, some guys started asking around town, looking to see if anyone knew you."

I stiffened. "Who?" I asked. "Did they say why they were looking for me?"

She shivered. "No, but they were ugly people, Sarah. Two men. One was gorgeous, but he had funny features, maybe Asian, but different. The other guy was a brute. Looked like he'd been hit in the face with a shovel a few times. They came by the Tae Kwon Do school and Sa Bum Nim talked with them. She's tough as nails."

"Yeah, I remember."

"But she told them that you'd moved away years ago and that no one had seen you since. They didn't like the answer, said some harsh things, but went away. Word of that got back to da and he started spinning out of control all over again."

I could see him, angry and scared—desperate to take action. What the hell was he running from? The guys sounded like some of Justin's cronies. I distinctly remembered killing two assholes that fit those descriptions. They'd tried to sacrifice Frick and Frack in their mad, necromantic schemes.

But they had no ties to me before I'd killed the dragon, Jean-Paul Duchamp. Da surely hadn't been running from that bunch of crazies. We'd been running far too long to be tangled up with them. Besides, I don't think da would've let us settle in Crescent Ridge if this were that close to the enemy.

No, he was running from something else. The jerks just happened to trigger his fears.

"So, about your hair?"

She ran her hand through it, pushing the bangs back over her head. "I was at school one day after we'd had a fight—"

She didn't have to say with whom. It was understood.

"—and my friend Bonnie brought the supplies from home. We ditched algebra that afternoon and went to the girls bathroom on the second floor, you know the one?"

I'd gone to the same school, only a bunch of years earlier. "Near the language arts rooms?"

She nodded. "LeAnn watched the door while Bonnie cut my hair. She'd read about how to do it specifically on the Internet. First she braided it into several braids, then she cut it. We were sending it off to Locks of Love. She took eighteen inches."

I smiled at her, nodding. "Impressive."

"Then she brought out the dye. We sat there talking while the dye set in. Bonnie and I have been friends for a few years." She paused, thinking. "She used to call us holy rollers, but only that first year we were in Tae Kwon Do together. Once we got to know one another, we became friends. Seems that most people are quick to judge."

"Got that right," I agreed. "Anything different is bad. Either beat it down, make fun of it, or cut it out of your life."

She looked up at me quick. I shook my head. "Not something I believe, but I've seen it enough times to know it exists."

She looked relieved. "Da has been mellowing, you know?"

Of course, I had no idea, but I let her continue.

"Ma convinced him to let me play soccer after I'd been so good at Tae Kwon Do. I'd earned it. Didn't rock the boat too much, not like you."

Too, true. From the time I was twelve, I fought against his worldview with every waking breath.

"Then ma and me convinced him that going over to the public high school would be good for me, how I could take some real science classes and languages and stuff."

That must've been a tough battle.

"But last spring things went sideways. I got in trouble for beating up a kid."

Woah … "Really?"

"It was Matt Abernathy. Prick."

She blushed at that.

"What did you do to him?"

She blushed even deeper. "Punched him in the throat."

I coughed. Geez. "You could've killed him."

She looked over at me with a fierce look in her eyes. "He was way out of line," she said, the anger fresh in her voice. "Grabbed me, kissed me. I pushed him away, but he called me a whore because of my hair and said he'd show me how men treated whores."

My stomach clenched. The Abernathy's were church people. Mom said Megan had been having trouble with them.

"He's two years older than me," she continued. "Big, strong. He was hurting me, had his big hands around my right arm, squeezing real tight, and he grabbed my breasts." She paused, suddenly out of breath. I knew that feeling, the fight or flight. I was proud that she fought.

"He was laughing, and there were a couple other boys there, watching the doorway to make sure no one interfered." There was a faraway look in her face then. "I think he'd have really hurt me, laughing about my purple hair and how I deserved what I was getting."

"Bastard!" I growled.

"For a minute, I thought about letting him, you know. Just giving in and letting him do whatever he wanted. Maybe I did deserve it—"

"Megan, no." I grabbed her shoulder, but she shrugged and went on.

"—but I thought of you, Sarah. Thought, now what would Sarah do in this situation. He'd ripped my blouse and was trying to get my skirt up around my waist when I just made my choice. I figured it was kill him, or he'd beat me unconscious. So I did the one thing I could think of."

"Good for you." I was breathing harder now, my heart racing. Jesus, I hated men like that. What the hell was wrong with people? I was so sick of big folk preying on the smaller ones.

"What happened then?"

She turned to look at me, a look of fierce determination on her face. "Short knuckle strike to the throat."

There was a look of satisfaction on her face at those words. She'd bested a bully.

"His buddies were quite surprised. Matt stumbled back clutching his throat and fell down onto his knees."

"Good for you."

"Then I round-house kicked him in the head."

I almost laughed. It wasn't funny, but I imagine he did *not* see that coming.

"I started screaming at the top of my lungs and the other two bolted, cowards." She had her hands clenched into fists, her whole body rigid. "I would have totally kicked their asses."

She trailed off, but I caught the mumbled word, "… pansies".

I grabbed her and pulled her into a hug. "I'm sorry," I said.

She remained tense for another few seconds, then melted into my arms.

"I'm sorry I wasn't there for you."

234

She pushed back, looking into my face. "I can take care of myself," she said, suddenly cold. "I don't need you to protect me."

Ice pick meet heart. I smiled despite the pain and nodded. "Apparently not. You've become quite the warrior."

The anger that had flashed onto her face fell aside and she quirked up one corner of her mouth. "Yeah, well. He was a jerk."

"Was he really hurt?"

"Just his pride," she said. "School expelled him, and he got community service for aggravated assault."

"What did you get?" I asked, half afraid.

She shrugged. "Grounded for a week and a lot of thanks from girls at school who never used to give me the time of day."

No telling how many girls the jerk had terrorized, or worse.

"He's lucky I didn't kill him," she said, watching her hands. "Lucky for me, too. I don't think I could live with myself if I'd killed him."

I didn't say anything to that, just sat there for another twenty minutes, holding hands and talking nonsense. I didn't want to think about who I'd killed.

"Speaking of warrior," Megan said, pointing to my bike. "Is that a sword?"

I looked over at the Ducati to where Gram was nestled along the side. "Oh, yeah," I said, grinning.

"Can I see it?"

I shrugged and got to my feet and walked over to the bike. "Sure." I flipped over the locks and pulled the scabbard and blade away, walked back over and sat down by Megan, holding the scabbard and blade to her.

"Careful," I said. "She's sharp."

Megan grabbed the handle and slid the blade half way out of the sheath. Far enough to see the first couple of runes along the fuller. "Wow," she said, looking up at me. "This is the real thing. Not for show?"

"Definitely not for show," I said, smiling at her. "She's the real deal."

"Why do you keep calling her she? Does she have a name?"

I held out my hands and she handed the sword to me, handle first. I stood, stepping away from her, and drew the blade free.

"She's Gram," I said, holding her in a fighting stance. I doubted the name would really mean anything to her.

"Like Fafnir's bane?" she asked.

I was surprised. "Good, yes. Like Fafnir's bane. Where did you hear that?"

"Wagner," she said, grinning. "We listened to a bit of it in school, so I read up a bunch. Dragons and gods and lightning and such."

I slipped Gram back into her sheath and sat down again, holding her across my lap. "World is full of crazy things," I said. "I like to have a little insurance, and I don't like guns."

She watched my face, studying me. "You were in that movie last year, right? The one where all those people died?"

"Not in," I said. "I'm the props manager. I deal with the equipment and such."

She just nodded, thinking. "Interesting." I could see wheels turning in her head. Did she suspect something?

We chitchatted about nothing for another ten minutes. Eventually Dennis got out of his car and called over to us. He could get her back to town and drop her off at the Tae Kwon Do school in time for our parents to pick her up, if they hurried. Save a lot of grief.

We said our goodbyes and I watched her get in his car and drive away. She was crying again, but the tears were mixed with her beautiful smile.

Why the hell had I stayed away so long. I'd missed a lot of really good years with that one. I was so proud of her.

She was facing her demons, not like me.

I gripped Gram, the pommel feeling natural in my palm. Some things could not be solved with hammer or sword. Sometimes the only way to win was to give up the fight.

All in all it was a fucking awesome visit. I just wish I could've shared it with Katie. Hell, I hadn't been out to Black Briar for a few days. It just made me feel so damned useless.

Powerless and useless. Not two of my favorite things.

But I'd go back out to Black Briar and visit Katie. It hurt to be that close to her and not be able to talk with her, to see her smile.

But I could be there for her all the same. Talk to her, tell her about stuff. Maybe it would bring her some peace?

FORTY-SIX

I took Jai Li out to Black Briar twice the next week. Nothing had really changed since Katie had gone into that seizure. The fact it happened around the time I was lost in the Sideways was no coincidence. I hated that I didn't know anyone who was an expert on this. Would have been nice to just sit down and ask questions. It reminded me that we were connected, at least. Maybe me, maybe the diary. But there was something there.

I also started jogging again. I needed the physical release, and my legs and lungs were damn unhappy with me for a while. After my run on Monday, I showered, grabbed some coffee, and took Jai Li to the park for a couple of hours. She was a fiend for the slides and the merry-go-round. I shouldn't have bothered to get up and jog that morning, I did enough running around in circles keeping that contraption spinning or running under her as I pushed her on the swing. She liked that the most, me pushing her so high she could see above the top of the swing set. Girl loved to be excited.

We had grilled cheese with roasted peppers and tomato soup with Edith once we got back to the farm. Julie was working a small farm out in Redmond and Mary was in town picking up some things from the Grange. She had three mares in foal, and Julie had two. There was much excitement around here on that subject. Jai Li was disappointed that the baby horses wouldn't be showing up until next March, but that's how horses were.

I completely missed the breeding part of the whole thing, but I've seen it before. There were no stallions on the farm as it was. Mary knew a woman she trusted who had a good breeding stallion. Jai Li missed all that as well. Edith thought she was too young to be watching such things. We agreed of course, but I doubt it would have mattered too much. Edith was a cranky old bird when she wanted to be. Good thing she loved Jai Li or I'd be concerned.

Lunch was pleasant enough, but my mind was elsewhere. I'd decided to head down to see Megan again, and I needed to get on the road down toward Mt. Rainier and Crescent Ridge.

I told Jai Li I was going to visit Megan and she wanted to go. I wasn't ready for that. If I wasn't taking Katie, I sure wasn't ready to take my foster daughter. Too much crazy there. We colored a while and read a few books before I had worked up enough courage to take off. I was taking the bike. Felt like the better option.

I wanted to feel the wind. I had this haunting memory of riding Meyja, the winged horse. And thinking of her made me think of Gunnr, the hot Valkyrie who I'd met a year ago. That was another pleasant, if guilty memory.

Jai Li conked out on the couch listening to Mozart and I boogied. Edith warned me to be careful and I was off. The bike was in the garage with the tractors. I kept her covered when I wasn't riding her. Kept the dust and such off. I made sure my hammers, energy bars, and water were in the saddlebags and slipped Gram into the rig on the side of the Ducati. I was ready for war. I just hoped it didn't come down to that. Things were quiet on that front and it made me nervous. I had a feeling like a storm was coming. There was trouble brewing, I just couldn't place it.

I pulled my helmet on as I straddled the bike. With a quick twist of the key and a likely unnecessary torque of the accelerator, I started the bike, letting it growl between my thighs. That was a moment of heaven.

I kept the throttle low until I got off the farm. Once I had the gate shut behind me and the open country road ahead of me, I opened that mother up and screamed down the asphalt. That was living. I loved how the adrenalin cranked through me as the speedometer spiked past seventy and headed upward past eighty to just above ninety before I backed off.

I stopped in Puyallup at a welding supply shop I'd read about—mom and pop outfit, but well stocked. I spent some time browsing the shelves. I needed to kill some time until the first classes at the Tae Kwon Do school.

Didn't want to get into town too early. Couldn't risk running into the folks at the grocery or something. Around three-thirty I got back on the bike. I had three brochures for various pieces of welding gear in my saddlebags and a nice warm "thanks for coming" to speed me on my way. I needed to expand my tool kit. Welding was something I was okay at. Practicing it would be a good idea. These folks were nice enough to give my money to, I'd definitely be back.

I got into Crescent Ridge fifteen minutes early, so I sat in the parking lot in the back by the Dairy Queen and waited for the Tae Kwon Do school to open. The school parking lot turned into a circus as dozens of cars cruised around—parents dropping off their kids mostly. I lost count of the cars and didn't always have a clear view of the doors, so I didn't see Megan show up. More the better, means I didn't risk seeing da either.

The school was doing a good business. There were at least two different classes going on at all times, and by the look of the parent-parade, they would be pretty full.

Megan was supposed to teach today, so I was hoping to catch her. I walked into my old dojang at straight up four-thirty. Sa Bum Nim Choi, the chief instructor was leading a class of young kids, six to eleven year olds and didn't notice that I entered. I remembered that class from when I taught. Not the same kids, though I was pretty sure I would run into some I knew if I hung out long enough. They'd be a lot older now.

"Good evening," a male voiced said through my haze of memory.

I looked over to see this young boy, fifteenish, sitting at the front desk manning the phones. "Anything I can help you with?"

God he was young. But the black on his belt let me know he knew his stuff. Sa Bum Nim Choi didn't promote you unless you were damn good and ready to move up.

"Mind if I watch the class?"

He shrugged and turned his attention back to the computer on the desk. At least his return to being a bored teenager wasn't that far from the surface.

I slipped out of my boots, bowed past the desk, and crept down the aisle between the wall and the railing, along the long row of benches. Butterflies battled in my abdomen, and the runes on my calf itched. I was totally wired to run. Being back in the school after all these years was nerve-wracking. I had a lot of history here, so much respect and reverence. Yet another place I missed.

I sat on the bench, cross-legged, and watched the kids go through their forms. My muscles ached to be out there. After a few minutes, Sa Bum Nim Choi noticed me and paused in her counting. The class faltered and turned around to follow her open-mouthed stare. The old woman didn't move for a full thirty seconds, then clapped her hands, calling her assistant instructor over to lead the children through their first Ki Bone.

"Ms. Beauhall," Sa Bum Nim said, her voice as thin as her lips. That was not the face of joy.

I stood quickly and bowed. "Sa Bum Nim. How are you?"

She looked me up and down, starting and ending at my hair.

"I see you have taken on a new look since I saw you last."

Damn, it was like I was fifteen all over again, being tested for a belt.

"Times change, people change." Not my wittiest, but the woman made my brain freeze up.

She walked toward the front of the school and bowed off the floor, then she came and sat beside me, watching her class. "You have been missed in this school."

We watched the class for a few minutes in silence.

"Where's Megan?" I asked.

She turned her head to look at me. I never realized how old she was. The lines around her eyes and mouth spoke of more years than I was prepared to ever see. The face was kind, that much I remembered. Firm and supportive.

"Ms. Beauhall, the younger, has called in sick once again," she said, the ice in her voice a familiar enough sound. "I fear she has not been keeping up her obligations as of late."

That was odd. Megan adored this school and that boy who'd given her a ride home said she was well thought of here. Her home away from home. Why was she ditching? Unless she was really sick or something?

"What happened to her?" I asked, my heart leaping into my throat. "She's not hurt or anything, is she?"

Choi shrugged her thin, bony shoulders. "Not to my knowledge. Your mother stopped in this afternoon to pay her tuition and she seemed to be unconcerned."

Ditching then. That was totally uncool. I never ditched teaching. "Must be something pretty bad if she's called in sick," I said, hoping she'd agree.

She didn't. "Megan has struggled more than usual these last few months. Her behavior has grown more erratic and her temper has become a bit of a problem."

"Worse than me?" I asked.

She studied me for a moment and patted me on the arm. "Sarah, you always put the training first and foremost in your life. Even when you warred with your father, you did not allow that to interfere with your responsibilities."

So, Megan was distancing herself from the school.

"I was hoping to see her tonight. I saw her last week, did she tell you?"

"Oh, yes." She got up, stepped to the rail and corrected two of the students, showing them the correct hand position for the form basic they were practicing.

"I really need to get back to my class," she said, shooing the children back to their group. "With Megan skipping out tonight, I'm down an assistant."

"Sure," I said, shrugging. "Thanks for talking to me."

I stood, but Sa Bum Nim took me by the elbow and followed me to the front of the school. "Sarah, I worry about you. There are things in the news, rumors of dangerous people, and now I see you ride a motorcycle." She pointed to the helmet I'd left on the seats by the front door with my boots. "Your behavior is reckless. Are you doing okay?"

I loved this woman, trusted her with every fiber of my being. But how did you tell your old Tae Kwon Do instructor you killed a dragon? Would she really understand? There had been nothing I couldn't tell her when I was growing up.

"You should come back to the floor," she said, patting me on the arm. "You could do with a bit of discipline in your life. An hour or two a week where the mind settled and the body relaxed into the flow of the form."

I started to say something, but I couldn't find the words. Crescent Ridge was over an hour from home, and further if we moved north.

"I can't," I started, but she shook her head and smiled.

"You left me once already, I don't need to relive those moments."

I felt the heat flashing up my neck and across my face. I hated leaving here, this was the one safe place when home was unbearable.

"Megan will follow you sooner than we all expected," she said. "You need to speak with her, go see your family."

I shrugged, fighting with the words that stuck in my throat. I couldn't, and she knew it. Knew the things I fled from.

"He's a good man," she said, stepping away from me. "He is frightened and lonely. You do not know how deeply he grieves for your distance."

Did she talk to da? They never did when I lived at home. Or did she?

"Your mother told me that you have some nice friends in your life, and that you are seeing someone."

"Yeah," I said, a small smile breaking some of the ice in my throat. "Katie. She's the best."

"I would wish no less for you." She stepped forward and hugged me. The action was so quick, I barely had time to squeeze her back before she was bowing back onto the floor.

"Holy crap," the fifteen year old said from behind the desk. "Who are you?"

I glanced back at him, shrugging.

"No one," I said, sitting down to put on my boots. "I trained here a long time ago."

He tapped on the computer a bit then looked up at me, startled. "You're Megan's sister, right?"

I nodded, tying my Docs as fast as I could. I needed to get out of there.

"Damn," he breathed, looking at me with a totally different gleam in his eye. "You're Sarah Beauhall. Did you know we use your creative form from your black belt test as one of our regular forms now?"

I looked up quickly. "No, seriously?" That was news.

"Sa Bum Nim added it last spring," he was looking at me like I had two heads. "First time in the school history they added a new form. I had to learn it for my belt." He stood, stepped around the desk and held up the loose ends of his belt. "First degree requires that form in addition to the normal stuff."

I looked out on the floor, and Choi was demonstrating the proper foot position for a front kick to several students. She honored me way beyond anything I'd ever imagined.

"What did she call the form?" I asked, remembering I'd called it something like *Angry Woman* form. Choi hadn't liked that name, said while it fitted the student, it was not in keeping with the school's goals.

"Dragon Warrior," he said

I nearly dropped my helmet. "Seriously?"

"Totally," he said, holding out his hand. "Megan is awesome," he smiled, a little color flushing across his cheeks. "I wish I was as good as her."

"She's a good kid," I said, shaking his hand.

"I'll tell her you came by," he said. "Sorry she's sick. If you swing by the house, tell her that Josh was asking about her. I'm covering her five-thirty class tonight since she's sick."

"Yeah, absolutely."

I found myself out in the parking lot, putting on my helmet, and starting up the bike. She used my form. And Megan was ditching. No wonder she was competing against me or worse the memory of me. I was a shadow she had to live under here. That had to totally suck.

I started the bike and cruised down toward our house. I almost turned into the court, but da's truck was in the driveway.

Not today.

But soon. I had to face him. I know I was being a coward, but inside I was a scared kid. I hated that. I cruised out of town, making sure to keep the bike under the speed limit. Didn't want any trouble here.

I stopped near the cutoff to Mt. Rainier and got off the bike, leaving the helmet on the seat, and walked off the breakdown lane into the chest high scrub that lined the road. Once I was through the bracken, I had a clear view of Rainier looming above me, stark and imposing. You could see the bones of the earth here, ragged mountains peaks and miles of deep green forest. I especially loved the way those colors crossed into the deep blue of the sky.

Not like Kansas when I was a kid. There the sky seemed to go on forever. It was so large, it seemed to swallow the ground whole. I used to think if I went far enough in any direction that the world would just cease to exist, like I'd walked off the edge of a painting or something.

Now with all I knew about the world, I couldn't help but imagine loud hungry things living in those mountains. Maybe Katie was right. Maybe Tolkien's work was more history than fiction. If it were me, I'd rather hang out with the hobbits than the goblins any day.

I stood there, letting the cool of the early evening soak into me, letting the sun fall toward dusk. There was something in the air, a smell maybe. More the memory of a smell I think. I thought back to the way Katie smelled and how much it excited me. How Jai Li smelled and how it made my belly hurt in a way I'd never expected.

Then I thought of the dragon fire, the giants and the trolls. The memory of their smells triggered different feelings. Part of me wanted to hide, to run away and crawl in a hole, but another part of me, that part that set aside the fear and did what needed doing. That part of me purred a little. Thinking about the sharp scent of blood and the acrid stench of burning tickled the lizard brain. That set the adrenaline to running and the endorphins to kick in. Then I was ready to charge forward toward the chaos, a war cry on my lips and Gram in my fist.

I walked back to the bike, my shoulders aching from the tension in them. I stretched a bit, swinging my arms in wide circles and twisting my torso from side-to-side.

I leaned against my bike and closed my eyes and thought long and hard about who I'd become.

And that woman—killer of dragons and trolls, giants and necromancers—was a child still, afraid to face her parents, afraid to go to her sister and make amends for seven years of abandonment.

That smell I was used to. That was the smell of shame and defeat.

FORTY-SEVEN

I was pulling through Kent when I decided to stop by the apartment on a whim. I wanted to grab the mail, see how things were. I parked on the street on the rare occasion that there was actually a space. Wasn't much of one, but I could slide the bike in. The huge ass pickup that was taking one and a half space wouldn't mind. I grabbed Gram, slung her over my shoulder in her normal and natural position, grabbed my saddlebags and helmet and headed into the building

Going into the vestibule was strange. There was a note from the super that said we had a new neighbor, and that she'd been complaining about the noise, could we stop by and check on things. He knew that Katie had been in the hospital, so he wasn't being weird. At least I didn't think so until I got to the top of the stairs.

The door to our apartment had a great white cross painted on it. All along the doorjamb there were burned out candles, at least a dozen. Two were actually still burning. What the fuck? I had my keys out and was going to unlock the door when I noticed someone had jammed a key in the lock and broken it off. Damn it. It would take a locksmith to get that out, or I could break the door down. And that was a heavy-duty door. We'd had them replaced last year after I kicked it in looking for Katie before I found out the dragon had kidnapped her.

I must've sworn out loud because some mousy gal poked her head out of the apartment across the hall and looked around. So, this was the new neighbor? We'd been neighbor free the entire time I'd known Katie.

"You new here?" I asked, leaning against the wall. I was pissed, but I was learning it's better not to yell at strangers.

"I've been here a few days," she said. She wasn't very pretty, with lank, greasy hair and eyes that flitted everywhere but on me when she spoke. Nervous sort.

"Well, welcome to the neighborhood. I'm Sarah." I stepped over to her to shake her hand, but she backed up, pulling the door mostly closed and peeked out the crack.

"The super said that a girl named Katie lived there," she said, talking louder than was normal for the situation. "I've called him several times. There are weird noises coming from inside."

I looked back at the door. "Did you paint the cross?"

She gave a curt nod.

"And the candles?"

"Protection," she said, quietly. "I can feel something inside there. It's hungry. I can feel it through the wall in my bedroom. Like it wants to come and get me."

Girl was smoking something righteous, that's all I could figure. I wasn't comfortable with that thought. I couldn't bring Jai Li back here if the neighbor was unstable.

"Do you have a cross and all in your bedroom then?"

She grasped the cross around her neck and nodded, this time slowly. "I pray every night and every morning, but sometimes I hear a man calling, or a boy, I can't tell."

"A television, maybe?"

She shook her head. "No, not a television. Something evil is hunting him, something he's hiding from."

Well, some people thought television was evil. I wasn't very fond of it.

"So, you're not Katie?" she asked.

"No, I'm Sarah and I live with Katie."

"Roommates?" the girl asked, looking at the floor.

I was getting annoyed. "Lovers, actually."

She winced when I said that. It felt good to say it out loud.

"Yeah we can get a little loud, you know, with all the sex." She was pissing me off. "Is that what you heard?" Of course, if it was, who was having sex here? I haven't been here with Katie for a couple of months.

She winced again and shuddered. "Abomination," she said, quietly this time, not talking to me or anyone else. I knew the words, knew the look. Here was one of those people from my prior life. It had been a while since I'd encountered it. It took me by surprise.

She shut the door and locked it. I heard her throw a dead bolt and put on the chain. Anger and shame rushed up through my abdomen, but I tamped them both down. Now was not the time. The runes on my calf flared to life, and the ones on my scalp remained cold and dormant. I tried to breathe through it, but I kept seeing those people from my past, my da, the churchie people, and all the rest of the close-minded idiots.

I punched the wall.

Felt good, damn it. I still had on my riding gloves, so I didn't scrape up my knuckles when I went through the cheap paneling. Fortunately there was only about four inches of space before I encountered cinder block, and I was up to my wrist in splinters. I let out my breath and carefully pushed the splinters aside, widening the hole, so I could pull my hand out of the wall. That was awkward, but worked to let the final juice run out of me, leaving me frustrated and a little hurt. Lucky I didn't break my wrist, or at least a few knuckles.

I went down the stairs and out the door, fuming. Elmer's Gun and Knife Emporium was still open, and there were a couple of high school age kids inside looking at swords.

I went inside and walked up to the counter. Elmer was an old guy, older than da even—late fifties. He looked like someone's grandpa: nice as could be, clean shaven, short hair, soft eyes. No one would peg him as a merchant of death. He preferred purveyor of home protection. I guess it depended on your politics. He kept spare keys and such to the apartments above, worked a deal with the super. I didn't need a key, though. I needed a locksmith, or a crowbar.

"Hey, Elmer," I called as I crossed the store. He looked over at me and smiled.

"Afternoon, Sarah." Elmer liked me. He sold a few knives for me on consignment. Pretty pricey stuff for him, after the markup and all, but he had some high-end clientele. Knew the value of a good blade. "What's up?"

"Crazy neighbor upstairs has painted a cross on our door, burned a couple dozen candles to the stubs all along the floor and wedged a key in the lock."

"Huh," he said, stepping back in front of the high schoolers who were debating on pulling a samurai sword from its sheath. "Don't even think about it," he said, placing his hand on the wooden and lacquered scabbard. That was a handmade dealio. I'd had a look at it once at Elmer's insistence. Good folded steel, not anything like I did. Not my style of blade. Nice, though.

The kids shuffled away, more interested in fantasizing about sword battles than ponying up the twelve hundred dollars for that blade.

Once the testosterone machines had gone outside, Elmer put the sword back in the case and nodded his head in my direction. "You driving that fancy motor bike out yonder?"

I glanced out his windows and looked at the Ducati. "Oh, yeah. Sweet ride."

"She's a damned fine machine," he said, smiling.

"You heard anything funny?" I asked. "Upstairs, I mean."

"Beside miss crazy neighbor, you mean?"

I nodded. "Yeah. She claims to hear things from inside the apartment."

"One of you girls leave a television on or something?"

My last trip I'd rushed out pretty damned fast, after Megan's call. But did I have the television on? Maybe the radio? "Probably it," I said to him. "I'll call a locksmith and get things under control."

"Let me know if you need anything," he said as I headed to the door. "Oh, I could use a couple more of those Elvish short swords you make. Had a run on them lately. Sold the last three I had."

Nice, that would be some nice scratch rolling in. "I'll get some out to you next week." I promised. "We can settle up on money then, okay?"

He waved, and I pushed back out into the great outdoors, fishing my cell phone out of my jacket.

Television made more sense than crazy neighbor hearing voices in our place. Of course, there was the possibility that she'd heard Gletts. He'd called to me through the mirror once upon a time, and I hadn't seen him since Julie pulled me out of the Sideways. And the wall between our bedroom and the mirror opposite the room in the neighbor's place had an old doorway to the Sideways. I'd almost been sucked in once. Maybe that's what she was sensing.

Oh, crap. The book and the shield were both in the apartment. Would they be part of the problem? I jogged up the stairs to the hallway between our apartments and pulled Gram from her sheath holding her in front of the apartment door.

The sword jerked forward, nearly striking the door. I pulled it back at the last second, stopping the blade from smashing into the metal plate.

Maybe I should get some professional help. Of course, Qindra was probably tired of me calling her all the time. Last time a book had almost killed her. The time before that she'd gotten locked inside the house out in Chumstick battling ghosties. But she was the resident expert on weird shit. I was obligated to call her. Right?

She answered on the first ring with a sigh in her voice. "You never call for pleasure. What can I help you with this time?"

I filled her in on the weirdness.

"You want me to come out and open the apartment?" she asked.

"I have a bad feeling about this," I said. "Wouldn't you rather be on the scene for once when I was going to start something?"

Qindra sighed heavily. "You are a piece of work, Sarah Beauhall."

I knew I had her.

"I take the shield with me when I leave," she said, exasperated. "And anything else dangerous we find."

Yikes, didn't see that coming. But still, would be good to know what the hell that shield was capable of. "Yeah, okay. Whatever makes sense. Could you hurry?"

"Sarah, you are definitely a magnet for the strange and dangerous. Hang loose, I'll be right over."

Now all I had to do was wait. I walked across the street to Frank's place, a dive watering hole Katie and I drank at sometimes. Mainly served neighborhood regulars. Frank hadn't worked there in years. His son, Bobby Joe, ran the place and he watered down the drinks for most folks. Not me or Katie, though. I think the old dude had a crush on Katie. It was early, so I got a rum and coke, sat at the bar with a view outside and waited.

Katie was going to be pissed if something bad had gone down in our apartment. You know, something else. Crap ...

FORTY-EIGHT

Qindra showed up thirty minutes later. I think she had one of those clicky things the fire department used to switch lights all red except for her. She denied it, but there was no way anyone else got through Seattle traffic that efficiently. Unless, maybe her Miata has been enchanted or something. That would be great for the Ducati. Maybe I'd broach the subject for my birthday or something.

She climbed out of her Miata, leaving it parked in front of Elmer's behind my bike. The pickup truck was long gone.

"Shall we?" Qindra asked as I joined her at the curb.

"Neighbor is still home," I warned as we crossed the street. "Real jumpy sort."

"Don't worry about her," she assured me. "I'll give her some peace."

We went up the stairs and looked around. The place looked just like I'd left it, only the candles in front of our door had burned out.

"Early American Séance?" she asked with a wry grin.

"Whatever. Crazy religious person is the best I got."

Qindra knocked on the neighbor's door, but no one answered. She pulled out her wand, cast a few squiggles in the air and shrugged. "She's inside, scared, but unharmed."

"Can you show me how to do that?" I asked.

"No."

That was blunt. At least she was smiling when she said it.

She walked back toward our door, stopped at the hole in the wall, and looked back at me. "Your work?"

"Oh, yeah," I admitted.

She just shook her head at me and went to our door. More squiggles glowed in the air as she examined things. "Nothing magical here," she said with a shrug. She tapped the lock and the broken key leapt out and clattered to the floor. She tapped the lock a second time and the door swung open.

Now, I am by no means a good housekeeper. I kill houseplants, goldfish, and anything else that can't fend for itself due to absent mindedness and neglect. I do not pick up my underwear nor my socks. I have been known to leave a gallon of milk on the counter for a week or more and never, ever do I dust or do windows.

All that crossed my mind as the door swung open.

Everything we had in the apartment was gone. I had a moment of panic thinking about the book and shield I had stashed in the bedroom. What the hell had happened?

It's not that the apartment was empty. There was just nothing mundane there. The walls had shiny white spaces where Katie's pictures had once hung. The floors were completely bare, cabinets were devoid of contents and even doors. But more than that, everything glowed like phosphorescent white porcelain. It was creepy. Starting just inside the doorway crystal formations covered every flat surface, oozing out of the gaping cabinets, pooling into stalagmites all around the kitchen and along the bar. Great webs of crystals covered the windows and hung down from the corners of the room.

"This is new, I take it?" Qindra asked as she stepped toward the door.

"Wait!" I shouted, reaching for her, my hand landing on her shoulder at the same time her foot crossed the threshold, breaking the plane between outside and in. A wave of dizziness washed over us both. Qindra stumbled, breaking my contact, but pulling me into the room. I recognized this stomach churning sensation. I'd felt it the last time I'd been plunged into the Sideways. Of course, then I was astral, out-of-body. This was lighter, somehow, but just as disorienting.

"That's strange," Qindra said, turning toward me, her wand in front of her face.

That's when the feeder dropped from the ceiling, knocking her to the floor.

It looked like a giant spider, with thick glassine spines and a myriad of glowing eyes. I lunged forward and caught the huge creepy with a crunching crescent kick to its body. Glass shards scattered across the floor as the nasty thing flew off of Qindra and shattered two crystalline formations near the bar before slamming into the wall. He was a big sucker, but didn't have much mass. I slid the sheath across my body, pulling Gram free with one practiced motion. I crossed the room and sliced through the creature's abdomen. It squealed and kicked as it parted into two twitching pieces.

I glanced up to make sure there were no more bitey things on the ceiling and stepped back to Qindra, my free hand out to her. The feeder had stabbed Qindra with its stinger, gouging a long gash across her left arm.

"Oh, damn," Qindra said, staggering to her feet. "Was that poisonous?"

The way it was bleeding, I doubted any poison was going to get into her system, but I didn't know. "Can you stop the bleeding?" I asked, scanning the apartment for more surprises.

"Yeah, hang on." She picked her wand up off the floor and waved it over her arm. At first nothing happened. "What in the name of the seven hells?" she gasped.

Uh oh. "That's not good."

She looked up at me, panic flickering over her face. "Not good at all," she said, the color draining from her. "Let's try that again." This time she really concentrated. She held the wand so tightly, her knuckles went white. There was a moment of straining on her face, as if she were lifting something heavy. Finally three yellow sparks shot from the wand and faint blue and green lights appeared, forming a lovely little rune above her arm. In just a few short seconds, the bleeding had stopped and the wound was closed like it was a couple of days old. "Why is this so hard?" she asked, breathless. "It will leave a scar, but I won't bleed to death."

That was encouraging, but I didn't like the whole magic-won't-work-right thing she had going there. Reminded me too much of how guns and things stopped working around too much magic.

"I guess the neighbor isn't totally crazy," I said.

"Sarah!" Qindra barked, pointing past me. I whirled and caught a second biter in mid-flight. This one had more than eight legs and resembled more of a millipede than an arachnid. Either way, it didn't like Gram at all. It stank of rotted meat and something I couldn't identify, but it was sharp, acrid. I backed away and hacked it a couple more times for good measure. It had mandibles the size of garden shears.

Qindra swirled her wand and a stuttering yellow stream flew across the room toward the bedroom where the second critter had emerged. The light struck it and it screamed, but it didn't slow down. This one looked more a dung beetle with a large, hard shell. I stepped in front of Qindra, avoiding a large and very sharp looking crystalline formation, and stabbed forward, shearing off one long, spiny leg. The damn thing was fast. It shifted, reared back, and sprayed a cloud of purple fog. I staggered back, coughing, swinging Gram in front of me as my vision blurred.

"Down," Qindra shouted. I ducked behind the counter that was to my right, and the crystal beside the beetle exploded, showering the room with shrapnel.

The beetle screamed as it fell back on its shell. I could make it out enough to roll forward and stab its lightly armored underbelly. Gram sliced through the chitin with a crunch and black blood spewed across the floor.

"Damn it," Qindra said behind me, her voice full of pain. I whirled and saw that two long shards of crystal jutting out of her chest. One had impaled her right breast, the second just below her ribs. She'd been turned with her right side exposed.

The counter had protected me from the blast.

"We need to get you out of here," I said, wiping at my burning eyes.

"NO!" she said, leaning back against the wall by the door. "We need to get in there and close that breach."

"Breach?" I asked, looking back. "The doorway you think?"

She grunted, but nodded. "Pull these out, will you?"

She had her wand poised and I stepped over to her, I was glad I still had my gloves on. The crystal was cold, colder than ice. The areas around the wound weren't bleeding, but they were black. I adjusted my grip on the first shard and pulled.

Qindra gasped as the crystal came out slowly, shredding the blackened flesh around the edges of the wound and allowing a quick welling of blood to come to the surface. I threw the crystal back against the counter where it shattered.

"Hurry," she said, her voice strained and breathy. I glanced over my shoulder, making sure nothing else was coming out of the bedroom.

The second shard was smaller. I could only get one hand on it, but it came out much quicker. She settled down onto the ground, sliding down the wall as her legs gave way. I caught her, slowing her fall.

"Keep watch," she said, raising her wand.

I glanced at the bedroom and then over at the doorway out of the apartment. The door was no longer there.

"The door?" I started, but she shook her head at me.

"I know, let me concentrate, please."

The wand sputtered and small flashes of red and blue flew from the wand.

"Not strong enough," she whispered. I knelt down beside her, pulled the glove off my right hand and closed it over hers. I'd used Gram to channel away the excess energy when I opened Katie's book, maybe I could reverse that and flow some of my chi, or whatever, into Qindra.

I held Gram tightly and concentrated on the way my body felt. I willed power to flow forward into Qindra. The runes across my scalp flared bright enough to cast a red glow on Qindra's face. She didn't seem to notice.

At first nothing happened. I concentrated, imagining a tap opening inside me, pulling magic from Gram, letting it flow through my hand and into Qindra.

A fat blob of blue goo burped out of the tip of her wand and blue light sprang forth. The blob fell onto the porcelain colored floor and sputtered like a bit of fat on a hot griddle.

Qindra bathed the blackened wounds in the light from the wand, and the skin closed, returning to a color more resembling the flesh of her belly.

I held her hand long enough for her to close both wounds. When I let go the energy from the wand waned, but didn't sputter out like before.

I knelt down, placed my naked hand on the sputtering blob of magic goo, and it leapt upward against my palm, vanishing into my skin. The oddest prickling sensation ran up my arm and into my head. For a second the runes on my forehead felt like ice instead of forge fire, but the sensation was not unpleasant.

"That was surreal," I said, standing. I pulled my glove back on and turned to watch the door to our old bedroom. Katie was going to freak.

"That threshold was trapped," Qindra said. "It bollixed up my magic in a way I've never encountered before. It was almost as if I were constipated."

Great, I thought. Magic is like taking a dump. Nice to know.

"Are you okay?" I asked, helping her to her feet.

"Sore and weak," she said, smiling at me. "But we must see to the rest of this apartment and close the breach. This cannot be allowed to spread."

My adrenaline was definitely in high gear at this point. The runes on my leg had me dancing from foot to foot, anxious for the next foe.

Qindra raised her wand and a stream of yellow sparks shot across the room. For a minute they seemed to punch a hole through the wall, then I realized it was just allowing us to look through the wall. Handy trick.

"There's a nest in the bedroom," she said. "There is something alive in there, as well as one or more items of power. Anything I should know before we go?"

"The book's in there," I said, remembering I'd stashed it in the bottom of the closet under a pile of winter boots.

"The Book?" she asked me, shock painted on her face. "You said you buried it somewhere."

I shrugged. "I didn't say in the earth. I buried it under a pile of old boots and coats."

"Unbelievable," she said, letting the yellow streamers fall away and sending green globules against the bedroom wall like paint pellets.

"There's also a weak barrier to the Sideways," I added, thinking. "A mirror and ... oh, and the shield."

"Great," Qindra growled. "You go first. We have to clean that mess out and see what's left of the room."

She was good with that wand, now that it was operating, even at partial force—used it like a popgun. There were several more feeders of various shapes and leg configurations in the room. I got most of them, but Qindra brought down two on her own. I have no idea what spell she was using, but when the pretty lights struck the feeder, one melted and one burst into flames. Green flames that didn't seem to burn anything other than the creepy.

Once we had killed everything that wanted to eat us I stood in the middle of what used to be a bedroom and examined the situation. There was definitely a nest here and an opening to the Sideways. The wall between our apartments was more of a gaping crack into a land of glass shards and fluorescent skies. Crystals spread all over the room reminding me of the melted candles on our threshold.

"This I can fix," she said, standing in front of the wall and weaving a net of energy across the opening. I watched her as the critters and the webbing and such in the room began to melt away. Without the connection to the Sideways, they had no real place in this world.

Qindra looked like she was patching the wall with fiberglass like da used to do on our old beater cars. A mesh of energy went over the hole first, then a wide swath of various colored light melted it all together. The more layers she put over the hole between worlds, the stronger her magic grew. By the time the room was clear of debris, the wall was completely whole once again and her power was back to full force. She took a few moments to tend to her previous wounds and helped with a couple of small cuts and bruises I'd gotten in the purging.

Once the mess cleared, three items remained. The shield, the book, and the mirror.

"They took everything else to the other side?" Qindra asked. "How strange. But they left two powerful magical items?"

I had no idea what feeders collected or not. "Maybe they couldn't touch the book. You couldn't."

"True. Or maybe they didn't think of it as an item of power. I've never understood this Sideways as you called it."

"Something you don't know about?" I asked, honestly perplexed. "Seriously?"

Qindra shrugged and pushed the mirror with the toe of her fancy black wedges. "Getting something odd about that mirror," she said, glancing up at me. "Something you need to tell me?"

"No," I said, squatting down and glancing at my own reflection. "Maybe something happened to it while this place was open to the Sideways."

"Maybe." She did a bit of fiddling, testing out various spells, and nothing seemed to please her. "Can you pick up the book?" she asked.

I grabbed the thing without hesitating, and she stepped back from me.

"Okay, good enough. And the shield?"

I held the book between my knees long enough to re-sheath Gram, scooped the shield up off the floor and grabbed the book in my left hand.

For some reason they felt equal. They both had a strong, nearly sentient feeling of protection. The book scared the hell out of me, but the shield had been mine.

"You getting the mirror?" I asked.

She glanced around the room one last time. The porcelain sheen to everything had finally dispersed. She knelt, picked the mirror up and stood, holding it out in front of her, looking at her own reflection. Her clothing was torn and bloodstained, and her hair was not its usual coifed perfection. She was pretty damned sexy in a disheveled badass sort of way.

"I'm taking the shield when I leave," she said, walking to the door to the rest of the apartment. "I'm thinking you should keep the mirror," she offered, setting it on the crystal-free bar top.

I nodded without really thinking anything about her comment. She tapped me on the shoulder as I stepped past her, and she turned me to look at the mirror. In the bottom corner there were several words scratched into the reflective surface of the glass.

,haraS
?uoy era erehw
.deracs m'I
.emoh yaw ym dnif t'nac I

Oh, damn! "Katie?"

Qindra looked up. "She was here? Looking out through this mirror?" she asked.

"Is that why I keep being drawn back here?" I asked, running my hand over the mirror. "I'll need to figure out where this place is in context to the Sideways," I said, glancing up at Qindra. "And we just sealed a breach. Maybe it opened because of her trying to find her way home."

"But her body isn't here," Qindra said, as if it were the most obvious thing in the world. "Even if she could come through, she has no place to go into."

Before I could answer two things happened. A screeching came from the hallway, the high-pitched squall of a woman in danger, and Skella appeared in the mirror.

"Sarah?" Skella asked, her face streaked with tears. Her eyes were red and puffy, and for the first time since I'd known her, there was no hint of make-up on her face.

"I got this," Qindra said, stepping to the door that had reappeared with the closing of the Sideways.

I nodded at her and turned back to the mirror. "Hey, Kiddo. What's up?"

A sob caught in Skella's throat. "It's Gletts," she said, scrubbing his face. "He woke up today."

I glanced down at the words scratched into the mirror. "Holy cats, really?" the little pisher. He'd been gone for weeks now. I thought I'd lost him in the Sideways. "That's great news," I offered, grinning. "Is he going to be okay?"

"Sarah?" Qindra called from the hallway. "I need—"

"Smith?" a male voice called. "Is she here?"

"—you out here."

"What's that?" Skella asked, looking past her fingers.

"No idea," I said. "Maybe you should pop over here. I gotta check on ..."

"Sarah?" Qindra's voice was loud and an octave higher than normal. Not a good sign.

"Hang on," I said to Skella, holding Gram up to the mirror. "Trouble."

She nodded at me, and I bolted for the door. Another scream rattled the apartment as I careened around the doorframe, nearly smashing into Qindra.

In the hallway, the chick from next door was pinned against the wall at the head of the stairs by a crazed homeless man. He was dressed in a mishmash of ragged clothing and a long grey overcoat. His head was a shaggy mess of grey hair and he had a wild beard halfway down his chest. He had the girl pinned against the wall with a long staff.

This wasn't Joe, the homeless guy who was also Odin. No, this was another in his place, a mummer like I'd seen before, a puppet dancing to the strings of the mad god. "Calm down," I said, stepping past Qindra who had her wand raised. "What's the problem here?"

The old man turned his head toward me, and I saw the glint in his eyes, the frigid blue and the light of worlds.

"Smith?" the man asked me, his swollen lips pulled back from his broken teeth.

"I'm here," I said, stepping forward. "Let the girl go."

"This whore?" he said, grinning. "She defiles this holy place."

Holy place? What the hell was he talking about? "She can't breathe," I said, noticing how purple she was getting. "Will killing her help you deliver your message?" I reached forward with my right hand, placing it on his where he held one end of his stave. At my touch he stepped back, letting the girl fall to the ground along with his cane. He grabbed my hand in both of his, turning to face me, massaging my hand with his.

"Dragon fire," he whispered, turning my wrist, looking at the palm. "I can feel the taint. Yet the flesh is whole."

"You're welcome," Qindra said, squinting at me before stepping past us to check on the girl who lay on the floor, gasping.

"Yeah, thanks," I said, as she knelt, passing the wand over the stricken woman. Qindra had helped heal me after my hand had been maimed by dragon fire.

"Blackened flesh, white bones, and the smell of burnt meat," the old man said, his voice husky, his eyes brimming with tears. "Is it truly you, dragon slayer?"

I pulled my hand from his and stepped back. "Yeah, that's me. Who are you?"

He looked at me, quizzically. "The shriven king bids you listen," he said, a glint of the madness in his eyes. "Let the world tremble at his words."

Qindra looked up at me with one of those incredulous looks.

"I know you are here, witch," the man said, his voice suddenly a richer timbre, the words smoother and clipped with a rough accent. "Tell your mistress her sins are unanswered and the time of her reckoning is coming."

Instead of righteous indignation, Qindra lowered her gaze and bowed her head. "I will share your words, o' king of old."

The old man chuckled and turned back to face me, his shoulders back, and his head high. "Listen to my words, heed my warning. Worlds are breached."

He held his hand out, palm down, and his staff flew up into his hands. "The well has returned. The hidden bridge fills the sky once more."

Well? Bridge? Did he mean the rainbow bridge? The one that Heimdall had shattered the day the dragons destroyed the gods?

"What bridge?" I asked, feeling the amulet on my chest throbbing in time with the runes on my scalp and calf.

"The secret way," he said, lowering his voice. "A winding track back to the golden throne." His face shone with victory and zealotry. "A way home."

I stared into his eyes as a vision exploded in my mind.

I stood on a field of bones before a great burning city. The old man stood at my side, taller, grander, but broken all the same. On the far hill, atop a golden longhouse, a great white dragon perched, sending gouts of flame roaring into the sky. I'd had a dream like that once, of Frederick Sawyer attacking a dwarven village, but this was older. This was a vision of the sacking of Asgard. The flames roared in my ears as the dragon beat her wings, fanning the fires to greater heights.

"Nidhogg," I breathed.

The old man blinked, coughing. "Carrion eater," he spat. "Filth and shame."

"Sarah!" Qindra broke in, shattering the vision. "This girl needs an ambulance. I am too weak to do what must be done."

Ambulance, right. I reached for my cell phone and found I had Gram in my fist, the old man stood before me grinning.

"You must slay the Corpse Gnawer," he said, poking me with his cane. "The wheel must spin, the cogs must grind forward once more."

"Sarah, now!" Qindra barked. Her voice was full of a strange new sound. Was it fear?

I shook my head, breaking eye contact with the old man, who turned and stumbled down the stairs toward the street. I sheathed Gram again and pulled out my cell phone. The girl was breathing, but I could tell she was hurt by the way she whimpered.

The vision faded from my mind slowly, like an afterimage. Kill Nidhogg? Could I do that? Should I?

I called 911 and sat down in the hallway, watching Qindra soothing the young woman, my mind a whirl of flames and smoke.

In the distance the long warble of the approaching ambulance echoed up the staircase, and I thought of a lonely god, lamenting his fallen. The homeless man collapsed before the ambulance arrived, burned out by the possession of the mad god.

FORTY-NINE

After the ambulance left, Qindra and I walked across the street to Frank's and both had a very stiff drink. We sat in the back and studied the bottoms of our shot glasses for a long time.

"Was that truly him?" she asked, her voice as soft as a breeze.

I nodded. "Well, sort of. A proxy, one of those who channel him, carry his voice."

"And this has happened before?"

I thought back to the young man who had the basset hound, and of course, Joe, the homeless guy that could very well be Odin. If not, he'd been channeling the old dead god for so long, he'd started to look like him. He also didn't die from the experience. Three data points there. Something to consider, I supposed.

"Yes," I said, letting my shoulders sag. "More than once. Odin himself. Are you surprised?"

She waved at the bartender who brought us fresh drinks. "No," she said, seeming to try on the word for the first time. "My mother thought that one had somehow slipped through the purging. I'm not sure how, but no. I am not surprised." She pulled her wand out of her jacket and placed it on the table between us. "There is much to the world that I do not know," she said after a bit. "But if He is manifest, what does that mean for my mistress? Could this be what she meant? Is this what has spurred her," she looked around and leaned in closer,

"… subterfuge? What does it mean for the world?"

"For starters, it means that Jean-Paul is dead," I said, matter-of-factly. "Things that were quiet in the world are starting to make noise. Maybe Nidhogg feels things changing, or perhaps they're changing because of her actions." I shrugged. "The die is cast. We just need to figure out how to help it along where possible and protect those that we can."

She let the side of her lip quirk up, almost a grin, but sad. "Part of me thinks it is you, my dear Sarah. You're the catalyst. If I were to kill you, would the world would settle back into its complacency?"

I stiffened at that. "I think you give me too much credit," I said, tossing back the remainder of my drink. "And there is Jai Li to consider."

"Quite," she said with a small nod.

I watched her, looking for a sign that she was going to attack me. She was looking down at the table rolling her wand from side to side.

I had Gram over my shoulder. No one commented on it when we came into the bar. Frankly, I just didn't think about her as a separate entity most of the time. We were becoming so in tune, she was like an extension of my own arm. If Qindra really decided to do something now, I'd have been wide open to the attack, because in my heart of hearts, I just didn't think she'd do it. Call me optimistic or better, foolhardy.

"I won't do it, you know," I said, finally breaking the silence. "I won't attack Nidhogg. Don't get me wrong, if she attacked me or mine, I'd fight her, but I have no intention of hunting her down or anything."

Qindra rolled her shot glass on the tipped edge of the bottom for a few moments, lost in thought.

"Who are you?" she asked, finally, keeping her eyes on her glass.

"I don't know," I answered, truthfully.

She looked up at me, her eyes were haunted. "Our destinies are intertwined," she said. "I saw it when I was immersed in the Chumstick Ley line. We are bound by fate."

I shrugged. "Really don't know anything about fate. I'm just trying to keep my head above water most days."

She studied my face, really watching me to the point I blushed.

"What?" I asked, shrugging my shoulders and trying not to be defensive.

"Gods help me, Sarah Beauhall, but I do like you. Life would be so much easier if you were a heartless bitch who I could just kill and get it over with."

Nice. "Sorry to be of value," I said.

"I'll have to do some research," she said, pulling her wallet out and dropping a twenty on the table. "I'll take the shield with me and see what I can learn. In the meantime, go home, check on Katie."

"Yeah," I said. "Coma or no coma, I still tell her what's going on. I just hope she's hearing me." I sat there for a moment, thinking about the mirror and the words etched into the silvered back. "I want to get things battened down before another storm comes in."

She patted me on the shoulder as she walked out of the bar. I sat there for a few minutes then took out my cell phone and called Skella. I'm sure she was freaking out about Gletts. And I really wanted her input on the whole mirror thing. Maybe I'd go to Vancouver, chat up Unun, check on the boy. I needed a better plan than the one I'd been operating under. For every step forward, I felt like I was three steps to the left. Close, but off the mark.

FIFTY

I called Julie from the now pristine apartment to let her know what had happened and that I was on my way to Vancouver. She already knew. Jai Li had drawn something about the elf boy Gletts. The girl had a real knack for freaking me out.

Skella showed up a few minutes later. She'd had to travel over to the cupcakery downstairs, as our hallway mirror was gone. She came into the apartment, handed me a cupcake, and stepped over to the mirror. She touched its surface, making the silver shimmer like water.

"She's been here," she said, quietly. "Recently. But she's flailing about, her energy signature is full of panic and fear. Like she's drowning."

"Fucking great," I growled. I was so tempted to step into the mirror, go back into the Sideways that it took an act of supreme will to hold back.

Skella put her hand on my shoulder and squeezed. "Let's go talk to Unun. Maybe she can give you some advice."

"Yeah," I said, wiping my hands over my face. "Let's."

We propped the mirror against the bar and stepped through it into the hidden cavern slash shrine that Gletts had kept. There were three mirrors there along with a shrine of my assorted crap he'd collected in the short time he'd stalked me. Boy had it bad for me. I hoped he lived. He'd been gone from his body for a very long time.

We hustled to the main village. As always we were in much too much of a hurry for the populace. Though I noticed that there were fewer hostile glances and stares now that we'd defeated the necromancer. Also fewer elves in general. Unun had been very surprised to know just how many of her people had thrown themselves in with the blood cult.

We hustled into the healing hall, making enough noise to cause Unun to cringe at us as we slid to a halt beside Gletts's bed.

"How is he?" I asked, barely out of breath. I felt pretty good about that, considering how little I'd been exercising lately. Maybe being Odin's favored had some additional cardio benefits I hadn't noted before.

"He's resting," Unun whispered, her voice hollow and thin. Her eyes, however, they told the true story. For the first time since I'd met her, I saw hope in those eyes. "He's come home to us," she said, looking up at me. "I suppose we have you in part to thank for that?"

I shrugged. "I just told him he needed to go home, that you folks were missing him."

She reached over and took my hand. I sat beside her and for a moment we watched Gletts breathing, his eyes closed in sleep.

"True sleep," she said, squeezing my hand. "Not the near life he's suffered under lo these many months."

"Will he recover?" I asked, glancing over to Skella who hugged herself, her face a stoic mask of anxiety.

"Perhaps," Unun said, releasing my hand. She leaned forward and brushed the hair out of Gletts's eyes. The hair was white, whiter than mine, and brittle. It used to be dark.

"He's so pale," Skella said.

"His body nearly failed," Unun said. "It will take time for him to recover."

She paused, turned to me, a small frown on her face. "My granddaughter tells me your young Katie is in similar straits."

I took a deep breath and nodded. "Yeah, going on two months now."

"I would've said your journey has been fruitless," she blinked at me, tears rolling down her cheeks. "I am truly sorry you cannot find your heart, but you brought mine back to me, and for that I will be forever grateful."

I bowed my head, the sudden pain of it all burning the back of my throat. "Gletts could've come back before," I said, hoping it didn't hurt them. "He was looking for something, for a way to take you home to Álfheim."

Unun nodded. "I know of this. Skella told me of your conversations with him on his wanderings." She reached over and pushed my chin up with her crooked finger. "You were like a burning torch, blazing through the darkness of the other worlds, calling out the dark things, the eaters and worse, each of them drawn to your love and your passion like moths to a flame."

Skella sat on the edge of the platform, placing her hands over top of Gletts's "But he saved her," she said, smiling through her tears. "That has to count for something."

Unun shook her head. "There is no scorekeeping, I am afraid. No ledger or balance. We are where we are, who we are, what we are at this moment in time. Our past deeds, good or ill, have no bearing on future deeds."

"He was a hero," I said, looking into her face, daring her to argue with me. "He saved me when I was lost, helped me find my way out of the dead places. Helped me flee the most vile spirit I've ever encountered."

"Yes," Unun agreed. "He is a very good boy. But these deeds will not bring him back to us. Only time and healing will show us if he will survive."

"Is there anything else I can do?" I asked. "I could give him some of my energy, if that would help." Worked for Qindra back in the apartment. How was I to know what worked and what didn't.

"No, Sarah," Unun smiled at me. "We need none of your essence. If anything, we should take some time and help heal you from your trials. So much time in those vile places has left your spirit bereft and forlorn."

"It's Katie," I said, the pain back in an instant. "I'm so scared I'll lose her. She isn't gone away of her own will, like Gletts was. He could find his way home. Katie is lost, scared and alone." I paused, breathing deeply to keep the sobs from coming. I couldn't prevent my eyes from stinging, but didn't wipe them. Let the pain leak, I needed the reminder of my failure.

"Perhaps she is looking for her body," Unun suggested. "You've moved her from where the incident occurred, I take it."

The question was like a smack in the face. "Yeah, of course. They took her to the hospital." I told her the whole story. About the book, and the magical explosion. Then about the hospital and how JJ had died. She listened patiently while I finished and sat there, silently, watching me.

My breath was ragged, like I'd been running or fighting. God I wanted to do something, anything. I wanted to lash out and stab something, or break something, I wanted to confront the enemy and smash it.

Unun said something I didn't understand and touched the side of my face. From her touch a cold spread, quelling the berserker, pushing aside the grief and leaving me clearheaded and calm.

Qindra had done something similar once, the night I fought Jean-Paul.

"Perhaps you need to unite her with this book, near the place where she fell. Have you considered that she is trapped in the locale she fell? Have you explored those possibilities?"

I stared at her, dumbstruck. What the hell was wrong with me? They'd taken her away in an ambulance, but she fell in Kent. The apartment was in Kent. The hospital where she'd banished Qindra from the ICU was in Kent.

I was looking for her from the apartment, but maybe I was off by a few miles. She loved the school deeply. Could that be the safe haven she hid in? Was that where she went, from where she forayed to find her body? Had we kept her spirit and her body apart by moving the latter to Black Briar? If that was the case, Jimmy would never forgive himself.

"I'll try it," I said, wishing I was there now. "I'll make some calls, get things in motion." How the hell was I going to get her body to the school without calling too much weird attention to it? And I'd have to go Sideways again, help guide her spirit home.

"Skella, can you take me to Black Briar?"

Unun nodded. "Go child. Let us attend to our family. Go and bring your lover home."

Skella and I ran through the forest back to the cave. Neither of us said anything, but I dared to hope. Was it this simple?

Would this really be the final piece to the puzzle?

I just needed to figure out how to get her body to the school without freaking out the staff. School was nearly out. Maybe a couple of more days. But there was no way I was waiting. No way I was going to sit around with this possibility and do nothing while we waited.

Luckily, that choice was taken out of my hands.

When Skella and I arrived at Black Briar, Deidre told me that Jimmy, Gunther, and Stuart had just left to visit the Order of Mordred folks.

"Jimmy wanted you there," Deidre said, her face a mix of fear and anxiety. "I told him not to go, I don't trust those people."

"Why did he go?" I asked, confused.

She looked lost, forlorn. "They said they had news of his parents. And they said they had other secrets. He thinks they know how to bring Katie home."

I looked from Deidre to Skella. Skella looked dubious, but shrugged. "Could be," she said.

Deidre was a wreck. I put a hand on her shoulder, lending her my strength. "I'll go to him," I said. "Don't worry."

I looked at Skella. "Back to Kent, then?"

Skella nodded and took my hand.

"I'll do what I can to keep them safe, Deidre. I promise you. In the meantime, can you call Melanie? Get her out here. We need to talk about moving Katie."

"I'll call her," Deidra said, as Skella touched the hallway mirror. "But watch out for that crazy woman. Gottschalk, I think her name is. She called ranting about something that had Jimmy freaked out."

"I'm on it."

Skella took my hand and waved at Deidre as we stepped back into the Kent apartment and I saw how truly devoid of life it had become. The breach, the stripping away of all items; this was truly a desert.

I grabbed the book and Skella beat feet back to Gletts.

"Call me," she said. "I'll help where I can."

I nodded, and she faded back through the mirror.

I grabbed the book and my gear and headed out of the apartment, calling Jimmy on my cell. He answered as I was climbing on the bike, and he texted me the address of the meet. It was at Gottschalk's place. Pretty gutsy on her part.

Time to rock and roll. Not the goal I wanted, but it was a place we could take action. And if they knew something about Katie, mores the better.

FIFTY-ONE

I pulled up to the address Jimmy had given me in Kirkland, surprised how much the place looked like a gingerbread house. Visions of Hansel and Gretel came to mind. Too clichéd, frankly. Jimmy's truck, Stuart's car, and Gunther's bike were all parked out front, along with a smattering of other vehicles. It looked like a block party. I wondered if the neighbors would complain.

I parked my bike beside Gunther's and walked down the long picket fence. Near the gate there was a small sign warning to beware the attack cat. It was cute and disarming. Gottschalk certainly cultivated the crazy old cat lady mystique. I wonder if the attack cat was the same one that talked to Charlie?

I opened the gate, which squeaked on the backward swing, closing with a neat little click. The yard was well maintained with raised flowerbeds, hearty rhododendrons, and several styles of birdbaths.

The walk was white stone, rough-cut and laid out in clean lines up to a wide porch with a swing and another little sign warning that solicitors who were not selling Girl Scout cookies were not welcome.

I rapped on the door and a young woman answered. She had a look about her that tickled the back of my mind—thin, brunette, pug nose, bright brown eyes, and dimples when she smiled. Very cute. Almost too cute. I was positive I'd seen her somewhere, but for the life of me I couldn't place her. Maybe she had spied on me at some point, or maybe I'd just run into her at the market. The runes on my scalp tingled, though. She had power of some measure, something flagrant and itchy. Her aura caused the hairs on my arms to stand up. Like a quick swipe of static electricity.

"Madame will be most delighted you have arrived," she said, sweeping me down the short hall to a sitting room. Jimmy sat on a rather rickety chair with a television tray propped in front of him and a small cup and saucer set in the center of what had to be the face of Don Adams. I glanced to where Gunther sat and saw the dented face of Barbara Feldon. They were a *Get Smart* set.

So I watched too much Nick at Night. I'm not sure if they saw the irony. Move along.

Stuart stood behind Gunther, staring out the window, his hands clasped behind his back and his shoulders bunched like he was ready to fight. Gunther looked slightly amused and winked at me when I stepped into the room. Jimmy did not take his eyes off Gottschalk.

"You've missed the tea," Madame Gottschalk barked, waving her hands at the woman who'd escorted me down the fairly short hallway.

"Would you like water?" the young woman asked.

"Yes, thanks."

She nodded, not glancing at the seething Madame and left the room. No one said a word until the young woman returned with my water. She left the room and Madame began talking again.

"As I was saying," she started at a rather high volume. "Your people are stirring things up, especially her," she said, jerking an arthritic hand in my direction. She looked like a goblin or something, squat and fat, with knobbly knuckles and spotted skin. Maybe a toad in a housecoat.

"What have I done?" I asked, having no patience for this type of BS.

She whipped her head around, eyes bulging and her cheeks quivering. For a moment, I thought she was going to spit on me, but she mustered up a throat-bobbing swallow and opened her mouth with a sneer. "Don't think I don't know you truck with the dragon," she said, the anger so apparent that her skin flushed red. "You were supposed to be an ally. You were supposed to be a watcher. Now I don't know what to do with you."

"Implying what?" Gunther asked, leaning back in his folding chair.

"You compromise us all," she crowed, flapping her hands in front of her. "And this one," she pointed past Gunther to Stuart. "He consorts with the witch."

Jimmy dropped his head into his hands. I could see the veins in his temple throbbing. I'm sure he had a hint that Stuart and Qindra had met a few times since he and Katie had rescued her before Christmas. I'm just not sure it had been so blatantly thrown into his face.

Stuart didn't turn around, but he clenched his hands into fists and hunched his shoulders even tighter.

"Just take a breath," Jimmy said, lowering his hands and raising his head. "We don't know you folks. We came here on good faith. Do you have information to trade, or do you just want to berate us for our personal relationships?"

Gottschalk took two gulping breaths, looking around the sitting room. A tabby cat strolled across the top of the bookcase to her right, dropped to the arm of her chair, and pushed his head into her shoulder, purring loudly.

"Oh, take their side," she groused, but scratched the cat behind the ears.

"Look," Jimmy said. "Did you know my parents?"

Gottschalk nodded once, the breath causing her nostrils to flare.

"Do you have information about their disappearance?"

Gottschalk raised her head to the point she was looking down her nose at Jimmy. "We may have some middling information. What do you have we could possibly be interested in trading?"

Jimmy started to rise from his chair, but Gunther put his hand on his friends arm and leaned forward on his own.

"If you have knowledge of Olivia and Paul Cornett, perhaps it would be a show of good faith to tell us, a gift perhaps, to seal a new friendship."

Sarah watched him as he spoke. His words were not singsong, but they carried the tone and weight of ritual.

"New friends?" Gottschalk asked, licking her lips. "It only seems fair." She fussed with the cat a moment, keeping her eyes locked onto Gunther's.

"And of course," he continued. "We would offer you a gift in return."

He looked over at Jimmy who reached between his feet and pulled opened a knapsack. Inside were three items: a scroll, a small dagger, and a necklace of dark stones. He laid each of them on the television tray in front of him.

"Trinkets?" Gottschalk asked. "Pretties?"

Jimmy took a deep breath and picked up the scroll. "This is the account of certain activities which occurred in Minsk nearly one-hundred years ago." He sat that back down. "They may be of interest to someone close to you."

Gottschalk's eyes narrowed, but she only nodded.

He picked up the dagger holding it between his thumb and one finger. The scabbard was plain leather, but worked with some symbols. My runes itched at the thought of them. "This item is reported to have belonged to Rasputin—"

Gottschalk sat forward, pushing the cat aside. Of course the furry prince would have none of that. He arched his back, hissed once, then strutted off the edge of the chair and sauntered to twine himself against Stuart's legs.

We'd all followed the cat's progress—all but Madame. Her eyes were only on the dagger.

"And the third?" she asked, the greed eager in her voice.

"A trifle," Gunther said, waving his hand over the lot.

"It came out of Iceland," Jimmy said, gritting his teeth. "I don't know the history of it, nor its importance." He paused, glancing at Gunther who just nodded once. "This is what convinced my parents to go to Reykjavik."

My head snapped up, gazing hard at Jimmy. I'd never seen that necklace, and I'm willing to bet Katie hadn't either. Man, she was going to be livid when she came out of her coma. She and Jimmy had only just begun to fix their relationship after the whole Fafnir's ring incident.

"Where did you get these?" Gottschalk asked.

"The dagger and the scroll were hidden in a safety deposit box," Jimmy said, aiming his words to me.

That's where he'd recovered Fafnir's ring. His parents had left them three clay statues, each with a secret inside.

"The necklace has been in the safekeeping of others," Gunther said, looking at me briefly then focusing on Gottschalk. He needn't have bothered. Gottschalk had no eyes for anything or anyone beyond the dagger.

I caught Gunther's eyes, and he casually fingered his own necklace—a crucifix. So, his order had been examining the Reykjavik necklace. I wondered what they knew about it and just why the hell Jimmy was willing to give up these three items.

"These are trifles," Gottschalk said, sitting back and waving her hand in front of her face. "Minor trinkets. What could you possibly want in return?"

Gunther sat back, smiling. Gottschalk and Jimmy had locked eyes and were not budging.

"First we want to know everything you know about my parents, what they were doing, where they went, and how or why they disappeared."

Gottschalk smiled demurely. "That's a fair trade." She rolled herself forward, leveraging her girth out onto the edge of her recliner, her one arm outstretched, reaching for the items on Jimmy's tray.

Jimmy closed his hands over the tray, blocking her reach.

"Second, we want access to your archives and your people," he said, unsmiling. "We want to interview them about what's going on in our area, the dragons in general, and anything else you may have discovered about this region."

That was too much. Madame sat back with a thump, her face distorted with disgust. "Are you mad?"

"Third," Jimmy want on, his voice rising to overwhelm her sputtering.

"Third?" she raged, rising out of her chair, knocking over her own television tray, sending a bone white china cup to the hardwood floor with a crash. "You demand too much."

"Third!" Jimmy cried, rising on his own to loom over the tray with his artifacts. "You will stop following my people, stop attempting to infiltrate Black Briar, and stop spying on us for your sister in Minsk."

Gottschalk sat back with an *oomph*, her face suddenly pale. "My sister?"

Gunther sat forward. "The scroll will appease her," he said, his voice like steel. "Baba Yaga is a powerful witch," he said. I shook my head, trying to make sure I'd heard him right. Baba Yaga of the chicken-legged hut? What the hell?

"She ..." Madame gulped once and coughed.

The young woman appeared at my side again. "Yes, Madame?"

"Water," the old woman croaked.

We waited while the young servant brought forth a tall glass of water, and watched as Gottschalk drained it in one long pull.

She handed the glass back to her servant and waved her away.

The young woman bowed and turned, winking at me as she did so. Damn, I know her from somewhere. I just couldn't place her. That was going to bug the crap out of me.

"I will send someone to you before the next full moon," she said, her voice quavering.

Was she scared? Was her sister truly Baba Yaga? And if so, why did Black Briar knowing this frighten her so much?

"Seven days," Stuart said, his voice a tight ball of pain.

"Quite right," she said, brushing her hair out of her face and composing herself. "I will send you a report of what we know of your parents," she held up one finger. "I will have my people stand down, but there is a caveat to that."

Jimmy frowned. "Such as?"

"We meet regularly, and exchange news, ideas, and plans. That way we may coordinate our activities, share the resources, and perhaps learn more by duplicating less."

Jimmy glanced at Gunther who shrugged. Then he looked at me for the first time. His eyes were bloodshot. "Sarah?"

I nodded. It seemed reasonable.

"Fine," he said. "Sarah will meet with you. What else?"

Wait, what? "Um ..." I began, but Gunther shook his head quickly and I subsided. Like I needed another job with no paycheck.

"Finally," she said, "You may inquire of us, anything you wish, and we shall do the same. But we will not freely give up all we have gathered. We do not know if that is a fair trade."

Jimmy scowled, but nodded. "Fair enough."

Madame sat forward, her hands out, reaching toward Jimmy.

I stepped forward, picked up the three items, and stepped toward her.

"If I'm to be the lackey here," I said, grinning down at the old woman, "I'll listen to your requests and pass on to Black Briar things I feel are worthy." I didn't even look back at the guys. Either they agreed, or I didn't play.

I placed the scroll in her hand, and her eyes lit up.

"Second," I said, holding up the necklace. "This stays with me until Katie has had a chance to examine it and ask questions." I glanced back at Jimmy then, and he was absolutely not happy. "No secrets, Jim, remember?"

He nodded stiffly. Stuart turned then, watching me for the first time. I think there was a bit of admiration in his face. That or gas. I was going for the admiration.

"And finally," I said, holding up the dagger.

The energy signature off that dagger was scary high. It made my whole arm tingle. This was some powerful magic. I looked to Gunther who nodded, smiling.

"You can have this," I said, sliding it into the jeans of my pocket. "When you put Olivia and Paul's wedding rings into my hands."

The room exploded.

"What the hell?" Jimmy shouted.

"How dare you?" Gottschalk started, then sat back as I leaned into her personal space. I was so pissed I could feel the berserker dancing in the background. It wouldn't take much to call it forth and punch this manipulating old bitch in the face. "I know you have them. Don't pretend."

I stepped back. Jimmy grabbed my arm. "What are you talking about?" he asked, the anger and shock bleeding through his words. "Their wedding rings."

"Later," I said, pushing his hand off my arm. "Those are my conditions."

I turned, walked down the hallway, and let myself out the door.

The house erupted into shouts, but I didn't go back inside. I walked out and sat on the back of Jimmy's pickup waiting for the fireworks to settle down.

After a few minutes, Stuart walked out of the house.

"Must you always kick the hornet's nest?" he asked with a grin.

I shrugged. "I don't like her," I said. "And I sure as hell don't trust her."

He leaned against the truck next to me and crossed his arms. "Pretty sure she's a witch," he said. "You sure you want to piss her off?"

"Hey," I said, poking him in the arm. "We have a better witch on our team."

He stiffened, suddenly uncomfortable.

"Qindra really digs you," I said, quietly. "I don't know what you've said or done, but that girl is seven kinds of flummoxed over you."

"Really?" he asked, turning to look at me.

For a moment he looked fourteen hearing about his first crush liking him back.

"Totally," I said. "She wants you to escort her to Portland, but she's afraid you'll laugh at her."

He stood up straight, his face very serious. "I would do no such thing," he said. "She is an intriguing woman." He looked passed me, his eyes a little unfocused. I turned to look over my shoulder making sure there was no one there and smiled. He was smitten.

"Take her to dinner," I offered, nudging him.

He focused his eyes on me and smiled a shy little smile. "I was thinking of asking her on a real date."

I patted him on the shoulder. "Someplace fancy," I said with a smile. "Let her dress up, pick the wine, gush all over her. She'll melt in your arms."

He blushed at that and looked toward the house. Gunther was striding down the path toward us.

"The scroll is the real win for her," he said to me. "The necklace is untapped. We couldn't make any sense of it. There doesn't appear to be any reason this drove Jimmy's folks to run off like they did. Just makes no sense."

"And the dagger?"

He sighed and shrugged. "Real as real. Rasputin had it on him when he survived several assassination attempts. Theory is it kept him alive, but none of us were willing to test that magic."

I cupped my hand over the dagger bulge in my pocket. "Maybe we don't want her to have this."

"It betrayed him in the end," he said. "There are only so many times you can tempt fate. At the end he trusted this would save him and it did not."

"Was Rasputin a dragon?" I asked. It would only make sense.

"Rumor has it," Stuart said, causing Gunther and me to both turn to look at him. He grinned and shrugged. "Hey, I may not be in any secondary guilds or anything, but I am a member of Black Briar. I do my research."

"My demands stand," I said. "You want me to play along, this is my price."

Gunther glanced at Stuart and shook his head. "Remember when she was unsure of herself?"

Stuart chuckled. "And how much she used to want to be just like us?"

"I never wanted to be you," I said, laughing. "I just liked having you both around as mentors."

They both got serious at that, and they each took one of my hands.

"Our little girl's all growed up," Stuart said with a syrupy southern drawl.

"About damned time," Gunther said.

"How did you know about Baba Yaga?" I asked. "And the dagger? Your order knew Gottschalk would drool all over it?"

"Yes," Gunther replied. "They've known about this Order of Mordred since they first came to town with the gold rush."

"Gold rush?" I asked. "That's a long time."

"And Madame Gottschalk is very old," he said. "The dagger was truly Rasputin's. It will help Gottschalk with some political matters back home. She and her sister do not always see eye-to-eye, let's say."

"You're the man in the know here," I said, slipping my hand in my pocket to grasp the dagger. "So, we're just gonna give her the knife?"

J.A. Pitts

He nodded. "In exchange for the rings," Gunther said, smiling. "That was quite the surprise. I'm curious how you knew about them."

"Long story, better told out of earshot," I said, hiking my thumb toward the house. "I need to head out of here, check on Jai Li. Can you two make sure Jimmy gets out of there alive?"

They chuckled.

"We've kept him out of trouble since the early days," Stuart said. "We'll be okay."

I walked over to my bike, and put on my helmet. As I pulled down the street to turn around, I glanced over and saw that Gunther and Stuart had their heads together talking.

I missed them both so much. We needed to get our lives back to some level of normalcy. And in all that, nothing was mentioned about Katie.

It only took me about fifteen seconds to have the bike back down the street to where Stuart and Gunther were talking. They looked up as I stopped the bike and flipped up the face shield.

"Did she say anything about Katie?" I asked over the bike's idle.

Stuart's face fell, and Gunther shook his head.

"I'm sorry," Gunther said, stepping over to grasp my shoulder. "Jimmy asked, but Gottschalk was perplexed. She doesn't know anything."

"Maybe she's lying?" I doubted it, but I had to ask.

"No," Stuart said, smiling. "She's not lying." He glanced at Gunther who nodded. Stuart reached into his shirt pocket and pulled out a small silver disk.

"If she lied, I'd know," he said, handing the disk to me.

I examined the disk, peeling off my gloves. The second I made flesh contact to it, I got a shock that set the runes along my scalp into overdrive. Light exploded from the disk, and I closed my fist around it, damping down the white flare.

"Lie about something," Stuart said.

I looked down at my fist and said, "I hate coffee."

The disk throbbed, a dissonant pulse that grated my teeth, but only for a second. "I love coffee." The disk hummed quietly, a smooth sensation.

282

I handed the disk back to Stuart.

"Damn," I said, frowning. "So, back to plan B."

Gunther looked up. "Plan B?"

"Let's regroup tomorrow out at Jimmy's," I said, glancing toward the house. "I'm not comfortable sharing secrets here."

They both nodded, and I shifted into first, swung the bike around and headed back toward Redmond.

Tomorrow I'd try something new. I just hoped that Jimmy would listen. After this little scene I'm not sure he would be too open to things.

FIFTY-TWO

The next day, Jimmy, Gunther, and I reconvened back at Black Briar. Stuart went off to see Qindra. It was very cute to see him so crushing on her. I laid out my ideas for taking Katie over to the school, doing a bit of a séance, maybe doing some astral walking and explore the surroundings. I couldn't tell them about the diary, however. If they knew Katie had taken it, they hadn't mentioned it to me yet, and I did not want to go there.

I wanted to get Qindra involved, but with Stuart currently asking her out to a super spectacular dinner and the whole wooing thing, I thought it would be better if I used the resources I had. Jimmy was dead set against me taking her on some damned fool's errand, and he was out on the deck talking with Deidre about it. Gunther and I planted ourselves in Katie's room to wait out the storm.

I'd kidnap her if I had to. I had to try something. I was pretty sure I could talk Melanie into helping me. Mostly sure.

I took out the necklace that we were going to give to Gottschalk. Katie's hands were crossed on her chest, so I turned them palm up and lay the necklace into them.

"Your parents had this necklace," I said to her.

Her hands closed over the cut stones, but her eyes didn't open

"Did she …?" Gunther began, standing up.

"No," I said, covering her hands with mine. "She grasps things when you put them in her hands. Some instinct, I think. She's not in there."

"How can you be sure?" he asked, sitting back down.

I sat beside him, took out my knitting and began to work on sample piece for a new scarf I was working on. This one used a lot of beads. It was going to kill me, I'm sure.

"She's lost somewhere," I told him as I began the soothing dance of the needles. "I've seen evidence of that. I just need to find out where."

He humphed and crossed his hands behind his head, crossed one ankle over a knee and leaned back against the wall, watching her.

"I watched her grow up," he said, quietly. "She was hell on wheels, this one."

I looked up. He had that faraway look of old memories.

"And when she told us about you," he said, grinning. "Jimmy about lost it. We knew you from the Ren Faire, but you were a little rough around the edges. All anger and bravado."

I squinted at him. "It wasn't that long ago," I said. "Like what, two, three years?"

"I think Katie carved it in the old barn. She was convinced you were the real deal, her one and only." He looked up, his face suddenly sober. "Not mine to tell, though. Sorry." He smiled at me with a very sad smile, his flowing hair and wild Viking looks suddenly sensitive and vulnerable. "She does love you, kiddo. With all her heart."

"Ditto," I said, looking at her with watering eyes. "God, Gunther. I can't lose her." My breath caught, and I thought I was going to cry for a moment. I cleared my throat and took a deep breath. "I have to bring her home, show her the way, put out a light, something."

"I'll talk to Jimmy," he said, quietly. "He'll see reason."

"Yeah, right. Jimmy? He only believes things he can see on his own."

"Brilliant idea," he said, smacking his open hand on his thigh. "Why don't you and Skella arrange to take him sideways. You can, can't you?"

I thought about it. Not astrally, that took a special skill. I don't know when I'd acquired it, but my bet was that Gram had something to do with it.

"Good idea. You wanna go?"

He laughed again and held up his hands. "Hell no. I'll trust you. I don't need some crazed spirit or giant spider like eating machine chasing me across Hel's domain to trust you're telling the truth."

"Jimmy thinks I'm lying?"

He shook his head. "Delusional, most like. He knows you love her and would do anything for her, but look at his life, Sarah. He's terrified he'll lose her, so he's keeping a tight rein on her."

I could see his point of view. Guy was just scared for her. Maybe I'd take Jimmy and Bub with me next time. Get Skella to drop us off someplace relatively safe. If that even existed in the Sideways.

"How's Anezka?" I asked him, changing the subject without signaling.

He turned and looked at me with a smile on his face. "She's a little ray of sunshine," he sniggered. "When she's not out of her gourd with anxiety and nightmares."

"Sorry."

"Well ... accepted. She says you've been stirring up the nightmares, making the dark things creep out of their hidey-holes and slip into normal people's dreams."

That sucked. "Skella's grandmother said pretty much the same thing," I said, dejected. I put the knitting down in my lap. "I guess when I go tromping through the dreamscape, I'm a little loud and annoying."

He laughed at that, a real belly laugh. "Jesus and Mary, Beauhall. You are the epitome of understatement."

I punched him and picked my knitting back up. Luckily I hadn't dislodged anything. I hated casting on.

He stared at me for a while, a look of concentration on his face.

"What?" I asked after a few minutes. It was unnerving.

"Well, we've been talking, me and Jimmy and Stuart."

"Yeah?"

He turned his chair slightly to better face me. "You see, we don't think you're one of the elder gods come back."

"Well, that's a relief. Especially after learning that the dragons want to keep them all killed off."

He waved his hand at me, smiling. "And you aren't a dragon or anything else my order can understand." He tapped two fingers against his lips, thinking. "It's like you're a white blood cell. Whatever is wrong with the world, you've been brought in to clean things up. Preserve the ecosystem by removing things that are harming the host."

I had to consider that for a moment. "Like magical penicillin?" I asked.

"Which makes the dragons STDs?"

We both laughed at that.

"But it's more than dragons," he said, tapping his hands on the seat of the chair. "The current theory is that you are an antibody that is trying to heal the one-true-being."

"Odin?" I asked. Didn't seem right, but what the hell did I know?

"No, not Odin. He's just another piece of the whole. No, I think you're a servant of the world tree."

I looked at him, thinking that maybe Anezka's nuttiness had infected him in some way.

"Let me tell you a story," he said, holding up his hands to forestall my clumsy rebuttal. "But I need something to draw on."

He left the room and returned with a drawing pad and a black ink pen. He flipped to a blank sheet, passing things I was sure Jai Li had drawn. Then he drew a rough tree with a long trunk, three massive roots and three tall branches.

"This is Yggdrasil, the world tree."

"Qindra drew it for me once," I said "Nine worlds, yadda, yadda."

He shook his head. "Yadda indeed. Do you know the mythos? The denizens? Do you know the worlds, truly?"

I shook my head. "No, truthfully I was a little worried about Anezka at the time she was telling me. We were waiting for her cleaning crew to show up out at Chumstick. She was showing me to bide our time."

"Just as I thought. May I tell my tale?"

I rolled my eyes. "Sure, I guess we're not going anywhere. Jimmy is still pouting with Deidre."

He sniggered and tapped on the page with his pen. "Pay attention then. This may help you someday."

FIFTY-THREE

There is evidence of the world tree," he began. "A giant tree that encompassed the entirety of the universe. Yggdrasil it was called in the old tongue. Off the branches and roots of this tree were the nine worlds.

In the heavens or the upper branches of the tree there were three worlds: Múspellsheimr, Álfheimr, and Ásgarðr.

Múspellsheimr is the world of Muspell or fire. This is where Bub is from originally. Before he became a servant of the amulet."

I fingered the amulet through my shirt. It was a constant reminder of the kobold. I missed him, I needed to stop and touch base with him, recruit him to my little Sideways outing.

"Also fire giants. They're definitely bad news."

I thought back to the time I battled Bub. "Fire extinguishers, got it."

"Álfheimr is the world of the Ljósálfr, Skella's people," he continued.

"Ásgarðr also known as Asgard is the world of the Æsir, Odin's people.

"The three central worlds," he pointed to the middle of the tree, "are Vanaheimr, Miðgarðr, and Jötunheimr."

"Vanaheimr is the world of the Vanir, the old gods that came before Odin and his ilk." He paused, considering. "There are those who believe the civilization collapsed before Asgard fell, but it is only speculation and rumor."

"Like maybe the legends of Atlantis or something?"

He looked at me, appraisingly. "Perhaps," he said. "Hadn't combined those two legends together before, but I can see the connection."

I smiled at that. I was getting better at pulling together puzzle pieces and solving mysteries.

"Miðgarðr or Midgard is Earth, the lands of the humans."

"Got that, easy enough. Home, sweet, home."

"Yes. The third is Jötunheimr, and is the land of the Jötunn or Giants."

Legend said you could walk from giant land to Asgard, so they must be connected somehow. "Oh, yeah, I'm very aware of them."

He smiled at me and pointed to the roots of the tree.

"These are the tree roots, the underworld. This is made up of Svartálfaheimr, Niflhel, and Niflheimr."

He looked at me. "Svartálfaheimr is the land of the dark elves, or the Dvergar, Durin's folk."

"Rolph's people?" I asked.

"Yes, precisely. They are considered dark elves because of their nocturnal nature."

"Doesn't mean they're evil, though. Right?" I didn't want Rolph to be evil. The guy was wonky at times, but he had a good heart. Now, some of his kin, like the dwarves who were messed up in the blood mead, and the necromancer's, shit, they were rotten to the core.

"Niflheimr is the land of the ice giants. They, along with the fire giants from Múspellsheimr are who were supposed to bring down Odin and his crew and trigger Ragnarök, the end of the world."

Ragnarök. Is that the only way to repair the wheel? Is that the final game? I know Nidhogg wanted the wheel repaired. So did Odin. But did I have to destroy the world to fix it? Seemed counterproductive, but we were talking mythical shit way above my pay grade.

"And Niflhel?" I asked, fearing his answer.

"Hel, the land of the dead."

I shuddered. "Oh, yeah. I got that one down. No desire to ever go back."

"Quite." He drew a bridge between Midgard and Asgard, then drew an X over it. "This is the rainbow bridge that Heimdell shattered when the dragons took Odin's halls. This kept the dire wolves from joining the battle. Frost giants and their younger goblin brethren made it to Asgard, but the ship the fire giants were to sail on was never built. Loki had been betrayed to Nidhogg, so Ragnarök never happened."

"Who betrayed Loki?" I asked.

"Ratatoskr—bore-tooth, or the gnawer. He's a big damned squirrel who carried messages between Nidhogg and the unnamed eagle that lived at the very top of the tree."

"Why unnamed?" I asked, forgetting all about my knitting.

"This is where the etymologies mix," he said, putting down the pad and standing. He paced the length of the room.

"In Genesis, the text states that thou shalt have no gods before me."

I nodded, well aware of the scripture.

"My order believes that the eagle represents God, the one true god. And that the others are lesser beings."

"So, you're saying that Christianity and all this Norse mythos stuff works together?"

"I don't see why not," he said. He scratched his chin. "You come from a pretty strict Christian upbringing. The scripture is full of ambiguities and plot holes big enough to drive a donkey through. Who's to say the myths and the gods don't live together perfectly well?"

"Well, da for one." No way the old man was going to buy Odin, dragons, and the like. Of course, I'd seen, battled, and lived through all of those. What I didn't have was hard evidence for was da's vision of the God Almighty.

"So, maybe God as my father believes him to be, doesn't really exist."

Gunther shook his head and clucked his tongue. "Oh, ye of little faith. Open your mind Sarah. There is ample evidence for both."

I moved my knitting over into my basket and stood, stretching.

"So, I'm this squirrel or something, narking out Loki and generally helping to break the wheel, betray Odin and give the throne to Nidhogg?"

"Not quite that," he said. "But there is evidence your true calling is to fix the wheel. Didn't Nidhogg say the same to you?"

I hadn't gone into detail on my last meeting with Nidhogg, just given them the highlights. Perhaps I was just a lackey to go between head and tail. I scrubbed my hands over my face and yawned.

"Okay, so say I'm this white blood cell squirrel thingy. Now what?"

Gunther sat down, his shoulders dropping. "Good question. We've never gotten past that point. Just deciding this was a huge leap of faith."

I laughed. "Berserker, Fist, Lover, Mother, Squirrel, and White Blood Cell. I am one complex individual."

We both laughed. "I'm going to roust Jimmy," I said, patting Gunther on the arm as I went passed him. "Squirrel...." I couldn't stop chuckling.

"I'll stay here," he said, sitting back down. "I'll just watch her sleep a bit longer."

I kissed him on the top of his head and went down the hall toward the kitchen and the back deck. Time to kick Jimmy into high gear. I wanted to bring Katie home.

Just in case, maybe I'd say a quick prayer. Couldn't hurt, right?

FIFTY-FOUR

I guess Deidre had worked Jimmy over pretty well. When I went out onto the back deck, he was walking across the grounds, heading out to the war memorial. Deidre patted me on the arm as I went past her and I gave her a quick hug.

Jimmy must've heard the door because he'd paused out by the old ruined barn.

"Hey, Jim," I said, jogging up to stand next to him.

He was staring into the ruins, the fallen timbers, the ash that refused to go away, even after more than a year of being open to the weather.

"This is where it happened," he said, his voice barely a whisper.

"What? Where Deidre fell?"

He turned to look at me, his eyes haunted. "This is where we lost our innocence. This is where we stopped being children and started being jaded and wounded grown-ups who struggle against the sharp edges, opening old wounds, lost in our past."

"That's pretty heavy stuff, Jim." I said. "Ever thought about tearing it down? Letting the new memorial the dwarves built pass for our historical memory?"

"Bub lives here," he said, pointing through the interlocked beams to a small corner in the back where a convergence of roof pieces had created a small cave of ash and burnt wood.

"We can find him a new place," I said, staring into the barn. "Where is he this afternoon?"

"No idea," he said, shrugging. "Can't you call him with that amulet of yours?"

I grabbed the stone beneath my shirt. "Yeah, I suppose. Let me give it a try."

The stone pulsed a quiet red as I slipped it out from my shirt and held it in my hands. "Bub?" I asked the air. "Bub, where are you my friend?"

There was a popping sound behind me, and the quick stench of sulfur. Jim and I both turned. Bub sat on the picnic table against the new barn across the yard. He squatted down with his knees up around his ears. A great yawn cracked his face, forcing his jaws open as wide as I've ever seen them. Half his head practically unhinging and tilting backward. I was willing to bet we could drop an anvil in his gullet and he'd just burp and smile.

"You tired, Bub?" I asked, crossing the yard.

He stretched his arms above his head and arched his back. His scales shone dully in the light of the late afternoon.

"I was taking a nap," he said.

Jimmy shook his head, but a smile touched the corners of his mouth.

"Nap where?" I asked.

"With Frick and Frack," he said, stretching upward, coming to his full four feet with his talons clicking above his head.

"I'm glad you could make it," I said, sitting on the table beside him. "Saves me from having this conversation twice."

Jimmy stood by the end of the table, one foot up on the bench nearest my boots. I leaned back on my elbows, and Bub dropped back down like a frog. He had the boniest damn knees.

"I want to do something with Katie," I started, not looking at either of them.

"You want to take her sideways?" Bub asked, his voice tight.

"No chance in hell," Jimmy said at the same time.

I held up one hand, leaning back on my right elbow. "Not exactly. I want to take her to Kent, drive around to a few spots, and the three of us, with Skella as a guide, to go into the Sideways and see if we can help guide her spirit back to her body."

"Intriguing," Bub said, swiveling his head to look at me. "What makes you think this will be any better than the excursions you've already made?"

"Good point," Jimmy said.

I paused a moment, collecting my thoughts. This was the right thing, it had to be.

I laid out a more detailed history of my other trips sideways, added in the information from Unun and the things I'd gleaned on my own.

"And you want me to allow her near all that?" Jimmy asked, his voice so tight, I think he'd vibrate if I plucked him.

"She's dying, Jim. I know what the signs are. I know Gletts was going through the same things, and you don't have a magic house of healing to help her along like the elves did for Gletts."

"Take her north, then," Bub said. "Wouldn't that improve her chances?"

"No way," Jimmy said, slashing the air in front of him with an open hand. "I'm not letting her out of my sight."

"Fair enough," I said. "But damn it, Jim. I won't let her die because you're so fucking pigheaded, you can't see beyond your own fear."

He dropped his foot to the ground, squared up to face me, and ground his teeth. "She's my blood," he finally managed to say. "She thinks she loves you, but I'm beginning to wonder if she wouldn't be better if she'd never met you."

Bub stood on the table hissing, his eyes two narrow slits. I reached over and put my hand on his calf.

I'd expected this tact from him. He'd lost control of the one thing he had sworn to take care of, and he was lashing out. Still hurt like a bitch. But I couldn't let him see it.

I took several breaths, letting the calm flow through me like an icy fog. When I knew I could talk without firing back at him, I sat up, shrugged my shoulders to loosen up the muscles from where I'd been leaning on one elbow, and slowly turned to look at him.

"I'm gonna pretend those words were never said." I sat forward, closing my eyes, and rotating my head on my neck, letting the tension bleed away. "We can do nothing and before another month passes, she'll be too far gone to matter."

I looked at him, putting every bit of anger and fire I could muster in my stare. "Stop being a damned child and listen to me. I have a plan, and I need your help."

He opened his mouth to speak, but I placed a hand on his arm. "Listen, please."

The muscles of his arm were so tight, I couldn't understand how he didn't have a cramp.

"I need you to help me search. You know her better than I do. I need your help in looking for clues. She's hiding somewhere, but it's a crazy funhouse landscape and I can't tell where she's hiding. I followed her, the trail growing colder and colder, but I couldn't catch her."

Bub sat down beside me and put his head in my lap, whimpering slightly.

"She's scared, and she's running, Jim. And I think that evil spirit I told you about wants to kill her, or wants to kill me and is using her for bait."

He didn't shrug off my hand, but I saw his shoulders drop a bit. I placed my other hand on Bub's head, stroking the scales on the side of his face.

"I need you to have my back in case things get bad. And I need you to help me find her, Jim." I took a breath, keeping back the pain. "I can't tell you how much I love her. There are no words."

He blinked a few times, turned his head away from me, and rubbed his eyes while stepping away. "Yeah, all right. But we go in with a plan, and I want you to go over it all again. From the beginning. Nothing left unturned, no secrets. Anything may help."

I felt a pang in my chest. But I know what had to be done.

"Same with you, right?"

He nodded. "Let me get some things together and we can meet back here. I'll arrange to have Katie driven down to Kent. I think we can hire an ambulance. Dena will know who we can call."

Dena was Melanie's girlfriend. She was an EMT and drove an ambulance.

"Let me get Skella to cart me around," I said.

Bub sat up. "I get to go too, right?"

"Absolutely, big guy. You're my ace in the hole."

He grinned broadly, showing off most of his business teeth and hopped down off the table. "I'll go tell Trisha that I'll be gone a bit," he said, scampering toward the barracks where she lived with the troll twins. "So the boys don't worry when I'm gone."

"Good idea," I said, feeling my heart lighten.

Jimmy was already on the porch heading into the house.

"Tell Gunther, will ya?" I called after him.

He waved at me over his shoulder and went into the house.

I pulled out my cell phone and called Skella to make arrangements. While I was at it, I thought maybe I'd call Rolph. See if he wanted in.

I'd love to take Qindra, but she's off with Stuart.

I started making a list in my head as I walked out to the smithy. I wanted a few things just in case, including my armor. I called Julie, warned her that Skella and I were coming out and that we'd explain everything when we got out there.

I just hoped that this didn't turn into a true cluster fuck. God knew I was okay risking my own neck, but taking others into that crazy place had me nervous.

But I was not letting her go. Not if I had to scour every square inch of that hellish place.

Besides, what could go wrong? I was asking for help. That's what I'd been doing wrong all along, right? This had to be the best thing.

I was running out of time.

FIFTY-FIVE

Stuart watched Qindra as she spoke to the concierge at The Governor hotel in downtown Portland. She'd booked the Lewis and Clarke Suite—a two-bedroom suite which caused him to wonder about the signals she was sending. If Sarah had been right about Qindra liking him, what did this mean? Not that he needed things to move along too quickly, it was just strange to be sharing a suite, but not a room.

Was there any chance he was leaving this city without kissing her? He knew there was much more that he wanted to do to her, but he just couldn't tell if she wanted him in the same way.

"It's a short walk from here," she said, breaking his thoughts. He blushed which drew a curious look from her, but she didn't pursue it.

"What time is our meeting?" he asked, checking his watch. The drive down had taken nearly four hours, longer than they'd anticipated, but the company was good and they talked a lot. He couldn't really remember much about the subjects, but her voice filled his head in a way that left him feeling drunk.

If anyone had asked him a year ago if he'd be all googlie-eyed over the dragon's witch, he'd have decked 'em for the thought. Now he just wondered what this breathtaking beauty could possibly see in him.

"I've called Mr. Philips," she said, placing a hand on his arm. "He's offered to send a car around at six."

"Or we could walk?"

She shrugged. "Walking is nice, but we still have time to kill either way. We could just go upstairs, have a drink …" She threw him a sultry look that made his brain stop working momentarily.

God, was he reading that right? Why was this so damn hard?

"It's entirely up to you," she continued, when he didn't say anything.

That was sultry, right? Not shy, not demure? His mind ran about ten thousand miles an hour. Signals and innuendo. How was he supposed to understand what was going on in that amazing mind of her?

He looked at her face, gauging her, trying to discern her mood, her thoughts. Maybe it was time to throw caution to the wind. In an obtuse and defensible way.

"I'm afraid if we were alone in the suite for several hours things could get a little out of control."

He blushed again, but he meant it. She was intoxicating.

She stood a head taller than him, but he didn't mind. She was beautiful and smart, elegant and way, way out of his league.

Of course he'd carried her out of that house in the fall. She seemed quite pleased then. And since, their conversations had been like dancing—exotic and enticing.

"Why don't we take our chances?" she said, leaning in and kissing him ever so lightly on the lips.

Magic was all he could imagine, the way the fireworks were going off in his head. He just stared at her numbly as she took his hand and led him back to the elevators.

"Perhaps we'll skip dinner altogether," she said as she pushed the elevator button.

His brain finally lurched into gear. She'd kissed him. That was definitely an opening move. Did he dare try it himself? He took a deep breath and plunged ahead.

He stepped closer to her, placing a hand on the small of her back and pulled her to him. This time the kiss lasted until the elevator chimed its arrival.

"Oh, my. That was nice," she said, smiling at him, a hint of color rising in her cheeks. "Let's do that more, with a bit of privacy."

She pulled him into the elevator and slipped her card in to unlock the suite before she was kissing him with a passion and energy he couldn't remember ever experiencing with any other woman.

When the elevator door opened, she kicked off her heels and ran down the hall ahead of him, laughing like a schoolgirl.

He picked up her shoes and made it to the door just as she got it opened. He followed her into a huge room. It was two adjoining suites with a conference table in the middle, in case they needed to take a meeting, he supposed.

He dropped the shoes by the door and swept her into his arms, kissing her while he carried her around the table.

"My room," she whispered to him, starting to pull at the buttons of his shirt. "The view's better."

"Oh, the view from here is marvelous," he said, covering her mouth with his.

To hell with the dragon, he thought. They could see Sawyer in the morning.

FIFTY-SIX

Jimmy, Bub, and I drove down to Kent, swung by the apartment, and grabbed Katie's mirror before heading over to the school. We waited until after six—had to make sure the place was abandoned before we got started.

Katie was in the ambulance with Dena and Melanie in the back of the school while I snuck Jimmy and Bub into her classroom. There had been a substitute in here for the last month or so since Katie had fallen, and the room had an odd vibe. None of the posters had been replaced or anything, and the classroom looked the same, but there was someone else's energy in the room. Another person led this menagerie of children. It made my heart heavier than I anticipated.

I set Katie's mirror up in the back of the classroom and called Skella on my cell. Within a few minutes she was in the classroom with us, adjusting a rather bulky fanny pack. She just glared at me, daring me to say something, but I declined. Really didn't go with her Goth outfit, but the bright purple was quite pretty.

I hadn't turned in Katie's keys, and the school hadn't asked. I figure they were still too freaked out to contact me for something that trivial. I walked around the room, explaining things to Skella, Jimmy, and Bub, pointing out pictures and such that Katie had favored.

I stopped at her desk and opened the drawer where she'd kept her purse and pictures of me. It was empty except for a box of crackers. I coughed to cover up the sudden pain in my chest. Where were those pictures?

"There's a box back here with Katie's name on it," Bub said, calling Jimmy and me back to the long case where the children stored their jackets and lunch boxes. Jimmy picked up the box with Katie's name on it, opened it, and found the pictures inside, along with a stack of drawings her students had made.

"Guess they were going to send these home to us," I said, repacking the box.

Jimmy watched me for a second and patted me on the shoulder. He was decked out in a shirt of Kevlar with plate over the top it, strap on plating over his jeans like football pads, and his sword in a sheath at his side. His helmet sat on one of the desks within easy reach, and he had a horseman's hammer over one shoulder, slung opposite how I had Gram over my shoulder. He was a righty, and me a lefty. I had on my chain, jeans, Doc Martens, and my hammers on my hips. I wish I had the shield, but that was at Nidhogg's place, over in Qindra's secret research facility. I think it doubled as her bedroom as well.

Regardless, I was feeling a little naked, but I had the book in my pack. I had to tell Jimmy at some point. The book was my beacon. I planned to hold it in my right hand, like I'd seen that statue in the dead lands. A beacon to guide me through the dark wild lands. I had a hunch that once I was through the mirror, the book would act differently. At least that was the theory.

"Is this where she fell?" Jimmy asked, pushing open the bathroom door and flicking on the light.

The room felt a lot smaller than the last time I'd been in there. It looked the same with the supply cabinet pushed against the wall like it should.

"You think she's stuck in here somewhere?" Skella asked, poking her head around the door frame. "Like stuck in with the toilet paper or something?"

Jimmy shot her a look, and Bub laughed a crackly little titter.

"Doubtful," I said. "But we can't assume. I'm willing to bet she was here a while, maybe even while Qindra and I explored the place, before we found the ..."

I paused. Show time.

"Jim, I have to show you something. Skella, can you and Bub grab the mirror and set it up back here?"

She nodded, and they walked back to Katie's desk where we'd left the mirror from our apartment.

I opened my saddlebags and pulled out the diary, wrapped in Katie's scarf. I peeled it back, letting the book show, but keeping a safety net between my fingers and all that magic.

At first Jimmy was confused, looking at me, then the book. Then recognition kicked in. He took a step back while reaching his hand out, like he wanted to take the book. The look on his face spoke more of horror, however.

"Where did you get that?" he asked, his voice quavering. "You had no right."

I lowered my arm, letting the book ride against my thigh.

"I didn't," I said, keeping my voice steady. "We found this in here," I motioned to the cabinet. "Shoved under that cabinet, after Katie had been taken to the hospital and before they reopened the classroom. Back when Qindra and I came to check it out."

Jimmy sat down on the closed toilet lid and covered his face with his hands. "Then she did take it from the house." It wasn't a question.

"Looks like it," I said. "She was angry, Jim. Mad that you'd kept secrets from her. You know Deidre showed this to her?"

His head snapped up and he glared at me, his mouth open and his eyes wide.

"Apparently not," I continued. I leaned back against the cabinet and crossed my arms with the book tucked against my breasts. "Look, Jim. What's done is done. You can ground her, yell at her, whatever you need to do, but after we bring her home. You know? Anger won't help us here. Hell, it's likely to draw more monsters. I need you calm and focused. We need to find her before it's too late."

There are some men who are petty, and some who are scared. Jimmy was a man of resolve. His baby sister was in trouble and we had a plan and a path forward. Nothing else mattered. At least I hoped.

"Damn it," he breathed, standing. "I can't tell you how much this sucks."

"Aye," I agreed.

"You think this is what caused the explosion, her going dark, the whole nine-yards?"

I explained to him about my experiments with the book. About the way it showed up in the Sideways with the Viking woman, then with the statue in the village there at the end of my last journey.

"It's a beacon for her," I said, feeling it in my gut. "She was searching for the book, searching for me. I think we can use it, let it send out its mystical signal or whatever the hell it does and see what happens."

"Can I touch it?" he asked. His eyes were haunted. This was his mother's book, and it had killed him, stopped his heart. Now here I was, not blood, and I could handle it. He was hurt and frustrated.

"I wouldn't advise it, Jim. Deep breath."

His shoulders slumped and he relaxed his fists.

"We're ready out here," Skella said, poking her head into the room. "If you don't get moving, Bub's gonna eat one of these desks."

Jimmy looked at me, nodded once, and walked out of the room, putting as much distance between me and the book as he could and still leave the bathroom.

"When this is over, we'll talk about the book," he said, putting on his helmet. "Maybe I'll get to stab a few things on the way to finding her."

Skella gave me a wincing look, and I shrugged at her.

"Be careful what you wish for," I said.

Skella went to the mirror, touched the surface, and teased the silver surface of the Sideways. "Give me a minute to find what I'm looking for," she said, sliding her hand across the mirror like flipping pages. "Getting to the Sideways isn't that hard, but we want to make sure we are anchored so we can get back home."

"Are you sure it's safe for you to follow us?" Bub asked, stepping next to me and slipping his clawed hand into mine.

I think he was a little scared.

"That's what you're here for, big guy. If we can't get back for some reason, you're gonna port back here with Skella and have her open the mirror again."

He looked up at me, his little round head reminding me even more strongly of a Muppet. "Are you sure about this?"

"Definitely," I said, grinning down at him. "You're a badass kobold. With you with us, and your ability to teleport, we are so covered."

He smiled at me and nodded.

"So, we start with the other side of here?" Skella asked. "Then follow any leads we can find after, right?"

"Yep, that's the plan."

Jimmy walked over to the pack he'd brought and opened it up, pulling out a teddy bear and strapping it to the bicep of his shield arm with a velcro tie. Then he wrapped a scarf around his neck, one I recognized from pictures of Katie when she was a kid.

"The scarf was mom's," he said. "Katie loved it more than anything—carried it night and day after they disappeared."

I smiled at him. He had a soft gooey center after all.

"And the bear."

He just looked at me without saying another word.

I turned away. Of course it was hers, but he wanted it to be his secret, what the hell.

We stashed our packs and my saddlebags in the supply cabinet and closed the door before gathering around the mirror. Skella had it opened and ready to a point that looked like a reflection of the classroom, only with some oddities on the walls and a long wispy spirit floating against the far wall of the Sideways room.

I looked back in this world, looking for the equivalent in our world, but didn't see anything. Not like there was always a correlation.

"Okay, let's go," I said.

We were a ragtag bunch. Once we stepped through the mirror the lights went out, and Bub screamed.

FIFTY-SEVEN

I t's quite simple," Frederick said, nodding at Mr. Philips who poured coffee into the cup at Sawyer's elbow. "I had a plan in place, a contingency in case one of my brethren took it upon themselves to remove me from the game."

Stuart waved Mr. Philips away from his cup, instead he picked up his water and took a sip. He'd had two cups of coffee with breakfast and he didn't want to confuse the taste with the image of Sawyer. Right now, the taste of coffee went quite well with his vivid memories of Qindra sitting naked in bed eating strawberries while they talked.

Qindra had already made a cup of tea and was sipping it when Mr. Philips returned to the table and took out a small notebook from his inside jacket pocket.

"A daughter?" Qindra asked.

Stuart wasn't sure why this was an important point, but Qindra knew her business.

"Yes," Sawyer said, steepling his fingers in front of his face. "A conceit, perhaps, but one I am willing to pay the consequences for."

"What are your intentions, then?" Qindra asked, setting her cup on the table and picking up a thin chocolate wafer.

Mr. Philips leaned over and said something to his master that did not escape their general orbit. Qindra watched them, her exquisite face a mask of serenity and calm.

The fact that Sawyer had somehow hatched a daughter was disturbing news. There had to be huge political play in motion here. Was he making a move on the Vancouver, BC territory?

"I have not decided yet," Sawyer said, finally.

Mr. Philips leaned to the side once more, but Frederick waved him back. "I know my own mind," he said to the stoic man.

Mr. Philips sat up straight and crossed his hands in front of himself, covering the small notebook and pencil under his manicured hands.

Qindra turned her teacup around, facing the handle toward her and kept her eyes focused exclusively on Sawyer. "Will you foster her, then?"

She was a cool one, but what did she mean by foster? Like sending the kid for someone else to raise? What would that entail? Stuart thought.

"I will not send flesh of my flesh to the great sow as a prisoner, if that is what you imply."

Qindra picked up her cup and took a demure sip, her eyes never leaving Frederick's. "And what of the …" she paused, "egg donor?"

This was a game they played, Stuart realized. This balance and feint, parry and thrust.

He cleared his throat. Parry and thrust made him think of their evening, and his face felt suddenly too hot.

The other three looked at him.

"Does she have to be fostered with another dragon?" Stuart asked. "We have quite the menagerie out at Black Briar. Maybe you'd want to send her up our way to raise." The idea was a stroke of brilliance. Sarah would love it and Jimmy would come unglued.

Qindra raised her eyebrows and pursed her mouth. Interesting idea, it said to Stuart. Mr. Philips remained stoic and unfathomable.

"Are you mad?" Frederick asked, turning his gaze to Stuart for the first time since they'd arrived.

Stuart looked at him, saw the fire in those ancient eyes. Despite the well-appointed look and the clean and modern office, he had no doubt that Frederick could destroy him where he sat, before he could react, without a single iota of remorse.

"Sarah protected you," Stuart said with a shrug. "Saved your life and refused to claim you for her own. I don't think you can overlook that."

Qindra winked at him, and the corners of her mouth turned up briefly. Neither Mr. Philips nor Sawyer noticed as they were staring at him as if he'd just grown a second head.

"You dare," Sawyer began with a sputter. "You imply ..."

Mr. Philips leaned forward. "Are you suggesting there is a debt here?" he asked, flipping to a blank page in his notebook and jotting down several words that Stuart could not read. Code perhaps.

"Call it what you want," Stuart said. "I don't know why you can't raise your own child, frankly." He looked at Qindra who did not respond.

"But if you really need someplace to have her looked after, I don't think you'd find a better group of folk to keep her safe and sound."

Sawyer sat back, scoffing. The look on his face was one of utter contempt.

"Your input is noted," Mr. Philips said, then turned to face Qindra.

"The girl is safe where she is. We both know there is no rush to make any decisions at this time. Her safety is not currently in jeopardy and there will be no internal house conflict until such time as she comes of age."

"She'll have her own territory at that point," Sawyer said, his voice tight and his anger barely concealed below the facade of proprietary.

"Of course," Qindra said. "As I said when we arranged for this meeting, we are here simply as a courtesy. Our conversations at the young Montgomery's funeral called for a follow-up in my mistress's mind, and here we are."

She sipped her tea, watching Sawyer, the mask affixed with natural aplomb.

"Please tell your mistress that her concern is noted," Sawyer said, sitting forward once more.

Nidhogg had stood over Sawyer's fallen form at the end of the Chumstick battle. Kept the Trisha dragon from killing him. He owed Nidhogg as well as Sarah.

"Nidhogg sends her warmest regards," Qindra assured him. "Things have shifted in the kingdoms of late, and Nidhogg would count you as friend rather than foe."

Sawyer nodded. "As would I. The whole incident with Jean-Paul has left us all a little on edge. The Reavers seek to undo much of what we've accomplished over the last four hundred years."

"Agreed," Qindra said, placing her napkin over her plate and leaning back in her chair. "I pray you consider your options with the child."

"There is much to consider," Sawyer agreed. "Too many moving pieces to get a good picture of the world today. The blood cult that dared confront us will not be the last, I am afraid. There are other factions, more desperate and radical, who may seek to do us, or our kingdoms, great harm."

Something about all this was bugging Stuart. He thought Qindra was the cat's pajamas, but this talk of kingdoms and factions was not happy making.

"Would you join me for dinner this evening?" Sawyer asked, nodding to Mr. Philips who took a note. "You could come out to the house, meet my darling daughter. What say you? Surely the great mother would like a firsthand report. Say seven this evening?"

It was barely eleven now. If they got out of here they could hit a museum, walk the Pearl district, or maybe even hit Powell's.

He glanced at Qindra. Or see if there were any strawberries left back at their room. He was sure he could think of something creative to keep them busy for a few hours.

"Splendid idea," Qindra agreed, standing and holding her hand out to Sawyer.

Frederick stood, taking Qindra's hand, and turned it, kissing her on the knuckles. "Enchanting as always," he purred.

Stuart squinted at him. *Don't push it bud.*

"Mr. Philips will show you out," Sawyer said and strode to the great window overlooking the financial district.

"Follow me, please," Mr. Philips said, coming around the table and motioning toward the door.

Qindra slipped her hand into Stuart's, causing his blood pressure to rise several points. She had nice hands, firm grip, long fingers.

There was nothing about her that he disliked, he decided. Even her loyalty to Nidhogg. As Sarah had stated over and over—not all dragons are created alike. Maybe Nidhogg was really remorseful of her past and wanted to change things going forward.

Of course, if she wasn't, there wasn't a whole lot he was going to do about it anyway.

Qindra leaned in a kissed him once they were on the elevator down to the lobby. "I think we should continue where we left off this morning," she said, licking Stuart's earlobe.

"Definitely," he said. "But at some point I'd like to know what the hell is going on in general."

Qindra laughed and kissed him on the cheek. "Politics, my dear Stuart. The dance of the moneyed class, what those individuals of immense power do instead of making love. They dance."

"I'm as poor as a church mouse," Stuart said to her.

A broad grin broke across her face. "Then we shall do what we shall do."

FIFTY-EIGHT

The book flared to life with a flash of bright green light as I peeled back the scarf and grasped the book in my naked hand. The classroom on this side of the mirror was suddenly swarming with crawlies. Skella clapped her hands once and said a word in Elvish I didn't recognize, but a flash of clean, white light exploded from her, shredding a dozen or more shadow creatures that had materialized around us.

Jimmy and I drew steel while Bub backed against the wall, hissing.

"What the hell were those things?" Jimmy asked, glancing around.

I looked up, making sure there was nothing about to drop on top of us, and pushed a desk aside.

"Some form of eater?" I asked, glancing at Skella.

"Shades," she said, shaking her head. "Lost souls who are drawn to places of power. Something has been going on here, drawing them to this place."

"Residual from Katie's accident?" I asked, walking across to the door to the hallway.

"Wouldn't surprise me," Skella said, drawing a small pouch from her belt and pinching out a bit of shiny dust. "Here," she said, stepping to Bub. "Unun sent me with this." She sprinkled a bit onto the top of Bub's head, and a light flowed over him like a golden cocoon.

"It tickles," he said, tittering.

Skella smiled and turned to Jimmy. "Could you squat down?" she asked.

Jimmy looked at me once, but did as she asked.

Once we were all adequately bathed in golden light, she put the pouch away and dusted off her hands.

"Why didn't we do that on the other side?" Jimmy asked.

"It doesn't exist on the other side," she said, looking at him like he was an idiot child. "This is magic."

"What does it do?" I asked, trying to keep a straight face.

Skella looked at me and shrugged. "All I know is that it helps keep you safe when travelling here. Unun wouldn't talk about all it does. Only that it allows us to see each other and helps mask our emotions as we wander the shadow lands. There are things here that feed off your baser feelings."

Eaters, crawlies, ghosts, shades, and on and on. "Is there anything here that doesn't want to eat us?"

Skella shrugged again. "There's a reason Gletts and I avoided this place."

Right. Awesome. And Katie had been lost here for going on two months.

We moved to the hallway door, watching for surprises. The hallway was quiet and longer in both directions than they were in the normal world.

"This is strange," Bub said, cocking his head from one side to the other.

"Emotional distortion," Skella said.

"Maybe you should write a book," Jimmy said, facing down one length of the hall, while I faced the other.

Doors lined the hall, but they were dark. To the right in our world there were a couple more classrooms, then an exit out to the playground. To the left was the main body of the school as well as several wings off for more classrooms. The school was like a giant failed Tetris game, with hallways going off at intervals leaving courtyards interspersed throughout. Some of these were roofed, with skylights. Those near the perimeter of the building were open to the outside, like the courtyard outside Katie's classroom.

Old classroom, I guess. This year was lost to her. I wondered if she'd ever come back here to teach. Made my chest hurt. She'd be devastated.

On the north side of the structure were the central offices and cafeteria. In the heart of the complex was a huge, sprawling library.

Twice we were attacked by shades as we opened classroom doors, but they were easily dispatched. Skella said they'd just reform later so we shouldn't dawdle.

While Katie's classroom had been fully rendered, there were other areas that were shadowy or almost non-existent. Places where people rarely gathered. Places of strong emotion—good or bad—were solid as our world.

Several times we paused as Jimmy picked up a hint that Katie had been there. There was a distinct difference from the memories of her etched into this place. The teachers' lounge had a strong impression of her. The cafeteria had her mark as well, but it was so faint, only Jimmy had picked it up.

"More like the memory of a feeling, you know?" he said.

I wondered if it was the love or the blood. The fact I couldn't sense that she'd been in a couple of places stung a bit, but they were blood related and knew each other longer.

"There's a hub ahead," Skella said after we'd explored the northern half of the school. "Near the middle."

"That'll be the library," I said.

We slowed our approach. There were two large doors ahead, each ornately carved with the figures of dragons.

Bub stepped forward and touched the door on the left. The dragon there flexed his great wings and turned his head toward us.

"Careful," Jimmy said, taking a step forward.

"Guardians," Skella said. "They wouldn't let any of the riffraff inside there, but it could be dangerous," Skella said. "Place like that has a lot of portals, lots of places to get lost."

"Why?" Bub asked, moving to the second door and looking up at the female dragon carved there. She lowered her head to be level with Bub and a puff of steam rose from her nostrils.

"Let me," Skella said. She opened her pack and took out a flaming torch.

"Nice," I said. "That burning the whole time it was in your pack?"

"More magic." Bub said, leaning forward and examining the dragon on the door in front of him.

"Of course," Skella said, smiling. "Unun gave me a few items. Seems maybe she'd done some exploring in her youth. She's a sly one, very secretive."

Skella stepped forward and bowed.

"We would like to pass," she said, smiling.

The male dragon turned away, saying nothing. His door did not move.

Skella turned to face the female. "And you, majestic one?"

She lifted her scaled head and shook it sideways.

"That's a no," Bub said.

"You try," I suggested, squatting down next to him. "You are kin, are you not?"

Bub looked at me, tilting his head from one side to the other, thinking.

"Kith, not kin," he said. "But I believe you hold the key here." He pointed to the book.

I patted him on the shoulder and stood, holding the book high. The light pulsed when I held it near the door, and the dragon blinked at me twice before stepping back.

The door swung open revealing a chamber crisscrossed with glowing ribbons of light.

Let the book guide you, a voice said inside my head.

I stepped forward, pausing to look back and make sure the others followed. Bub grabbed the back of my chain shirt. I smiled at that. He had a look of sheer amazement on his little round face. It was cute how expressive he could be with all those scales.

Skella came next, followed by Jimmy. Once we were all inside, the door closed with a quiet click, and the room lit up like a discotheque.

"It's the books," Jimmy said, stepping up next to me.

We stood on a marble staircase going down to a grand cathedral of shelved books. The place was a palace.

"This is the dreaming place," Skella said. "Where minds are opened and worlds created."

We descended the marble staircase and crept across the thickly carpeted chamber. In the distance we could hear children laughing.

"Echos," Skella said, urging us forward.

Bub paused at one point, falling behind. The lights were dazzling.

I walked back and put my hand on his shoulder. "Come on, big guy."

"I thought I heard Jai Li," he said, looking around.

"She's at home," I promised him. "Julie, Mary, and Edith are watching her."

He looked at me, blinking for a moment and nodded. "There is much here to explore. I think I could become lost here."

I took his hand. "Come on, I won't let you get lost."

We made our way after that with no interruptions.

"How do we know Katie isn't here?" Bub asked as we climbed the stairs on the other side of the expansive hall.

"She's not," Jimmy said, pointing to his left arm.

I looked at him as he turned halfway to show us. The teddy bear he'd strapped to his arm was reaching toward the door to the rest of the school.

"Well, that seems clear enough," I said. I led them to the huge doors and pushed the metal bar that opened them. Just like the doors in the rest of the school. The Sideways was a funny place.

Once the doors closed behind us, we saw immediately a glow coming from down one hall.

Bub pulled away from me, scrambling down the hall. "She is here," he said, looking back with a grin. "Can you not feel her?"

"Bub, wait," Skella called, reaching out with one hand.

But it was too late. Shots rang out from one of the side passages. Three bullets smashed into Bub, and he fell back, a bloody ragdoll.

"No!" I shouted, running forward. This could not be happening. Not here. Not the soldiers.

FIFTY-NINE

Out of two hallways came a scattering of the monster men. On the right a scrum of burly men with the heads of bulls roared forward swinging clubs and axes. On the right, two smaller men with the heads of cats held rifles, while a half a dozen more poured out of the other corridors with swords, axes, and clubs.

Skella ran to Bub and slid to her knees at his side. I turned and rushed the men with rifles, screaming. Jimmy's own cry reached me as I smashed into them.

One of them got off a shot as I slammed Gram down, severing both arms, and cutting the rifle in half. I staggered as the bullet thumped into my chest, knocking me back a step. I'd feel that later. I assumed the chain stopped it since I didn't fall over.

The armless guy fell back screaming, the stumps of his arms flailing, spraying me with black blood.

His partner stepped forward and swung his rifle around, catching me in the shoulder, causing me to lurch to the left and nearly go down in the slick blood. I careened against the wall, caught my balance, and juked to the side as he stabbed the bayonet forward, missing me by a hair's-breadth. The steel rang as it sparked off the cinder block wall and the blade snapped.

I smashed my right hand forward, catching the bastard in the face with the book. He dropped his rifle and brought his hands to his smoking face. I stepped back as his head caved in on one side, melted by a flare of purple light that exploded from the book.

In the flash of light, I saw the Bowler Hat Man back in the deep shadows. These were the shock troops. He'd enter the fray after they'd won or fallen.

I backed out of the hall, glancing around to see how the others were faring. Skella had Bub's head in her lap and his wounds were a glowing swath of light casting her face in awkward shadows. He was breathing, but she did not look pleased.

Jimmy had taken down three of the other fighters, but was having a hard time keeping the rest from either bringing him down or getting past him to Skella and Bub.

I launched myself into the flank of the oncoming baddies, smashing one with the book, causing another explosion of energy—this one green. The light slashed through several of them like shrapnel causing two to drop and a third to fall back holding his face. I dropped him with a quick thrust of Gram, kicked a second to the side and engaged the final man in that hall.

"About time," Jimmy grunted as he parried a poorly aimed strike with a short spear and swept the tip of his blade across the monster man's eyes. The ugly fell back with a cry as two more stepped forward to take his place.

Skella screamed.

"Skella," I shouted, dancing with my own enemy.

I glanced over, and she was dodging a blow from the Bowler Hat Man. He had come forward too quietly for me to notice, what with all the battle going on. He wielded twin axes, dancing an intricate web of flashing steel and verbal derision.

I made out a few words my mother would blanch at. Skella had no place to go and had just missed getting hit with one of the axes when Bub lurched forward and swiped the inside of the man's thigh with his claws.

The man roared like a banshee, which thankfully he wasn't, and I put down my last bad guy. Jimmy was being hard pressed by four of the burly men with clubs. "Hold the fort, Jim," I called as I swung around toward Skella. The Bowler Hat Man smashed an axe down, catching Bub in the shoulder. He crumpled, lifeless and broken.

"Fuck you," I cried, leaping over Bub's body. My vision started to blur as the berserker finally kicked in. Skella fell to the side as she caught a glancing blow from one of the axes, but I dove over her, catching the man in the chest and knocking him back into the hallway he'd come down. We landed hard, my shoulder in his chest, and he grunted, dropping the axes. I scrambled back, looking around. I'd dropped the book, but managed to keep my hands on Gram.

I was on one knee, debating standing or just fighting the guy on the ground, when something very pointy stabbed me in the back. The world sloughed sideways, the walls running like melted cheese. My body seized up, poison flowed into me, pumping from the bulbous poison sacs of a huge millipede that had dropped from the ceiling.

That's gonna leave a mark, I thought as my vision blurred.

I lurched to the side, trying to bring Gram around to stab the damn thing, but I couldn't lift my hand. The Bowler Hat Man had his knee on my wrist and was trying to wrench the blade free.

I was rightly fucked. I punched upward, striking the millipede with my right fist, but I was growing too weak to make much of a difference. Then it bent itself back, extracting its stinger and screaming. Skella stood there, blood running down her face, with her torch thrust into the great thrashing creature.

The Bowler Hat Man stumbled back, giving up on getting Gram and picked up one of his fallen axes. I rolled to the side, vomited once, and pushed myself up onto my hands and knees.

Skella pushed the millipede thing away with the torch, and it curled up in a ball, smoking and writhing, the screaming rising in pitch. The sound pierced my head with such pain that I vomited again. I gripped Gram with both hands and forced myself up onto my knees, then let gravity help me smash the sword down on the beast, severing it in two.

The screaming stopped, and I fell back against the wall on my backside, Gram in one hand and my other on Skella's leg. She stood over me, waving the torch, keeping the Bowler Hat Man from advancing.

"Tut, tut," he clucked, a grin spreading across his face. "You are already dead, my pretty. I'd prefer to play with you a bit before you fade away, but I think you'll be entertaining even after you're dead."

"Try me now," I said, almost too weak to talk. "Give me your best shot. See how you like it."

My vision faded in and out as he laughed at me, standing there, just out of reach with one axe in his hand, and his hair a disheveled mess. Funny, I'd assumed he was bald the way he kept that damn hat on all the time.

I could hear battle coming from the main hall. Jimmy was still fighting. I just wish I could stand up.

Skella waved the torch in front of us, and the man laughed, his voice like a nightmare.

"Don't you worry, missy. I'll be having a go with you as well. It's just this bitch that's been haunting me. Her I want to hurt. You I'll take my time with, let you linger a while. I bet you'll be delicious."

I looked to one side, then the other, looking for the book.

The man followed my gaze, stepped to my side, and knelt down next to the book. "Is this what you're looking for?" he asked. "I want to thank you for bringing it to me, after all these years, it's finally mine once more."

"Don't touch it," I said, half hoping he would. Maybe it would burn him up. But there was something about him, something older and fouler than the other denizens of this fucked up dimension. I had a feeling that if he touched it, he'd turn it, corrupt it.

Wait. Did he say the book was his?

"I saw what you did to some of my boys with that little book," he said, keeping a fair distance away. "I think I'll let it sit for now."

He stood, stepped over the book and walked past us toward the mouth of the hallway.

"Now, if you'll excuse me, I'll see to my great grandson."

"Warn Jimmy," I said, but the world slid sideways and I fell over. *Grandson? Jimmy?*

Screams filled the corridor, and a roar like a grizzly echoed down the hallway. I truly hoped it was on our side.

SIXTY

I woke up with Skella's face inches from my own.

"Wake up," she said, smacking me again. She was pouring something over my shoulder out of a small glass phial, but I couldn't tell what it was. It smelled heavily of urine and roses. Not the most pleasant combination.

"Take the book," she said, pointing to my left. "I can't touch it."

I glanced down at her as my head began to clear. I definitely wasn't one hundred percent, but I wasn't going to fall over again. Not yet, anyhow.

She pulled my shoulder and cried out as she did it. I glanced down and saw that her hands were burned badly.

"Book doesn't like me," she said, wincing.

"Doesn't like anyone," I grunted, forcing myself to my hands and knees, aware of the sound of carnage in the main hall. I had to get up, had to get the book and Gram. I didn't want to face whatever was making that noise, but I couldn't leave Bub and Jimmy out there alone.

The second I touched the book, flame rushed over me and through me, entering my mouth, nose, eyes, and every single wound on my body from the slightest scratch to the gaping hole in my back from the millipede.

I lost conscious for a while, not sure how long, but I battered myself pretty good as the power surged through me. I think the only thing that stopped it was Skella slid Gram toward me, shoving her against my outstretched hand.

As soon as the sword made contact with my hand, I grasped it convulsively, and the power overload dialed it back several notches. My hair hurt, the soles of my feet hurt, hell, my fingernails hurt, but I was alive and the power of the book had burned the worst of the poison out of me.

Unfortunately, it also burned off all my body hair. At least what I could feel and smell without disrobing. Things were uncomfortable everywhere. I didn't want to check anywhere else. But I had a bad feeling.

I sat there smoking, trying to get my mouth to work when a giant of a man came barreling down the hall toward us. Skella screamed and flung herself aside, but the bull-headed man didn't even try to accost us. One of his huge horns had been ripped off, and there were long gouges down his left side. He whimpered as he passed us, limping into the shadows.

The eaters would finish him. They didn't take sides, really.

Skella helped me up and I leaned against the wall, getting my sea legs.

"What about you?" I asked. "Any healing potions in that kit for you?"

She shook her head. "No healing potions, period. This isn't a game."

"So, what did you do to me, then?"

She looked at me and shrugged. "Think of it as smelling salts for your spirit."

That wasn't strange.

Another roar echoed out of the main hall, so I started shuffling my way forward, Gram held tight in my left hand and the book in my right.

"Come on, then," I said, not looking back. "Don't dawdle back here without me."

"You don't have to tell me twice," Skella said, edging past me to glance out into the main battle.

She stood mouth agape when I caught up with her.

There in the middle of the courtyard a battle was happening between a dozen or so monster men and a bear the size of a small house. She was wounded with a dozen spears and axe strokes, but the dead around her rose in heaps.

"Where's Jim?" I asked Skella who pointed to the right hall toward the glowing light we only assumed was Katie. He was down, his sword broken, and his helmet smashed on the ground beside him.

Bub still lay in the middle, at the bear's feet, unmoving. He wasn't dead. He'd just reappear again later. He just needed to melt like he always did. I knew he would. I brought my hand to my throat and tried to grab the amulet with the same hand I held Gram in. Did it feel any different? Was it cold? That damned kobold better survive.

"Check on Jimmy," I said, feeling more of my strength creeping into my veins.

Skella nodded and careened around the right side of the battle, well out of the way of the bear's brutal attacks.

Okay the bear was on our side. That was good to know.

But she was not going to survive without help. I went to the left, away from the glowing light, toward shadow. I sensed more than saw the shades gathering along the periphery, waiting their opportunity to feed on the fallen.

"Not today," I said, holding the book up and waving it toward them. The shadows fell back, but they didn't leave.

The monster men were dwindling, but were in a good defensive position, keeping the bear back with spears. Unfortunately for them, they didn't realize I was still in the fight.

I rushed forward, swinging the book in one hand, and Gram in the other. Green and purple light arced through the bad guys like chain lightning as Gram cut a swath through them, totally destroying their flank.

The bear took advantage of their sudden confusion and took down the biggest of the bull men, shredding his face and chest with her foot long claws. After that, the remaining enemy turned and fled, dropping their weapons and not looking back.

The bear dropped onto all fours and galumphed after them for a few paces.

"Wait," I called after her. "Too risky."

The bear paused, looked back at me and snorted once before turning back and ambling into the room. It walked to Jimmy,

322

sniffed him from head to toe, and dragged its long tongue over his face.

"Eww," Skella said, sliding back away from the bear. "That's gross."

Jimmy spluttered and sat up, holding his head.

"Not dead I see," he groaned, reaching for his dented helm and placing it back on his head. It mostly fit.

"The bear was unexpected," I said, kneeling beside him, looking into his face.

The teddy bear that he'd had strapped to his arm was gone. Right, of course. Too obvious.

"Probably kept me from getting my brains totally smashed in," Jimmy said, struggling to stand up. Skella helped him and he got unsteadily to his feet.

"When the new squad arrived, I knew we were screwed. Just as that big bastard showed up," he pointed at a huge man, eight feet tall with the head of a rhino, "I went down. The bear was getting big fast, and totally threw me off balance. Kept my brains inside the helmet and my head."

The bear snuffled Skella then began to walk down the hallway to the glowing white light.

"Where's the Bowler Hat Man?" I asked.

Skella shrugged and looked after the bear. "If he's that way, the bear will get him."

"I'd rather not risk it," I said, following the bear. "Jimmy, can you bring Bub? I don't want to leave him here for the feeders."

I didn't look back. If Katie was ahead, I needed to find her, needed to know.

The Sideways is a really strange place. There was no way that damn bear could've fit inside the school, but when I got to the next classroom she'd pressed herself into the room and curled up next to a glowing white rabbit.

There was no sign of the Bowler Hat Man.

Skella stopped in the doorway, allowing Jim to bring Bub into the room and lay his motionless form beside the bear.

"Close the door," I said, motioning for Skella to come into the room.

"Is this her," Jimmy asked, shock and pain painting his features.

"I think so," I said, pointing to the bear. "She's pretty bent on protecting that rabbit." I knelt and reached toward the bunny. The book flared, a green aura spreading from me to the bear, then to Jimmy.

He squawked, desperately pulling his mother's scarf off his neck and flinging it at me. His hands and neck were burned, but he'd live.

"Yeah, okay." I knew what to do.

I sheathed Gram, set the book on the ground, reached over, and picked up the bunny.

The bear snorted, swinging her huge damned head toward me and sniffed once, then lay back down, licking the wounds on her paws and arms.

The rabbit slept, nestled in my lap.

I took the scarf and wrapped it around the bunny, stroking its long ears.

"Katie, love," I said.

The rabbit stirred, but did not react in any other way. It slept on.

"You sure that's her?" Jimmy asked again, confused.

"Let's get her out of here," I said, grabbing the book and shoving it in my saddlebags. Then I picked up the rabbit, cradling it like a baby against my chest. I stood up and paused as the room swam. Maybe I wasn't doing so well myself.

"Sooner the better," I muttered. I was flagging. Maybe the poison wasn't as burned out as I thought.

The bear stood and snorted, so Skella pulled the door open and stepped back.

I don't know why I didn't react sooner. Hell, I don't think I'd ever get the image out of my head.

The Bowler Hat Man stood on the other side of the door, leering, his hat cocked to the side as he swung both axes forward.

"Watch out," Jimmy said, stepping forward, pushing Skella out of the way.

The two axes flashed. One caught Jimmy in the face, the second in his chest.

It was brutal and sudden, so sudden I reacted on instinct. I shoved the rabbit into Skella's hands and pulled Gram free. Jimmy fell to his knees first, wrenching one axe from the bastard's hand, and fell forward with a clatter of armor and axe handle.

"No!" I shouted as I stepped forward, stabbing forward, catching the Bowler Hat Man in the throat. The cartilage in his neck parted like cutting whipped cream, and the grin on his face faded to a look of shock and surprise.

I stepped around Jimmy, drew Gram back and hacked at the man, catching him in the arm as he dropped the axe and brought his hands to his throat. I hit him over and over, smashing his body and carving away great bloody globs of flesh. I was out of my mind, far beyond the berserker. I had no thought, no feelings, just hacked and hacked until my arm grew tired and I could no longer lift Gram.

"He's gone," Skella croaked.

I glanced at her, my eyes coming back into focus. She and the rabbit were covered in gore. The door, the walls and the hallway were covered in it.

I stepped out, making sure that there were no other monsters, ready to kill and kill and kill.

When I turned back, Skella was on her knees at Jimmy's side. She was struggling to flip him onto his back with only one arm and not succeeding.

"Here, let me," I said, laying Gram on the ground at my feet. "Just keep Katie safe."

SIXTY-ONE

Dead is dead, Gletts had told me a lifetime ago in the dead lands. Hard to argue with logic like that. But I was sure as hell gonna try.

Jimmy's helmet caught the brunt of the axe stroke, which surprised me once we got a look at him. It looked like the bones in his face were crushed.

Skella poured the last of her little bottle of white smoke over him while I was working on wrapping his face in bandages. I was surprised that the wounds didn't close once the smoky liquid had washed over him.

"Thought that was a healing potion."

She looked at me with disdain. "This isn't a game, Sarah."

Jimmy's plate had turned the axe aside, but it had bitten deep into the chest muscle peeling it back in a thick slab. It bled like hell, but we packed it as tight as we could and wrapped his face in bandages.

"So, what does that stuff do, then? If it doesn't heal. What did it do for me?"

She smiled a bit that spoke of pain. "Keep your spirit tied to your body," she said. "So you don't get lost and wander here forever, or until something eats you."

"A last resort when one of us was close to dying?" I asked, both shocked and impressed.

She only nodded.

We constructed a travois from the assorted weaponry and clothing of the fallen. The bear didn't argue one bit when we lashed it to her. We managed to get both Jimmy and Bub onto the structure and made good time going back. Twice we had to fight off shades, but they were no real trouble. Good thing, too. Most of them were driven back by Skella's torch. When I asked her why she didn't do that clapping thing with the flash of light, she assured me it was a sometimes treat.

By the time we found our way back to Katie's classroom, Skella and I were wiped out, emotionally and physically.

She opened the mirror, giving us access to the real world. Skella scrambled through to keep the mirror open. The bunny vanished as she crossed into the real world, like a bit of smoke in too much wind.

"Katie?" Skella said, looking back at me it the mirror.

"It's fine, I said, looking back at the bear. I think she's found her way home. Call Melanie, get her in here."

Skella nodded and ran to the supply cabinets where we'd stashed our gear. Soon she was standing in front of the mirror, talking on her cell phone.

The bear nudged me with her large nose, pushing me toward the exit.

"Yeah, I know," I said. "Time to get this mess home."

The bear stepped forward through the mirror, though it was too small for her bulk. The travois hung half-way, in both worlds, when she fell to the ground, a battered and bloodied stuffed animal once again.

Melanie and Dena were able to pull the travois through the rest of the way and begin working on Jimmy.

Bub hadn't moved, hadn't breathed.

"Did you use that spirit smoke on Bub?" I asked Skella.

"No," she said, tears running down her face. "He isn't like you and me. It wouldn't have any effect."

I sat down beside the small form, stroking the side of his scaly face. There was a second ambulance on the way. Not sure how we were going to explain all this, but I didn't care.

We sat there in shock as Melanie and Dena worked on Jimmy. It was surreal. All the things we'd done, the battles, the library, the monsters. Yet here we sat in a colorful classroom where the children's desks had been pushed aside and the floor was sticky with blood.

At first I thought it was just exhaustion. The sound started to fade to a low buzz then ended altogether. I glanced up, nearly numb but surprised at the creeping quiet. The world was pushed aside as a greater power imposed itself on the scene.

Then I heard them. Horses. My mind froze for a moment, realization striking me. The door to the classroom opened at the same time Melanie sat back, wiping hair out of her face with the back of her bloodied hands.

"Sarah?" Gunnr said from the doorway

"Gunnr?"

There she was, shield maiden, Valkyrie. Spear maiden for Odin and chooser of the fallen.

The rest of the world grew still, frozen. Melanie, Dena, and Skella stopped moving, caught between one breath and the next.

Skuld and Róta came into the room next, their winged helms under their arms. "Rest assured," Skuld said, nodding at me. "We are not here for you."

I looked down at Bub. Him, surely.

"Not him, either," Gunnr said, squatting next to me and touching Bub on his forehead. At her touch he melted, a rapid transformation from kobold to vapor.

"He will return in time," she said, looking into my eyes and touching the side of my face. "We are here for the other one."

The breath caught in my throat. "No," I whispered.

"I know this pains you, dear one," her eyes bored into mine, the depths a swirl of galaxies. "He fought to save those he loved and has died valiantly," she said, smiling. "Let us take him home."

"No," I said, pushing her hand away. "He's not dead. You can't take him."

Skuld shook her head, and Róta stepped past her, stepping toward Jimmy. "We have no time for this," she said, her voice firm but without anger.

"Leave us a moment," Gunnr said, glancing at her sisters.

Skuld jerked her head toward the door, and Róta backed away, shaking her head.

"It is always this way," she mumbled as they left. "He should be honored for his glory. Why must they weep and wail?"

The door shut off any reply that Skuld may have made.

"Please," I said, trembling at Gunnr's touch. "He's a good man. He deserves to live."

"He has lived," she said, smiling at me. "And he has led his people with honor. But he has fallen, sweet Sarah. To hold him here would be a horror beyond reckoning. Let him ride with us. I promise you it is for the best."

"What do I tell Katie?" I asked, the numbness spreading through my limbs.

"You have brought her home, have you not?" she asked, motioning toward the door. "She has rejoined spirit to body. Her brother died saving her, died saving her true love." She paused at this, letting out a deep sigh. "As much as I crave you," she said, touching my lips with her fingers. "I cannot deny the love you share. She will wake in due time. And you will be there to help her through the pain."

I couldn't help it. Tears ran down my cheeks, tickling the flesh and making my eyes sting.

Gunnr leaned forward and kissed me on the left cheek, kissing away the tear.

"Rejoice," she said, sitting back. "He will be a true leader among the Einherjar. His glories will multiply until the time the old man returns to us and we have the final battle."

I bowed my head as the tears fell in earnest.

After a moment, Gunnr leaned forward and kissed me on the top of my scorched head. "Your locks were comely," she said. "Even when shorn in the odd fashion you favored."

I choked out a laugh. My locks were comely. And Jimmy was dead.

"He is a great man," I said, wiping my face.

"Of that there is no doubt," she said smiling. "Let him ride with us, give us leave to take him from this place."

Why was she asking my permission? What if I refused, that then?

"My fierce warrior," she said, standing and pulling me up by my hands. "He will remain dead, no matter your decision. You only choose the manner of his eternity."

What was I going to tell Deidre? What about Gunther or Stuart?

"Take him," I said, pulling my hands out of hers. "He deserves a glorious afterlife. But don't think I'm doing this with a glad heart."

She stepped around me, knelt at Jimmy's side and touched his shattered face. "So very handsome, he was. He will be even more so in the next world when his valor will show through."

She rose, and Jimmy rose with her. Rather his spirit did.

"What is this?" Gunnr asked me, brushing thick strands of white from Jimmy's spirit.

"Something of the elves," I said, pointing to Skella. "To keep his spirit from being lost in the Sideways."

Gunnr glanced down at Skella and smiled. "She was right to do so," she concluded, brushing several more strands of white goo from Jimmy's form. As a spirit he looked as handsome as the day I'd met him, tall and strong, his gaze confident and his will strong.

"Tell him I'm sorry," I said as Gunnr pulled him free of his body finally.

"When he is ready for the hearing," she assured me. "But let us go."

She walked to the door, Jimmy trailing behind her, staring forward as if he were in a trance. I guess he was, being newly dead and all.

"Look for your friend," she pointed to where Bub had lain. "In a day or so, he will come to you, drawn to the amulet."

"Thank you," I said. I really wanted the little guy back, but I couldn't think through the pain.

"Take your love home," she said, opening the door and ushering Jimmy out. Skuld and Róta took him by an arm each and walked him to a large horse. I stepped out of the classroom, stunned. "Blue Thunder?" I asked, and looked back at Gunnr who smiled. "Every warrior needs a worthy steed," she said. "We would not let a beast such as this escape into oblivion."

I watched them mount and gallop into the sky. Jimmy never looked back, but Gunnr did. The look she gave me was as much lust as loss.

"I'm sorry," I whispered.

"Sarah!" Skella yelled from the classroom.

I looked back at the classroom. "Out here," I said. But when I looked back to the sky they were gone.

Skella careened against the doorframe in a panic. "Jimmy's ... dead ..." she said between sobs. And Bub's gone. She swiped at her face, pushing the tears away with anger. "Why are you out here?"

"Long story," I said, putting my arm over her shoulder. "Let's get all this crap out of here. I'll need to tell Deidre."

Dena took the ambulance and headed back to Black Briar. We debated on calling the authorities for Jimmy but then thought better of it. If Qindra could make people disappear, I'm sure she could help us fake Jimmy's death in a way that wouldn't raise suspicions.

But I wanted to get his body back to Black Briar. Deidre would want to bury him, or whatever. For all I knew she'd burn him on a pyre. I would.

We loaded Jimmy into the back of the truck, covered him with tarps, loaded the mirror and the travois, making sure to gather up any stray bits of cloth or wood.

I set the teddy bear on the dashboard. She needed to be washed and mended. There were several rips and she was soaked in blood. Katie would want her when she woke up.

We took the time to mop the place up and reset the desks. When we were done, the classroom smelled of bleach. I'd ask Qindra to come here and do a cleansing. The kids didn't need this form of energy.

Skella rode back to Black Briar with me instead of taking the mirror home. She wanted to be there, wanted to help with Jimmy, with Deidre.

I couldn't call Deidre. I was too cowardly. But we called Gunther. He'd need to be there. It was only right.

I called Stuart as well. He and Qindra were on their way home from Portland. I didn't say what the problem was, but I told him to bring Qindra to Black Briar. That alone told him something horrible had happened.

SIXTY-TWO

We pulled into Black Briar, the ambulance first, then me in the pickup. When I crossed onto the property, the fence erupted, shooting flames a hundred feet into the air. Not just near the house, but the whole fence, all the way around the property. As far as we could see from the house, anyway. The flames burned long enough for me to pull around the house and park in front of the deck.

The yard was jammed with vehicles, and more were coming in behind me. Not sure if the flames cut off the driveway. Looked like Gunther had called the whole phone tree.

I was out of the truck and half way to the back porch when Deidre came rolling out of the house.

"Where's Jim?" she asked, looking from my truck to the ambulance where Dena and Melanie were standing. Skella stayed back leaning against the truck.

I kept walking, eyes dry, looking at Gunther who stood behind Deidre, his hand on her chair. I know I looked like hell, covered in blood and bandages.

"Where's my husband?" Deidre asked, her voice shriller and higher.

Gunther put his hand on her shoulder, but she pushed it off.

"God damn it, Beahaull," she broke, a sob breaking her composure.

I dropped to my knees at her side, taking her hands in my own. "I'm sorry," I said, looking at her, watching the light go out of her eyes.

"No," she whispered. "Not Jim." She pulled her hands away from mine.

"We found Katie," I said, my throat felt like I had swallowed broken glass. "He saved her, Deidre. Saved us all."

"Where?" she begged, reaching over her shoulder to take Gunther's hand suddenly. He gently placed it on her shoulder where she grabbed it like she was drowning.

Gunther looked at me and I stood, turning back to the truck. "We brought him home," I said, feeling the way the crowd that had formed held their breath. "It's not a show," I growled, scrubbing my eyes. I walked back to the truck. "Somebody open the barn," I shouted, climbing into my truck. "And the rest of you clear the fuck out of here."

I started the truck, pulled it around to the barn, where Trisha was pulling the big doors wide. I drove into the center of the barn and stopped, my head on the steering wheel. This was where we sparred, where no vehicle had ever been. This was Jimmy's domain. The heart of it all. He'd built this place with his own hands and the hands of his clan after the dragon had burned the last barn. This was the focus of the rebuilding—not just of the buildings, but of our spirits.

Once inside, the big door shut and for a brief instant I was alone in the darkness with Jim in the back, quiet as a church mouse.

After a minute, the side door opened and Deidre rolled into the barn followed by Gunther. No one else. It seemed right for the moment.

Gunther flipped on the overheads and I climbed out of the truck, walked around and opened the lift gate.

"I can't see anything in this damn chair," Deidre said, her voice icy.

"Raise it," Gunther said, walking around her to hop into the back of the truck.

Deidre fumbled with the controls of her chair, and the hydraulics began to whine as she raised the seat. It was the Harley

333

Davidson of wheel chairs. She could damn near stand up in the thing, the way it contorted up all the while keeping her strapped in.

Once she was tall enough to see over the lip of the truck bed, Gunther knelt down and lifted the corner of the tarp. He dropped it quickly, looking back.

"It's true," he whispered, his face ashen.

Deidre began to wail. I sat on the lip of the truck, frozen in horror. Gunther knelt there, staring down at his hands and the world grew darker.

Time stopped with that wail. It was the worst sound I'd ever heard, worse than the dragon roar, worse than the necromancer curse, worse than the nightmares that haunted me night after night.

And Deidre wailed, her voice cracking and failing, only to renew again within seconds.

Soon an echo rose outside the barn, the voices of Black Briar rising to let the world know that their leader had truly fallen.

SIXTY-THREE

Bub showed up on Tuesday. He looked thinner than normal, but he remembered everything that happened up until the point he'd been killed. He never wanted to go back into the Sideways, understandably. We got him fed and bedded down with the troll twins that first day, keeping the harsh news about Jimmy from him.

But we couldn't keep him in the dark forever. When we told him about Jimmy he cried and cried. The troll twins consoled him as best they could, but it wasn't until Jai Li stepped in that he finally calmed down.

Deidre was in shock, as you might expect. She promised she didn't hate me, but she wouldn't make eye contact with me. I explained to her about the Valkyrie, but she didn't seem to hear me. Gunther assured me he'd make sure she understood in the end. Stuart and Gunther rallied their squads once things got into motion. They took over the running of Black Briar while Deidre hid herself away in the great house. Qindra stayed briefly that first afternoon, but went back across the water to break the news to Nidhogg. She and Stuart held each other for a long time before she left, a mixture of two worlds. It felt right. She promised to go to the school as well. She'd make it right there, keep that from the students.

There was no dissent from the troops. While Qindra was an outsider, and a servant of the enemy, things were not quite so simple. All that was in transition. Jimmy had been the hardest to bend on that subject of who was an enemy, and his passing had broken the spirit of the most ardent hater. It helped that Gunther supported her being there, and Stuart was quick to defend her to anyone who made any noise.

Deidre voiced no opinion, glanced once at Qindra and Stuart holding hands, nodded her approval and looked way.

We had no idea what it meant that the fences burned. Gunther sent crews out to check on the entire length of it and start the rebuilding. I guess bringing Jimmy's lifeless body home had broken the magic that protected the farm.

We'd have to do something about that.

In the meantime, Katie didn't come out of her coma, not that day or the following days. Doubt began to creep through the farm. The thought that Jimmy had fallen for nothing was passed around the barracks from time to time, but Trisha and her crew squashed it whenever they heard it. It just took time. Her body was a mess, they reminded everyone. She'd recover any day now.

We waited, hoping, praying that she'd wake, but she didn't.

Eventually we had our pyre, sent Jimmy's mortal remains into the sky amid the smoke of ash and birch. We added sage and lavender to the flames to keep any stray spirits at bay. I knew his had gone on to Valhalla, but it was best to be sure.

Deidre insisted on making a huge meal for the wake, and Black Briar pitched in. Old members from days gone by returned to visit, folks I'd never met. There was one gentleman in his late fifties, Jeremiah Fletcher that Gunther and Stuart treated with a reverence one would expect of a respected elder. He had been a friend and compatriot of Jim and Katie's parents. I didn't talk to him, but caught him looking my way from time to time.

I sat in the back of the crowd with Mary, Edith, and Julie hovering in my orbit. It was strange to be alone in this crowd of comrades. I was a part of Black Briar and separated at the same time.

Trisha ran the kitchen despite Deidre's best attempt. Her heart just wasn't in it. At one point Jai Li broke away from the other kids and went to Deidre, crawled into her lap and held her while she cried.

It was something I had no power to do, but that child of ours had a gift.

Later that night, as the drinking and singing began, Deidre came to me and hugged me, forgave me for Jimmy's death, though she assured me I wasn't responsible.

Sometimes you needed to assuage the guilt whether it was rightly owned or not. I know I'd carry it in my heart 'til the end of days. It just as well could've been me going through that door first, confronting the evil bastard. It didn't have to be Jimmy. But that was his way. Saving Skella from that murdering bastard was something Jim did on instinct. No thought to his own safety. Always a protector.

It was a glorious celebration and the bleakest day in my life. Long after dark fell, while the wake roared into a raucous party on Jimmy's behalf, I found myself in the old barn with Bub. He knew exactly where Katie had carved her love to me. It had been spared from the dragon fire, back in the corner that he'd claimed for his nest.

Light from the celebration was enough for me to see where she'd carved my name in the wood. She'd tied our names together with an intricate chain of Celtic knots. The word love glowed as the light from the halogen lights around the farm found its way into the ruins.

I couldn't breathe in that space, the smoke and ash of the old life choking me. In the end I fled, out past the lights, out to the copse of trees where I'd once kissed a Valkyrie. Here I could think. Here I could breathe.

But I couldn't stand. I fell to my knees and wept, my tears cutting through the ash that covered my face.

The pain was too much, the hole in my soul too deep. If she didn't wake, I was lost. I had no concept how I could possibly go on without her.

And I knew without Katie, Black Briar had no place for me.

SIXTY-FOUR

A week passed like blinking. Black Briar was a house under siege. Gunther and Anezka stayed out there most nights, and Stuart was there for dinner every night. Jai Li and I stayed out at Circle Q after the funeral. I just couldn't handle the blanket of pain and anguish that smothered the place.

It was Wednesday a week later that I got the call from Charlie Hague. The meeting with Madame Gottschalk had been so long ago, I'd blocked it from my memory. He said he wanted to make the exchange for the rings, bring Rasputin's knife back to the Mordred crew as we'd promised.

I had the knife, wondering if that's what kept me alive in the Sideways. It had kept Rasputin alive through a dozen assassination attempts, or so the story went. I wish Jimmy had been carrying it.

There was a park down on Kirkland's waterfront—a small thing with a single pier and a few benches. Basically the lovely green swathe of grass they had was covered in goose shit and the benches were full of senior citizens watching the sun rise and fall, but the pier was quiet and isolated. You could have a conversation at the end of it and not be overheard by those on the shore.

I agreed to meet Charlie there at sundown. It would be a quick exchange, a matter of formality. I didn't trust Gottschalk, and Charlie was guilty by association. He seemed nice enough, but I'd decided to wash my hands of him.

The sun was going down as I stood out over the water. The night was warm, one of the glory days of Seattle summer. I'd ridden the Ducati out there, promising Jai Li I'd be home in time for her bath and a story. Julie and Mary had been treating me with kid gloves. I went to work every day, dealt with the horses and the mules, giving them what I couldn't give anyone else. Well, anyone but Jai Li. I clung to that girl like I was drowning. If it wasn't for her, I'd have packed my kit and fled, driven so far away I couldn't find my shadow again. Part of me started to understand da a little in that.

I spent my days wanting to vomit and punch things, breaking into unaccounted for rages and black moments of melancholy. I couldn't go back into the Sideways. Gunnr told me that we'd done what we needed to, that we'd brought Katie home, but she would not wake the fuck up.

I leaned against the railing of the pier, looking at the water as the sun crept toward the horizon. It wouldn't go true dark to damn near ten in the evening this time of year. This was the twilight time, the longest period of transition from one state to the other that we knew of out this way.

It was a reminder of those innocent summers of my youth where the days lingered on forever and it felt like winter would never come.

"Sarah?"

I turned to see Charlie Hague walking toward me, a shy smile on his face. He was cute in a boyish way, with his sleeves rolled up and his hands in the pockets of his khakis.

"Thanks for meeting me," he said, stopping back far enough that I couldn't lunge forward and grab him.

For some reason that thought buoyed me a bit. He was afraid of me, and damned right to be. I had no love for his people.

"Sorry this took so long to get to you," he said, pulling his right hand out of the pocket. He held up one of those little jewelry boxes.

I stepped toward him and to his credit he didn't flinch. The box was grey with a soft cover, fuzzy like those you always see in movies when a guy is asking a girl to marry her.

I looked into Charlie's eyes and laughed, taking the box into my left fist.

"Thanks," I said.

He nodded and dropped his hand. "You can check," he said, encouraging me with a head bob.

I cracked the case open and saw the rings I'd glimpsed once before. Paul and Olivia Cornett's wedding rings. There were three rings, one was his, the other two were hers: a wedding band and an engagement ring. The diamond sparkled in the light of the waning sun. I closed the box and put it in the pocket of my work shirt. I'd come straight here from smithing, and I knew I smelled of sweat and horses.

"I need to tell you a few things," he said, stepping to the rail beside me and leaning forward on his arms. "Something I shouldn't be discussing, but with the way things are going ..." He trailed off, but I didn't prompt him. I turned and leaned against the railing beside him and watched the way the light played across the water.

"I'm sorry about James," he said, quietly.

"Is that an official response?"

"No," he said, looking at me.

I turned to look down at him. He was several inches shorter than me.

"Not at all," he went on, his voice suddenly angry. "Madame Gottschalk is thrilled with James's death. Claims you're crew will be easier to control."

I took a deep breath, letting my anger bubble at the edge of the world. I'd been needing a battle, something to smash. Maybe this Order of Mordred wanted to get ugly. I could deal with that.

But not Charlie. He'd said he was sorry.

"Look," he said, seeming to come to a decision. "There's a split, factions forming. Madame's sister has more play here than any of us knew. Spies within the organization. Madame seems to be on one hand oblivious to what's going on under her nose, and the rest of the time in a petulant tirade about how unfair life is."

"Fair's in August," I said, automatically. Something da always told me as a kid.

"True enough," Charlie said. His shoulders relaxed.

Maybe he'd decided I wasn't going to throw him in the lake. Funny I hadn't decided that answer quite yet, though.

"I heard from the cat," he looked at me, a sheepish grin on his face.

"The talking cat?" I asked.

He nodded. "There's something coming in from Minsk, and it ain't Madame's sister."

"Baba Yaga?" I asked, my curiosity piqued.

He turned to me in a panic, hands up, pushing them in my direction. "Shhh ..." he said, his eyes wide. "Don't say her name. Jesus, are you nuts?"

I shrugged. "Yeah, probably. You telling me saying her name may get her attention."

He shivered. "Not something I want to test," he said, rocking his shoulders back. I heard his back and neck pop when it did it. Boy was tense.

We talked for a while, both watching the sun slip toward full dusk. He was nervous and scared. In over his head.

"I think I'm one of those expendable players," he said, finally. Voicing the fear I'd watched him dance around the whole conversation. "I think they'd kill me if it supported their cause."

Sure as hell wouldn't surprise me, but I couldn't tell him that. Did Captain Kirk ever tell the redshirts they were all gonna die? Seriously.

"You could be a double agent," I suggested, liking the way it sounded as I said it. "Keep us informed of what's going on over there."

He didn't respond right way. I could tell he was thinking about it. Heck, maybe he'd already thought about it. "Would you protect me?"

"I'll talk to them," I said. Gunther and Stuart would go for it. But I wanted Deidre to have a say as well.

"Not them," he said, reaching out and touching me on the shoulder. "You. I want your word."

He pulled his hand back when I looked down at it and up to his face.

"Sorry," he went on. "But seriously. I want your word. Black Briar is in flux. They may not recover from this. With Jimmy gone, and Katie still ..." he glanced at me, but I didn't respond. "Anyway. We know about the defenses flaring up. Anyone with any magic sensitivity in the whole region caught that bit of fireworks."

Damn. Why hadn't I thought of that? I needed to talk with Qindra. Figure out a way to get something back out there.

"You help us," I said. "I'll promise I'll do anything I can for you."

A smile broke across his face. "Excellent," he said, holding out his hand.

I took it, giving it a good, honest shake, and he stepped back, looking as calm and pleased as the first time I'd met him.

"Oh, yeah. I almost forgot," he said, a sheepish look on his face. "I need that dagger. Madame doesn't know I took the rings. She was holding them, thinking we could keep them and use them somehow."

Wow, the dude went against Madame. Impressive. "She's gonna flip her shit when she finds out you took them, right?"

He shrugged. "I'll give her the dagger. That'll keep her busy enough. Besides, I'm nobody. She needs to be looking out for her sister." He gave a facial shrug, twitching his mouth to the side and raising one eyebrow.

"Okay," I said, pulling the dagger out of my back pocket and handing it to him, sheath and all. I'd examined it, had Bub help me. It wasn't the dagger at all, frankly. It was the sheath. That's what protected Rasputin from all those attacks. Just like the one that Yeats carried. I needed to look that part up. Old magic.

I stayed on the pier long after Charlie left, thinking about all the shit that had gone down. At least I had the rings. I'd take them out to Black Briar. They were Katie's now. She deserved to have them.

SIXTY-FIVE

I called Circle Q and asked them to keep Jai Li up late. I was
going out to Black Briar. These rings belonged with Katie,
and I wasn't waiting a minute longer than I had to.

It was going on nine by the time I rolled down the long
drive at Black Briar. The fence was brand new, twice as high as
the last one and blocked the farm from the road. The old one had
been a split rail. This one looked like something the Department
of Transportation put up to keep the sound from bothering the
rich folk. Made Black Briar look even more like a compound
rather than a farm. Not sure how the locals would react, but this
far back in, there wasn't a lot of local traffic—mainly forestry
people and kids looking to drink in the national forest that backed
up to the farm.

I parked the bike and left Gram strapped to the side of the
bike. I wouldn't be needing her here. Not tonight. I set my helmet
on the seat and climbed up onto the deck, two steps at a time. By
the time I was knocking on the door, Stuart had the inside door
open and was beckoning me inside.

"What's up, Sarah," he said, mildly surprised. "Didn't figure
we'd see you until the weekend."

I shrugged out of my leather jacket and laid it on the kitchen
table. Deidre was in the living room with Trisha, Bub, and the
twins watching something on television. I don't know what it was,
but they were laughing. Well, not Deidre, but she wasn't as dark

as she'd been. Mourning takes time.

"I need to see Katie," I said to Stuart. "I got the rings back from Charlie Hague tonight. Thought I'd take them in to her, you know …" I shrugged.

He smiled at me and patted me on the arm. "You go ahead. I'll get Deidre to come back. You give 'em to Katie and sit with her a bit. We'll make sure they get put up someplace nice."

I leaned in and kissed him on the cheek, which surprised him. He smiled, though. That was good.

The hallway was dark and the only light in Katie's room were the glow of several of the machines. She wasn't on a breather, that was good. She was breathing on her own, but she was so thin. She'd been on a feeding tube for a while, one of those direct to the stomach things, punched through her abdomen. It made me sick to think about it, but it was keeping her alive. Qindra had spent time with her several nights after Jimmy died. The nurses were doing a helluva job, but there was only so much you could do when a body just doesn't move around.

She was as healthy as she was going to be in a coma. Deidre agreed that Qindra could come out again in a week or so to see how Katie was progressing. Seems Qindra could encourage the body's own healing abilities, accelerate things like a time-lapse camera, but there was nothing beyond that. No magical healing, no magic potions, no laying of hands. All this dragon and Norse god horseshit and we couldn't muster up a good cleric?

It would've been funny if it wasn't so fucking depressing.

The room was warm and smelled of unpleasant things I had no desire to decipher. The human body was not made to lie in a bed that long and unpleasant things happened.

I flipped on the bedside lamp, allowing a small warm glow to light the center of the room. Katie was so beautiful lying there, even though she was so thin to be pinched, her bones showed more than normal, and her face was gaunt.

I leaned forward and kissed her. The skin was dry and papery, but she smelled like her, underneath the antiseptic and the sick.

"Hey, baby," I said, brushing the hair off her face. It didn't really need to be moved, but I had to do something. She was well cared for, I had nothing to do but sit and fidget. Sit and watch.

"I talked to Charlie today," I said, pulling a chair around to sit beside her. I put my hand on top of her left one, the one closest to me. She was a good listener, that's for sure. I told her about my day and about my conversation with Charlie.

At one point I heard a cough and turned to see Deidre and Stuart hovering back in the doorway—giving me space.

"Come on in," I said, waving at them. "I was just about to get to the best part."

"You think she's getting any of that?" Stuart asked, not unkindly.

"Hell yeah," I said, the bravado strong in my voice. "Every damned word."

Deidre patted Stuart on the arm, and he looked down at his hands, not saying anything else.

I was crying again, damn it.

"I got these tonight," I said, pulling the small box out of my pocket. "Traded that stupid knife to Charlie Hague."

I opened the box and showed it to Deidre and Stuart, who looked up and smiled.

"Good girl," he said, quietly.

"Are those ...?" Deidre asked, not finishing.

"Yes," I said, turning to Katie.

"Katie, love," I said, opening her hand. I took out each ring and placed them one at a time in her palm, explaining. "These are your parents' rings. Your mom and dad's wedding bands, and your mom's engagement ring."

I glanced back at Deidre and saw that she was clinging to Stuart's arm with one hand, her other over her mouth. Tears shone in her eyes.

I folded Katie's hand closed and moved it over her heart, pulling her other hand over it. She clutched the rings and kept her hands together when I stepped back. Reflexes, I'd explained to Gunther a long time ago.

We sat there, crying quietly for a long time, listening to the heart monitor and dreaming of better days.

Eventually Deidre and Stuart went back to the front of the house and I sat there alone, lost. "I'm sorry," I said, giving up. I was done in. Everything I needed, everything I loved lay in that bed and was beyond my help.

Finally I got up and pushed the chair back against the wall. Jai Li needed me and it was late. Going on midnight.

I bent down and kissed her once more, tracing my fingers across her cheek and wishing

Then she spoke. It was so quiet and so rough I leaned in to make sure.

"Yes," she said.

Holy jumping Jesus fish! "Katie?" I asked, torn between collapsing and exploding.

"Yes, what?" I asked her, laughing and crying.

"Yes," she said again, her voice a little clearer.

"Stuart," I shouted. "Deidre."

I darted to the doorway and shouted again. "She's awake!"

By the time they came barreling down the hall, I was back to her side, my face pressed against her chest, my hands over hers.

"Yes, what?" I said again, my voice as hoarse as hers.

"Yes, I'll marry you," she said, opening her hands in mine and fading into sleep.

I sat there, staring at her, feeling her heartbeat and marveling at the sound of her voice after so long.

"Get Melanie," I said. Stuart took off running back to the kitchen. I knew it wasn't Deidre because she was on wheels.

"Jimmy would've liked that," Deidre said close to my side.

I straightened up and looked down at her.

"A wedding," she said, patting me on the arm. "We need a wedding here, something to bring some hope back into this place."

"May be a while," I said, looking down at Katie. "She's not out of the woods yet."

"True, but you brought her home finally. I'm just sorry Jim isn't here to see it."

The night was a mad scramble. They came by ambulance and took her back to the hospital. They needed to get her stable, get her moving, remove the tubes and the lot.

She'd live. She was awake. That was the best thing.

I rode to the hospital in the back of the ambulance.

Maybe there was some hope in the world. Jai Li was going to be out of her mind with joy.

When we pulled up and they opened the doors, Mary, Julie, Edith, and Jai Li were waiting for us.

"What are you doing here?" I asked, confused.

Jai Li held up a drawing she'd made. One where Katie was awake.

I looked at the picture and down at the girl.

They took Katie into Evergreen while I stood in the parking lot, holding my girl. "You are amazing," I said, hugging Jai Li. "How did we ever get along without you?"

She giggled and that was the best sound in the world.

Katie … home … she signed.

"Yes. Katie's come home."

It would be a long recovery back to a normal life, but the options were there, the hope had paid off.

Jimmy would be happy. I hope the Valkyrie told him the good news.

IF YOU LIKED...

Working Stiff
Kevin J. Anderson

The Love-Haight Casefiles
Jean Rabe

Pockets of Darkness
Jean Rabe

ABOUT THE AUTHOR

J. A. Pitts is an award-winning author who lives in the Pacific Northwest. In the dead of winter he can be found battling the elusive tree squids in the world's only temperate rainforest.

OTHER WORDFIRE PRESS TITLES

Our list of other WordFire Press authors and titles is always growing.
To find out more and to see our selection of titles, visit us at:

wordfirepress.com

CPSIA information can be obtained
at www.ICGtesting.com
Printed in the USA
LVOW12s1453260317
528508LV00006B/643/P